Kirov Saga:

Darkest Hour

Altered States
Volume II

By

John Schettler

A publication of: *The Writing Shop Press*
Kirov Saga: *Darkest Hour*, Copyright©2013, John A. Schettler

Discover other titles by John Schettler:

The Kirov Saga: *(Military Fiction)*
Kirov - Kirov Series - Volume I
Cauldron Of Fire - Kirov Series - Volume II
Pacific Storm - Kirov Series - Volume III
Men Of War - Kirov Series - Volume IV
Nine Days Falling - Kirov Series - Volume V
Fallen Angels - Kirov Series - Volume VI
Devil's Garden - Kirov Series - Volume VII
Armageddon – Kirov Series – Volume VIII
Altered States– Kirov Series – Volume IX
Darkest Hour– Kirov Series – Volume X
Hinge of Fate– Kirov Series – Volume XI

Award Winning Science Fiction:

Meridian - Meridian Series - Volume I
Nexus Point - Meridian Series - Volume II
Touchstone - Meridian Series - Volume III
Anvil of Fate - Meridian Series - Volume IV
Golem 7 - Meridian Series - Volume V

Classic Science Fiction:

Wild Zone - Dharman Series - Volume I
Mother Heart - Dharman Series - Volume II

Historical Fiction:

Taklamakan - Silk Road Series - Volume I
Khan Tengri - Silk Road Series - Volume II
Dream Reaper – Mythic Horror Mystery

Mailto: john@writingshop.ws
http://www.writingshop.ws ~ http://www.dharma6.com

Kirov Saga:

Darkest Hour

Altered States
Volume II

By

John Schettler

*"Two qualities are indispensable: first, an intellect
that, even in the darkest hour, retains some
glimmerings of the inner light which leads to truth;
and second, the courage to follow this faint light
wherever it may lead."*

— Carl von Clausewitz

Kirov Saga:

Darkest Hour

Altered States – Volume II

By
John Schettler

A note on the Kirov Saga

The *Kirov Series* is a long chain of linked novels by John Schettler in the Military Alternate History / Time Travel genre. Like the popular movie "The Final Countdown" which saw the US Carrier *Nimitz* sent back in time to the eve of Pearl Harbor in 1941, in these books the powerful Russian battlecruiser *Kirov* from the year 2021 is sent back to the 1940s in the Norwegian Sea, where it subsequently becomes embroiled in WWII.

Like episodes in the never ending *Star Trek* series, the *Kirov Saga* continues through one episode after another as the ship's position in time remains unstable. It culminates in Book 8 *Armageddon*, then is resurrected again in a 9th volume entitled *Altered States*, the book immediately preceding the volume you are now reading.

How to read the Kirov Series?

The best entry point is obviously Book 1, *Kirov*, where you will meet all the main characters in the series and learn their inner motivations. The series itself, however, is structured as sets of trilogies linked by what the author calls a "bridge novel." The first three volumes form an exciting trilogy featuring much fast paced naval action as *Kirov* battles the Royal Navy, Regia Marina (Italians) and finally the Japanese after sailing to the Pacific in Book 3. The bridge novel *Men Of War* is a second entry point which covers what happened to the ship and crew after it returned home to Vladivostok. As such it serves as both a sequel to the opening trilogy and a prologue to the next trilogy, the three novels beginning the fifth book, *9 Days Falling*.

The *9 Days Falling* trilogy focuses on the struggle to prevent a great war in 2021 from reaching a terrible nuclear climax, and features much modern era combat. It spans book 5, 6, and 7, covering the outbreak of the war as Japan and China battle over disputed islands, and the action of the Red Banner Pacific Fleet against the US Fleet. It then takes a dramatic turn when the ship is again shifted in time to 1945. There they confront the powerful US Pacific Fleet under Admiral Halsey, and so this trilogy focuses much of the action as *Kirov* faces down the US Navy in two eras. This second trilogy also launches several subplots that serve to relate significant events in the great war of 2021 and also deepen the mystery of time travel as discovered in the series. The trilogy ends at another crucial point in history where the ship's Captain, Vladimir Karpov, believes he is in a position to decisively change events.

The next bridge novel is *Armageddon*, Book 8 in the series, which continues the action as a sequel to the *9 Days Falling* trilogy while also standing as a prologue to the next trilogy that begins with book 9, *Altered States*.

In this third trilogy, *Kirov* has moved to the year 1940 where it becomes trapped in the world made by its many interventions in the history, an altered reality. It is important to note that the ship's position here *pre-dates* all the action of the first eight books in the series by a full year, which raises the possibility of paradox when the officers wonder what will happen to them in a year's time when the ship was first supposed to appear in July of 1941.

The opening volume, *Altered States*, continues the long saga with the ship slowly becoming enmeshed in the war, now taking sides against the one navy of WWII it has not yet fought in any of the other books, the Kriegsmarine of Germany. In this alternate history, however, the world's navies have all built many of the "what if" ships that were never built during the war. Britain's flagship is the powerful G3 Class battlecruiser HMS *Invincible*. Germany has built powerful new ships from their Plan Z naval building program, and there are new ships in the French and Italian navies as well… all as one consequence of *Kirov's* earlier actions.

You can enter any of these three trilogies that may interest you, though your understanding of the characters and plot will be fullest by simply beginning with book one and reading through them all! Here now is book 10 in the long saga, *Darkest Hour*.

Part I

Ragnarök

*"Axe-time, sword-time, shields are sundered,
Wind-time, wolf-time, ere the world falls;
Nor ever shall men each other spare.*

*Much do I know, and more can see
Of the fate of the gods, the mighty in fight."*

—Valuspo ~ Nordic Poetic Edda

Chapter 1

Tovey watched his new flag staff officer turn and hasten away with his message to the bridge. Yes, he thought, now you may run. The time is come. All the planning and maneuvering and deployment was finished now. The bow of HMS *Invincible* was pointed, the ship's course set, her guns manned and ready with battle at hand.

The ship had cleared her throat in the Norwegian campaign, providing shore bombardment briefly, though she mainly ran with the carriers as their primary covering force against the possibility of German intervention at sea. Thus far only the Twins had dared to engage, but now the Germans were bringing out a pair of much stronger ships. Let us hope we live up to our name, he thought as he took a last look at the plotting map. Then he straightened his hat, adjusted the fit of his jacket and started for the bridge himself. He would walk, not run. His order to turn for battle had already proceeded him on the swift footfalls of Mister Wells. Now he would follow, a steely calm settling over his mind. It was the witching hour.

"Admiral on the Bridge!"

Captain Bennett was waiting in his chair in the armored conning tower, his eyes lost in the cups of his field glasses. HMS *Invincible* was a truly novel design, Britain's heavyweight at just under 54,000 long tons full load, she was in fact the heaviest ship by displacement in the Royal Navy. With three triple turrets mounting 16 inch guns, she had tremendous firepower and an unusual turret arrangement that saw two mounted forward of the conning tower, and the third directly behind it, amidships. This meant her engineering sections and twin funnels were pushed aft in the latter third of the ship.

Her main armor began at A turret and stretched to C turret with all of 356mm or 14 inches of hardened steel. Behind this it thinned to 305mm and eventually tapered to 254mm in the stern. Yet this gave good cover to the engineering plant and vital propulsion systems. Even the boiler room and funnels were surrounded by an armored box. With armored decks between five and eight inches, the ship had a tough shell against air attack or plunging fire. And the business end of the ship saw turret face armor of 17.5 inches and 9 to 12 inches on the conning tower. Her anti-torpedo bulge could withstand a blast from a 340kg warhead. All in all she had better protection than any other British ship of her day, and the oblique 18 degree angle of that heavy armor made it even more effective in stopping plunging fire at longer ranges.

What *Hood* lacked, *Invincible* had in abundance, and to go with it she could hit harder, range farther, and even had better speed than *Hood*, a truly remarkable design considering it was conceived in the 1920s. There was only one other ship in the world at that moment with a more innovative design—*Kirov*, and only the secret mega ships being built by Japan and Germany, *Yamato* and *Hindenburg* were bigger.

To be standing in the armored bridge of a ship like this gave one a heady feeling. This is the best we have, thought Tovey. If I could have hastened the workout of the *King George V* class ships I would dearly love to have them at hand now, but this ship is the might and sinew of the Royal Navy. We are facing Germany's newest designs as well, unproven, but fearsome on paper. Now we will put them to the test. I'm going to come in at just the right angle, with all guns blazing. We'll outgun *Bismarck* if we find her, but *Tirpitz* has been reported as well, and that is a tall order indeed.

There had been no further word from Admiral Holland on *Hood*, and they were no doubt engaged at this very moment. Yet that ship was already hit by those damnable *Stukas* off *Graf Zeppelin*. Tovey nonetheless believed he could still outgun the Germans—if only he could get *Invincible* to the fight in time. The Twins were also vectoring in behind him, set to arrive like Blucher at Waterloo... He did not like the thought of casting himself in Napoleon's shoes, but there it was.

He was rushing to the scene like Napoleon's Old Guard to restore order, but those damnable Twins were on his heels, and he would have only a brief time of advantage when he came into range of the heavier Germans ships before those two battlecruisers were nipping at his flank with their 11 inch guns. Let's see what C-turret has to say about it, he thought, turning to Captain Bennett.

"Captain, let us train C-turret on those two wolves bearing on our flank. Perhaps we can discourage them."

"Aye sir, that we can. Mister Connors!"

"Sir!"

"You heard the Admiral. Give the Twins our calling card."

"Very good sir."

Half a minute later the roar of all three 16-inch guns on the amidships turret shook the ship with their anger as *Invincible* engaged the shadows lurking to the northwest. Forty seconds passed and then Tovey heard a jubilant shout, prompting him to raise an eyebrow as he turned to Captain Bennett.

"Am I to assume we've a hole in one, Captain?"

"Aye sir, right amidships on the number two ship. Straddled the bastards with the first salvo!"

Tovey knew that was a proverbial long shot, and a bit of very good luck, but the Twins had done the same when they crept up on HMS *Glorious*, and now Britain had evened the score when it came to long range gunnery. The hit was obtained at just over 24,000 yards.

"They've had enough of that, sir," said Bennett. "Both ships are breaking to the north."

"I shouldn't count them out of the game just yet, Mister Bennett. They'll undoubtedly slip over the horizon, but will still be running parallel to our track. Make sure the lookouts are sharp."

"Let them peek into the shop window again, sir, and we'll give them another black eye."

They were running full out, and even the two destroyers in the van, *Fortune* and *Firedrake*, were laboring to keep up speed at a whisker under 32 knots. This ship is the pride of the fleet, thought Tovey. She is one of a kind, with no siblings, and there is nothing like her for raw power and speed in the entire fleet. Look how she just sent the Twins off with one good stiff jab. She'll outgun the German

Bismarck class battleships, and she can outrun them as well, and all with armor every bit as good as the protection the Germans gave their ships.

He passed a moment of regret, thinking he should have deployed the ship together with Admiral Holland on *Hood*, but there was simply too much sea room to cover. At least the two battlegroups were not too far apart. He'd get there in time, he knew. Last notice from *Hood* had her steering 280, coming towards his own ship now. They could already hear the distant boom of naval gunfire, rolling like the low rumble of thunder on the horizon. He expected that the mainmast watch would see the smoke of that battle any moment now, and the tall spires of *Hood's* mast soon after. They had already seen planes on radar all throughout the battle zone as pilots from *Ark Royal* mixed it up with the Germans off *Graf Zeppelin*.

"Air alert!" The call came in with strident alarm, a bell ringing to underscore the urgency. "Formation low off the starboard aft quarter!"

Invincible had four 2-pounder gun mounts, each with ten barrels, the same pom-poms *Hood* had deployed against the *Stukas*, but this alert was for low flying planes, and her six 4.1-inch quick firing deck guns could also be brought to bear. Crews were already at action stations and, as Tovey went to look over his shoulder at the direction of the sighting, he could see the guns beginning to train on distant targets.

Not very sporting of Jerry to jump right in with an air strike again, he thought, but something about this one didn't seem to fit. As far as he knew the Germans had not yet deployed a torpedo plane capable of operating from a carrier. The modified *Stukas* were their only strike asset, and they would certainly not come in this low. He went to the nearest viewport to have a look and was soon convinced these were British *Swordfish*. They had been ordered north to look for the German fleet, and here they were, but at this altitude he had the sickening feeling they might have mistaken *Invincible* for an enemy ship. He turned swiftly, with every second counting now.

"Belay that air alert and send up recognition flags and flares, gentlemen. Those are *Swordfish* off the *Illustrious,* if the mainmast would care to have a better look at them. Mister Wells, kindly go to the W/T room and see that those planes are vectored northeast on a heading of 040."

"Right away, sir!"

Wells walked briskly off the bridge until he was out of the Admiral's sight. Then, seeing he had a clear ladder down, he hastened away at a run. Tovey heard the man's footfalls echo from the open hatch and smiled.

* * *

Lt-Cdr. Williamson was leading in 815 Squadron with two sub-flights of three *Swordfish* each, and his planes were lined up well on the target ahead. They were coming in on the aft quarter after descending from 4,000 feet to make their attack run. Lt. Scarlett was ready on the rear gun mount, and fussing about with his W/T headset.

"Signal the lads, Mister Scarlett. Target ahead. Sub-flight B to the right. We'll swing round the other side."

Scarlett was fated to win a Distinguished Service Cross later that year over the Italian Navy at Taranto, and Williamson would be admitted as a Companion of the Distinguished Service Order, but instead they would get their medals early for the events that were now about to unfold. John Scarlett thought he heard something in his headset, tapping it again and thinking he had a dodgy wire. Then a voice came through and his eyes widened. At that same moment, Williamson saw two flares go up, an expedient measure that was seldom used by a warship in combat, as it would clearly mark its position. He counted them, one… two… three… blue! "What the hell? Hold on, Lieutenant. Belay that order! That's Royal Navy up ahead!"

Scarlett looked over his shoulder, saw the flares, passed a fleeting moment thinking the Germans may have worked out their signal sequences, but he had heard a frantic voice in his earpiece, right in the clear. *"Lookout ahead! HMS Invincible!"* The message came in just as the planes were beginning to swerve off to make their attack approach. "They want us to fly on zero-four-zero, sir. It's HMS *Invincible* up ahead!"

"Good of them to introduce themselves," said Williamson. "Thought we had already passed the Fleet Flagship long ago! If this is *Invincible*, what was that ship we left in our wake, Johnny?"

"Might have been *Sussex* or *Devonshire*, sir. They're both off to the southwest."

"What about those other ships up ahead at ten-o-clock?" Williamson had spotted two more dark silhouettes on the horizon.

"The message says our target is on 040, sir."

This was the first combat mission *Illustrious* had been handed, and just three days after she had finished initial trials on air wing operations. There seemed to be ships everywhere, and the men had not had enough time over the fleet to drill on ship recognition profiles, or anything else. He would have seen what was in front of him in time, as *Invincible* had a profile that was impossible to miss, but they had been coming in on the ship's aft quarter, making identification more difficult. He took a long look at the contact at 10:00, thinking it had to be German ships, but orders were orders and so he steered 040.

Several sub-flights had already fluttered off to their attack headings, as per training, but Lieutenant Scarlett was quickly signaling them to reform. Sub-Lieutenants Sparke and Macaulay were quick to respond and maneuvered off either wing. Lieutenants Kemp, Swayne and Maund were already down at a thousand feet, but he saw them nose up to rejoin. The last two sub-flights in his squadron were well back and got the message before they broke to attack. A few minutes later Williamson had his eggs in the basket again and the *Swordfish* came up and then veered right to bypass *Invincible*, wings wagging in salutation. Thankfully not a single round came up for them, but it was a near run thing.

"Did Hale get the message?"

"Right, sir," said Scarlett. "819 Squadron is coming up behind us and will follow our heading."

High overhead a sub-flight of three *Fulmars* surged ahead. They were accompanied by six *Skuas* of 824 Squadron under Lieutenant Commander Charles Evans, off to sweep out in front in case the Germans were waiting with more Messerschmitts, though no sign was seen of enemy planes.

The whole formation veered right, roaring away toward the spot on the horizon where *Invincible* hastened to join the battle, and within seconds they saw the smoke and fire of battle. Zero-four-zero it is, thought Williamson. Now that we've sorted out our target heading, let's hope the lads can remember how to make a decent attack. This time the Germans won't be shooting off flares.

Chapter 2

Aboard *Bismarck,* Captain Lindemann knew he was not firing flares. The 15-inch guns had opened the action at a little over18,000 meters, with both his own forward turrets firing along with Anton turret on *Tirpitz* behind him, the first spotting salvos to see if they had the range. True to form, the shots were very close, good enough to begin firing for effect with only minor adjustments.

"Port ten and steady on," he ordered, swinging around a bit to allow his aft turrets to begin training on the targets. "Looks like our *Stukas* had the first dance," he smiled. "That second ship is already burning. What do you make of it, Mister Oels?"

Fregattenkapitän Hans Oels was the Executive Officer aboard *Bismarck,* making ready to go below decks when Lindemann turned to him. Tall and straight, he was a man of few words, but a strict disciplinarian and not one to cross in the line of duty. Oels stepped up and took the field glasses Lindemann handed him.

"Hood," he said calmly. "And trouble with one of their forward turrets from the look of it."

"There's another battlecruiser leading her," said Lindemann.

"It would have to be *Repulse.* Werner says *Graf Zeppelin* drove off *Renown* and its back in Scapa Flow by now."

"There's no way it could be out here then. Excellent! Two battlecruisers. Good guns but they haven't the armor to stand with us in a fight like this. Today we prove what the Kriegsmarine can do, Oels. It looks like Schneider already has the range." He was referring to Korvettenkapitän Adalbert Schneider, the ship's First Artillery Officer.

"Good shooting, sir," said Oels. "I had better get down to the Damage Control Center." Oels action station was the central damage control command post, deep in the bowels of the ship. If anything happened on the bridge he could have an overall view of the situation by reading the lights winking on the damage control panel, and he could command the ship from there if necessary. It was, in effect,

Bismarck's equivalent of a reserve bridge.

"Don't worry, Oels, I won't keep you busy. *Hood* is already burning!"

The roar of *Bismarck's* second salvo punctuated his remark, rattling the bridge with its power. Oels was not there to see the results a short minute later when Lindemann saw the tall water splashes straddle the target. "A hit!" he said jubilantly. "Right on the conning tower! That will give them a headache or two, and let them know just who they are dealing with."

Now we get our chance, he thought. I have the two finest ships available in the German navy. When *Hindenburg* is ready we will be even stronger, but at this moment we are more than a match for *Hood* and *Repulse*. The *Invincible* is another matter. If that ship is close by, as I believe it is, then the odds will be even. So we must reap every advantage while we can just now. Schneider has the range. Let us sink these ships before the British can do anything about it!

"Watch reports aircraft bearing two-one-zero, Kapitän." It was Korvettenkapitän Kurt Werner, the ship's Intelligence Officer, who had just come up from the signals deck. "Low altitude, sir. Most likely *Swordfish*."

"Then they must have another carrier nearby," said Lindemann. "Signal the fleet to repel air attack. It would be nice if *Graf Zeppelin* had left a few fighters over us."

The Kapitän would get his wish, for Marco Ritter had lingered after the *Stuka* attack and still had two wing mates with him of the seven fighters that had broken up much of the strike wing off *Ark Royal*. There they had tried their hand against the veteran British pilots, but now the wing from *Illustrious* was tasting combat for the first time. Lindemann saw what looked like a flight of falcons drop out of a cloud bank and come swooping in on the low flying *Swordfish*, their wings lit up with machine gun fire. Trails of thin smoke bled from the tails of two British planes, then he saw that a Squadron of enemy fighters came on the scene from above and the German planes were soon in a swirling dogfight.

The flak guns were firing now, filling the sky with dark grey puffs of smoke as their rounds exploded, but the *Swordfish* were so lumbering in their approach that it actually threw off the sighting mechanisms on the German guns, which had been calibrated to oppose more modern aircraft flying much faster. He saw six, then twelve planes coming right in at the center of his battle line, and on their right another ragged line of planes appeared, slightly behind, all flying low on the deck as they began their attack run.

Bismarck was heavily provisioned with anti-aircraft defenses. The ship had sixteen 4.1-inch guns arrayed in eight twin turrets, another sixteen 3.7-inch guns, and twelve more 20mm flak guns, which were perhaps the most effective guns against the *Swordfish*. The 3.7s were only semi-automatic, with a fairly slow rate of fire. If they hit a plane it would probably knock it down, but those hits were few and far between. By contrast, the 20mm guns could rattle out a good stream of lead, the tracers clearly marking the firing path to allow the gunners to get a better aim. With *Tirpitz* in her wake, all this fire was doubled, and *Prince Eugen* had also opened up with everything she had. Many of *Bismarck's* bigger 5.9-inch secondary batteries joined the fray, and the sound of all these weapons firing at once was deafening, a crescendo of doom punctuated by the enormous roar of the main turrets as they fired their third salvo.

The German gunners had some success, particularly against Lieutenant Commander Hale's 819 Squadron where Lt. Lee and Sub-Lt. Jones went down after luck favored the Germans and they took a direct hit from a 3.7-inch round. Diving into their attack, Lieutenants Wellham and Humphreys were found by the 20mm guns off *Bismarck*, which set them afire and caused severe aileron damage. Wellham struggled with the yoke, the aircraft out of control for a time, but he managed to kick his tail around and straighten out.

"Let's get that fish in the sea!" he yelled to his mate, and they dropped the torpedo at about 900 yards aimed right at the *Bismarck,* but it was clearly too late and bound to miss, running into the ship's wake. Wellham kicked himself for aiming directly at the ship and not leading it properly, but in the heat of the moment, struggling for control on the yoke and stick, it was the best they could do. As he banked away, his plane received further wing damage from AA fire and it was only good fortune that allowed him to get his heavily damaged *Swordfish* back to *Illustrious* in one piece.

The Squadron Leader, Hale, could see several of his pilots had fired much too soon, doing exactly what Wellham had done and taking aim at the broad side of the big leading German ship. They would have to be in at 500 yards to have any chance of a hit, he thought, the bloody idiots. So he pressed on through the flak, determined to get his torpedo in the water at the last possible moment and get that second ship in the line. Lieutenants Hamilton, Skelton and Clifford followed him in, but Morford and Sub-Lt. Green in plane L5Q developed engine trouble and had to abort, dropping their torpedo to gain altitude and limp off to the south.

It was Hale's group of four planes and an equal number of intrepid pilots from 815 Squadron on their left that got the right idea and bored in to take aim at the gap between the two big German battleships. The flak gunners got two of eight planes in this sector, but the remaining six all got their torpedoes away and they were well aimed, right ahead of *Tirpitz*, which was running on at high speed.

Lindemann looked to see *Tirpitz* make a hard emergency turn to port, her bow frothing up the sea, the blood red water awash and gleaming on her forecastle. The ship turned smartly, but her forward momentum was too great to allow it to get inside the line of enemy fire.

Topp's only chance now was to see if he could run with the torpedoes, thought Lindemann. *Tirpitz* was surging along their same bearing to present a slimmer target. In doing so he was dangerously exposing his turbines and rudder to the line of fire, but in this case he was lucky enough to avoid damage there. It was the great beam of the ship, 118 feet wide, that ended up being his downfall. *Tirpitz* was right between the wakes of two torpedoes after making the turn, and the gutter between them was too narrow for the mighty ship to avoid the deadly lances. Both torpedoes hit, one on either side of the ship, but Lindemann saw only one tall water splash on the starboard side indicating a successful detonation. The second torpedo had failed to ignite on contact, scudding off the side of the ship and angling away off to the left.

Lieutenant Commander Hale got credit for the hit, just below B turret but in a place that saw *Tirpitz* well protected by the anti-torpedo bulge and good armor. The second torpedo from Williamson's 815 Squadron struck well aft, on the port side in a much more vulnerable spot, but had no teeth. Hale's planes veered right, taking murderous fire from *Bismarck* in reprisal that saw Skelton and Clifford's planes shot to pieces. The other two planes, including Hale would make it back to *Illustrious* alive. Williamson's Squadron banked left over the broad frothing wake of *Tirpitz* and had only the lighter flak fire from *Prinz Eugen* to deal with. They would all make it home alive.

The gallant attack had begun with 24 planes. Marco Ritter got two before he was embroiled in a fight with the British fighter cover, the flak gunners got four more, and only nine of the eighteen remaining got torpedoes in the water that had any chance to score a hit. Yet it was enough to send *Tirpitz* wheeling off the battle line, where Lindemann knew damage control parties were now rushing to inspect the starboard hull.

"Signal *Tirpitz* and see if they have any real damage from that torpedo hit."

Lindemann had the heat of battle on him now. The fourth salvo from *Bismarck* boomed out again as the flak gun fire subsided, and the Kapitän swerved back to the real battle at hand. He could see that *Hood* was damaged in three places, her B turret, conning tower, and a bad hit amidships after the *Stukas* came in. Thus far his own ship had not been struck by enemy fire, though two big geysers had wet his bow with a rain of glittering seawater. The sense of power under his feet was overwhelming as the *Bismarck* forged ahead, her turrets blasting away at the enemy, engines running smoothly.

Smoke shrouded the scene, but Kurt Werner was back with a signal from *Prince Eugen*. "Another ship sighted," he said, "coming in on the same bearing those planes hit us from—two-two-zero."

Lindemann peered through his field glasses, unable to see anything in the dim light, with smoke from his own guns rolling out of the side of the ship as *Bismarck* fired again. We should have launched a seaplane, he thought. I am relying too much on Böhmer and his planes aboard *Graf Zeppelin*.

"And what about *Tirpitz*?"

"They report minor damage on the starboard side torpedo bulge. Nothing serious. The second torpedo failed to detonate."

"Then they got lucky. Good, we can always use a good throw of the dice, because now it comes down to armor and guns, Werner."

"*Tirpitz* is coming around again to match our heading, but we are between their ship and the enemy now. Shall we have them fall back into line with us?"

"No. Leave them where they are. It will force the British to split their fire at two different ranges, while all our gunfire can focus on one point."

He raised his field glasses again, and some thirty seconds later he saw another bright flash and explosion down his line of fire. The plot was thickening with the arrival of another British ship, but *Hood* had been hit again.

He looked at his watch. It would probably be another half hour before he could expect more air support from *Graf Zeppelin*. How many more planes were out there on those British carriers? Where were the rest of the German fighters? Don't worry about the planes, he chided himself. You're a gunnery officer, the best in all Germany. You've taught most every lead Artilleryman of any note. See to the guns, that's what will do the job here. See to the guns.

The Nordic poetry he so often read was running through his mind now. It was Ragnarök, the clash of the gods in a mighty battle to decide their fate. Here we decide the fate of nations at sea, he thought. If we can defeat the Royal Navy here, then anything is possible in this war. The echo of the guns pounded out the tempo of the battle, and the words of the Poetic Edda ran through his mind like the hot pulse of blood at his temples.

> *"Axe-time, sword-time, shields are sundered,*
> *Wind-time, wolf-time, ere the world falls;*
> *Nor ever shall men each other spare."*

Chapter 3

Out on the weather deck Admiral Volsky stood watching the ochre light on the sea, deceptively calm, and the silver tint of the fat moon over it all. It was a day when no night would come, no place to fold oneself into the darkness and shadow, into the silence. The light gleamed on ragged shards of floating ice, like the cold white teeth of a great shark emerging from the sea. The ship was thrumming beneath his heavy soled boots, the metal hull pushing through the ice floes. A cold wind was crisp on his face, and above him he caught the ceaseless sweeping turn of the big Voskhod-2 "Dawn" Navigation and weather radar, the highest mast of the ship, and saw the silhouette of the watch posted there.

They had lost their original set in the Pacific, and this was a new model, hastily fitted before the ship left Vladivostok, though the umbilical cables and wire tentacles that would integrate it into the ship's systems had just been connected in recent days. Engineer Byko managed to get it back on line to improve their radar coverage, but the Admiral knew it would only be the bringer of more bad news. They were sailing at the edge of a great battle at sea now, and steel gladiators hastened to converge in the watery arena where only death and destruction could possibly result.

Behind him he could see the glow of the red combat lighting in the citadel of the main bridge where his officers sat dutifully at their posts, their eyes fixed on their computer screens and system panels. Fedorov was standing like a shadow by the Plexiglas navigation panel, marking off the positions of the ships that had been fingered by the radar. Brave Fedorov. He had lost his tether to the history, and now joined the stream of ongoing events like anyone else, an unknowing participant, swept inexorably forward into the moment with each revolution of the ship's powerful turbines.

Then he heard a distant rumble in the deep crimson of the midnight hour, the growl and thunder of a distant battle. Guns were firing, the big steel barrels of the battleships of this era blasting out their red anger. Admiral Tovey was now facing a trial by fire. *Hood* was engaged with two powerful enemies, the heart of the German battle fleet, *Bismarck* and *Tirpitz*. Tovey was racing to the scene aboard the battlecruiser *Invincible* arriving like the cavalry at the 11th hour to join the action. Off to the south *Kirov's* radars had also spotted flights of aircraft, fluttering low and slow over the sea like moths drawn to the flame of battle. These were the *Swordfish* torpedo bombers off the British carriers, or so Fedorov had told it.

Yet the Germans had more reinforcements at hand as well. The dark shadows of another battle line were only now emerging at the edge of the horizon to the north. Volsky had come out to the weather bridge to have a closer look at them himself with his field glasses. He could have stayed in the heated battle bridge, watching the scene on the overhead HD video feed from the Tin Man, but somehow seeing the foe with his own eyes, feeling the cold air on his face, smelling the sea and hearing the distant guns was what he wanted now.

The Admiral knew that he could turn away here any time he wished, and avoid becoming embroiled in the conflict, withdrawing into the gloaming of this hybrid dusk and dawn. Yet somehow the grinning smirk of the near full moon seemed to taunt him with recrimination.

Yes, we do not belong here, he knew. We are uninvited guests, interlopers, trespassing on the sacred ground of years lived long ago, but he could say that very same thing to both the British and Germans now. None of this should be happening, as Fedorov would attest. The HMS *Invincible* that now carried the flag of the Royal Navy into battle was never supposed to have been built! *Bismarck* and *Tirpitz* should not be at sea either, not in 1940. The fact that this was happening at all sat heavy on his shoulders, a burden he knew that he and his crew would now carry for some time, perhaps for all their remaining days.

We did this, he said to himself. This is the face of the war that we shaped with our own meddling, the war we sculpted with missile fire and the hard chisel of a nuclear warhead. It is ours now, a world of our own making, and no, we cannot shirk from battle here and slink away into the shadows. We have chosen, I have chosen, and now we must own that choice and do what we must here. It could be no other way.

The dark shapes on the sea ahead were the very same ships *Kirov* had engaged earlier, *Scharnhorst* and *Gneisenau*, with the heavy cruiser *Admiral Hipper*. They were hastening to the sound of the guns, even as *Kirov* was, latecomers to the battle, but ships that might weigh heavily in the balance and decide how fate would rule in this crucial engagement. Rodenko's radar report told the tale. The British would be out gunned if these ships arrived on the scene. *Invincible* had scored a stunning long range hit, causing the Germans to veer off, but they had just skirted north to slip over the horizon and continued on.

Volsky knew this brief moment of calm, a breathless anticipation, would soon slip from him like his frosty breath. He could not wait here, watch here, a simple bystander letting the history they had created play out as it might. They had made a choice.

The time for battle was again at hand, but what should they do? They had no more than 26 SSMs remaining, and perhaps five long years of war ahead if they could not find a way to move forward to their own time again. Each missile was worth its weight in gold. Even if they could move forward, what would they find? The world might be fractured beyond all recognition. Is that what Gromyko found when he shifted on *Kazan*? What would he do? What if he shifts again? These and a hundred other questions ran through his mind now as he turned and opened the outer hatch to the citadel bridge. The red light of battle stations fell on him as he entered, like a baptism of blood and fire.

"Admiral on the bridge!"

"As you were." Volsky pulled off his gloves and pocketed them, reaching for a handkerchief to chase the chill from his nose. "A cold summer night," he said. "But the sea is calm."

"Aye sir," said Fedorov. "Those planes have veered on a heading of zero-four-zero and engaged the Germans. I thought they had mistaken Admiral Tovey's ship as the target for a moment, but it appears they sorted things out."

"That is good," said Volsky. "I'm glad they did not find us here and we were not put in the uncomfortable position of having to fend off an attack. But now we must look to the action ahead. I just had a good long look at that contact to our north." Volsky pointed to the overhead Tin Man video screen that was now tracking the ships vectoring in from the northwest.

"It looks like those ships will arrive at a most inconvenient time for Admiral Tovey. What should we do about this, Fedorov? I would be prepared to take further action here, but what would you recommend?"

Fedorov thought for a moment, hearing and seeing the launch of a missile in his mind's eye, with all the drama and spectacle that would create. It would be clearly seen by the Germans again, and by Tovey's ship. Perhaps it would make their claim as a warship just a little more convincing, he thought, but it would certainly raise quite a few questions should they ever share lunch and gin with the British again.

He remembered his thought, moments ago... *They will see every shot we fire, and my god, what would ever happen if it became known that we were not born to this time and place, that we are strangers in this strange land, interlopers from another time with power beyond the imagination of anyone alive this day?*

"How many cards do we want to show here, Admiral? Our missiles will be a shocking addition to this battle should we engage now. It will raise more than a few eyebrows, and not just with the British should we meet with them again."

"Well the Germans have already seen what one of our missiles can do."

"That was expedient and necessary given the circumstances we found ourselves in. Yes, that will have consequences too. They will think we were a British ship, and perhaps conclude that this is a new weapon system being deployed by the Royal Navy. It could have effects we cannot foresee just yet. Remember, the Germans already have interest and activity in rocket development. Even in the history we know they fielded radio controlled glide bombs, the V-1 cruise missile, the V-2 ballistic missile and jet aircraft before 1945. That effort could now be accelerated."

"Yes, the cat is out of the bag, but we cannot control what they do now that they have seen our MOS-III."

"Yet if we keep our missiles close, the lesson will not be repeated, sir. Perhaps they might see it as a fluke, a lucky shot, and the effects could be mitigated."

"Perhaps, Fedorov, but we will never know. What was done was done. The Germans have see our fire, even though the British did not seem overly impressed with our ship."

"That will change if we fire SSMs to intervene in this battle now sir, but it isn't just the British I'm worried about."

"No? What is on your mind, Fedorov?"

"Ilanskiy, Admiral. That strange time shift effect on the back stairway of the inn at Ilanskiy. I went down those steps and found myself in 1908! A journey up that stair took me right back to where I was, 1942 again, but Sergei Kirov also came up that stairway after me, and from what Deputy Director Kamenski told us I now suspect that Naval Intelligence officer may have taken that stairway as well— Volkov. If that is true, who knows how far back in time that would have taken him? What if he reached the year 1908 as I did, but never deduced that the stairway was the means by which he did so? He would have been trapped in 1908, which could explain how he would have seized the reins of power with the knowledge he had. If this is the same man who now seems to control the Orenburg Federation, then news of a ship firing advanced rocketry and SAMs may also have an unpredictable effect."

"You suggest that Volkov might discover we are here?"

"That is inevitable if we continue with this intervention. He will know that no ship could possibly have such weapons in 1940, and if he ever does conclude that we have also come here from the future, then he will also know that we have other weapons on this ship as well."

"How would he discover that?"

"Did you see the cameras the Royal Navy had on us when we made that rendezvous? Of course I understand why we did so, but now there are photos of us, of this ship, and if one ever comes to Volkov he will immediately recognize our silhouette. Remember, he is Russian Naval intelligence. If he does hear about a strange new British ship he will do everything possible to discover what it is."

"This is all very disturbing, and I have not yet had time to consider it since Kamenski voiced his suspicions. How very odd… Volkov seemed to be a man in his later twenties or early thirties."

"He was 32 years old, sir," Fedorov put in. "I looked up his service records."

"Then he would be twice that age now if he went all the way back to 1908 as you say you did on those stairs. To think that he has been here, shaping the history all that time, is very alarming. Of course, we have had no time to stop and take a remedial course in history. It seems we have been moving from one crisis to another, all with the aim of preventing damage to the time line, but each one wreaking more and more havoc."

"We could still veer off and try to shift forward again," Fedorov suggested.

"Yes, but that control rod is not reliable, Fedorov. You yourself said that we could end up marooned on dry land if the same thing happens and we move in space again as well as in time. That and the strain to our reactors leaves me very reluctant to wave our magic wand again."

"What about the third control rod, sir? It has never been used, and it might work as Rod-25 did."

"Possibly, but can we take that risk? I know if we accept that, then we must also accept we are already marooned here. It would mean we live out the rest of our lives in this time."

"There may be other ways we can move in time, sir."

"Other ways? What do you mean, Fedorov?"

"Kamenski has told us that intense explosive events can also rupture the time continuum. That is how we now believe *Kirov* was shifted back to 1908. Remember, they had no control rod at all when Karpov sortied from Vladivostok. It was the eruption of that Demon Volcano that sent the ship to 1945, and then Karpov's use of atomic weapons that sent *Kirov* further back to 1908."

"And where does this lead us?"

"I'm not sure... but *Kirov* was blown decades into the past by the Demon eruption of 2021. That might mean we could move in the same way, and we also know there is one other way to create an explosive event capable of moving us in time." Fedorov stopped there, his point obvious.

"I know what you are suggesting now, but that is a dangerous alternative. And these events always moved us further into the past, yes? That would do us little good, and would be fraught with uncertainty. All I know is that we are here now, and at the edge of a moment where we may soon have to act. Something tells me that if the British lose this engagement, and are badly hurt, then their position becomes even more precarious."

"I agree, sir." Fedorov had an idea, but he kept things to himself for the moment. The Admiral made a telling point. They already had their foot in the door here, and trying to slip away now seemed a bit craven in some sense.

"We decided to intervene here," Volsky continued. "The time is now at hand. What do we do? That is the question. I could put missiles on the German ships and end this fight in one decisive blow, just as Karpov would argue if he were here. But what you have said about all this gives me pause."

"If need be, we can engage with deck guns to assist Admiral Tovey. The German *Stukas* are another matter. You said you would extend our SAM umbrella over Tovey's fleet, but that may soon lead to some rather spectacular fireworks in the sky, Admiral. If the

Germans manage to turn over and launch another strike from *Graf Zeppelin*, that could decide the battle in their favor. The British have just played out their air attack, and it will be some time before their carriers can recover any survivors and regroup for another strike. The surface action may be concluded before that happens, but the German air strike broke off and returned north over an hour ago. Those planes could have already landed on *Graf Zeppelin*, and they could be airborne again in twenty minutes."

"You see the carrier as the real threat now?"

"The German *Stukas* hurt the British once before, and it is clear that they have already engaged and damaged ships in Admiral Holland's task group."

"Apparently so, but what about those German battleships?"

At the moment, sir, it looks to be *Bismarck* and *Tirpitz* against HMS *Invincible, Hood* and *Repulse*. That is even money. Perhaps your thought of allowing that battle to proceed without our intervention there is wise now."

"What about those ships to the northwest, Fedorov?"

"*Scharnhorst* and *Gneisenau?* We can stop them, sir. We did that once already. As for the carrier, here is what I suggest."

Part II

Fire in Heaven

"The sun turns black, earth sinks in the sea,
The hot stars down from heaven are whirled;
Fierce grows the steam and the life-feeding flame,
Till fire leaps high about heaven itself."

—Valuspo ~ Nordic Poetic Edda

Chapter 4

Commander John Warrand held firm at the wheel of HMS *Hood*, the smoke and shock of the hit the ship had sustained finally abating. Like another young navigator aboard *Kirov* who was thrust unexpectedly into the Captain's chair, Warrand suddenly found himself the only senior officer on the bridge, with the battle thickening about him and the sea erupting in wild geysers of blood red water.

He had served as a navigator aboard the carrier *Furious*, and cruiser *Neptune* in the 1930s, and more recently as Navigating Officer aboard *Devonshire*, and finally the venerable battleship *Rodney*. He had just settled in, arriving aboard *Hood* months ago in March of 1940 to assume his post as Navigation Officer, Battle Cruiser Squadron.

Even as he struggled with the wheel, he was haunted by the face of Ted Briggs, the last man he had spoken to before the shell struck the conning tower and killed so many men on the compass platform. The men were crowding in there to get a look at the action, and he thought to have a look himself when he met Briggs at the door, gracefully stepping aside with a gesture and a brief word: "After you, old chap."

Then he remembered Captain Glennie had asked him to get a map from the chart room, and so he went there instead. It saved his life. The compass platform was a long way up from the Admiral's Bridge, which was tiered up over the forward gun director behind B turret. He doubted if any man there had survived the spray of shrapnel that must have exploded upwards after that shell struck home and hit the compass platform like a shotgun blast.

"Coming left twenty," he shouted, maneuvering to instinctively avoid the fall of heavy shells ahead of the ship, but also with the thought that he would be opening his rear turret firing arcs to enable them to get into action. "Hoist Blue Two!" Now *Hood* would at least bring all her functioning guns into the fight, and along with *Repulse* that would give them twelve 15-inch guns.

He gave an order to slow the ship down, hoping to briefly throw off the enemy's calculations and also stabilize the ship. *Hood* ran very low in the water, and when running at high speeds the spray from her own bow wash could often mist and veil the lower gun directors mounted on the forward turrets.

There came a loud roar and Warrand knew the finger of the Gunnery Officer had just squeezed the trigger on his firing pistol again, blasting with every gun trained and ready in one mighty salvo. Headless, bloodied and bruised, *Hood* was still fighting. No, he thought, not headless. Use your own noggin, Johnny. You're the man at the helm now. This fight is yours.

Smoke still trailed from the damaged B turret, and the anti-air rocket system there was completely destroyed, not that it was any great loss. The weapon basically deployed long trailing cables from a parachute in the hopes of snagging a passing airplane, and it had never been effective. The real damage was the loss of those two big guns in the heat of the battle.

Warrand had no idea what was happening on the boat deck amidships where the *Stukas* had planted a bomb that seriously damaged the aft funnel. Now, at least, he had someone on the Flag Bridge to hoist ensigns and he soon learned that there were still men alive on the compass platform above when someone shouted through a voice pipe that they had sighted another contact.

Then the ship shook again, and Warrand was nearly thrown from his feet. At the same time he could see what looked to be an explosion on *Repulse* ahead. The Germans had quickly found the range again, but the voice of 1st Gunnery Officer Lieutenant Commander Colin MacMullen was reassuring him that they were still in the fight.

"Down 200 and steady on bearing. Four guns ready. Fire!" MacMullen had been adjusting his fire using down-ladder corrections in 200 yard increments, and this time he was spot on.

Hood's mainmast soon called out a hit amidships on the lead German ship, presumed to be *Bismarck*, and Warrand took heart. A yeoman came running with more bad news, however, and he knew that a clock was ticking on the ship's prospects for survival.

"Sir! That last hit amidships has slipped our armor and we have damage in the number four boiler room!"

Two guns down, speed off a third, fires amidships, a hull breach that will mean we'll be taking water, all the senior officers wounded or killed but me, and now *Repulse* takes a hit for good measure. The question in Warrand's mind now was whether he could risk further damage to the ship by holding to this course and trying to stay in the battle, or whether he should attempt to break off and live to fight another day.

We're wounded and down on one knee, but we can still hold a sword, he thought. Then came the news he had longed to hear. It was shouted from the mainmast top watch, clear and high through the voice pipe and relayed to him by a Yeoman.

"Sir! Ships sighted on the horizon off the port bow!"

Anything on his port side was likely to be British, he thought. Dear God, let it be Tovey. Let it be HMS *Invincible* and then let's get on with it!

* * *

John Warrand's prayer would be answered that day. It was, indeed, Admiral John Tovey on *Invincible*, and with him, running like hounds to either side of the big battlecruiser, were the destroyers *Fortune* and *Firedrake*.

"Signal destroyers to swing round to zero-two-zero and make a run at the enemy," Tovey said coolly. "Gunnery officer, what do you make the range to that big fellow second in line?"

Lt. Cdr. Edward Connors answered, clear and confident. "I make it 23,400, sir. Right in our wheelhouse after that hit on the Twins, with all guns training on target now."

"Very well…" Tovey clasped his hands behind his back, even as his signalman runner Wells returned, breathless from his running climb back up to the Admiral's Bridge. "Hoist battle ensign. Good of you to rejoin us, Mister Wells. Please take up a post at the signal room voice pipe and let's give you a chance to catch your breath. Kindly call down and advise the W/T room to signal *Hood* and ascertain the condition of Admiral Holland's squadron."

Wells was quick to reply, his high voice echoing the Admiral's mannerly order, which prompted Tovey to smile again.

"You may reserve that octave for the order to abandon ship, should it ever come, Mister Wells. Otherwise a clear and calm order is best served to your purpose."

"Yes sir, of course." Wells had the heat and excitement of going unto his first combat at sea aboard a real battleship, but he took a deep breath after his climb, calming himself, yet alert and ready to execute any order that came his way. Somehow Tovey's cool was infectious, and he noted that every man on the Admiral's Bridge seemed to be standing his post with a steady, calm professionalism. He raised his chin, proud to be there, and waited.

"Gentlemen, it may interest you to know that a locket of hair from Lord Nelson himself has been sewn into the battle ensign we raise this hour," said Tovey, "and we're all the better for it." He gave Wells a reassuring nod, which did much to bring a measure of confidence to the younger officer.

"All guns trained and ready sir," came the call.

"Then let them know we are here. We'll see how they like our sixteen inch guns. Hoist Blue Five. You may begin, Mister Connors."

A bell rang three times, and this time it was Connors finger on the firing pistol, and the guns fired the first ranging salvo, using only the centermost barrel on each of the three turrets. If he was close again he had six more rounds ready to fling at the enemy at once.

* * *

Aboard *Graf Zeppelin* the air crews had completed the recovery of their strike wing and were now feverishly working to re-arm and re-fuel the planes on the hanger deck. Marco Ritter's Messerschmitt was one of the last to return, his right wing studded with dings where a *Fulmar* had managed to get a bite out of him. His sub-flight had managed to break up and harass the *Swordfish* strike from *Illustrious*, and he labored to note the direction the enemy planes took on their return leg.

"If one of our seaplanes can swing round and have a good look to the south we may be able to catch their carriers," he said to one of his pilots, then he spied the young Hans Rudel standing by his *Stuka* and smiled. My lucky eighteen, he thought, striding over to the man and clasping him on the shoulder.

"I saw what you did again this time, Rudel! Keep it up! Three more hits and you'll be in line for your first Knight's Cross."

"Thank you, sir. I did my best."

"Yes, and the British know it! You put that egg right in the nest, just like the first time. And where is that stupid Maintenance Chief, eh? He said you could not fly combat missions, but he can eat those words now. Tonight we'll drink to success, but for the moment, maybe you can get one more hit before Lindemann sinks those ships!"

"I'm ready, sir. As soon as they patch that hole in my tail, we can go out and hurt them again."

Ritter finished his tin of coffee and set it down. "Let's get up to the flight deck. They'll serve up your plane in no time." Together they took the ladder up.

Graf Zeppelin was a big ship, over 860 feet in length and 119 feet abeam, the ship displaced as much as *Kirov* would at a full load of over 33,000 tons. 1700 officers and men crewed the ship, which had sortied *streikschwere,* with a strike-heavy compliment primarily composed of modified *Stuka* dive bombers. As such, the ship was configured for an offensive role, instead of loading up with fighters and playing defense for Lindemann's fleet. The decision had paid good dividends, largely due to the discerning eye of Marco Ritter and his discovery of a top notch pilot in Hans Rudel.

Up on deck Ritter saw they were already finishing the mounting of two BF-109s on the forward catapults, perched right near the ship's bow. Behind them the main hanger deck yawned open, and the sound of the air crew chiefs shouting orders echoed up from below. High above them the tall yet graceful curve of the black stovepipe funnel darkened the sky. The ship was making speed into the wind, ready to launch. Already the first of the black winged *Stukas* were coming up on the elevator and being maneuvered aft to their pre launch positions.

Three planes had been lost in the 1st Squadron, two hit by flak and one caught by the British fighter defense. This left nine there, and two had damage enough to keep them below decks in the maintenance bays. Seven remaining planes were spotted and ready. The twelve planes in 2nd Squadron had all made it back, with eight still serviceable and being armed for action, including Rudel's plane.

Ritter offered Rudel a cigarette, but he declined, never indulging in the habit during those rigorous and challenging years in naval flight training school. All he could think of now was getting back in his plane and hearing the thrum of the engine as he pulled away from the deck of the carrier.

The sleek destroyer *Sigfrid* was cruising just off their starboard side, and its brother *Beowulf* was off the port side, effectively screening the ship's vitals from any possible torpedo attack by a lurking submarine. Both ships were new, the *Atlantik* class project that had conspired to build a fast destroyer that could run with the carrier and have the endurance to stay at sea. Sometimes called *Spähkreuzers*, or "scout cruisers," the ships were larger than any other German destroyer, with a dual propulsion system that used diesel engines for long cruises, and steam turbines for emergency speed.

The destroyers had six 5.9-inch guns in three twin turrets, a pair of 88s for high altitude AA defense, and a lavish battery of eight 37mm flak guns with another eight 20mm caliber. Ten 21-inch torpedoes amidships finished off this impressive weapons suite for a ship displacing just 5,700 tons. Two depth charge racks were also mounted astern so the ships could also provide ASW defense. Unfortunately their designers could provide no defense for the enemy they would soon encounter.

Ritter saw it first, thinking he was seeing a shooting star, a fast moving light in the hazy ocher sky. A billow of slate grey clouds drifted across the glowing orb of the low sun, dimming the light and making the contrast of the fire in the sky more noticeable. It was high up, then began to fall rapidly, towards the sea.

"Look there, Rudel. Are you sure all our planes are back?"

He thought it might be a fallen angel, one of the missing *Stukas* that had managed to get close enough to the carrier before eventually being forced to ditch. But no plane could move like that. Seconds later his eyes widened as he saw the light swoop low over the ocean and then accelerate! Its movement was inherently threatening, as it came, heading right for the ship, surging in like a hot star thrown down from the heavens. Then it smashed right into the hull of the Destroyer *Sigfrid* where it was keeping station two hundred yards from the carrier. The resulting explosion vibrated the air and an angry red fire scored the red twilight. Fire leapt up in a terrible sheet of flame.

"Mein Gott!" he exclaimed. Then a massive secondary explosion nearly shook them from their feet, and Rudel heard the hard chink of metal on metal as fragments of the ravaged destroyer were flung against the carrier's hull. He felt a nudge on his foot and looked to see one small piece of shrapnel had scuffed the toe of his boot. The torpedo mounts amidships had gone up in the fire, and the destroyer's back was broken.

Graf Zeppelin swept on, leaving the stricken destroyer behind. Ritter looked at Rudel, a stunned expression on his face. "That demon was meant for us, Rudel! It must have been a rocket! *Sigfrid* was just in the way. Get to your plane. I'll be damned if I'll get caught on this deck if another comes in." he eyed the heavens darkly, as if another star would suddenly shake itself loose from the sable sky and come hurtling from above, like a javelin cast by a vengeful god.

Ritter threw his cigarette down, tapped his companion on the shoulder, and ran to the forward catapult, making for his fighter. Rudel wasted no time either, his feet taking him aft as shouts of alarm and the signal for air alert resounded through the ship. The growl of the hydraulics on the elevators seemed more urgent now. They were under attack, but he could see no ship near them on any horizon save the foundering *Sigfrid* and now destroyer *Beowulf*, which had slowed to render assistance to its fallen brother.

Stop gawking and get to your plane, he thought. Ritter is correct! The sooner you get aloft, the better. Yet even as he had that thought, he wondered if the carrier would still be there when he returned from this last mission.

Chapter 5

"**Something** has gone amiss," said Rodenko as he hovered over the radar scope. He pointed to the screen, noting how the contacts they had been tracking had separated, one moving on ahead, and two behind.

"Any change of speed or heading?" asked Fedorov.

"No, I still read the primary contact as bearing on eighty true, and look, those look to be aircraft now. I think they are launching."

"Could our missile have missed or failed in some way. It's almost certain they could not have any chance to shoot it down."

"No sir, we detected the detonation. I think we must have hit one of the smaller ships. The contacts were very close to one another in that formation—so close that we almost read it as a single contact until I did some signal processing."

"The carrier was probably being screened by those destroyers. If that is what happened then we may be too late to stop them from launching."

"I'm reading at least seven aircraft up already, but we can put another missile on them in three minutes." Rodenko folded his arms, waiting for a decision.

Admiral Volsky had been listening from across the Captain's chair, brooding as he watched the dull red sky. "It is clear we must have struck one of those destroyers," he said.

Their plan to disrupt the carrier's launch operation had been foiled by the lucky positioning of the destroyer *Sigfrid* close off the carrier's starboard side—lucky for *Graf Zeppelin*, but not for *Sigfrid*, which took the P-900 that was meant for its bigger brother right amidships, and died an agonizing death.

"We might have used the Vodopad system," thought Fedorov. "But we were just not close enough. The range was well over 200 kilometers from our present position, and the Vodopads max out at 120 klicks."

"The same result could have happened, even if we configured it to wake homing mode as you suggested Fedorov. These weapons make a target selection, and it could have run right up the wake of one of those screening ships. Remember, our systems were never designed to fire in isolation at a battlegroup like this. We have always fired in salvos or three to twenty SSMs, enough to completely saturate a modern defense and obliterate the target. If that were a modern American carrier we would have fired with nearly every missile we had. As it stands, one of their screening units was just hit, and now they must be wondering what happened."

"Well, we've stuck a big stick in the bee hive," said Rodenko. "I'm reading another eight planes up—make that ten—seventeen planes aloft now."

"Are they bearing southwest to the scene of the surface action?"

"Not yet, but where else would they be headed?"

Volsky shrugged. "We tried a little surprise attack, just like our late Mister Karpov would have advised, but I think he would have put at least three missiles to this task. We had to be stingy, and now we got nothing for our trouble, and our missile inventory slips another notch."

"This means we will have to extend our SAM umbrella over the battle zone, sir." Fedorov knew that would also have a cost. They wanted to try and be discreet, applying the tremendous power of their modern weapons incrementally to try and affect the outcome here, but it was going to take something more. Beyond the missiles they would have to commit, the visibility of their SAM defense could have unforeseen consequences.

"Mister Samsonov," Volsky said quietly. "What is our SAM inventory?"

"Sir, my board reads thirty S-400 *Triumf* missiles remaining, and all conversions to full SAM mode have been completed. On the *Klinok* system we have ninety-eight missiles ready, and our *Kashtan* system still has fifty missiles available."

Volsky thought. "Then if we had to shoot down all those planes Rodenko is now reporting we would use ten percent of our SAM inventory, but after that I think this German aircraft carrier will pose no further threat. If, however, we decide to use an SSM now, it may take several hits to disable that ship, and its planes are already in the air. Very well, secure SSMs. Extend SAM shield over the battle zone, and let us hope the British planes are not so eager to return to the action."

"We may not have to shoot them all down," said Fedorov. "And once we let those missiles fly they are going to turn every head within sighting range."

"Well, gentlemen," said Volsky. "Time for the fireworks."

* * *

Aboard *Bismarck*, Lindemann was exhilarated with the excitement of the battle, until he felt the hard impact of an enemy shell, the sea erupting as a 15-inch round from HMS *Hood* plummeted in to strike the ship's heavy side armor. Seconds passed, then he received the call from Oels, who had gone down to his damage control post. The armor had stopped the shell, and the ship had not been hurt.

"*A little higher and we would have lost one of the secondary batteries, Kapitän. The hit was very close to one of the 5.7 inch gun magazines, but it did not penetrate our side armor.*"

"That is good," said Lindemann, smiling. But the Kapitän did not have time to savor his good fortune. *Hood* had found the range, and he immediately altered course ten points to try and throw the British gunnery off. The message that came next was as puzzling as it was disconcerting.

"Kapitän—a message from Böhmer on *Graf Zeppelin*. They have come under fire from what appeared to be a rocket of some kind!"

Lindemann had been too focused on his firefight with *Hood*, lost in the fire and smoke of battle now, and he had not seen the solitary

P-900 rise and fall in the sky as it arced over the scene, racing north another 150 kilometers to where *Graf Zeppelin* was cruising in the rear.

"A rocket?" Now Kapitän Hoffmann's words returned to haunt him. Rockets... fired by a mysterious British cruiser—a battlecruiser—a ship the size of *Hood* itself. He tried to warn us all that the British had these new weapons. But clearly *Hood* has nothing of the kind. No. They rely on good artillery, as we do.

"Was the ship damaged?"

"No sir. But the weapon struck *Sigfrid* and Böhmer thinks we may lose that ship."

"*Sigfrid?* Sunk?" This was something else entirely now. Hoffman's wild story of a fiery tailed rocket striking *Gneisenau* still seemed unbelievable. He had not seen the damage personally, but if he had, the news might have made more sense to him. Whatever this weapon was, it must have tremendous striking power to be able to sink a ship like *Sigfrid* in one blow. That was no ordinary destroyer! It was nearly 6,000 tons in displacement.

Beyond that, *Graf Zeppelin* was far to the northwest, well over the horizon. There was simply no way the British could have reached it with such a weapon from their present positions... unless... unless the ships to his south were not the only enemy units now vectoring in on the scene of the battle. *Nelson* and *Rodney* had been at sea for some time, but he heard nothing from Wilhelmshaven as to their current position. Suppose they continued west, following his own wake north of Iceland, and were even now bearing down on the Denmark Strait from the north?

His mind was in a whirlwind of possibilities now, and the sound of the battle seemed like a storm of steel all around him, the guns were elevating, firing, belching out their anger in tremendous salvos that shook the entire ship. The sea was a churning lake of fire, with tall geysers jetting up as the ships continued on a slowly converging collision course, the range diminishing by the minute. He had to think!

Could that rocket have been fired by a plane? Was it in fact a rocket weapon as reported, or might it have been a bomb? Could it have been a torpedo from a submarine, or even a flying rocket torpedo? He knew that Doenitz had toyed with that concept, a rocket that might be fired from beneath the sea to cross a longer distance before falling back into the ocean to approach its target as a torpedo. Naval Intelligence also believed that Italians were trying to develop flying torpedoes that could be dropped by parachute and then activated to circle and search for enemy ships. The roar of *Bismarck's* guns shook the ship again, rattling his attention back to the moment with the jarring sound of battle.

"Ship sighted! Bearing 220 degrees true!"

Lindemann pivoted to search the smoky red horizon, barely seeing the growing shadow of another ship on the sea. It had been reported earlier by the air units, and now was making its prominent appearance on the horizon. At that very moment Admiral Tovey was sending up his battle ensign and remarking that it bore a lock of Nelson's hair. Seconds later Lindemann knew that his battle was evolving to something more than he expected. He saw the bright flash of gunfire from the shadow on the horizon, heard the low booming peal soon after.

That will be HMS *Invincible*, he thought, perhaps the best ship the British have. He could see the high arc of the shells catching the sunlight, a small spotting salvo to test the range, but he knew this ship would soon follow with a full broadside if these shots were close.

Now his mind raced on. An attack on *Graf Zeppelin* from an impossible range… Could the British have another battlegroup to the north that he did not know about?

"Send to Böhmer," he said quickly. "Ask if he has sighted any enemy ships to the north of our position. That rocket had to come from somewhere. If the British are behind us…" He said nothing further, but the concern was obvious in his voice.

* * *

The missiles leapt up from the forward deck of battlecruiser *Kirov*, the hatches snapping open and the sibilant hiss of the declining jets orienting them to the correct angle of fire. Then the roar of the main rocket engines ignited, and the deadly lances were on their way. One by one the S-400 *Triumf* missiles rose into the sky, accelerating rapidly and scoring the ruddy sky with their long white tails that seemed almost luminescent in the midnight sun.

They formed a great smoky rainbow in the sky, arcing up, their tails bright with fire, the noise of their haste a roaring howl that seemed to shake the air itself. They were a weapon that could not have even been conceived in the minds of any man of that day, capable of finding and hitting a supersonic target as much as 400 kilometers away, and doing so with near pinpoint accuracy. And they could reach the mind numbing speed of just over 4000 meters per second, which amounted to 14,400 KPH!

Aboard the battleship *Bismarck*, every man on the bridge was staring at the sky. There came a lull in the gunfire, and he knew that the British crews must be equally spellbound. There were three, then five missiles clawing through the sky like shooting stars, high up, and then descending like meteors, bright with fire to explode on the heedless formation of *Stuka* dive bombers that was fast approaching the scene of the battle. One by one they exploded, then they saw the flaming wreckage of aircraft falling from the sky… one by one…

Lindemann was astounded by what he saw, the inner voice of the skald chanting the demonic verse from the Eddas…

"The hot stars down from heaven are whirled;
Fierce grows the steam, and the life-feeding flame,
Till fire leaps high about heaven itself."

Till fire leaps high… What in the name of heaven was happening? His eyes followed the long arcing trails through the sky, tracing back towards the smoky red horizon to their point of origin.

There, he thought. Whatever blighted *Gneisenau* and struck at *Graf Zeppelin* was there. He could feel the sinister presence of something dark and unseen beyond that horizon, a fateful nemesis that lurked at the edge of history itself, looming, brooding, a hidden menace on the high seas that was wholly unaccountable.

This is not possible, he thought. *Not possible!*

Then something jarred him to action, the harried worry snapping at him from all directions like the snarling teeth of a wolf pack. It was as if he acted on pure reflex, sensing a danger so profound here that his only recourse, the only sane thing to do, was to step back, to turn, to get his ships as far from that unseen danger as he could until he could assess what was happening.

At that moment one of the fiery streaks in the sky swerved and dove, racing down at breakneck speed and plummeting to the sea. At the last moment, it pulled up and then came streaking in, aimed right at *Bismarck*, just a meter or two above the water!

"Left hard rudder! Come round to ten degrees north and signal all ships follow!" Lindemann's voice was ragged as he shouted.

"Rudder left and coming hard about!"

The maneuver might have avoided a slow moving torpedo, or even frustrated the aim of an oncoming plane—but this was no plane. The rocket came hurtling in, right for the heart of the ship and then struck home with jarring fury and fire. It was as if Thor had hurled his hammer from the sky, the hammer of God striking his ship and igniting a horrid hot fire on his starboard side.

Bismarck wheeled off course, just as a narrow spread of two more heavy rounds from *Hood* hissed into the sea where the ship had been a moment before and exploded, magnifying the sense of imminent peril the Kapitän now felt. Then Lindemann saw the distant ripple of fire as the newly arriving British ship let loose with its first full broadside.

Hoffmann tried to warn me. I could see it in his eyes; hear it in the tone of his voice. There was fear there, and awe, and now I know what he had tried to convey. Now I know what killed *Sigfrid*. Yet

Lindemann had not even seen the enemy ship that had fired the terrible weapon at him!

The range opened at once, and Lindemann looked to see that *Tirpitz* and *Prince Eugen* had both matched his maneuver. The destroyer *Heimdall* was also churning about and accelerating to its top speed of 36 knots as the German ships veered off angle and began to break away to the northeast, guns still firing with wrathful anger.

Now the situation had taken a sudden and dramatic turn. Oels called up to the bridge saying he had red lights across two full compartments on the starboard aft quarter, and a bad fire. *Gneisenau* had been hit like this, by this terror weapon with precision accuracy and amazing range and striking power. *Altmark* obliterated, *Gneisenau* hit, *Tirpitz* hit, his own ship damaged, *Sigfrid* sunk and *Graf Zeppelin* under attack! This was more than he bargained for when he strove to persuade Raeder to allow him to engage here. Suddenly the lure of fat convoys to the south no longer seemed promising. Now he could think of only one thing he must do.

I must get these ships to safe waters. We must disengage at once. Hoffmann was correct and I should have listened to him.

This changes everything.

Chapter 6

"**That** seems to have done the trick," said Rodenko, his face registering satisfaction. "The German main battle group has turned on zero-one-zero. They look like they are breaking off, Admiral.

"And the planes?

"We got all seven in the lead group with that S-400 barrage. The rest are still near the carrier, but they now appear to be circling."

"Let me know if they proceed south on a heading to make any further attack."

The Admiral looked at his acting Capitan now. "Well, we could not avoid the fireworks as you had hoped, Mister Fedorov, but it appears we have made just a bit more of an impression than our deck guns did when the British had a look at them."

"Agreed, sir, and we will have some explaining to do should we meet them again, but I suppose it could not be helped. All things considered, it was a fairly economical cost to affect the outcome of this battle. Those five SAMs and the two SSMs we expended may have saved thousands of lives."

"On one side of the equation," Volsky reminded him. "Remember that we may have also killed a good number of German sailors with this intervention. Rodenko now believes the destroyer that took our P-900 has now sunk." He let that settle in for a moment, more for the sake of the younger officers within earshot than to lecture Fedorov. He knew his young Captain would have done even less if he could have found a way to impose an outcome here with minimal violence. Where Karpov was heedless of the human cost his actions levied, Fedorov seemed to count every soul lost on his fingertips.

One man heedless and headstrong, the other compassionate and overly cautious, yet daring in many ways. It was Fedorov's plan that safely rescued Orlov, and also his plan that put my bottom in this seat again and pulled *Kirov* out of 1908. We may have just arrived there aboard *Kazan* in the nick of time. Another hour and Karpov would have destroyed most of Togo's fleet. Who knows what the world would have looked like then?

He looked at Fedorov, seeing a distant look in his eyes, as if he was considering something, his mind grappling with a problem of some kind.

"Your thoughts, Mister Fedorov?"

"Sir? Oh, I was just thinking about our chances… of moving in time again before 1941."

"You are still worried what will happen come late July next year?"

"I am sir, in spite of what Director Kamenski has said. He believes this to be an altered reality, separate from the line of causality we left in 1908. That may be true, but it could also simply be the same world, only one badly fractured by what happened that year."

"But what did happen of any great consequence, Fedorov? We do not know this yet. Yes, Karpov sunk several old ships in Admiral Togo's fleet, but then we spirited the ship away and no one was the wiser."

"Yet that had a significant effect, sir. I spent two hours from my last leave with Nikolin listening to radio traffic. That incident re-ignited the Russo-Japanese conflict. Japan repudiated the Portsmouth treaty, and almost immediately occupied all of Sakhalin Island. We could not get all the details, but there was a news item about Urajio, and that was the Japanese name for Vladivostok. Japan now controls that city, sir, and it is not any exaggeration to think that may also be the result of the incident in 1908."

"That certainly would have changed the history in the Pacific."

"Yes sir, and I have learned one other thing. Josef Stalin died as a young man—in 1908. There was a broadcast out of Orenburg that mentioned his death in Bayil Prison. Apparently he was executed, though the narrator used the word assassinated. There is a statue of him there in Baku, and his name was etched on a monument as one of the instigators of the early revolution."

"Yet you must see this as good news, yes Fedorov? Think of all the millions sent to the death camps under Stalin's regime."

"Of course, sir, but there is another side to that coin. The strength of his will and personality was also a decisive factor in building the Soviet Union as we knew it. Without Stalin, Russia remained divided in a contentious civil war that apparently continues even now. There is fighting today again at Volgograd. This world may simply be the result of things that happened in that decisive year—in 1908. It was the year Russia lost its only Pacific port, the year Stalin died, and one other thing—it was the year something fell from the deeps of space at Tunguska, something that found its way into Rod-25."

"Suppose you are correct, Fedorov. What then?"

"Then we have reason to fear our own coming, sir. I keep going back and forth on this. On the one hand I think that for us to be here on this ship, this very moment, then this saga had to begin somewhere—with that accident on *Orel,* and our displacement to July 28th of 1941. Then on the other hand I think that for any of that to happen it must result from a history that remains sufficiently intact so that this ship is built. The events that lead to the design and commissioning of *Kirov,* the placement of Rod-25 aboard—well they have to remain perfectly intact. It's a house of cards, sir, and we are an Ace sitting at the very top. Anything that changes the history significantly in the past could easily affect our very existence. I wonder if the changes we see, and our presence here now, will prevent the ship from ever being constructed—or worse, Admiral. I wonder if these alterations in the history could even lead to changes in our own personal histories. Remember those men on Doctor Zolkin's list. It could be that our names are written in that same ledger now, and that time is simply waiting for the right moment to make an end of us."

That was a fairly dark assessment, and it gave Volsky pause for a moment. "I know how you feel, Fedorov, and what you must fear. Sometimes I think of my wife, and I am sure many others here think of their own loved ones we left behind so long ago. It is 1940. The dear woman I married over forty years ago will not be born for another seventeen years! Believe me, to think I am now in a world where her soul does not yet exist has left me feeling very empty at times. This heart of mine was half filled, or more, with the love that woman gave me, yet she doesn't even exist, except in my memory at this moment."

"Yes, and forgive me Admiral, but she might never even be born at all. This is what I fear now, and while it remains troublesome speculation and worry on my part at the moment, come July 28, 1941 we will be facing a dangerous paradox. We cannot be here, alive, the ship intact in this world at the moment *Kirov* is supposed to first arrive here. This is what I fear, and Director Kamenski's reassurances have not yet been sufficient to allow me a good night's rest here."

"Yet what can we do about that, Fedorov?"

"We can leave, sir. Something tells me we must leave before that date. Call it a hunch, but I just have this feeling about it. So I have been looking at any possible way we could resolve our dilemma here, given the fact the this new control rod we used seems unreliable."

"So you have been brooding over volcanoes; looking for a way out of this world."

Fedorov smiled. "Yes, I suppose I have, sir."

"I know you too well, young man. You are scheming again, correct?"

"Well sir, I thought I would see if there were any significant eruptions in this year or early next year, but I haven't found anything useful. Most of the volcanic activity was in the Pacific—a few eruptions in Japan, the Kuriles, Kamchatka. Now that we are here in the Atlantic, we will miss a moderate eruption on Miyake-Jima off the southern Japanese coast. That will happen July 12th, and there will be another moderate eruption in Indonesia on July 20th."

"Well I don't think it would be wise to try and spin the roulette wheel again and see if we end up in the Pacific."

"True, sir. But there won't be anything else until Asama on Honshu, Japan on July 13th next year—that's just two weeks before *Kirov* first appeared in the Norwegian Sea. They were all moderate eruptions—nothing like that Demon Volcano in 2021. The biggest event near us in time and space now would be Hekla on Iceland, but it isn't scheduled to erupt until November 2nd, 1947."

"That is of no help to us."

"Perhaps," said Fedorov. "But that eruption had been building for more than a century. Hekla is the most active volcano on Iceland, producing explosive eruptions on a fairly regular basis. The 1947 event was very explosive, though it was much smaller than the Demon Volcano, just a VEI 4."

"You have been digging, Fedorov. And you are thinking we have our own way of lighting a candle whenever we choose with our special warheads."

"I suppose so, sir. It's something we may have to consider if we cannot sort our this control rod issue."

Volsky gave him a look of admiration. "Well I will consider this with you. But remember, these explosive events always send things to the past, not the future. That is a caveat we must not forget. We will discuss it with Kamenski and perhaps Zolkin as well. The Doctor always has some interesting insight on these matters. After all, it was he who suggested we simply have Dobrynin fiddle with the reactors to get us home, and that has worked for us more than once. Now, however, I think we have our foot in the door here, and we must look to what is happening with the Germans. It is in my mind to continue north now, for Severomorsk and Murmansk."

"You're going to sail *Kirov* right into port, sir?"

"Possibly. If the situation permits and it seems safe and prudent. You have told me that Sergei Kirov is leading the Soviet State now. I want to speak with the man—in fact, I think you should speak with him as well. After all, you two met years ago." The Admiral smiled.

John Schettler | 53

"Do you think that is wise, Admiral? Look what happened after I met him in 1908. Just the slightest word form me may have caused all this."

"I told you to lay that burden down, Fedorov. You must not blame yourself. It may be that we vanish next July as you fear, but Kamenski could also be correct and we may simply be forced to live out our lives here if these new control rods no longer work. Oh, we will keep your volcanoes in mind, but we may be here for some time, and this ship will need a friendly port. There is no other way to say it. We'll need food, water, supplies. Beyond that, I have the men to consider. Perhaps sight of home would do them some good."

"But you can't be considering shore leave there, sir. Wouldn't that be very dangerous?"

Volsky remembered how Fedorov fretted in the Pacific when they had put men ashore. He wanted all his eggs safe in the basket where he could keep count. "I know you still hope we can avoid further changes, further contamination here, but that may not be possible."

Fedorov sighed. "I know that, sir. One night I was standing a quiet watch and seemed to be able to let all those concerns go and just accept the fact of my own existence here—that this was my life now, here, in this time and place. It was very liberating, far better than carrying these troubled thoughts around in a big burlap sack on my back."

"Yes? Well have you considered this, Fedorov? You say Sergei Kirov followed you up that stairway at Ilanskiy. It may be that he discovered what was happening there in some way, even as you did. He was a clever young man back then as well. Suppose he did discover that there were two different worlds joined by those stairs. Then what?"

"I've thought about that, Admiral, but how can we know this?"

"By speaking with Kirov, that's how."

Fedorov was silent for a time, finally realizing what the Admiral was driving at. Yes, he thought, we could learn a great deal about what happened in such a meeting. For that matter, if we do make port somewhere, then I could get my hands on some history books and read all about it. This would clear up many questions, but it would also be very risky, and he said as much to Volsky.

"Yes, yes," said Volsky. "It's risky to get out of bed each day. But we still get up. Breakfast is waiting. So we must take a few risks here if we want our eggs and sausages, eh?"

"Or a good blini and jam, sir."

"Exactly. But there is one more reason I think we must speak with this man, and this is one you may have considered yourself. If what I have said is true, and Sergie Kirov did learn the peculiar nature of that back stairway, then he knows it still—to this day. There is one other way we can move in time, Mister Fedorov, and without control rods, nuclear bombs or volcanoes. That stairway may still exist, and if it does, it is the single most important place in all of Russia. You understand? The innkeeper at Ilanskiy may be the most powerful man on earth and not even know it! But that said, only a very few people on this earth may know about this. Aside from a select club on this ship, Sergei Kirov may be one of those people."

"I see…." Fedorov suddenly realized that Volsky had been thinking a great deal about things, and had plans and schemes of his own. Then the Admiral held up a finger.

"There is one other man who may know of what we speak, that Intelligence officer Kamenski told us about, the man who shares the name of the current leader in Orenburg—Ivan Volkov."

The name fell like hot coals hissing in a bucket of water. They passed a brief moment, with a palpable sense of dread between them, clearly evident in the eyes of both men.

"So you see, Fedorov, we may have more to worry about here than this rendezvous with fate on July 28th next year. We have business of our own making to attend to first, and something tells me time has left us here for that very reason."

Part III

Prodigal Son

"The pattern of the prodigal is: rebellion, ruin, repentance, reconciliation, restoration."

—Edwin Louis Cole

Chapter 7

The madness that overtook him was a raging storm, yet something within him struggled to restrain it. End it! *End it!* The shame was too great, welling up like bile in his throat, and he raised the gun to his head. At that moment Admiral Tovey intervened, steady at the wheel of HMS *King Alfred*, bearing down on the ominous shadow ahead. A shell from his guns fell very near the ship, sending a hail of splinters up when it exploded, one scoring Karpov's face even as he began to squeeze the trigger. The pain and blood shocked him to the realization of life, harsh, stunning blood-red life that was still pulsing in his veins.

The ship lurched and he was thrown off balance, careening against the gunwale as *Kirov* rolled, and he was thrown completely over, falling from the weather bridge and scudding off the Korall BN-3 space communications system dome cover, which sent him flying right off the ship and headfirst into the sea! He plunged into the water with a hard thump, dazed and yet moving with an instinctive frantic impulse to save himself.

Beneath the frothing sea, he opened his eyes in a moment of panic, gaping at the shadow of fear itself in the shape of a submarine, like a phantom from his own private hell. There it was, lurking like a predatory shark very close to the ship! It was as if he had been flung into his worst nightmare, and he flailed, nearly gasping in the seawater as he struggled to reach the surface.

The broad hull of the ship had passed on, looming up as it slid away on the turbulent waters. He found himself batted about in the swirling wash of the ship's wake, the sea suddenly alive with energy, a scintillating seafoam green radiating out in every direction. Only his adrenaline kept his limbs moving, thrashing and flopping to keep his head above water. In one last terrible moment he saw the horizon studded with the squat iron shapes of the enemy ships, dark and threatening, iron monsters churning forward, their bows biting into the waves as they converged on the scene.

From the bridge of *Kirov*, with the power of the ship at his command, they were no more than heedless targets for his anger and ambition to squash on a whim. But here, alone in the wild sea, they loomed as steely devils, belching steam and black smoke, their guns training and firing, booming out reprisal.

It was over, he realized in a sudden moment of lucid thought. This was his end. Death waited for him here in the cold, merciless sea. Then he closed his eyes, his struggle finished, feeling a sensation of feathery lightness, his skin tingling as with the prickle of a thousand needles. There was no pain, only the strange sensation that he was slipping, falling, sliding away into the unseen depths—the infinite sea of time itself. His vision faded to grey, his consciousness fleeing as he lay in the hand of fate that moment. Yet its resolute grasp did not choose to close upon him with the finality of its crushing weight. Not yet... not now... not this day...

It was *not* over. Death was not waiting hungrily for him as he hoped it might, and when he finally awoke he felt himself adrift, still floating, his body moved by some unfathomable power beneath him that he instinctively recognized as the rise and swell of the sea. Karpov was alive. The sun was warm on his face, but something else was there. Eyes closed, he reached his hand, still feeling the soreness in his shoulder where he had fallen against the ship... coarse cloth... a bandage on his face. He opened his eyes, squinting up at the azure sky, studded with fluffy white clouds and resounding with the call of seabirds. A quiet bell rang, very close. The salty marine smell and an odor of fish was all about him. Then a shadow loomed over him, and he saw a face.

The eyes held a smile beneath cinder brows, the face of an old Asian man. The sudden memory of that headlong fall from grace and power to what seemed a clear and imminent death was on him again, and he struggled to sit up, almost as if to flee from the vision in his mind—*Kirov*, the guns and missiles firing, the faces of the crew, Samsonov and Rodenko, stony, adamant, full of recrimination. Doctor Zolkin slumped against the bulkhead... the blood... then the wild fall into the nightmare sea and his vision of the one thing that sent chills through his frame and haunted his thinking whenever he stood at the helm—a submarine! His breath came faster.

He felt gentle hands on his shoulder, pressing him down, bidding him to lay still, then the cool splash of water from an old tin ladle on his face and lips. He stared at the face again, an old man with charcoal brows, grey hair tied off on a short topknot, clearly Japanese. The only way he could place this element into any sensible context was to think he had been found adrift and captured by one of Admiral Togo's ships. The rhythm of the tide was evident, yet when he opened his eyes again he could see that he was not aboard a cold metal ship, but lying on the sun-bleached teak deck of a weathered fishing boat.

"Osore o shiranai," the old man said, then gestured to his own chest. "Watashi wa Tanakadesu. Ima yasumu. Ima iyasu. Surīpu." He pantomimed sleep, his clasped hands forming what might have been a pillow, eyes closed.

Karpov did not have to be persuaded. A weariness was on him that felt leaden, a lethargy of the mind and soul that seemed to paralyze him. He lolled back, closing his eyes, and drifted off, lulled by the quiet ding of the boat's bell, the call of the sea birds, the warmth of the sun. Sleep…

Sometime later, he knew not how long, his senses roused him again, this time with the smell of something cooking on charcoal. He ate, receiving small morsels of grilled fish and rice, more water, then warm tea. The old man was dutiful in tending to his needs, and then sleep came again, night and day blending in a seamless wash, his mind adrift on a sea of fitful dreams.

The images and the faces would not leave him for many days, long days at sea on the tiny fishing boat where he slept, ate, drank and slowly revived himself. Another day passed. Watching the stars, he knew the boat was headed north, though he did not know where it was going, or why. They came to an island and the old man threw a stone tied to a rope over as a makeshift anchor, then he went ashore, speaking to Karpov in his unintelligible language, but gesturing that the Captain should remain where he was. Karpov was still too weary to be curious. The long weeks of stress and tension had sapped his vitality. Now all he wanted was rest and sleep, so he lingered in the boat, sheltered by a flat tin roof in a small compartment beneath the mast and sail.

The old man returned, with gourds of fresh water and something just a little stronger, which Karpov soon came to know as Sake. But in his wake there soon came other men, uniformed, looking official. They carried a stretcher and the Captain found himself lifted and carried away by these newcomers, who spoke to one another as they walked. Some of the words fell into his memory through languorous, drowsy sleep... *Oshima... Nagata Maru.... Urajio...*

Soon they came to a small bay, and when he opened his eyes Karpov could see a squat tramp steamer tethered to a wooden dock. He was carried aboard, his eyes catching the name on the hull in faded block letters. *Nagata Maru.* They would sail another four days, always north, the seas accommodating and calm. He was quartered in a room below decks, given simple meals, and a Japanese man who seemed to be a physician called on his room once to give him a cursory examination, seemingly satisfied that he was not seriously ill. On the fourth day another man appeared, tall and swarthy, and obviously European. The sound of his voice speaking Russian was a welcome relief.

"Wake up!" The man strode into the room after the barest knock on the door. "No more free loading for you my friend." He introduced himself as Koslov, a pilot aboard the ship, and planted himself on the old wood chair as Karpov sat up, shifting his feet off the simple cot where he lay and onto the floor. He was glad to see someone at last that he could talk to.

"Where am I?"

"You're on my ship, the *Nagata Maru.* God only knows what you were about. They tell me a fisherman plucked your hide out of the sea way down south off Iki Island. Said they found themselves a Russki. What were you doing there, mate?"

Karpov frowned, giving the man a cursory glance, noting what looked to be military grade boots, a waistcoat, thick leather belt and fleece cap, but no sign of insignia or rank. He could obviously not tell this man anything resembling the truth, so a little *vranyo* was in order here, and he easily served it up.

"I was out in a launch and got caught in weather. A big wave swamped the damn boat and I went into the sea. Didn't think I had a chance then, the next thing I know, I'm on a fishing boat, and turn up here. Where the hell are we now?"

"Urajio," the man folded his arms. "That's the Japanese name for Vladivostok. They told me you were here, but we get more than a few vagrants thrown aboard on a typical run. Don't mind those bandages. You had a bit of a nick, but it's healing well, or so the medic tells me. But don't be surprised the next time you look in the mirror to shave. You'll have a scar."

Karpov touched the bandage on the left side of his face, remembering now, the pain, the blood, life in his veins that stayed his hand on the trigger. I spared *Key West*, he thought, and I spared my own life as well.

"This here is *Nagato Maru* out of Sasebo," said Koslov. "We came up on our weekly run. Not anything glamorous, but a fairly new ship— commissioned last year in fact. I was lucky to make pilot, cause I know the waters here well. Golden Horn Harbor was home to me for many years. You look to be military. I know a Captain's stripe when I see one. Who are you?"

The Captain could see no reason to lie, so he gave his name. Who would know him here if this was still 1908? He realized he needed to confirm that as soon as possible. "Karpov," he said. "Yes, I shipped out from Severomorsk on another steamer. Went ashore on that damn island, got drunk, and missed my boat!" Another convenient lie to close that door of inquiry. Then he quickly angled for more information. "Was so woozy with rum and seawater after I went into the drink that I don't even know what year it is any more. Must have hit my head on the gunwale when that storm swamped me. What day is it? What year, for that matter?"

Koslov gave him a narrow eyed smile. A cagey one, this one. Nothing he says makes much sense. Came here on a steamer? What ship? Where was he bound? What's the man doing in that garb with those stripes on his cuff and shoulder insignia?

"Tenth of June, thirty-eight. Get your wits about you Captain, if you *are* a Captain. Something tells me there's more to your story than you're telling, but I could care less. It's not my watch. I just came down here to say we've made port. If your ship was headed here, you've made it. If not, too bad for you. Jappos round up any Russki they find these days and ship them here—at least those without any papers. So here you are."

"Tenth of June... did you say thirty-eight? You mean 1938?"

"Of course that's what I mean. Are you daft or still groggy? Doctor says you've a clean bill of health. They watch for fevers and such. No sense shipping in a plague, eh? Well, you're clean, he says, and you're here. But now you're a landlubber again mate, unless you can find another ship to jump. You're lucky that old fisherman found a steamer like this one to turn you in, and not a military ship. Otherwise there would have been a good many more questions than the lot here would care to ask. As it stands, I'd think twice about parading about Urajio in that uniform. Russian military comes under a good deal of scrutiny here these days. There's a war on, you know."

Karpov did not understand. The news he had already heard was jarring enough—1938? What was this man saying now? "War? Here? The Japanese and Russians?"

"The Japanese and whoever they damn well take a dislike to. No, they've finished with us—at least for the time being. Now it's the Chinese they're after. Troop ships coming in and out of Urajio every week now and shipping out on the rail line through Harbin into Manchuko. You want out and can't find a steamer here, then you might try that. You can get all the way down to Ryojun from here, but it will be risky."

"Ryojun?"

"Port Arthur. Get used to calling it that way too, Captain. Jappos hear you speak of Vladivostok or Port Arthur and they get damn foul tempered about it since they took the place. Best be watching your manners here, if you know what I mean. That uniform of yours is going to be trouble, I can tell you that much. If you want some good advice, throw on an overcoat and be less conspicuous here. Then head inland if you're trying to get anywhere where one good Russian can speak to another. Siberia is the same as it always was, but there's Jappo military all the way out to the Amur river now, and don't you forget that. They find you wandering about in a uniform like that and you could be shot out there. That's mean wild country out on the river zone. Then again—if you are a sea faring man, you might get lucky like I did and get work on a steamer here. You'll need to learn some Japanese now, and how to bow and scrape and all, but it isn't a bad living. I'm seven years at it now and they gave me a new ship just last year—Pilot of the *Nagata Maru*, eh?" He thumped his chest, smiling through his bristly black beard.

"What do you mean—The Japanese have invaded here? Their army is on the Amur River?"

"What, have you had your head in the sand the last thirty years— or maybe in that jug of rum? Japanese kicked us out of Vladivostok long ago and we never got it back. You know that. In fact, we may never get it back now with another war brewing. It's too damn important to them now, right at the heart of their empire. Some say Ryujun is a better port—warmer waters there and not so much trouble with the ice in winter. But the Sea of Japan is well named now, isn't it? It's nothing more than a Japanese lake, and the route here is a whole lot safer than in through the Yellow Sea to Ryujun. Chinese haven't much of a navy, but pirates and Wakos still raise hell between Shanghai and Ryujun along the Chinese coast. Jappos have to escort most shipping there in convoys with military ships to keep watch, but not on the run up here. No sir. From Urajio you can throw a stone six hundred miles in any direction and it will still land in Imperial territory."

"Six hundred miles?"

"You must be European. You ship in from Kirov's lot? I suppose they're too busy with the fighting on the Volga to worry about what happens out here. Well, there's a lot happening, and you'll soon find out."

Chapter 8

Karpov seemed startled at the mention of Kirov, but the man went on, and it was soon clear that he wasn't talking about the ship, but the man. 'Kirov's lot' seemed to refer to European Russians from the far west, or so he reasoned, though he could not understand why.

"Out here you can forget all those nice European ways, and don't think anyone here will cut you any notice, whether you've come in from Leningrad or Moscow. Here the Japanese empire is all that matters. Yes sir, and they've started expanding again. If they don't know that back west in Orenburg or Moscow they soon will I suppose. Like I say, there's troop ships arriving here every week. Rumor is that my own ship will be commandeered soon for similar duty. Taking Vladivostok, Sakhalin and all of Primorskiy and Amur province wasn't enough after the last war. No sir. Now they've got all of Korea, Taiwan, Manchuko, and they may just push all the way to Lake Baikal if they have a mind to. Siberians can't do much about that, can they? Kolchak will try, but he'll be no match for these little weasels. Brutal when they get to war, and that's a fact."

Karpov was astounded by what he was hearing now. The last war? The man seemed to be saying the Japanese invaded and occupied Russian territory long ago. He knew that had happened once. Japan sent troops to Vladivostok in the midst of the Russian Civil War along with troops from many other powers, British, French, Italians, Czech, even Americans. They occupied the place in 1918 to support the Whites but after Kolchak's White Army collapsed in the war against the Bolsheviks in 1919, the Japanese remained in Vladivostok until 1922, fearing the rise of a communist state so close to their Imperial homeland.

"So 600 miles is nothing," said Koslov. "It's nearly a thousand miles to Zabaykalsk on the border. There's Japanese troops there, or so I hear tell. More coming every week. And they're in Mongolia now too. Rumor has it that they've pushed all the way to Ulaanbaatar. Damn industrious, these Japanese. They ran us out of the only port we had on the Pacific. That was inevitable after what happened before the war."

"This war?"

"The *last* war—the Great War as they called it. Something tells me this next one will be even bigger. All the ships are bigger, and now they have planes—planes on ships, mind you, and submarines too. No. *This* will be the great war, but maybe we can stay out of if this time around. After all, we're still at each other's throats, eh?"

Karpov did not know what to make of all this, and was very confused. Was this man telling the truth or exaggerating. 1938? How could he possibly be here? Did something happen to the ship? Did it move again and pull him along with it? But how was that possible? *Kirov* had no control rod this time, and there was no great explosion, nuclear or otherwise, that could have moved the ship. Then the image from his nightmares returned, that horrible moment when he plunged into the water, opening his eyes in a panic to see the long, evil shape of a submarine lurking in the shallows beneath the ship. Could it have been real?

"Are you sure you are well?" Koslov was watching him closely now, but Karpov just looked at him, saying nothing. "Well or not, it's time you were on your feet and off this ship. Considering you were put on by the Jappos, I'll grant you free passage this time. Get ashore and hole up in a good hotel for a while. The whole harbor district is overrun with Asians, but inland the city is still much as it always was. But mind what I said—wear an overcoat and don't flash those stripes on your cuff on the street or you'll likely be picked up by the Jappos for questioning, and you won't like that one bit. No sir, not one bit."

Karpov rubbed a cramp from his neck. "I will take your advice, Koslov, if I can find an overcoat as you suggest."

"Look in that locker, Captain. Help yourself... Tell me, are you regular navy?"

"I was."

"No longer?"

"It seems not. At least I have no ship now."

"Where were you headed?"

"Look, Koslov. I would rather not talk about it."

The other man gave him a knowing look. "Very well," he said. "A man has a right to bury his troubles, and it looks as though you have been digging for quite a while." He reached into his pocket and produced a handful of coins. "Here, take these. The medic says you haven't two rubles to rub together. A man needs to eat, and there's enough here to get a modest room in the Moscow Hotel if you choose. But unless you want to bow and scrape to the Jappos rank and file every time you see them—and you better learn a proper bow, mate—then I would head straight to the train station and get on train number four. It will take you up to Khabarovsk. Japanese took that as well, so stay on the train. Once you get up over the Amur bend you don't see them much at all. Get to Irkutsk, my friend. Then you hear good Russian. Old Man Kolchak is still there trying to re-organize the White Army. Otherwise the Japanese will take that too. Yes, get to Irkutsk. Once you get there, you can breathe again."

Karpov gave him a wan smile. "Thank you, Koslov. I will remember you."

"God go with you."

Karpov took the advice given him, along with a plain trench coat to conceal his uniform. He removed his service jacket, stuffing it inside a pillow case and using it for just that, something to lay his weary head on for the long train ride he contemplated. As he stepped ashore on the quay, the recollection of the last moment he had stood on this place was a sharp barb in his mind. The waterfront and piers were crowded with onlookers, the Mayor and his entourage were lined up with their tall hats, and out in the bay sat the mighty *Kirov*, its crew assembled on deck in dress whites, and the sound of the Russian national anthem resounding from the surrounding hills. There he stood, his Marine honor guard around him, a demigod to these men. That was only days ago… days… thirty years… a lifetime now it seemed. Then he was Vladimir Karpov, Captain of the most powerful force on earth and the new self-appointed Viceroy of the Far East—invincible.

He wondered what had been recorded of that moment, and what was written about the engagement he forced against Admiral Togo's fleet and the Japanese Navy. It was all history, the first domino to fall that set off a long chain reaction to produce the world he found himself in now, a world made by his own hand. This is all my legacy, he thought. I was going to restore Russia to its rightful place as a Pacific power…

Now look at me, he thought. Now I skulk ashore, head down, scarred and broken, humiliated, powerless, a lost and forsaken soul adrift in a world I can never escape from now. It was said that hell was a prison where every iron bar on the windows and doors was forged in the fire of your own mistakes and misdeeds. This was the hell I made for myself, and not just for me, but for everyone I see here now. The Japanese are certainly happy, but look at the suffering I have brought upon my own people.

He remembered all the many conversations he had with Admiral Volsky. The man had put his trust in him, and he swore he would not let him down. He remembered their conversation in the briefing room off the main bridge while they cruised for the Torres Strait. Volsky had discovered the special warhead still mounted to the number ten P-900, and wanted to make certain I had no more ideas about using it. The Captain remembered clearly what he had said.

"It would be just like me to say I assumed that you discovered the warhead earlier, and had it removed, but that would be a bowl of lozh, just another lie from the man I was back then."

Volsky had given him a long look. *"You asked me to give you a chance and I did so. I will not say that I have been in any way disappointed with your performance, but I wonder, Karpov… Is there any remnant of that old man still alive in you?"*

Karpov met his gaze, unflinching. *"A man may never purge himself entirely of his bad habits and faults, Admiral, or fully atone for his sins. But if he is a man, he can control himself and do what is right. This you have taught me well enough."*

"No, Karpov, that you learned on your own." He smiled, obvious

absolution in his eyes. *"I tell you this because it may happen, by one circumstance or another, that you find a missile key around your neck again one day. Then you will have to decide what you have learned or failed to learn, particularly if I am no longer here to weigh in on the matter with this substantial belly of mine."*

One day... And look what I did when I had that key around my neck. What did I really learn? Did I control myself, restrain those inner urges in me that wanted to do just what Dostoyevsky said was so gratifying? *Whether it is good or bad, it is sometimes very pleasant, too, to smash things...*

He could hear his own voice now, like a whining sycophant as he buttered the Admiral's bread. *"I would hope to find the courage to be half the man you are, sir, if I ever do find that key around my neck again."*

"Yes," Volsky had finished. *"If God dies, then we see how the angels fare..."*

Oh look how they fared. I tried to intimidate and destroy the American Navy in 1945 and got *Admiral Golovko* and *Orlan* in the soup instead. God only knows what happened to *Orlan*. But I sunk another big ship just to show the Americans what real power was, and then *Kirov* slipped away like a thief. What happened after that? I never took the time to try and find out. There was no way I *could* find it out. Suddenly we found ourselves in 1908! There would be nothing in any of Fedorov's books, but I can imagine that the Americans were not happy to see that Russians had atomic weapons too, and were more than willing to use them.

A strange thought came to him now. *It's 1938!* It's seven years before any of that happened. It's three years before *Kirov* ever showed up in this war in 1941. What will happen come late July that year when the ship is supposed to appear in the Norwegian Sea? But how can that happen now? Look at the world I have made. The Soviet Union doesn't even exist any longer, nor is it likely to exist in any form resembling the nation that built *Kirov*. Fedorov must be having fits with all of this. Serves him right for sticking his thumb in my pie.

What happened to the ship? Was *Kirov* still out there somewhere, its sharp bow cutting through the seas? Fedorov was aboard that submarine. Yes, the same one from my nightmare—*Kazan*. He had to use Rod-25 to get back and find me. He and the Admiral planned this whole thing! He would not leave Orlov when he jumped ship, and he moved heaven and earth to go and fetch him. It was no surprise that he came for me as well, only I underestimated him again. That damn intrepid son-of-a-bitch, Fedorov.

His thoughts unerringly led him back to that traumatic moment on the bridge. So that was *Kazan* that I saw when I went into the sea. Those bastards were so stealthy that they must have slipped right beneath the ship! That's what they planned! *Kazan* would shift and take *Kirov* right along with it, only something slipped. Maybe the big fish got caught in the net and *Kirov* and *Kazan* vanished right in the thick of that last battle. I was cast off, a little fish thrown back into the sea, unwanted.

What was Tasarov doing, listening to his music again? I told him to find that submarine. He was probably in league with the rest of them, from Rodenko, to Samsonov, to Nikolin. I can understand why Rodenko and Zolkin did what they did, but Samsonov? That was the final straw. When he stood up and refused my order, I knew it was all over for me. I was a fool to think I could do whatever I choose simply because of the stripes on my jacket cuff. Did I let Volsky's rank deter me when I tried to take the ship? No… Not one minute. Those goddamned traitors stood against me in the heat of battle. But who betrayed who? Did they betray me, or did I betray them? Either way you learn the hard lesson, Vladimir. You can lead, but it is only those that choose to follow you that place the power into your hands. Without them you are nothing. Never forget that again.

He did not forget. It was a very long train ride up through Khabarovsk, following the same route that Fedorov, Troyak, and Zykov had taken when they set off to find Orlov. On occasion a Japanese guard would eye him briefly, but he looked so decrepit, his face still bandaged, lean and hungry, eyes darkened with sorrow and regret, that no one seemed to want to bother him. So Karpov rode the train all the way to Irkutsk, doling out the last of the rubles Kaslov had given him for food along the way.

He found an old newspaper, dated two weeks earlier and read. The shock of what he learned there stayed with him for some time. Russia was divided, and still at war with itself. Sergie Kirov was alive, though he should have been killed four years ago in 1934. There was no mention of Stalin, none at all. Another nebulous and shadowy figure named 'The Prophet,' Ivan Volkov, ruled the central province now named the Orenburg Federation, a principle antagonist against Kirov's Western Russian state centered on Moscow and Leningrad.

Here in the east, the wild steppes and thick taiga forests of Siberia remained untamed, a free state. It seemed loosely controlled by groups of warlords, like the Cossack clans that had once ranged in the heartland of Russia. The name Kozolnikov seemed to appear prominently in Irkutsk, along with that of Old Man Kolchak. He was still alive too. Apparently the Bolsheviks were never able to assert control beyond the Urals.

Orenburg, all of Kazakhstan and the Caspian region, along with all of Siberia had remained provinces of the White Russian movement. Now Volkov's forces in Orenburg referred to themselves as the Grey Legion. He saw odd line drawings of what looked to be airships in the sky. What had happened to the world?

This was my doing, he thought. I did this the moment I took it upon myself to challenge Japan. No! It was Fedorov's meddling that caused it all. If I could have finished what I started none of this might have happened! He could not leave things be. He had to come back in that goddamned submarine. Was it still out there somewhere too?

He thought for a long time on his sad state, with plenty of time for regrets. Yet something within him folded in on itself, a hard kernel of stone that refused to yield, refused the mantle of shame and held but one thought in mind—*revenge.* That's what I said to that Inspector General and his dog from Naval Intelligence. Yes... Revenge is a dish that is best served cold.

At Irkutsk he decided to go and find Old Man Kolchak and see what he was up to. The first thing he did was pull his uniform jacket back out of that pillowcase and put it back on, and proudly. Some would say he tarnished it with all he had done, but let them talk, he thought. I know more than anyone alive in this sad world. If there is any man who is rightfully a prophet, it is me.

This was what Orlov had in mind when he jumped ship, yes? Well, I had something else in mind, and I didn't jump. The world threw me here, and here I will stay. With all I know, power will come easily into my grasp if I reach for it. And what better place to find it than in the hands of the men who already hold the reins? Yes, he thought. Go find this Old Man Kolchak, and the other one, the young Turk, Kozolnikov. I will soon be very useful to them. That's how it will begin. But before long... yes... before long they will be answering to me!

Chapter 9

Alan Turing reached for his handkerchief again, still bothered by the pollens of early summer, as he always was in June. As deviously clever as he was, he had not yet discovered a way to defeat Mother Nature, or to defend himself from the perennial attacks of Hay Fever that beset him. Not even the full gas mask he wore as he rode his bicycle to Bletchley Park each day for his work in the cypher busting unit seemed to do him any good, and probably frightened scores of roadside passersby and children when they saw his macabre, masked specter, head down, peddling furiously and breathing hard behind the leering visage of his goggle mask.

The bicycle also seemed to conspire against him at regular intervals, its gear chain slipping and clogging the works, bringing him to an ignominious stop on the long country roads. Then he would be forced to remove his gas mask to see well enough to re-set the chain, and the pollens would find his nose, still breathing heavily with the exertion of his ride. So he took to carefully calculating the interval between gear chain failures, counting each rotation of the pedals, and cleverly intervened, tightening and adjusting it just before the average time elapsed to ward off the failure.

In spite of his Hay Fever, he remained fit and trim, sometimes taking to running the three miles from his cottage to work each day, a *bona fide* marathon man in his own rite. All the while, his mind was feverishly working on some problem or another, be it an equation or expression in his calculations, a thorny problem in his effort to crack some devilishly complex code, or perhaps dreaming up another of his strange devices, like the Universal Machine that stood as a good foundation to the modern understanding of computers. Find the flaws, he thought. Find the loose ends, the contradictions. From those you can get a lever into the code and deduce everything. Then all it required was the proper machine to aid the decryption effort, and of course good signals intelligence. He was determined to have a solution to the German Naval Enigma code in short order.

His associate, Gordon Welchman, has been working with him on a device, which they called a "bombe," but the work was frustratingly slow. It was a series of drums arrayed in rows that rotated at 120rpms with each setting off the next in a precise order, and the motion migrating down and down to turn the positions of the lower drums, almost like the gears of a clock...or a bicycle. By brute force of trial and error the machine would test the possible relationship or "connection" between two letters.

It might deduce that E was connected to H until a contradicting case appeared in its machination that proposed E was connected to J or some other letter. Since E could not be connected to both H and J at the same time, it was the contradiction that allowed the code breakers to eliminate one case or another and eventually arrive at the correct connection—a connection that corresponded to the assignments on the German Enigma code machine. In effect, Turing and Welchman were building and using a massive analog computer to help them break the German code. It was all much more complex than that, but the principle was sound, and it was slowly producing results.

They had it up and running just a few months ago, in the ides of March, 1940, and at times its clattering and churning could be heard throughout the whole facility. To Turing, it sounded much like the feverish pedaling on his bicycle, mixed in with the chugging repetition of a printing press. The only problem was that there were too few men on the job, and too few "bombe" machines clattering away to move the effort forward. Building on the work of several Polish cryptographers, Turing was also attempting to decipher the German Naval Enigma code. He boldly announced it could be broken, and eagerly set to work on it.

"Look Gordon," he said one day, "no one else is doing anything about it and I could have it to myself." That was an idea particularly appealing to him, as it could become a perfect testing ground for his methods and machines. He kept Peter Twinn busy on the project as well, and innumerable girls providing hands and eyes for the enormous clerical work involved. A little luck also helped when the British captured the German Trawler *Polares* on April 26, 1940, which held numerous pieces of equipment related to the code.

Known as the "Narvik Pinch" it aided the work immensely. The German Enigma machine operators also helped in many ways. Thinking the code unbreakable, they would often pair three letter sets with a second series that was easily related. It was found that the three letter code set for LON was often followed by DON for London, and the three letter set for BER was often followed by LIN, just as HIT was finished off by LER. If any one of the sets could be identified in a message, the related series was easily deciphered.

By May of 1940 Turing and other dedicated cryptanalysts, notably Hugh Foss, had a breakthrough that led to the deciphering of a complete day's messages. The success was celebrated ever thereafter as "Foss Day," but as the code changed daily, there was still a great deal of work to be done to allow reliable deciphering for an entire month.

Hut 8 at Bletchley Park, or Station X as it was sometimes called, was a very busy place. That day Turing was wiping his weary nose, lamenting that his gas mask did not seem as reliable as he hoped on the morning ride, even though he had successfully averted a gear chain failure by stopping at a precise interval to effect a repair. A bit weary and bedraggled by his Hay Fever, he went over to the cupboard and quickly unlocked the padlock and chain which he used to secure his favorite coffee mug from any "unauthorized use" as he called it. Coffee! That was what he needed now to get the gears, wheels and bombes of his own mind working and clattering again.

Just as he was settling back into his chair and savoring the aroma as he breathed in thin curls of coffee vapor to soothe his nose and sinuses, in came Peter Twinn, with what looked to be a large photo in hand and a thick manila envelope under his arm. Turing caught the return label and knew it had come in on the morning delivery from Whitehall and the Admiralty.

"Well," said Twinn, "we're in trouble, Alan. What, pray tell, do you make of that!"

"What is it?" Turing seemed uninterested.

"It's the prodigal son, that what it is." Twinn pressed the photographs into his lap.

Turing took the first photo, eying it suspiciously. It was a typical aerial reconnaissance photo of what appeared to be a large warship at sea. "Well it certainly is exactly what it looks like," he said. "A ship."

"Yes, but not a German ship this time, Alan. Take a good guess as to who owns this one. Then have a look at these close-ups under my arm. I think you'll be quite amazed."

Turing set down his coffee mug, reached for his magnifying glass, and took a closer look. "Russian naval ensign," he said definitively. "That's clear enough. Where was it taken—the Baltic?"

"Southwest of Iceland, right in the middle of this big operation underway out there now."

Turing looked again, this time his gaze lingering on the photo, eye roving from place to place behind the big round lens of the magnifying glass and a strange feeling coming over him that he could not quite decipher. It was an odd ripple, shiver like, that ran up his spine and tingled at the back of his neck, yet he could not see why he would react thus way to a simple photograph.

"Dear Alan," said Twinn. "Having another allergy attack, are you? Don't worry, I'm sure there's a reasonable explanation as to why we could have missed a ship like this in the Russian order of battle. After all, we've never seen them as much of a threat. It's the Germans we've been hot about, eh?"

Saying nothing, Turing extended an arm, gesturing for the manila envelope Twinn was holding, his eyes still riveted to the original photo, a furrow of growing concern creasing his brow. He had seen this ship before... That was the feeling at the back of his neck now, and it was bloody dangerous, a rising discomfort and warning alarm in his mind. He had seen this ship before, yet he could not recall the where and when of that, strangely bothered, as his mind was a steel trap that little escaped from once embraced by the cold steel of his logic. He took the envelope, opening it hastily as Twinn looked on, now somewhat concerned himself.

"My Lord!" Turing exclaimed. "How did they manage to get these? Why, it looks as though they were taken from a ship steaming right alongside this big bad fellow."

"That they were—taken from HMS *Invincible* just days ago and flown off to the Admiralty for the purview of Their Lordships. So now they've come to us. Quite a ship, is it not? Note the label. It was listed under the name *Kirov*, and they've classed it as a battlecruiser of sorts, though I can't see much in the way of armament."

"Yes, just a few twin secondary turrets, but my god, the damn thing is bristling with receiving antennae and what looks to be radar dishes. Look at all these features here." Turing pointed out elements in the photo, the feeling he was reliving something of grave concern still deeply rooted in his mind. He could even feel the rising magma of fear there, an old fear, something learned long ago, and he noted how his pulse quickened.

"Now here's the amazing part," said Twinn. "This ship was commanded by a Russian Admiral, and he was invited over for lunch and gin with our own Admirals Tovey and Holland! Word is the Russians offered to throw in with us against the Germans! How's that for news?"

"Officially?" Turing gave him a searching look.

"We don't know the details yet. Tovey is still at sea, and things are getting quite hot from the latest signals we've received. But it would be a rather welcome development. All we have to do now is explain how the Russians built this ship without anyone here knowing about it... and how it came to be found in the Denmark Strait! First word on that monster was apparently sent in by an auxiliary cruiser escorting convoy HX-49 out of Halifax. Then came that aerial sighting from a pilot off *Ark Royal*."

"So we missed something," said Turing. "Ship watch isn't our department."

"But signals traffic is. Admiralty wants us to listen in more on the Russians now to see what else they might have up their sleeves. I don't think they perceive them as a threat, at least not Soviet Russia, but with the Orenburg Federation throwing in with the Germans the situations is somewhat... fluid."

"To say the least. A lot of dominoes have been falling Peter, Italy, France, Belgium, Holland, Denmark, Norway and now Orenburg. Well, they haven't any navy to speak of, just those antiquated old airship fleets."

"That's their navy of sorts," Twinn countered. "They've twenty four big zeppelins, rigged out for aerial reconnaissance, air defense and even bombing missions now. Those new self-sealing gas bags have proven very resilient. A typical fighter group has fits trying to shoot one of the damn things down."

"Yes, yes, well forget about Orenburg for the moment." Turing's attention was still fixated on the photos of the Russian ship. "Something tells me this ship is hiding something beneath that long empty foredeck. See these hatches? I doubt if this is an armed steamer or cargo vessel. Admiralty will have noticed this as well and they'll be wanting us to sort it all out."

"I can ask Kendrick or Strachey if they could listen in on Russian signals. This ship is bound to be receiving orders."

"Good idea, Peter... and let me know, will you? Let me know the instant you hear anything at all about this ship."

"Finally got your attention, eh?" Turing seemed to have an unusual interest in the matter now. "Well, Alan, I've finally found something that can get you to interrupt your coffee time!" Twinn smiled, but as he looked at Turing he could see he was again lost in his review of the photos, a silence about him that seemed very troubled.

Part IV

Alliances

"Friendship is but another name for an alliance with the follies and the misfortunes of others. Our own share of miseries is sufficient: why enter then as volunteers into those of another?

— Thomas Jefferson

Chapter 10

June 20, 1940

The crews were working feverishly, the Air Commandant's voice harsh as he bawled through the voice pipes to the nose of the ship. *"Cast off! All lines away! Ballast Chief, release ground anchor an lighten load!"*

The sun gleamed on the round nose of the ship where the dull red of its serial number was painted on the slate grey canvas—S6, "Siberian Six," otherwise known as Siberian Airship *Abakan*. Its broad tail fins were prominently marked with the Cross of Saint George, the war time symbol of the Free Siberian State. The elevatorman was exerting himself to spin the wheel, his eyes fixed on the elevator panel to note the airship's pitch, deflection and inclination. A glass leveling tube told him much of what he needed to know, and his effort was to "chase the bubble" when he wanted to level off the ship.

Abakan rose slowly, its interior gas bags struggling to get the necessary lift on the cold morning air. This ship, like most all the others still in service, was a model by the inspired genius of the German airship engineer Karl Arnstein, one of the great pioneers of rigid airship design who had worked closely with Count ('graf') Ferdinand von Zeppelin. The airship was every bit as big as the ship that first bore the count's name, the *Graf Zeppelin*, all of 770 feet long and just over 100,000 cubic meters in total gas volume. A helium lifter, as all airships in the Siberian fleet, it had incorporated the new Vulcan self-sealing gas bags, eighteen in all from nose to tail, and this single breakthrough had extended the life of the airship for decades.

The first designs had used hydrogen, highly prevalent and easy to obtain, and the lightest of all gasses to give it the best lifting power. Yet its Achilles heel was its volatile nature and flammability, which was driven home during the First World War.

Overmatched in the deadly proving ground of the war, airship technology was once on the verge of dying out when the airplane was seen to be a much less costly and effective means of controlling the skies. The duels of bi-winged canvas fighters fluttering around the big airships like flies stinging the back of a rhino were legendary in the first great war. The Germans had found out the hard way over England when their hydrogen inflated zeppelins were ravaged by agile fighters with incendiary rounds. Too many had plummeted from the sky as flaming wrecks, prompting Germany to all but abandon its zeppelin fleet.

The Russian states had stubbornly held on to their fleets, finding them too useful on the vast open heartland as their lifting power saw them capable of transporting a full battalion of armed troops as an air carrier.

The planes were still a threat, but the greatest danger to an airship in the new war would come from the long range anti-aircraft guns that were getting bigger and more effective every year.

Non flammable helium was adopted as the key alternative lifting gas. After the *Hindenburg* disaster of 1937, not a single airship now dared to use the more efficient hydrogen. Instead, rigid airship frames were made lighter and stronger with "Duralumin," an alloy of aluminum with exceptional durability, and its composition and heat treatment were a wartime secret. But the real advance that had extended the life of the airship was the discovery of "Vulcan," a self-sealing gelatinized latex rubber lining that was used in the shell and all gas bags. If penetrated by machinegun fire from enemy aircraft, it could reseal within seconds, and the bullets would simply end up going right through the gas bags or clattering against the Duralumin frames and ending up at the bottom of the big interior air cells, which had special openings where the air engineers would remove the rounds and count them as trophies.

Abakan had already reclaimed over a thousand rounds on its many combat missions over the years, a veteran of the continuing infighting during the long Russian civil war, and more recently against the ever more aggressive Japanese. Machinegun fire was still a threat to the gondolas, which could not be too heavily armored, and had too many view ports to provide a safe environment. But here the AA defense of the zeppelin often saw eight or ten machine guns, and even heavier 20mm to 30mm caliber weapons that made any approach by a fighter plane a very hazardous attack.

The only problem was the scarcity of helium, until vast discoveries were made near Irkutsk in Siberia that provided an ample supply. Helium production increased dramatically after hydrogen was proved too dangerous during the war. In Russia, the breakaway Orenburg Federation had production centered on the fields around Kashagan in the Caspian Basin, and that state still maintained the largest fleet of airships in the world. In Siberia, gas and condensate fields unique for their massive reserves were located in the Irkutsk Region at Kovykta and Chayanda, and provided enough helium to keep a smaller fleet active.

With eight big ships, the Siberian fleet was only a third the size of the Orenburg air fleet, which was the largest in the world with 24 active ships. Yet the Siberian zeppelins served well in the vast, tractless steppes, where it was simply impossible to travel by any other means. The Trans Siberian rail was still operating, but it had fallen into disrepair east of Omsk, torn up by ceaseless war and the pillaging of Cossacks, Tartars and others. The trains were often seen as good prizes for roving war parties, who would ride in on fast moving cavalry units and board the train cars at the gallop. Ambushes were common, rail blocks always a problem, so traveling by airship avoided all that, and it was faster than the train as well.

Other powers still maintained a few airships in service. The British Farman Aerodrome and the firm of Armstrong-Whitworth, had produced Beardmore models that became known as "Pulham's Pigs" when they operated out of Royal Navy Air Field Pulham. The British "Pigs on the wing" became the backbone of the Imperial Airship Fleet for a time, but by 1940 only three were still used by the Royal Navy.

There were five German Junkers *LuftSchiffs* and two built by Parseval Engineering in Friedrichschafen. Italy deployed two Forianini airships and France had one Freres airship still assigned to the Lafayette Escadrille Aerodrome. Even the Americans got in on the game with the deployment of several airship carriers that could launch and recover up to five bi-winged aircraft in flight by means of a specially designed trapeze docking system. With substantial helium resources of its own, the U.S. still kept a modest airship fleet active with designs from Wellman and Goodyear, and the Japanese still used floating reconnaissance balloons and a few airships designed by Yamada and Fujikura.

The *Abakan* was taking off on a very special mission that morning, up from its mooring facility on the Ob river near Novosibirsk and heading west with a most important passenger. Troops of the 18th Siberian Rifles were aboard to provide security, and the airship would link up with two brother ships within the hour to form an air flotilla of three as it made the long 750 kilometer journey west to Omsk.

"Inflation?" Air Commandant Bogrov was carefully monitoring his status from the main gondola bridge as the ship rose into the mackerel sky.

"95 percent, sir, and all engines nominal."

A helium airship would never take off with its gas bags fully inflated. For longer journeys they would want to fly at high elevation and therefore take off at only 90% inflation. Helium expanded as the airship rose to seek out the fast moving jet streams above. If they began with 100% inflation their climb would be much easier, but they would later have to slowly vent helium to prevent the gas bags from overfilling with expansion, and helium was too valuable to waste.

So instead they took off at 90% inflation, or 95% on a short run like this where they would not be gaining much altitude. They would simply drop ballast to facilitate the climb, and then special air condensers on top of the ship could distill water from the atmosphere to take on additional ballast. They could even harvest rain in stormy weather, braving the certain threat of lightning to get open the rain catches to collect all the fresh water needed.

Up in a jet stream the airships could make remarkable speed, some achieving 160KPH with favorable prevailing winds along their intended heading. On their own power using four powerful ram air turbines, they could make over 70 knots, or 135KPH at lower altitudes, much slower than any plane, but twice the speed of even the fastest ocean going ships, which made the airship a very useful scouting vessel in a naval reconnaissance role. It's endurance could outlast most any other aircraft of its day, but one drawback was that it was highly visible in the sky, and also easily detected with the early development of radar.

Air Commandant Bogrov was soon satisfied that all was well, and he turned to the Admiral seated at the plotting table behind him on the bridge.

"*Abakan* is aloft, sir, and I make it a little under an hour before we rendezvous with *Angara* and *Talmenka*."

"Very well, Mister Bogrov. In spite of the circumstances I will want all aeroguns manned and ready at all times."

"We will remain at full action stations throughout the journey, sir. All systems manned."

More than a means of conveyance, *Abakan* was also a fighting ship, with one turret mounting a single 105mm recoilless rifle on the forward gun gondola, three more 76mm beneath the long main gondola and another two on the aft gondola. Normal artillery using heavy hydraulic gun recoil carriages were simply too cumbersome, and the recoil of such weapons would have thrown the ship off its axis, causing violent swings in the gondolas and jarring vibrations that made it completely impractical to use them.

The solution was the Kurchevski 'Dynamic Reaction Cannon,' (DRP), mounted in pods beneath the gondolas. The guns could have their back flash vented safely into the open air by means of a simple manifold that diverted the stream downward beneath the gun pod, and the pod itself could rotate a full 360 degrees. The weapons also offered stability and light weight, yet sacrificed range to do so. Being largely designed for ground bombardment, they could still engage other zeppelins, but with maximum ranges between 4000 and 6000 meters. Another drawback was that the guns could not elevate well with the gondolas above them and the massive bulk of the airship. So an airship duel was always a struggle to gain superior elevation on the enemy ship where you could blast the big target below while remaining safe from all but small caliber return fire. To correct this firing arc defect, one or more 76mm recoilless rifles were positioned right atop the airship, on a reinforced platform anchored to the central Duralumin frame.

Above the gondola structures, the interior of the rigid Duralumin airframe could also be accessed from the long "keelway" that allowed the crew to move from the nose of the ship to its tail. Ladders up allowed crews to man the 20mm cannons on the top of the ship, one fore and one aft, and a battery of four machine guns. There were eight more 12.7mm machine guns positioned along the sides of the main the airframe in small dimples, and accessible by ladders positioned outside the main gas bag sectors.

The ship could also deploy bombs for ground attack, fledgling Katyusha style rockets arrayed in light weight aluminum racks, and a new longer range rocket assisted 'glide bomb' for standoff ground attacks. Much of this rocket technology had come from the Orenburg Federation, which seemed to be one of the leaders in that field, spurred on by Volkov. Some alarming leaps had been made in rocket technology there, and 'the Prophet' insisted it would one day become the preeminent military weaponry.

Even with all these arms mounted, the airship was capable of lifting another 40,000 pounds of arms, men or equipment. The rear cargo gondola could even carry two small armored cars that could be lowered by an engine driven crane and pulley system.

"I trust the men are ready with the appropriate honor guard?" The Admiral was justifiably touchy, for this day would see a meeting that may decide the fate of all Russia east of the Volga for decades to come. It was a high level diplomatic mission, arranged during a tensely negotiated truce between the Free Siberian State and Orenburg Federation. The two nation-states had been warring along a ragged border that seemed to change daily with one side or another making claims and incursions.

Swift raids by the Siberian Tartar cavalry would seize hamlets and villages, plunder them for supplies and food, and then withdraw. This would lead to the deployment of regular army units of the Grey Legion of Orenburg, and the simmering conflict eventually erupted to a major action at Omsk the previous winter. The legion pushed towards the city, once the westernmost major settlement in Free Siberia, and they crossed the Irtysh river there, occupying the entire city and driving another forty miles along the rail line through Kornilovka to Kalachinsk.

More motorized than the Siberian forces, the spring thaw of 1940 had seen the legion bog down in the marshy steppe country beyond Kalachinsk, but there were plans for a renewed offensive. Old Man Kolchak and his Lieutenants were well aware that Orenburg seemed intent on pushing east.

"What are the prospects for peace, Admiral?" said the Air Commandant.

"That remains to be seen, Bogrov. The Grey Legion has its hands full on the Volga, yes? Their campaign against Omsk last winter has emboldened them, and perhaps they think they will have continued success against us—but not if I can help it."

"They will outnumber us, sir, both on the ground and up here as well. Were flying west with more than a third of our entire air fleet. Don't be surprised if they have five or six airships over Omsk at this moment, and planes on the ground at the ready, sir."

"We have cards to play, Bogrov. The battalion we carry here is but one of the entire 18th Siberian Rifle Division. Kolchak has moved the whole division west as a measure of our resolve. The Volga Tartars have been restless, and many will come to our side if this conflict continues. Volkov knows this, which is perhaps the only reason he agreed to this meeting. Together with our Siberian Tartars, we could put half a million horsemen in the field and drive a wedge through Orenburg all the way to the Urals. He will do anything he can to prevent that, so it does not matter how many airships he has at the moment. We have resources Orenburg needs, and a strong position for negotiations."

"Will we get Omsk back sir?"

"I will insist on it. It is either that, or I will tell Volkov that he will have to garrison the river as far south as Oskemen."

"What about the Japanese, sir? They already have troops in Mongolia. If they push further west Volkov will have them on his eastern border too."

"The Japanese are of no concern for the moment. They have already taken what they want from us, and will see little value in getting embroiled in a war in the heartland of Asia."

The Admiral was studying his map even as he spoke, gesturing with a pencil. "No. Mark my words. Japan will soon direct its main war effort to the Pacific. They will want the Philippines, Indochina, Malaysia, the Dutch East Indies for their oil and rubber. They may even look to war on Australia."

"But that will mean war with the British and Americans at once, sir. Surely they could never hope to win in such a conflict."

"The British Empire is not what it once was, Bogrov. They will soon lose the last of their Asian bastions. Japan will take Hong Kong and Singapore from them as easily as they took Vladivostok and Port Arthur from us. As for the Americans, that is another matter. They will not be prepared at the outset. The Japanese will surprise them with the ferocity and ambition of their war effort. In time events may take another course, but it will be of no concern to us here for years. If Japan loses its war, then we will pick up the scraps and retake our eastern Pacific provinces. But first—Ivan Volkov. First we settle accounts with him."

"I wish you good luck in the negotiations, Admiral. Old Man Kolchak had great faith in you, as we all do."

"Luck will have nothing to do with it, Mister Bogrov."

The Admiral looked up from his map, the red underway light of the main bridge painting his features red, and underscoring the prominent scar on his right cheek, an old wound he never spoke about. He stood up, folding his arms, his eyes gazing out the viewports at the gleaming river far below them now.

He was not a big man, slight of frame and a bit round shouldered as Bogrov regarded him. The Air Commandant was a burly man, taller and more husky than the Admiral, but there was something in the way this man moved, something in the way he looked at you with those dark eyes above that scar that was most unnerving. A man's strength was not always found in his arms and shoulders, Bogrov knew. The man had come on the scene a few years ago and now had more titles than the Air Commandant could count.

He was Admiral of the fleet, commanding all eight airships in the Siberian Aero Corps. That was the hat he preferred to wear whenever he was aboard an airship. Yet he was also Vice Chancellor of the Free Siberian State, thick in league with Old Man Kolchak and the young Turk, Kozolnikov. On the ground he was General Commandant of the Siberian Cavalry Corps, and growing his enlistments week by week.

Yes, he was a man to be reckoned with, this one, thought Bogrov. We all know his name now, don't we—Vladimir Karpov, and god help any man who gets in his way. Yes, Vladimir Karpov was going west to Omsk that morning, and he would not come back until he had sat eye to eye with Ivan Volkov. He would not come back without Omsk in his back pocket either, and that would mean another medal would soon be pinned on his chest by Kolchak.

Bogrov had no doubts about it.

Chapter 11

It was eight hours until they finally saw the smoke rising over Omsk. The sun had been up since 3:30AM, but now it hung low in the grey sky, waiting for the moon to rise in its stead and take its turn on the endless celestial watch. A full moon tonight, thought Karpov. We will make certain our ships cannot be silhouetted. They will have guns along the riverfront, and I will take no chance that they will be aimed my way.

Bogrov was correct. There were five airships hovering at intervals above the city, their bloated steel grey shapes looking like a school of barracuda. One had three dull red stripes on its dorsal tail, the *Orenburg,* flagship of the fleet. Undoubtedly Volkov had arrived here in that ship. Bold of him to risk the fleet flag like this. I left our own flagship, *Irkutsk,* behind, choosing *Abakan* for the journey. If there is treachery here then at least our better ships will still be safe. He stooped to peer through the sighting telescope, shifting from one enemy ship to another. Yes… *Orenburg,* 12 gun dreadnaught, *Pavlodar, Astana, Sarkand,* all with eight DRP recoilless cannon. Then he had a flash of anger when he read the name of the last ship.

Those bastards! They did this simply to goad me, and rub my nose in their shit. He could see that the airship's old name had been painted over, and it now bore the name of the very city they were hovering over, *Omsk.* It was a jabbing way to let him know that Volkov thought he was going to keep this place as his own, in spite of the outcome of these talks. Karpov stood up stiffly, his jaw set. We'll see about that, he thought.

Omsk was a place of extremes. Situated on the Irtush river, a ready source of fish and fresh water, it was founded by the Cossacks in the 16th and 17th centuries, and grew rapidly as a gold rush town when Colonel Ivan Bukholts made the discovery up river from the present city center in 1716. A trading town for many years, it was also a cold frontier outpost at the edge of Siberia, and a place where the cast off rabble of European Russia might be sent in exile when they fell on hard times.

Prisoners surviving the hard labor camps of Siberia settled there after they gained their freedom again, and so it became a city of hard men, desperate men, where hope was in short supply. But in drawing all these wild misfits and felons to its bosom, the city became a fortress of survivors, their faces branded with letters to indicate their crimes—K on the right cheek, A on the forehead, T on the left cheek to spell KAT, which was short for "katorjnik" the word for "convict."

Yes, thought the Admiral, a city of marked men in the midst of all this desolation. Karpov fingered the mark on his own cheek, branding him for crimes he had committed. I am no different, he thought, remembering. That was then, this is now. Forget the past. Focus on what is before you.

He looked out the airship gondola viewports, noting the wide streets and broad prospects, heavy iron bridges over the river, and the areas cleared for parks and gardens. They had tried to make the place a little like Saint Petersburg, he thought, but out here that is like putting a dress on a boar. Still there were some buildings in the city that remained unscarred by the war. He spied the tall gleaming gold spire of the Resurrection Military Cathedral where the meeting would be held, the walls of the old frontier fortress, the Siberian Cadet School and Governor's Palace, and the Old St. Nicholas Church. The rail yards seemed to be a hub of activity, and he could clearly see the grey uniformed troops of Volkov's Legion there, clustered in groups, a blight on the place.

Old Man Kolchak made his residence here and established Omsk as the capital of the White Russian movement, he thought. What would he think to see his white city muddied with grey? That is why I am here. I must get the place back again, and they can damn well re-name that airship as well! I've half a mind to blast that damn ship from the sky, but not before I see this Volkov eye to eye.

"Make ready to disembark the troops," he said to the Air Commandant. "The fleet is to remain on a full alert standing until I return. Yes, we come here under the protection of a flag of truce, but

I will take no chances with a man of Volkov's reputation. He might like nothing more than to get his hands on someone like me. Then he would have the city and a hostage to go with it! So stand ready, Mister Bogrov. If I do not return by the time that fat sun out there rises again, I want you to blast the hell out of those ships," he pointed, "and start with that one!" His finger was on the misnamed *Omsk*.

"Aye sir. We'll give them a hell of a fight."

An hour later the battalion of the 18th Siberian Rifles was marching proudly through the streets of the city to the site of the old Resurrection Military Cathedral, their forest drab green uniforms immaculate, black belts and boots shined and gleaming, the hard clap of their timed footfalls sharp on the cobblestone streets. The honor guard carried the flag and standard of the Free Siberian State, led by a select squad with drawn sabers. Theatrics mattered at times like this, thought Karpov, still remembering his landing at Vladivostok to meet with the Mayor.

He marched proudly, surrounded on every side by a thicket of guards. As they approached the cathedral he heard the orders to advance on the double shouted by the Major At Arms, as he had commanded. The entire battalion moved into a run, each stride precise and timed, like the workings of a great machine bristling with bayoneted rifles as it snaked around the last bend and then came to a halt.

There stood a troop of the Grey Legion, vastly outnumbered by the men the Admiral had brought with him, but he had little doubt that Volkov had ample reserves close at hand. He knew also that he would not be permitted to enter the cathedral grounds with any more than a single squad as an honor guard and escort, and that his battalion would have to move off a thousand meters to the open ground of a city park, as had been agreed. He looked up briefly, noting that two of the Orenburg Airships had been well positioned to bring that park within the field of fire of their guns, but this did not surprise him.

An hour later, after anthems and honorifics, the Admiral finally found himself politely escorted to the meeting room in the cathedral. There sat a solitary man, with short grey hair and brows, easily in his sixties, yet nonetheless of sturdy frame and build. Volkov stood and the two men shook hands briefly before taking seats on opposite sides of the table.

As he met the man's eye, Karpov had a strange feeling that he had seen him once before, which he quickly dismissed, thinking it must have been the photographs he had reviewed. There on the wall behind Volkov was a freshly printed war poster depicting the dark silhouette of a leader's statue, undoubtedly Volkov himself, his arm raised in salutation to a fleet of long, sleek airships above. Orenburg had the largest airship fleet in the world, and it was apparently a singular point of pride Volkov wished to make here.

Karpov could see that Volkov's eye lingered on his for some time. As they were seated he seemed to be studying him very closely, thinking, as if struggling with something in his mind. The moment stretched out in the silence between them and then Karpov had enough of it and spoke.

"Why do you look at me like that? This scar on my face cannot be that intimidating."

"Forgive me, Admiral," said Volkov. "I… I have seen you before, I'm certain of it, and your name is familiar too. Yes! I remember now! The resemblance is remarkable."

"What are you talking about?"

"You…" Now Volkov seemed very ill at ease, and clearly surprised. "This isn't possible," he muttered, but his gaze kept steady on, his eyes awakening as if with sudden surmise. "Why, it *is* you… Could it be so? You are different, yes clearly different, but thirty-two years have passed since I first questioned you, and I never forget a face—never. How can this be? You haven't aged!" Volkov seemed clearly surprised, then a flash of anger crept into his voice, with an edge of suspicion. "Who are you?"

Karpov was annoyed. Was this Volkov's way of working up an insult to begin these talks, just like that airship out there, bearing the name of our city? A bold man, this one. He folded his arms, fixing Volkov with an equally leaden stare, eyes conveying his displeasure.

"You know very well who I am. What is this drivel you begin with? We have important matters to discuss here, and I am not your long lost cousin. Why do you look at me as if I was a ghost?"

"Because that is what you seem, my friend, a ghost from the distant past that I had almost forgotten. The resemblance is uncanny! Look at me! Look closely! Are you sure you have never seen me before?"

Karpov was clearly unhappy. What was this man saying? How dare he begin negotiations with such a flippant and infantile manner? Yet, even as he thought this, a strange feeling came over him, a sensation of *déjà vu* as if he had indeed seen this man before, though he could not place the face in his memory. He leaned forward, eyes narrow, his face serious and drawn. Yes, there was something strangely familiar about this man. Then something the man had just said stuck in his mind and jogged loose a question.

"What is this you say about questioning me? I am not a prisoner from your days past sent to a Siberian labor camp, if that is what you mistake me for. What is this nonsense you speak now? Thirty-two years? Make sense!"

"You don't remember, do you. No, I don't suppose I look anything at all like I once did thirty-two years ago. Vladimir Karpov! Yes, I knew I had heard the name before, but there are probably 100 men in Russia with that name, so that is nothing unusual. But a name and a face together—this I do not forget. It took me a moment, and when I say more you will understand the shock I must've felt in realizing it, but let me be blunt now, Captain Karpov, are you certain you do not remember this face?"

Captain Karpov? That immediately jarred Karpov on a deeper level. What was this man saying? How could he know that? Might he have heard rumors that I first came to Irkutsk wearing the uniform of a naval captain? No, how would that be possible?

Volkov could see that he had hit a nerve, and so he pushed his finger harder. "Yes, Captain Vladimir Karpov, acting commander of the battlecruiser *Kirov*. I know you well enough. Once I was very intent on finding that the young officer you sent west on the Trans-Siberian rail—or so we thought… What was his name again?"

"Fedorov?"

"Ah, yes, that was the man. Yes, director Kamenski sent me off on a wild goose chase to look for Fedorov, yet I do not think he had any idea what would result! No, how could he? Because even after all these years I have no idea what really happened to me. Don't you remember me now? I am Ivan Volkov, former Captain in Russian Naval Intelligence, the officer you met aboard your ship in the year 2021. I was sent there with Inspector General Kapustin to determine what had happened to your ship after it disappeared in the Norwegian Sea, and look at me now!"

Karpov's eyes widened in shock and surprise. He leaned back, clearly staggered by what this man had just said. There was simply no way this could be possible. And yet, the more he looked at the man the more he began to recognize similarities to the younger man he had confronted aboard *Kirov*, the meddling intelligence officer, the man he called Kapustin's lap dog. Yes, Volkov had that same gray hair, dark aspect, penetrating eyes, and now even his voice sounded familiar. But he was older, so much older. Karpov was speechless. Could this, indeed, be the same man? How could anyone else have known about the facts he had just disclosed?

"Yes," said Volkov, "I remember all too well now. It was that night before you sortied with the ship from Vladivostok. You tried to explain away those missing men on your doctor's roster. I didn't buy it, of course, but somehow you managed to convince the Inspector General. We went to director Kamenski with the matter, and it was he who ordered me to pursue this man, Fedorov. We knew there was no way he could leave the city by sea or air, as we were watching very closely, but just in case he might've slipped away on the trans-Siberian rail, I was sent to look for him."

"But that is impossible," said Karpov. "The man I knew was no more than thirty years old, and you are twice that age."

"Yes, I am. You have a very good eye, Karpov. I am exactly twice as old as I was when you saw me last. How could I be here now, you must wonder? How could I have aged like this? Believe me, I wondered it myself for years. But in time I put my insanity aside and came to realize that I *was* here. Then I got busy."

"Volkov… Why it is you, but how could this be?"

"Let me be more direct, Karpov. I went looking for Fedorov on the Trans-Siberian rail in the year 2021, and I thought I almost found him. Yes, where was the place? The little railway inn just east of Kansk near the old naval munitions center. That's when the madness started. I was searching the premises with my guards, and thought I discovered a hidden stairway at the back of that inn. I found someone was hiding there, and herded the rascal down to the dining hall. The next thing I know I encountered men who seemed completely out of place."

"Out of place? What do you mean?"

"I was downstairs in the lower lobby, the dining room, with a suspicious character by the ear when I ran into a group of men who held me at gunpoint and claimed they were members of the NKVD! Imagine my surprise—no, imagine my anger—a pair of fools, or so I believed. Well, I dealt with them easily enough. I thought they were just stupid idiots playing with fire, but this fire burns. And yet… when I walked out of that inn later, the rail yard looked strangely different, nothing like the place I had come to. Beyond that, all of my guards had simply vanished. I could not raise them on my jacket radio…"

He smiled, inwardly remembering his indignant anger and surprise over what had happened, and realizing now that there was no one on earth who could ever possibly have received his plaintive radio call as he sought to reestablish communication with his men. That was thirty-two years ago.

"Yes, the year was 1908, though it took me some time to discover that. Imagine my surprise, Karpov. Imagine opening a door, stepping outside, and finding you are in a completely different world! Of course you immediately doubt your own sanity, and this I did, but in time the weight of reality builds and builds and you cannot argue the evidence of your own senses. It was some time before I could actually believe it. I was indeed in the year 1908, and I have been here ever since."

"1908?"

Karpov was completely amazed at what he was hearing now. Ivan Volkov! This man was telling him he was indeed the naval intelligence officer he had met aboard the ship. One part of his mind was able to accept what he was saying on one level. Karpov had been to the year 1908 himself, equally bemused, bewildered, and yet ready to make the most of the opportunity that madness presented him. He had been displaced in time, lost, bouncing from one era to another for months on end. The ship had finally moved again, after he was flicked from the weather bridge of *Kirov* like a flea off the back of a rhino. Then time just seemed to discard him, as if it had no place for him any longer. He was cast back into the sea like an unwanted fish and ended up in 1938. Then things had finally settled down when he was returned to Vladivostok on that old merchant ship. At least he had remained here, stable in time, for the last two years.

"You are telling me that *you* moved in time?"

"Don't be so surprised, Karpov. Your very presence here tells me you have done the same! Yes, how could you be here, I say this to myself? But the evidence of one's eyes is very convincing, is it not? You are Vladimir Karpov, Captain of the battlecruiser *Kirov*. Do you deny it?" Volkov could see that Karpov remained speechless, bewildered, and now somewhat ill at ease.

"No, you do not deny it. You *are* Karpov, the same man I spoke with. And given what happened to me, and your presence here, I now begin to understand what happened to your ship."

Chapter 12

"**This** is astounding!"

"Yes, it truly is, and I have lived with it for the last thirty-two years. Tell me, Karpov, how long have you been here? As I said, you do not look like you have aged much since I remember seeing you last, except for that scar you bear on your cheek."

Now that the awful truth was plain between them, Karpov's words spilled out, unrestrained.

"Thirty-two years? 1908 you say? There is something about that year. I don't suppose you know what happened to me after the Inspector General sent you on your way and I sailed out of Vladivostok later to face the American Navy. No, I don't suppose you have any idea at all what I have gone through. Face them we did, and we hurt them. Then that Demon volcano erupted in the Kuriles and blew what was left of my fleet into the past again. I say *again* because you are right, that is what happened to *Kirov* in July during those live fire exercises in the Norwegian Sea. All your suspicions were correct. You could clearly see that the ship had been in combat, that something was amiss, but the pieces of the puzzle did not add up. There was no way for you to see the big picture, and of course no way you could possibly believe what we might have told you if we had revealed the truth. But, as you say, the evidence of one's eyes becomes indisputable after a while, and so I, too, came to believe that the impossible was real."

"Demon volcano? I don't understand."

"It's a very long story, Volkov. Perhaps one day we will have more time to discuss it, but for now it seems we share one thing that few in this world could comprehend or ever know. Yes, *Kirov* moved in *time*. It was an accident, and just as you say you found yourself somewhere else in time, our ship did the same. We found ourselves in the 1940s, fighting in this damnable war, struggling to find any way we could to get home. At times that struggle was rather fierce, and I had to resort to some extreme measures. But it seems all I did was worsen our situation. Then we found ourselves displaced deeper in time, to the year 1908, as impossible as it sounds for me to casually say such a thing. Then, unaccountably, the ship vanished, but I was left behind... Somewhere else."

Volkov was trying as best he could to follow all of this, and only his own incredible experience gave him any reference point to understand it or accept it. But now each of the two men were coming to believe the impossibility that was before them, and Karpov's candor was evident.

"You say the ship moved to the1940s? How was it I had no word of that? My intelligence apparatus is very good, as you might suspect."

"Because you weren't here, Volkov. None of this had happened. There was no Orenburg Federation or Free Siberian State. The Japanese were not in Vladivostok, and Stalin ruled a united Soviet Union with an iron hand."

"Stalin? What about Kirov?"

"He was dead, just as he should be now. Yes. We were in the past, but the history had not yet changed. It was all our meddling while we were there—all my meddling to be fair about it. That is what gave rise to all of this." He waved his arm, encompassing the entirety of the world beyond the confines of that meeting room.

"Your meddling? So the entire ship did move in time as I suspected. How? Have you discovered that yet?"

"Yes, we thought we knew how and why it was happening, but now I come to feel that ship was cursed, along with every man aboard. Yes, we moved even as you did, Volkov. Then, in the midst of combat, I was thrown clear of the ship when we were struck by enemy gunfire, and when I awoke I was here... That was two years ago."

"Two years ago? You mean to say you appeared in the year 1938?"

"Correct, and I have been busy too! I see you have made the most of your situation, so do not be surprised that I made the most of mine. Cream rises to the top, does it not? You and I seem to be common fated, Volkov. We are two men cut from the same cloth."

"This is amazing!" Volkov put his hands flat on the table now, as if he were testing the reality of this moment, needing something common and tangible to get hold of and anchor him. On one hand the presence of Karpov in the room relieved the terrible burden he had carried all these years, that he was a derelict, and outcast in time, a lost soul condemned to this wicked torture, exiled in the past. Here was another confederate, someone he could finally unburden himself to, a man and face from the old life he had come from. So he *wasn't* insane, and this was not his private hell any longer. There was another fallen angel before him now, scarred, haggard in spite of his prim uniform and cap, and all those medals pinned on his chest.

"So you have been busy," he pointed. "Old Man Kolchak seems to have taken a liking to you."

"That is so. He knows strength when he sees it."

"How did this happen, Karpov?"

"We don't really know."

"You say it was an accident?"

"At first, yes, that is what we believed. Then we discovered it may have had something to do with our reactors, with a control rod we were using in a maintenance procedure. That's what we were doing at the Primorskiy Engineering Center that night, Volkov. We were testing that damn control rod, and the man you were sent to look for, Fedorov, he was behind it all."

"What do you mean?"

"Once we suspected the control rod may have been the cause of these time displacements, he thought he could use it to go back and fetch that last missing man you uncovered in your inspection— Orlov."

"Orlov... Yes, I remember now. He was listed as missing, the only officer on the ship casualty list."

"Well he was missing—in 1942! Yes, we were there—the whole damn ship and crew—and Orlov jumped ship. Fedorov thought he would cause nothing but trouble if we left him there, and he hatched this wild scheme to go and fetch him. War was at hand, and we could not take the ship back again. *Kirov* was needed in the here and now, at least as we once held it in 2021. So we installed the control rod in the Primorskiy test reactor, and Fedorov went back. He was going to travel west on the Siberian Rail if he made it back safely, and apparently he did. So I suppose Kamenski and Kapustin had the right idea—just the wrong time. You were on his trail alright, Volkov, but some eighty years late. Fedorov did make it back to 1942 with that control rod. What I can't understand is how *you* slipped in time."

"Nor can I."

"When did it happen again?"

"At that railway inn… Now I remember the name. Yes, the place was called Ilanskiy. I was searching every rail station and inn on the line."

"And you had men with you up until then?"

"Yes. Then I went downstairs with a suspicious character I found hiding in a locked stairwell, and that is when the madness started."

"Madness?"

"I met men there, as I said. They claimed to be NKVD." Volkov related the entire story.

Karpov shook his head. "This is truly astounding. Could it be that place has something to do with your disappearance, your movement in time?"

"That had not occurred to me. It took me months to believe I was even sane. Yet, now that you mention this, that may be something worth investigating."

Karpov paused, considering, taking this all in and accepting it, swallowing the impossible yet again. "It seems you and I have had a steady diet of madness and mayhem for some time, Volkov. Now I understand why they call you the Prophet. Well that makes two of us. You see how easy it was to use the knowledge we have and seize power here. They tell me Stalin was killed in 1908—was that your doing?"

"No. I had nothing to do with that. But I think Kirov killed him."

"Sergei Kirov?"

"Who else? Stalin and Kirov were going to be old friends one day—until 1934."

"That explains why Kirov now controls the Bolsheviks. He was far more popular than Stalin, which is probably why he was assassinated."

"Probably true…" Volkov took a deep breath. "Now what about us, Karpov? What about this little war we're fighting here while the whole world is choosing sides and getting ready to go crazy out there."

"I see you have allied yourself with Germany?"

"That seemed to be the thing to do at the moment."

"But you know what happens, Volkov. Germany loses this damn war. The Axis powers are utterly defeated."

"Perhaps. But who really beat the Germans in that war? We did! Russia! It was mostly our burden. The British and Americans stuck their thumb in the pie at the end, and wanted half of Germany for their trouble. That won't happen now, not with the whole country back stabbing in this civil war."

"Don't sound so sanctimonious," said Karpov. "What are your troops doing here in Omsk, eh? Renaming airships now, are you? Feeling comfortable here?"

Volkov smiled. "So you noticed. Well, don't get your dander up, Karpov. Now that I know who you are things will change. As you say, we are cut from the same cloth, you and I. There is much we can accomplish together."

That sounded like a good opening now, but Karpov knew he had to be cautious. "We have business here first, Volkov."

"Yes, and I see you've moved more than this single battalion of the18th Siberians west."

"You see much."

"Don't be surprised. I was an intelligence officer, remember? Very well, Karpov, you came here to see if we can settle matters, and I came here for the same reason. Let's get on with it."

"We can start with Omsk," Karpov said quickly. "Kolchak lived here for years. He has a sentimental yearning for this place. Beyond that, we invested a great deal in getting the rail yards in order here—before you showed up with your Grey Legion last winter."

"Life has its surprises, does it not?"

"Indeed, well Omsk must be returned. We begin with that. If you cannot agree, then we have nothing further to discuss."

"I lost a lot of men last December trying to take this place."

"You'll lose a good many more trying to keep it." Karpov folded his arms, adamant.

Volkov smiled. "I remember that face, that look, and the way you backed down the Inspector General with that load of *Lozh* about those missing men."

"Yes, and I could see you were quite upset about it, but Kapustin had a head on his shoulders."

"I suppose that is true. I was somewhat impulsive in my youth, but age and the careful winnowing of the soul that power brings to a man have changed me Karpov. Oh, don't mistake me, you will find me as headstrong and determined as I always was, it's just that age brings a certain wisdom. Yes? Very well, you can have your city back if that is what it will take to secure this border. Then we can turn our attention to more important matters once we bury the hatchet here."

"You will withdraw all your units west of the river? Well west?"

"I'll give the order tonight. We'll pull back to the old border, in fact, I'll quarter my men in Petropavlovsk and we can get away from these damn mosquitoes. Fair enough?"

"Done. We'll reoccupy the city five days after you withdraw to make sure there are no incidents with the men. I'll want a border checkpoint at Isilkul, and an outpost at Moskalenki, but other than that we'll leave the border zone alone."

"And what about the Tartars?"

"You noticed those as well, did you?" Now it was Karpov's turn to smile. "Listen, Volkov. This war is only getting started. You have an arm full of it right now on the Volga, and you certainly don't want us at your backside. For that matter, we'll need troops in the east to stop the damn Japanese. I came in through Vladivostok. You wouldn't recognize the place if you saw it now. They have warships in the harbor ten deep—troops all over the region. And you know they've moved into Mongolia as well."

"They are biting off more than they can chew."

"Of course. You and I both know where their real war effort will be directed soon, and how that turns out once the Americans get involved."

"I suppose we do."

"Yes, and so if I'm to restore what we've lost in the Pacific, first you and I have to come to an agreement. Let me be blunt. I can put half a million Siberian and Tartar cavalry in the field within six months. If I were to move west now in force the Tartars would rally to my banners by the tens of thousands from here to the Urals. Those are fast moving troops, and if we combine our airship fleets we can move thirty-six battalions, that's three full divisions of regular infantry, and all in one lift, and Sergei Kirov has nothing that can stop us. With our airships and the cavalry I command we can move like the wind. I can swing up through Perm and secure your entire northern flank, or set it on fire and raise hell for you—the choice is yours."

"Half a million? Yes, I suppose you could. But it's 1100 kilometers from here to Perm. That's a long way to go on horseback, and over very rugged terrain."

"My horsemen live there. They know that country like the back of their hands. They'll get there, and I'll organized them when they do. Believe me, we will give the Bolsheviks fits. I can take Perm, and secure the Kama river line all the way to Kazan. Then we have the Urals, the resources, and when Hitler turns his panzers east Kirov will have nowhere to run when the Germans drive on Moscow."

"You dream big, Karpov."

"Of course I do. I know you think you will live forever, Volkov, but you won't. Someone is going to have to take over when you go, and I'm your man. Kolchak won't be around much longer either. You are not yet old, however. I can see that in spite of your age. With what we know now, the two of us can shape the course of events for the next twenty years. Then you can retire and leave the work to me."

Kolchak gave him a narrow eyed grin. Then he did something unexpected, though it did not produce the reaction in Karpov that he thought it might. He reached into his inner coat pocket and pulled out a gun, aiming it right at Karpov's chest.

"So you think you will inherit everything I have given half my life to build here, eh? I could put a bullet in your heart right now, order my airships to blow those overinflated balloons of yours out of the sky, and have that battalion you brought with you for breakfast!"

Karpov didn't move a muscle. He just smiled. "Look under the table, Volkov. Before you can move a finger to release the safety on that pistol I could blow your balls off."

At this Volkov laughed, releasing the tension, and he set his pistol squarely on the table now. Karpov drew his hand up from beneath the table and he, too, was holding a pistol, which he set right beside Volkov's.

"I think we may have reached an understanding," said Volkov. "And now I think we should put our pistols away and drink on it. I have some very good Vodka on ice in the next room."

"Good, Volkov. Very good. Yes, I will drink with you now, and we have much to discuss. Oh… One other thing. Rename that damn airship, and have it done before I leave here today."

At this Volkov laughed, reaching in his pocket again. But this time he pulled out a pair of good cigars.

Part V

Homecoming

"*How puzzling all these changes are! I'm never sure what I'm going to be, from one minute to another… I wonder if I've been changed in the night. Let me think. Was I the same when I got up this morning? I almost think I can remember feeling a little different. But if I'm not the same, the next question is 'Who in the world am I?' Ah, that's the great puzzle!*"

— Lewis Carroll

Chapter 13

June 21, 1940

Kirov winked out a lamp signal in farewell as the ship turned north, easing away from HMS *Invincible*. In the heat of the battle they had made a very timely intervention. Just as the second air strike was vectoring in on the stricken *Hood*, five lethal S-400 SAMs had swatted the leading elements from the sky. Then a single P-900 had been sent directly against the presumed fleet flagship, the *Bismarck*, and its dramatic approach and impact had the same effect on Lindemann that it had on Hoffmann.

When Rodenko got the radar report that the Germans appeared to be breaking off to the north there was only one more consideration—*Scharnhorst* and *Gneisenau* had been hastening to the scene, and might arrive right on Tovey's rear left flank. Approaching on that same flank, Volsky decided to put on speed, and show his silhouette to the Germans. The sudden appearance of the same mysterious ship he had seen earlier, along with Lindemann's orders to alter course and withdraw, had been enough to cool the ardor of Hoffmann, eager as he was to lock horns with their adversaries.

"Don't count the Germans out just yet," said Fedorov. "They were not beaten here. Absent our intervention I would have given odds that the Kriegsmarine would have written a decisive victory into the history books in this engagement. My God, look at *Hood!*"

Once the pride of the fleet before HMS *Invincible* took those laurels, *Hood* looked like a beaten and broken fighter who had barely managed to hang on to the late rounds and was saved by the bell. Her B-turret was out of action, a boiler room severely damaged, her aft funnel all but shredded, leaving a constant pall of acrid smoke over the ship as it steamed pathetically along in Tovey's wake. Admiral Holland was wounded, but would recover, as would many other senior officers, though Captain Glennie had been killed in action and the ship was currently being mastered by a relatively inexperienced

Lieutenant Commander Warrand. Tovey made arrangements to immediately have a ranking officer flown out from Rosyth to Reykjavik to take over command of the ship, Captain Ralph Kerr.

Admiral Volsky had decided not to arrange a second meeting with Tovey just yet. He felt that it was necessary to first meet with those in power in the Russian homeland, realizing that he alone could not in any way guarantee or deliver on any offer of support or alliance.

"I am master of this ship, Fedorov," he had explained, "and I think we have won a measure of good will here that will come in handy in the months ahead. Yet we cannot commit Russia to a wartime alliance with Britain on our own, nor should our actions here be interpreted as such a grace by Admiral Tovey. What we must do now is meet with the man this ship was named for—Sergie Kirov. So I want to press on north as soon as possible. We can herd the Germans along as we go."

"I understand, Admiral."

"Where do you think the German fleet will head now?"

"I doubt that the fleet commander here had full authority in this engagement, sir. It is very likely that his commitment of capital ships to open battle with the Royal Navy was conditional. I think the attack we made on *Graf Zeppelin* was very shocking to the Germans, even if we apparently did not hit the carrier itself."

"Yes, I suppose they will be wondering just where the ship was that attacked them."

"Indeed, sir. Radar returns showed they flew wide area search patterns all around the ship's position. It seemed clear to me that they were trying to answer that very question. That uncertainty, the damage we put on *Gneisenau*, the loss of their destroyer and that tanker we sunk, and the hit we put on *Bismarck* all seemed to be enough rocks in the wheelbarrow to give them pause. It is my belief that Admiral Raeder gave orders that the fleet was not to be put at risk of sustaining serious losses."

"You believe they will return to Germany?"

"That depends on the extent of the damage they have actually sustained. These were very tough ships, well armored, very durable. I don't think we really hurt *Bismarck* that badly, though the damage we put on *Gneisenau* appeared to be more extensive. That ship may need to return to a German shipyard for repairs. *Scharnhorst* will most likely return to Trondheim or another Norwegian port. If the history I know holds true, that ship will need work on its engines and turbines soon, but for now it should still be considered an operational threat. As for the battleships, I cannot see that Raeder would want them in any Norwegian port at this time. They are too important to leave exposed to potential attacks by the R.A.F. My guess is that they will return to Bremen."

"Then if we sail north in their wake we may not have to face this entire battle group again anytime soon I hope."

"Once we get out of the Denmark Strait there is a lot of sea room in the Norwegian Sea, Admiral. I think we could sail North and safely avoid engagement, but you are correct, the Germans may no longer have battle on their mind until they can learn more about what has actually happened here. They will be very curious as to what these weapons we used are, and what ship fired them."

"Then I think we will pay our respects to Admiral Tovey, and be on our way."

"You're going to meet with him again, sir?"

"No, I think I will have Nikolin send over a message, and perhaps we might send a boat over with a box of good cigars."

That is what Volsky decided he would do, and in the box he enclosed a personal note to Admiral John Tovey, which he hoped would keep the door open for better days ahead. In this way they avoided the inevitable questions regarding the weapons they had put on full display here. The less said the better, thought Volsky, but he had at least avoided the scenario they had already lived through once in these waters—a hostile engagement with the powerful Royal Navy. As to their future cooperation, Volsky wrote that he would do everything possible to further such an arrangement and hoped to meet again soon.

Admiral Tovey, he wrote. *So today you have seen that there is a little more on the deck of my ship than three 5.7-inch gun turrets. We were pleased to be able to render assistance in this engagement, and look to better days ahead. I will speak with my government soon, and you should expect to hear from me again in the future. It may be that Kirov will sail south again and I would be most willing to shake hands with you if a welcome remains there for us. My respects to you, and regrets for any loss of life your fleet may have sustained in this engagement. I find it fortunate that the German Navy wisely elected to return home, and I will see to it that you are informed if any of their ships take a wayward course to the south. For now, I bid you farewell as I point the bow of my ship north, and think of home.*

Highest regards,

Admiral Leonid Volsky

The lantern winked out 'fair weather, farewell.' Then *Kirov* eased away from the big British battlecruiser, put on speed, and slowly slipped ahead into the night that would never be born that day. His intention was to sail north for the island and Jan Mayen, the frigid Arctic outpost that had been so instrumental when they first appeared here, a lifetime ago it seemed now. It was there that Fedorov had his first flash of genius, saying that all they needed to do was to overfly that island with a helicopter to look for the weather installation facilities to determine whether they were still in their own time or not. So it had been a key piece of the incredible puzzle they had put together to make it clear that something impossible had happened to them, and they were no longer in their own time.

As the ship sailed north there was a strange feeling of both completion as well as a growing uneasiness. These familiar waters are deceptively calm, thought Volsky. He realized their course was fraught with uncertainty, but he decided to take Fedorov's advice to heart. He knew it would be dangerous to allow the men to go ashore, and for that matter he was not even certain they would receive a warm welcome when they first appeared in the long inlet leading to Murmansk and Severomorsk.

There is really nothing there at Severomorsk, he thought, and we will not see tall Alyusha and the eternal flame if we sail up the channel of the Kola Fiord to Murmansk again. Alyusha was the tall grey statue of a Soviet soldier, 116 feet high and weighing 5000 tons atop a stone pedestal to commemorate the defenders of the Soviet Arctic during this war. They have yet to earn their laurels, he knew, thinking that the outcome of the war itself still remained unknown. The Germans have not yet come for the city that was so doggedly defended by the Soviet Moormen, the Polarmen as they were sometimes called—the icemen of the Soviet Arctic.

He was one of them, as were all the men on the ship. They had steamed from those waters and now they return. What will be the effect on the men when they do not see the familiar skyline of Severomorsk. It was just a small settlement in 1940, called Vayenga. There will be no shipyards there, no docks or quays, except at Murmansk.

"What can we expect in the Russian Navy at this time, Mister Fedorov?"

"Not much to speak of, sir. They will have five or six destroyers, a handful of submarines, two torpedo boats, and a few patrol boats and minesweepers. There is nothing there that could pose any threat whatsoever to *Kirov*, though I do not think they would see us as hostile with that Russian naval ensign on our mast. At this time they would be busy building up the White Sea military base as an anchor defending that region. They are also a bit preoccupied with the Finns, assuming that conflict occurred as it did in our history. That may not be the case, however. I have not had time to dig up any new information with Nikolin."

"Very well, then we can head home without undue worry."

The channel leading to Severomorsk and Murmansk is very long and narrow, sir. Were you thinking of going that far in?"

"No, I think we will be cautious at first and stay near the mouth of the inlet."

"Perhaps we could have a look at the area near Malaya Lopatka."

"Nothing was built there until 1950, Fedorov. That was the base we built for the old K-3, our first nuclear powered submarine. Don't worry. We'll have a look around with the KA-40, discretely, and then I must consider how to persuade Sergie Kirov to meet with us. The meeting will most likely have to be at Murmansk. Severomorsk wasn't even an operational base in 1940."

"I can bait your hook for you, Admiral."

"You have a suggestion, Mister Fedorov?"

"Yes sir. Why not send a message saying the man Kirov met at the inn at Ilanskiy in 1908 wishes to speak with you. Perhaps even mentioning my name would help trigger the recollection. If he remembers the incident, he may be curious enough to want to know more."

"That is a very good idea, Fedorov. Yes, I think we will do this."

* * *

The word Kremlin meant "fortress," and it had long been the heart of the Russian government in the center of Moscow, dating back as far as the second century BC. It sat on one of the seven hills of Moscow, 145 meters tall, and its golden spires and domes were known the world over as a symbol of Russian power. The first official buildings had been constructed there in the year 1156, and now the place was simply called "Kremlin Hill."

Its walls and towers had been improved and designed by famous architects during the renaissance. The 27 acre complex now comprised Red Square, Revolution Square, the Grand Kremlin Palace, the iconic gold domed cathedral, and many other squares and official government buildings.

On this morning the message received at the office of the Commandant was most puzzling. It had come in over radio channels, transmitted from the far northern outpost of Murmansk where there was apparently quite a stir. News of a large warship that had been moving north sounded the initial alarms, as it was thought that this must surely be a German ship, possibly intending to scout the Arctic waters. Yet when planes were sent out from the naval base to look for the intruder, they were astounded to see a large ship, prominently flying the Russian naval ensign, and crewmen waving eagerly in welcome as the old MTB-1 seaplane overflew the ship.

"What is this ship?" The Commandant noted that the naval authorities had stated that they were unfamiliar with the vessel, and had no record of it. Yet they were speaking with the ship's personnel over the shortwave, and they were clearly Russian. A request had been made, very odd, and one that might had been dismissed were it not for the mystery accompanying the arrival of the ship.

"They say it is a battleship, enormous," said the Lieutenant of Signals. "And this message is directed to the Secretary General."

"Oh?" The Commandant was justifiably curious as he took the message in hand and read it slowly. "What nonsense is this? You say Murmansk has been speaking with an Admiral aboard that ship? They say it is not ours? Could it be from the Black Sea, a ship defecting from Orenburg? And who is this Fedorov the message indicates?"

"We don't know, sir. It is very confusing. If this ship has come from Orenburg, we would be wise to follow up on this. It may also be a diplomatic overture."

The Commandant frowned, shaking his head, with half a mind to tear the message up and simply throw it in the trash bin. A man named Fedorov wanted to speak with Sergei Kirov! Someone he had met in 1908? Could this man be an ambassador? He mused on it for a moment longer, then did the most expedient and careful thing.

"Very well, send it to the Kremlin main office of the General Secretary, and then let them sort it out." The Commandant would not be the man fingered should any trouble arise from this. He simply passed the news on and then forgot about it.

Later that same day he was quite surprise when the Lieutenant rushed in again with even more news. "We must alert the General Secretary's security detachment at once, Commandant!"

"What is this all about, Lieutenant?"

"*Kirov*, sir. They say that is the name of that ship I reported on earlier this morning. And not only that, the Secretary General himself is making ready to leave for the airport. I am told he is flying north to Murmansk today, and we are to provide for all the security arrangements."

"Today?" The Commandant's face reddened, eyes widening and looking this way and that, as if to find everything he would need to assure security. The air force must be notified. Fighter squadrons must be alerted all along the intended flight path, men must be waiting at the other end, trusted men from the GRU, and base security must be heavily reinforced—and all this had to be done quickly and as quietly as possible.

Sergei Kirov was an impulsive man, he knew. The General Secretary had once received a message that there had been an air raid at Perm and flew there himself that very day to see to the organization of the ground defenses there in the event the Grey Legion was planning an offensive. He was impetuous, with ceaseless energy, and it was just like him to do something like this on the spur of the moment.

The Commandant would be a very busy man that day.

Chapter 14

June 24, 1940

They would meet near the first stone building ever constructed in the city of Murmansk, a stately red brick walled structure with tall concrete exterior columns and two high arched windows flanking the heavy wood door, framed in bright white paint. It sat adjacent to the rail yard on Lenin Street, at the edge of the harbor where Admiral Volsky's launch was tied off. Just a short distance beyond the broad rail receiving yard, they caught sight of the old Hotel Arctic, built in 1933. They were told that quarters had been arranged there, and a reception was planned at the main dining hall.

The men who received them at the quay when they arrived were military police, and they eyed Sergeant Troyak and Corporal Zykov darkly when they saw the burly Sergeant emerge from the cabin of the launch. He snapped off a crisp salute, which was then returned, and something about this time honored gesture of good will and perhaps the red hammer and sickle flag Volsky had retrieved from his sea chest and fixed atop the boat, seemed to defrost that the situation. When Volsky appeared in the uniform of a naval Admiral, the security men stiffened at attention, affording him the respect the uniform and rank was due, even if they did not know anything of the man who wore it.

"Right this way, Admiral." A tall man in a dark trench coat gestured to a waiting line of cars, and there was room in the vehicle for the entire party.

They could have easily walked to the meeting site that had been arranged. Volsky had suggested the location in communications exchanged with the City Commandant before the meeting. He knew of the old hotel, as his father had often spoken of the place. They drove through the familiar intersection known as "Five Corners" and arrived at the hotel just minutes later. Volsky looked around and noted the absence of the statue that would commemorate Gunner

Andre Bredov, who gallantly defended his position and then blew himself up when surrounded by Nazi soldiers when they tried to storm Murmansk during their Operation Silver Fox.

Not yet, Anrdre, he thought. That was in 1944. I used to have lunch there in the grounds near the place where they will erect that statue, assuming Bredov was still out there somewhere and was destined meet the same fate. The monument to the victims of political repression was missing as well. The town was dramatically different, with none of the tall brick and concrete buildings, and almost no vehicular traffic on the broad empty streets. There were many more buildings of wood, some using the unhewn trunks of pine trees to construct log cabins.

After a brief security check, and profuse apology for the necessity, they were ushered into the lobby, where Troyak and Zykov would wait, served hot tea and cakes. They had instructions to contact the ship using the hidden radio in the lining of Troyak's service jacket. A full contingent of well armed Naval Marines was ready on board *Kirov*, with the KA-40 loaded for bear. The Admiral did not think it would be necessary to call on them, but the uncertainty inherent in the situation prompted him to arrange for his extraction should he not contact the ship within 24 hours. All the men had hidden transceivers and could be easily located.

Volsky and Fedorov were then led off to the meeting room, flanked by four guards in the same dark trench coats, and they saw more security men at intervals along the long hallway. Doors were dutifully opened at the end by two more guards, and they were let into a spacious room, with an elegant crystal chandelier above a table dressed out with candles, oil lamps, and white linen. Tea service was waiting, and they were quietly attended by white coated hotel staff while they waited.

Ten minutes later a door opened and two men stepped in, taking up positions to either side of the entrance. The next man they saw seemed like a demigod walking out of the mists of time itself—Sergei Kirov. His stocky frame, broad face, ruddy features were unmistakable to any Russian, as they had been depicted in statues, postage stamps, posters and artwork for decades after his assassination in 1934... But that had never happened in this world. Stalin had died in Kirov's place.

The tallest guard, clearly a favored adjutant, announced the arrival in a clear voice. "The Secretary General of the Communist Party!"

Kirov looked at them as they stood in respectful greeting, both men removing their caps as though they were in the presence of a saint. Volsky saw the light of awe and respect in Fedorov's eyes, and noted how Kirov stared at him, an equal light of amazement plain in his expression. Then he smiled.

"All security personnel will leave the room at once," he said, still standing by the door. The men obeyed, though their officer's face betrayed some concern. Volsky noted a small hand gesture by Kirov, reassuring the man that all would be well. Then Kirov stepped forward and extended his hand to the Admiral in a warm greeting, yet his eyes were ever on Fedorov, glittering with silent realization.

A man of just 54 years, Kirov seemed in the fullness of his life, with just a touch of grey starting to appear in his thick head of hair, combed back above his broad forehead. A handsome man, he exuded an energy of confidence and authority.

"Admiral Volsky," he said smiling. "I must admit that we have no Admiral by that name here in Soviet Russia, and so imagine my surprise when I was invited to this meeting. And you... He turned to Fedorov, his eyes strangely distant, as though he were seeing back through the years to that moment when he had first laid eyes on this man outside the dining hall of the inn at Ilanskiy. "You are Fedorov, and if you can assure me that you are not working for the Okhrana, I would be happy to share my breakfast with you!"

Fedorov smiled. "Sergei Mironovich Kostrikov," he said warmly. "I am honored to make your acquaintance again, after so many long years."

"Not for you, Fedorov! You appear exactly as I have remembered you all these many years, even as I remembered every word you whispered to me on that stairway before I went down. Imagine my surprise when I received your message—a message only I could understand, and so I hastened here to this meeting, unwilling to believe it might be the same man I spoke to back then… in 1908. Ah, but it wasn't 1908 when we parted, was it Fedorov? It was 1942! Yes, I found that out as well. Yet every step I took down those stairs gobbled up two years! I counted them—seventeen steps, a nice prime number. When I got to the bottom all was as I expected, but I must tell you that the room where we spoke that day on the upper floor was not in the same world I left. Yes, I know that now."

He gestured to the table and they all took seats, with Kirov sitting opposite his visitors. Now he looked at Admiral Volsky. "I did not see your ship in the harbor, Admiral, though they tell me you have given it a familiar name."

"We have, sir," said Volsky.

"Well, when I first heard of this ship I came to believe you had come here from the Black Sea, sent by Volkov in a warship built by the Orenburg Federation, though that seemed surprising to me. We saw no sign of this at Sevastopol or any other port on the Black Sea, and we still control Odessa and the shipyards there."

"No, General Secretary."

"You need not be so formal. Just call me Mironov, for old time's sake. That is who I was when I first met this man. Then he told me he was just a sailor being transferred, but I had my own suspicions about him."

"Very well, Mironov, I must be forthright and tell you we have not come from the Black Sea, nor are we in any way affiliated with Orenburg."

"Oh? Then where have you come from? Surely not from the far east, unless you've managed to Shanghai a Japanese warship and sail it all this way as a prize."

Volsky smiled. "In fact, we have come from there, but not in a Japanese ship."

"I see…" Kirov thought for a moment, then leaned forward, lowering his voice to an almost conspiratorial tone. "I can see you hesitate to say more, Admiral. You must think that to do so would be too much for me to comprehend. Perhaps it would be so, but…" now he looked at Fedorov. "I am a very curious man, you see. So curious that I must tell you I took more than one trip up that stairway at Ilanskiy. Some of the things I saw and learned were quite shocking, and I think you know of what I am speaking."

"You went back up those stairs?" Fedorov's eyes registered surprise and just a touch of fear.

"I know you told me to get as far away from that place as I could, and never come up those stairs again, Fedorov, but that is one bit of advice that I'm afraid I did not take. It wasn't until I did go back up that stairway that I finally realized what you meant with that other bit of advice you gave me, that whisper in my ear as we parted. Yes, I learned more than any man should ever have to know—the very day, time and moment of my death! But as you see, I have avoided that fate. You wanted that, did you not? Yes, you did. Well then let me shake your hand one more time, Fedorov, and give you my thanks. Because of you the man that would arrange that unfortunate business scheduled for December of 1934 was not in the world to do so."

"Because of me?" Fedorov had a guilty look.

"Only in part," said Mironov. "The rest was my hand writing in the ledger of fate. It was I who made an end of Josef Stalin. Having seen the world that resulted from his reign of terror, no sane man could do anything else. Yes, I went to Bayil when I found out the Okhrana had him there. It was risky, the most dangerous thing I ever did in my life. I gave myself even odds of living out that night, but I gave Stalin worse."

Fedorov was shocked to hear this. "You killed Stalin?"

"I did. And thank god for that. Unfortunately I have not been as willing to cut off heads as he might have been, and so the effort to unify the country became mired in this endless civil war. I suppose I saved millions of lives by taking Stalin's, but now we have this damnable war. On the one side we sit watching the Polish border for any sign of the German buildup there that is almost certain to come. On the other we remain locked in this perpetual civil war with the Whites—with Volkov's Orenburg Federation as he has come to call it these days."

"It appears Time and Fate have a way of balancing their books," said Volsky.

"Very true, Admiral. I must ask you one thing now, though I believe I may already know the answer. When I met you in 1908, Fedorov, you were not born to that world. Am I correct?"

"Yes sir."

"You came from the world at the top of those stairs? From the world we live in now?"

"No, sir."

Mironov folded his arms, his brow registering some confusion. "No? Here I thought you waited all this time to arrange this meeting. You see, you look exactly as I remember you."

Fedorov looked at the Admiral, and Volsky nodded, giving him quiet permission to explain himself. He cleared his throat, thinking what he might say and how he could elucidate that they were from another time altogether. Then the image of the stairway itself gave him some graspable way of explaining things.

"You lived on the first floor back then, sir, in the dining room of 1908. That was a very memorable day. I suppose you now may know what we were looking at to the northeast when the sky seemed to be on fire there. Well… when you came up that stairway after me, you know where you ended up. Suppose that inn had a third floor. That is the world I came from. How I came to be there in the year you met me is a very long story, but we—the Admiral and I—we live on the third floor sir, if that makes any sense."

Sergie Kirov was quiet for a time, his eyes alive, thinking. "A third floor? Yes, I get what you are saying, Fedorov. Why not? Then you are telling me you came from years beyond that time?"

"We did, sir."

"But why?" The question was obvious, burning, unanswered in the whole impossible saga they had lived through thus far.

"At that moment I was looking for a man, a member of our crew in fact. I was sent to find him by the Admiral here."

"And how did you get to the place on that second floor where we spoke, Fedorov? How did you get back? Are there other stairways out there that wend their way through madness and time? Yes, I thought I was mad for a while, truly insane. But I got over it when I learned what was really going on at the top of those stairs."

Fedorov was not quite sure what to say now. Kirov would have no comprehension of nuclear reactors, and control rods. How could he explain what happened when he barely understood it himself?

"Sir... We are not exactly certain. There was an accident—in our time—and we found ourselves adrift on the oceans of your world."

"Just the two of you?"

"No, said Admiral Volsky. Now you have the explanation as to why you cannot seem to recall the construction of my ship."

Kirov leaned back, quite shocked now. "You mean to say your entire ship moved in time? My god, how many are you?"

"Our crew? About seven hundred men. Our ship was christened *Sergie Kirov*, yes, in your honor."

"When?" Kirov's eyes held intense anticipation as he waited for the answer.

Volsky looked at Fedorov, then folded his arms. "Well I don't suppose there is any harm in saying it now. The ship was originally laid down in the year 1974, launched three years later, and finally commissioned in 1980. It was later extensively re-designed, and re-commissioned again... in the year 2020. Since you, yourself, have been up and down those stairs, sir, you are aware that the stairway may continue on and on. We never know what lies beyond the floor we are born to, unless something very strange happens to us, but I think that stairway does go on into the future, and we are a small clique of men, fortunate or not, who have moved from one floor to the next."

"2020? This is amazing! Unbelievable. Yet you are correct in what you say. If anyone might hear what you have just said and not think it wild *vranyo*, it is I, someone who has walked that back stairway, more times than I should have. But what are you doing here now?"

"Fedorov here is saying hello to an old acquaintance," said Volsky. "Beyond that, it was our hope to make a new friend or two here. You see, General Secretary, as Fedorov said, we are not quite sure why we find ourselves here—but here we are and, at the moment, we seem to be marooned in this day and year. Believe me, I am as bewildered as you seem to be now about it all. I have spent hours wondering just who I really am now, in this world. You see, I am a little older than you are, Mironov, but I was born in the year 1957, and young Fedorov here… why, when were you born, Captain?"

"1994, sir."

"Remarkable," said Kirov. "This ship of yours… Why it must be very powerful."

"That it is, the most powerful ship in the world, and we have been tested against many others who might like to make that claim. It was our hope to minimize any contact with the world we found ourselves in after we first went down the rabbit hole. Now we have come to realize that we have already made a very grave difference in the world. Our presence in the past has had a shattering effect. Your presence here, at this very moment, is one result. You see… you *did* die on that cold December night in Leningrad, in 1934, but here you are. Everything is different now, in more ways that we can possibly have time to explain. Fedorov here calls it a broken mirror, and when we look into it now we wonder who we are at times. We thought we could reverse the damage, preserve it, put things back the way they were. Finally we gave up trying, as it seems it is an impossible task. So here we are, Sergei Kirov, beggars at your doorstep—a place we once called home. We left this very harbor in the year 2021, and sailed out on a bright sunny day. The weather has been very stormy for us ever since, but now we are finally back… not quite home yet, but we are here at long last."

Kirov had a grave expression on his face. These men have been through the same madness I suffered through, he thought. Yes, I can see it in their eyes. We are brothers, the three of us.

"Admiral Volsky, in one sense we are all in the same boat, the three of us here, and I, too, am a member of your crew."

They smiled.

Chapter 15

"I had hoped I could recruit your support," said Volsky. "Every moment we have been at sea these last months has been a hardship. The men have lost everything they had, everyone they ever knew, and while I have promised them we would find a way to get them home again, that may never happen for us. Once we thought we had come home, but here we are again, and I am no longer sure the world we came from even exists any longer."

Kirov had a very serious expression on his face, clearly empathizing with everything the Admiral was saying. "Well," he said, "I owe this man my life, and so in return I will do everything possible to secure yours, and those of every man on your ship. You are welcome to anything we have, food, fuel, quarters ashore. Anything you need can be provided."

"Thank you, Mironov, it was my hope that we could find a safe harbor here. Yet there is one more thing I must tell you. Our route here took us through the Atlantic and the Denmark Strait, and there has been a major battle there between the British and Germans."

"Yes, our intelligence has informed me of this, but the British seem to have prevailed. Their navy is the one force the Germans cannot break."

"It was much more serious than you may realize," Volsky said with a certain urgency. "Mister Fedorov here is somewhat of a student of military history, and he believes the Germans would have won this engagement if not for our intervention."

"Your intervention?"

"Yes, I'm afraid so. It is a long story, sir, and I cannot give you all the details now, but at one time we made an enemy of the Royal Navy. Finding ourselves in these waters again, and needing support, this time I thought to make them a friend. The Germans sortied with a very powerful fleet, and the situation did not look good for the British. I therefore elected to use the power of my ship to…

discourage the Germans, and we were able to see them off home again."

"I see…" Kirov was very thoughtful now. "I must tell you, Admiral Volsky, that we will not be able to stand neutral in this war for very much longer. When I went up those stairs at Ilanskiy, into Stalin's world, I learned that Russia and Germany were at war by 1942, and that the Germans had pushed all the way to the Volga! If they were to do the same again, then we are facing annihilation. So in some sense I look upon your coming here as a harbinger of good fate."

"We are a powerful ship, sir, but I do not think we can sail to the front line if the Germans push for Moscow."

"And they will," said Fedorov. "It is almost certain that they will. They called it Operation Barbarossa."

Kirov nodded gravely. "Even now we begin to see a slow and steady buildup on the Polish frontier, and yes, our intelligence had wind of that very name—Barbarossa. You may or may not know that the Orenburg Federation has declared open war on us and allied itself with Germany. At the moment they are also squabbling with the Free Siberian State. Last winter they crossed the border and took Omsk from the Siberians, which was good news for us. We made overtures to Kolchak, but he seemed indecisive. He, too, has a war on two fronts now, with the Japanese at his back and Volkov on the other flank."

"I must tell you something now," said Volsky. "This man Volkov, the man they call the Prophet, we believe that he was not born to this world."

"What do you mean? He has come from… from another floor in the inn?"

"That may have been exactly what happened," said Fedorov. "We have thought a great deal about that stairway and the strange effects we have both experienced there. When we learned of this man, Volkov, we began to suspect that he was a man by the same name that had also come from our world—that he has gone down those stairs as well."

"I see…" A light of realization was evident in Kirov's eyes. "That would explain much. Volkov was able to outmaneuver Denikin and everyone else—except me. I had the support of the Reds, so he settled into the White movement and consolidated power there. But he had been here for years, decades in fact. I met him twenty years ago, and could see that he was going to be trouble during the revolution."

"If what we believe has actually happened, he may have gone down that stairway, just as I did," said Fedorov. "If he ended up in 1908, then that would explain his presence here all these years. We know that he vanished in our day, and at that very place, Ilanskiy. This leads me to suspect that stairway can also make a connection to our world—to the third floor, Mironov."

"That would be very significant if it did. Do you think Volkov knows about this?"

"We do not know, but I am inclined to believe that he does not. If he did, why would he have remained marooned in the past? It would seem any sane man would try to return the way he came."

"Something may have prevented him," said Kirov, "the madness, the shock of what he experienced. I found it very difficult to bear myself."

"Yet he had years to try and return, but never did. If he does remain in the dark, that is good news, and we hope as much. Because if that stairway still exists in this world, and the effects continue, then it could be a way for us to return to our own time—a way for any man to do so."

Kirov immediately perceived the peril there. "That would be very dangerous."

"Yes," said Volsky. "Men who knew what they were about could use that stairway to cause a great deal of mischief."

"At the moment that inn may not see many travelers," said Kirov. "This civil war has been very hard. The railway east has degraded. Much of it has fallen into disrepair. The route from

Chebalyinsk to Novosibirsk is impassible now with Cossacks and Tartars at each other's throats. One or two trains still operate further east all the way to Irkutsk, but there are very few who dare to travel that route. We have men there from our intelligence arm. Things are starting to wake up now that Karpov has come on the scene."

The name fell like a hot coal in a bucket of ice water, and Kirov could see the immediate reaction in both the other men. Volsky leaned forward, giving Fedorov a worried glance. "Karpov? Tell me more of this man."

"I wish I could. He seemed to come from nowhere just a few years ago. Old Man Kolchak and his Lieutenant Kozolnikov were running things in the east. Then the name of this man Karpov began to appear in dispatches and signals traffic. We thought he was just another minor official, or perhaps a newly appointed military officer. Then we learned he was given command of the Siberian Air Corps. Now it appears that he exercises considerable influence over Kolchak. They call him the old man for a good reason. Kolchak is getting slow, and he has been unable to unite the disparate warlords ranging throughout Siberia—until recently. Karpov is whipping things into shape there. Yet you both seem very surprised to hear this name. What is your concern?"

"It may be nothing," said Volsky. "It is just that Karpov was an officer aboard my ship—one we believed was killed in action, though we never recovered his body."

"When? Was this a recent event?"

"Just days ago for us, but decades past in your time. You see, Mironov, our ship found its way to the same year when you first met Fedorov—1908. How it came to be there is a very long story, but this man, Karpov, believed he was marooned there permanently and took some rather aggressive action against the Japanese. He had it in his mind to reverse the humiliation of our defeat at the hands of Admiral Togo's fleet in 1905. Yes, he thought he might restore Russia to her position of power in the Pacific, but we knew this would cause grave harm, and so at that time I did everything possible to impede him."

"You were there with him on the ship? He opposed your authority?"

To make a long story short, Volsky decided to abridge his tale. "That is a fair assessment of what happened," he said. "But he was stopped. The crew would not follow him any longer, and that was his undoing. Then he disappeared. We believed he had been killed in action, but this mention of his name has been somewhat jarring. Our ship moved again in time after that—I cannot explain it fully here, but if Karpov also moved with us, and was still alive…"

Fedorov spoke now, very concerned. "You say this Karpov came on the scene some years ago?"

"We first began to hear his name a year ago. I would think he would have been fermenting in the power structure for many years before that, but we could turn up no history on the man, and no records. Nothing is known of Volkov's early life either. No one ever heard of the man until he began inserting himself into the revolutionary cadres in 1908. In time he co-opted Denikin's entire operation in the Caucasus, and from there he has expanded to control all of Kazakhstan. We've held the line on the Volga, but now, with the Germans building up on our western front, our situation becomes very serious. So you see, I need friends as well. Soviet Russia needs friends. Otherwise we may not survive this war."

Volsky extended his hand. "When I learned from radio intercepts that it was you, Sergei Kirov, who control our homeland in Stalin's place, I felt hope for the first time in a good long while. I told young Fedorov here that if there was one man in Russia I could fight for, it would be you. I will tell you now that we made contact with the British on our way here. In fact, I met face to face with their Admiral of the Home Fleet. He is a reasonable man, and one that could become a strong ally if you were so inclined."

"The British are hanging on by their fingernails," said Kirov. "Yes, if they go, then we are surely next. Then the whole word comes under the shadow of Nazi Germany."

Volsky was clear and direct, and Kirov could see it in his eyes. "That cannot be permitted to happen. Mister General Secretary, this has been an hour of many revelations. We sit here discussing the impossible fates we have both suffered, and now this news of Karpov chills my blood if this is, indeed, the man we lost. He is a man of great ambition, and could prove a grave danger. Now, however, I think that Russia's only chance at survival is in a speedy alliance with Great Britain and the United States."

"America? They are a neutral state."

"At the moment—but Russia is a neutral state as well. You and I both know that no nation with any power in this world will be able to remain a neutral bystander. We know how this war ended once, Kirov. It is only just beginning now, but it will grow and grow and become a whirlwind of chaos that will consume the entire world before it ends."

"Yet your presence here tells me Russia survives. I could spend days with you with the questions in my mind now."

"As I could with you, but we both have duties to perform. Yes, Russia survived—in the history we knew. In that war we were allies with Great Britain, but without their support, and the supplies and equipment that flowed to us through this very port, we may not have survived the onslaught Germany unleashed upon us. At this moment, all is in play. These years are the most dangerous of the entire war. Unless you get sound footing, the Germans could stampede all the way to Moscow, and now, with this Orenburg Federation and Volkov at your back, you have no refuge in the east as Stalin had when hard pressed."

"You tell me things that I have realized for some time now. Yes, I know we cannot stand alone, and for that reason I have already put out feelers to the British, and will now make a formal proposal of alliance. Do you think it will be well received?"

"It will. I am almost certain. Britain stands alone in the west, even as you stand alone here. You must join hands and become brothers in arms. There is no other way for either of you to survive. If Germany can turn its might on either nation in isolation, they would certainly win. It is only the strength of the Royal Navy that now shields Great Britain from destruction."

"The Germans are planning to invade England even now!"

"That plan will fail," said Fedorov. "At least it never came about in the history we know. Yet this is a new history book we are living in now, at least for me. The Kriegsmarine is much stronger than we knew it to be. Things have changed, and the Germans may now be able to pose a serious invasion threat to England."

"Not on my watch," said Volsky flatly.

Kirov smiled. "You sound very confident, Admiral. I like that in a man. A good boast is sometimes a necessary food for the soul, as long as a man has courage to go along with it."

"I do not boast, Mister General Secretary. The ship I now command has the power to assure England's safety from invasion. I could accomplish this single handedly, but the Royal Navy has great strength as it stands. If I commit my *Kirov* to their cause, then I can assure you that the Germans will not set foot on English soil."

"Well Admiral, then I urge you to do this. As for this Kirov," he placed his hands on his broad chest now, "he is committed as well. Now then, let us drink on this new day together. I will call my Lieutenants back and we will have a good meal and some good Vodka as well. Then we will get on with the business of trying to save the world, eh? I have only one hope, Admiral Volsky. You have told me your ship has moved in time, though I do not grasp how that happens. That aside… will you move in time again? Can you do this? Or might it happen again by accident?"

"We do not yet know," said Volsky truthfully. "All I can promise you is our friendship and support as long as we can stay put."

Kirov clasped his arm in a hearty handshake. "Then I can promise you the same."

The meal was delicious and very fulfilling, a taste of real home cooking, as Volsky described it. Troyak and Zykov were also seated at the table, and the obvious good will between the General Secretary and these visitors lightened the mood of the security officers.

As the evening concluded Kirov brought in a man in a naval uniform, introducing him as Vice Admiral Arseniy Grigoriyevich Golovko, currently serving with the Red Banner Northern Fleet. At first the man was surprised to see Volsky, as here was an Admiral he did not know. To forestall the questions this would surely raise, Kirov covered by saying he had just appointed this man, who was head of a very secret project.

"I will have to find a way to explain your presence here, Admiral," he had whispered to Volsky at the dinner. "And to explain your ship when it pulls into the harbor. So for now you are a state secret, a special project, and I can keep curious men under control if that will be a help to you. There is a good harbor north of the city here that we have been considering for a new shipyard. Perhaps you know it?"

"Severomorsk," said Volsky, smiling. "Yes, we sailed from that port... eighty-one years from now." It still sounded fantastic and unbelievable every time he considered it. "Admiral Golovko will make good company here. In our day we had a ship that bore his name as well."

"Good then," said Kirov enthusiastically. "The place is yours. I will marshal the resources to have facilities built there, and for now you will find it a safe anchorage. One day I should dearly like to see this ship of yours, but for now I am needed in Moscow."

"I will arrange a tour when next we meet," said Volsky.

"Then is there anything else I can do for you; anything you need?"

Fedorov raised his hand and Kirov leaned around Volsky to smile at him. "Yes Fedorov? You have a request?"

"If I may, sir. Books," he said. "History books."

Kirov smiled.

Part VI

Wunderland

"But I don't want to go among mad people,"
Alice remarked.
"Oh, you can't help that," said the Cat,
"we're all mad here. I'm mad. You're mad."
"How do you know I'm mad?" said Alice.
"You must be," said the Cat, "or you wouldn't have
come here."

— Lewis Carroll, *Alice in Wonderland*

Chapter 16

July 2, 1940

Kapitän Kurt 'Caesar' Hoffmann was brooding as he stared at the rocky Norwegian coastline off Trondheim. Raeder was upset over failure of the operation, and justifiably so. He had been convinced that it would succeed, and it should have been a great victory, until that strange vessel appeared.

"I knew there was something amiss the moment I set eyes on that ship," he said to the ship's chief gunnery officer, Schubert. "There was something wrong about it. What ship was that, Schubert? Is the Abwehr so inept that they could fail to notice a ship of that size in the British order of battle? I don't think so."

"It is very strange, sir."

"More than strange! You saw what it did to *Gneisenau*, eh?"

They were standing on the weather deck, and the grey sky above seemed to lower over the bay, deepening the gloomy mood that was on the Kapitän.

"I have never seen such a weapon, Kapitän. Such speed and accuracy for a rocket is incomprehensible. It must have been a lucky hit, just like that hit we got on that British aircraft carrier."

"Yes, and we should have sunk that ship, Schubert. That's another thing that slipped from our grasp. Yes, things have been slipping. I have the odd feeling that we have been denied our rightful victory. We got close enough to the main battle to see the smoke from the fires on that British ship. They tell me it was *Hood*, and we should have put that ship at the bottom of the sea. Then Lindemann lost his nerve."

"He was only following orders, Kapitän. You know Raeder made it clear that if our capital ships were in danger of sustaining serious damage, he was to break off."

"Yes, but we were so close. So damn close. I could almost see us feasting on those fat British convoys to the south, but that's another thing that slipped away."

"I'm afraid so sir."

"You are afraid? Well I'll tell you the truth now Schubert. *I* am afraid. If the British have these weapons then our fleet is good for little more than target practice for them. My god, you saw what those rockets did to the *Stukas* off *Graf Zeppelin*, and I spoke with Böhmer as well. Thank God his best pilots survived that hell. His squadron leader, Marco Ritter, made it back, and one of his new hot shots survived as well—the fellow that got two hits on the British! All these battleships and the *Stukas* do the real work. We should have built more carriers. Böhmer says that *Sigfrid* was not hit by a torpedo as we first thought when we got that report. No! It was another one of those damn naval rockets!"

Schubert seemed very surprised. "I had not heard that."

"I just heard it myself. It came in on this morning's unit traffic: Böhmer confirms *Sigfrid* lost to rocket attack. Single hit amidships."

"One hit?"

"Well having seen the damage on *Gneisenau* that does not surprise me. So there, we have lost one of our newest destroyers." Hoffmann took a long drag on his cigar, and exhaled, clearly upset.

"But sir, *Graf Zeppelin* was over 150 kilometers to the north. Are you saying the new British ship slipped by and got close enough to fire this weapon without being spotted by our search planes? We saw it well south of our position when we received the order to break off from Lindemann."

"You were in the gunnery director with your eyes fixed on the British, Schubert, so perhaps you did not see what happened. I was out here on the weather deck and saw everything. When those rocket weapons are fired there is one thing they do with that vapor trail they leave behind them. You can follow the trail like a smoky rainbow right back to the source of the firing ship. No. That enemy ship was nowhere near *Graf Zeppelin*, and that is what is so astounding about all of this. It hit *Sigfrid* from a position *south* of our own just as you say."

Schubert was dumbfounded. "But that would mean they would have had to fire from a range of 175 kilometers! That's impossible! How could they even see the target or know where to aim, even if a rocket could travel such a distance?"

"That is what is so astounding, Schubert. But they did see it. They knew the location so precisely that they would have put that rocket right into the belly of Böhmer's ship. *Sigfrid* just got in the way. Böhmer tells me they had just sent over a case of beer and sausages, compliments of the Kapitän, to congratulate *Graf Zeppelin* on their successful strike on the British. They were keeping station just a couple hundred yards from the carrier. Then hell came from the sky. A lot of good men were lost when that destroyer went down."

"Sir, they must have had a U-boat nearby to spot that ship. Maybe they have some way of sending course corrections via radio."

"That is my suspicion," Hoffman nodded. "If *Altmark* was hit by a torpedo, then that says the British had a submarine lurking nearby. It might be working in cooperation with this rocket cruiser."

"Rocket cruiser?"

"That's a good name for it," said Hoffmann.

"Then what happened?"

"Böhmer launched everything he had, but the initial squadron was cut to pieces. When Lindemann gave the order to break off the engagement, the remaining planes scattered like crows in a cornfield when you put a good 12-gague shotgun to work. They searched the immediate vicinity, but found no sign of an enemy ship. Of course not, I saw where that rocket came from. It was south of us I tell you, and I have told Lindemann that as well, but he did not believe me."

"Who could believe such a thing?"

"Yes, that puts your finger right on the heart of it, Schubert. We saw things that were completely unbelievable, and yet *Sigfrid* was sunk, *Gneisenau* and *Bismarck* both hit by these rockets, and don't forget what happened to *Altmark!*"

"I thought it was hit by a U-boat."

"Possibly, but did you hear what that oiler man said? Fritz Kürt. We pulled him out of the flotsam after *Altmark* went down, and I spoke with the man at some length. He says it was a torpedo, though no one saw any sign of a U-boat on the surface or periscope. But what he did see was a big fat battlecruiser, dark on the horizon. The man thought it was our ship, but then it turned away."

"Then it had to be British, sir."

"I think it was the same ship that fired those rockets. I've had this odd feeling about it since we first engaged those two British cruisers. At least we sent them packing, and sunk one to start things off. Everything was going so well, Schubert. Then the dominoes began falling. *Altmark* is sunk, we find this strange ship Fritz was trying to describe, and look what happened to *Gneisenau!* Don't you see? Everything that went awry had something to do with that ship."

"Perhaps you are correct, Kapitän."

"I can feel it, Schubert. I had the feeling something was watching me, watching our ships from a distance, something lurking behind those grey clouds. It was stalking us, nipping at our heels, taunting us, and when we got close, it punched my battlegroup right in the nose. We must find out what this ship is, and then we must sink the damn thing or this new navy we've built will be good for nothing. Lindemann should have continued the engagement. Now look at us, stuck in this miserable fiord, sitting here waiting for the British to sneak up with a couple aircraft carriers and launch those damn *Swordfish* at us again."

"We'll get another chance soon, sir."

"It may be a while. *Gneisenau* was ordered back to Kiel along with *Bismarck*. They left *Tirpitz* at Bergen, but Topp departs for Kristiansand and Bremen tomorrow if the weather is bad. They're pulling our horns in, Schubert. It's just us up here now, and a couple destroyers."

"What about *Nürnberg*, sir?"

"That light cruiser? What good is that?"

At that moment a signalman stepped onto the weather deck, saluting. "Message from Wilhelmshaven," he said smartly, and handed off the note to Hoffmann.

The Kapitän read it slowly, shaking his head. "Look here, Schubert. They managed to complete the refit on *Admiral Scheer*, and they are sending it up here tonight from Kristiansand as a distraction for the withdrawal of *Tirpitz* south. It's going to make a run west, as if it might be headed for the Iceland Faeroes gap, then it turns north to join us here."

"Here sir? What for?"

"Have a look, Schubert." He handed his artillery officer the message. "Read it yourself. Raeder must be getting curious about this ship we've been talking about. One of our U-boats reported a large warship moved north around the cape, and a plane out of Narvik spotted it again. That's why *Nürnberg* arrived last night. Misery loves company, eh? Now they are sending up the *Admiral Scheer,* and Raeder wants to have a look up north. They're calling it Operation Wunderland."

* * *

Wunderland was conceived to do exactly what Hoffmann had surmised—have a good long look up north to see what the Russians were up to. Naval intelligence had not been sleeping since the abortive engagement with the Royal Navy in the Denmark Strait. Information had been developed that suggested the strange ship reported by Hoffmann and other German assets may not have been a British ship at all! That seaplane out of Narvik got more than a sighting report that day—it got a photograph as well, and naval analysts could clearly discern the Russian naval ensign flying from the ship's aft mast.

Raeder needed time to consolidate the fleet after their ill-fated sortie—time for repairs, and more importantly time to refuel. The fleet had burned through months of petrol supplies, and the dwindling oil stocks were going to hobble the navy if the storage depots were not soon replenished. He could not afford to send out his big ships now, not with Hitler scheming over Operation Seelöwe, the planned invasion of England. So he sent the light cruiser *Nürnberg* north to Trondheim where there was enough fuel in store to replenish, and now that *Admiral Scheer* had completed her refit with a new Atlantic clipper bow and a lighter conning tower with new flak guns to give her more air defense, that ship was a perfect choice.

A *Deutschland* class 'Pocket Battleship,' the ship was now reclassified as a heavy cruiser in the shadow of so many other more powerful ships now in the German fleet. Hitler was of two minds on what to do next with his war machine. On the one hand he had Britain on her knees and waiting to receive the death blow. A successful invasion of England would probably decide the war in the West within six months, and the Americans would never get their foot in the door. On the other hand, Orenburg had just joined with Germany, creating a situation where the Soviet Union under Kirov was now badly flanked and already at war all along the Volga.

This, along with the fall of France and Italy's entry into the war, made it seem that Germany was now invincible, and destined to become the dominant power on earth. Eventually the Americans would have to be dealt with, but they had no army to speak of at the moment, and posed no threat to Germany.

In spite of all this, Raeder was suddenly edgy about the situation. If these reports were true, if this was a Russian ship fighting alongside the British, it could upset all his carefully laid plans. With Europe prostrate at his feet, Hitler had to believe, at Raeder's urging, that he could crush the Soviet Union any time he wished—but this was not the time.

"Why not now?" the Führer had asked him. "Half the Soviet army is already tied down on the Volga. My Generals tell me they can take Moscow in two months and knock the Russians out of the war!"

"We do not know that for certain, my Führer. The Russians may not capitulate as easily as the French. If there are complications, delays, then we would find ourselves bogged down in a two front war, repeating the mistakes of 1914. At the moment England is reeling from hard blows. Now is the time to finish them!"

Raeder argued that any invasion of Russia now would give England a respite. Could the British regain their balance and dig in well enough to hold out until the Americans came to their aid? This was the real strategic question that hung in the Balance in mid 1940. The issue of Russia could be decided later. Hitler seemed to agree, albeit reluctantly, and turned his thoughts to Operation Seelöwe. There might be enough time to finish the job against the British and still invade Russia before the winter set in.

But now this—a Russian ship perpetrating an act of war! Was it true? It could change everything, and Raeder had to know more. Operation Wunderland would be a reconnaissance in force to test the strength of the Russian Navy. Raeder proposed to send the heavy cruiser *Admiral Scheer* and the light cruiser *Nürnberg* from Trondheim to Narvik, and then around the North Cape. They would make a run for Svalbard, sneak across the upper Barents Sea while the ice was thin. Then they could scout the Kara Sea to see what the Russians might have hidden there.

If war came with Russia, Germany planned to move into Finland to flank Leningrad from the north. To do so Raeder knew that the Russian Fleet would have to be neutralized, and the main port of Murmansk occupied by German troops. Operation Wunderland was the first tentative probe north, a light shove on the shoulder of the Russian state to see what they might do, and to determine if the reports were true about this ship.

Admiral Scheer was capable of facing down anything the Russian Navy had, or so it was believed until this new ship had been sighted. So *Scheer* would head north, see what this mystery ship was up to, and test the mettle of the Soviets at the same time.

What the Germans did not know was that a ferocious bear was now sleeping in the long Kola Fiord that led to Murmansk, a ship with capabilities that would soon shock and mystify more men than

Kurt Hoffmann. Events were now about to unfold that would set the course of the war off in a startling new direction, and as always, the battlecruiser *Kirov* would have its hand on the twisting gyre of fate.

Chapter 17

July 2, 1940

Admiral Scheer was the second of three *Deutschland* class heavy cruisers launched and commissioned by the Kriegsmarine in the mid 1930s. Dubbed 'pocket battleships' when they appeared, they were built to be able to outrun most every battleship in the Royal Navy at the time, and outgun any of the fast British cruisers that could catch the ship. The ill fated sortie of the *Graf Spee* in 1939 proved that it would take at least two, and possibly three British cruisers to stand with these ships, and it was only because he believed they were facing even higher odds that the Germans elected to scuttle the ship in a neutral South American port.

With six 11-inch guns, *Admiral Scheer* was not as powerful as Hoffmann's *Scharnhorst*, nor even as fast, but Raeder did not want to risk any more of his better ships in the operation, though he felt the heavy cruiser would be capable of handling anything the Russians had. Light cruiser *Nürnberg* would sail with her on the planned mission to scout out the Arctic seas and determine the degree of Soviet naval buildup there. The ship was lighter, a bit faster, and fitted out with the latest Germans FuMO 26 radar. The Kapitän of *Admiral Scheer*, KsZ Theodore Kranke, came over to visit *Scharnhorst* at Hoffmann's request.

"So what is all this business about a rocket cruiser, Hoffmann?" he said flatly.

Hoffmann heard the same incredulous tone in his voice as the other officers had. Undoubtedly Raeder was even more dismissive of the claim. Well let him have a look at the damage to *Gneisenau* and *Bismarck*, and let him listen to survivors off the *Sigfrid*. Perhaps then he will understand.

"There is no other way to describe it," said Hoffmann. "We sighted what appeared to be a large battlecruiser, though it wasn't moving at anything more than ten or fifteen knots by our estimation.

We engaged and it stuck a fast moving rocket right into *Gneisenau's* belly. It was astounding, Kranke! You would have to see it to believe it, but I saw the whole thing with my very own eyes, and I will never forget it. This was the same weapon that sunk *Sigfrid*, and hit *Bismarck*. We had the heart of the fleet with us, yet this ship forced Lindemann to back off. Now they are sending you? Be careful!"

He did his best to forewarn Kranke, hoping he had conveyed the same sense of peril and urgency that he felt. *Scharnhorst* was ordered to accompany the newcomers as far north as Narvik, where Hoffmann would wait on 4 hour notice should Kranke's detachment run into difficulty. But what good can I do, he thought? Lindemann was not willing to stand and fight the British with ships like *Bismarck* and *Tirpitz!*

"Don't worry about us," said Kranke confidently. "*Admiral Scheer* is a good ship. I will take your advice—and one of those cigars you keep in your pocket if you can spare one."

Hoffman gave him three. "Smoke the first if you can find this ship," he said. "Smoke the second if you can get close enough to verify its identity and get a good photo or two."

"And the third?"

"Smoke that one if you get back here alive."

* * *

The last big German ship to come this far north into Arctic seas had been an airship, Zeppelin LZ-127, which carried an international research team in 1931 on an amazing 13,000 mile route from Berlin to the far cape Zhelaniya and back, with stops in Leningrad, Archangel, White Sea ports and Franz Joseph Land. They had promised the Russians they would share any photographs and research data they obtained after getting permission for the trip, but never delivered on that pledge.

The cruiser *Köenigsberg* had come up into the Barents Sea briefly in 1936, and *Köln* followed with a brief sortie in 1937 before the war.

The Germans had established a small supply base and weather station west of Murmansk at Kirkenes in Norway, but they also had plans to rapidly push a column from there to Litsa on the Molotov Gulf to provide them sea access east of the imposing Volokovaya cape landmass. From there they could watch cape area traffic and relay wind and weather front data. Code named "Base Nord," *Admiral Scheer* was tasked with secretly putting ashore a detachment of ski troops to make an initial survey of the location. Then they would scout the route west to Kirkenes again in preparation for the push east.

With war looming in the far east, Germany also thought about the prospect of exploring the Arctic passage to the Bering Sea. There were several German merchant ships and steamers that might find a quick and safe way home by that route. Raeder contemplated sending the armed merchant raider *Komet* north for this mission, but decided to send a ship that would not have to ask permission to sail where it wished. It was risky. An incident could spark hostilities, so he made sure to brief Kranke well.

"Just slip in the back door and see what's in the kitchen, Kranke. And be careful, don't break the china while you are there! The last thing we need is a war on two fronts."

The operation was happening two full years earlier than it might have in the history Fedorov knew. In his books the *Admiral Scheer* had sailed alone, under a different commander, and caused much trouble in the north. The history now, in the shattered world these ships all sailed in, would be an eerie echo of that operation—including the trouble it stirred up. Kranke's detachment was tasked with listening to Russian radio traffic, putting shore teams in at isolated Soviet outposts to look for anything of value, particularly maps, code cipher keys and related equipment. They would also scout sea conditions, ice floe patterns and ice density, and note prevailing weather.

The detachment sailed from Narvik on the grey morning of July 4th, 1940, and quietly made its way north around the northern cape of Norway. Kranke would sail east of Bear Island, past the ragged Spitzbergen Islands to the forsaken icy rocks of Franz Joseph Land. His first goal was to slip into the Kara Sea and collect as much information as possible. To facilitate that effort he took aboard a Kriegsmarine Funkaufklärung team. Experts in radio signals intelligence, these men also spoke fluent Russian to listen in on the radio traffic.

Their work would be aided by Oberleutnant zur See Peter Grau aboard U-46, which had left Narvik several days earlier to take up a station near Cape Zhelanlya for relaying radio intercepts. There the German U-Boat surfaced to catch a small Russian outpost by surprise. Then something happened that soon set events off on an unpredictable course. Two Russian guards fired at U-46, raking its exposed hull with machine gun fire. Grau replied by shelling the radio tower and two seaplanes, and then putting a team ashore to search the station. Declared or not, Oberleutnant Grau's first shot at the icy northern outpost on the 5th of July, 1940, was the opening round of the war in the east between Germany and Kirov's Soviet Russia, though no one knew that yet.

There had been no time for a distress signal before the radio tower was destroyed, and so the Soviets remained unaware of the incident, and oblivious to the steady northern incursion of *Admiral Scheer* and *Nürnberg,* which rendezvoused with the U-boat later that same day. There they received Grau's report, and Kranke ordered the U-Boat to scout down the long ragged western edge of Novaya Zemlya Island to look for similar outposts. Then the German flotilla turned north east into the cheerless waters of the Kara Sea.

"What are we doing here, Heintz?" Kranke was on the bridge with his Executive Officer, thinking about those cigars and wishing he was in the Atlantic. "There's nothing up here but these isolated weather stations and a few old Russian merchant ships. No glory here, just these tedious ice floes and cold hands and feet."

What Kranke did not know at that moment was that Soviet Intelligence had become suspicious of trouble when the weather station Grau had shelled did not report that day. They had a coast guard ship, SKR-18, the former armed icebreaker *Fedor Litke* in the Kara Sea, and decided to send it down to have a look.

"Lean pickings, I agree Kapitän, but we are not even supposed to be at war here. Remember, this is nothing more than a reconnaissance operation."

"Don't fool yourself, Heintz. I was only joking earlier. We have business here, as you will soon see."

Heintz did not quite know what that was about, but said nothing. A day later, July 6, 1940, the top mast reported a small ship sighted due east of their position. Kranke stepped out onto the cold weather deck to have a look through the better telescope there. Sure enough, he could make out the red flag, though the ship did not look all that threatening. Back on the bridge he waited until the distant ship began to hail them on radio, and when the call was not answered he saw they had begun flashing their search lights.

"They are ordering us to stop and heave to for boarding," said Heintz."

"Tell them to go to hell," said Kranke. "Once they get a look at those eleven inch guns out there they will see that I have more than ample means to send them there myself!"

"They will report our position, Kapitän."

"Let them. What can the Russians do about it?"

The Captain of SKR-18 was very insistent, and he did indeed report the contact in a message to the Archangel Party Commiserate that was soon followed by another message. SKR-18 was under attack! Kranke was in a bad mood that day, and when the coast guard ship fired a warning shot across his bow, under international protocols, the Kapitän answered with his forward gun turret. It might have been no more than a simple reflexive impulse of war, just as Grau had done, but Heintz soon learned that Kranke seemed to be deliberately courting conflict here. Five minutes later SKR-18 was a flaming wreck, sinking fast, but the last plaintive message had been sent: *Sighted German warships. Under attack!*

When the message was received at Murmansk, Admiral Golovko could not believe his ears. Would the Germans risk provoking a war with a minor incident like this? Should he take stronger action? He cabled Moscow for instructions and the word came back in no uncertain terms: *Protect Soviet interests, and all ships and personnel.* The means was left up to him, so he dispatched the heavy cruiser *Kalinin* and two destroyers, and they rushed east over the White Sea and north towards Port Dikson.

Kranke had immediately reversed his course after the incident, then looped southeast to creep up on the shoreline thinking to observe Russian convoy traffic north of that same port. He lingered in the area all the next day, eventually finding another old Russian icebreaker, the *Siberiakov*, a veteran of the northern Arctic route with many years service.

Lovingly nicknamed "Sasha" by the hard men of the north, the ship had two teeth, a pair of 76mm guns, along with two 45mm mounts and a couple Oerlikon 20mm flak guns. The lead ship in the "Icebreaker-6" naval team, she was bound for Port Dikson to the south when *Admiral Scheer* found her.

"Signal that ship to stand down, and tell them that this time *we* will be sending a boarding party over." The Kapitän thought he might pinch some signal equipment or code boxes, and it was a good idea. *Sasha* had played a dual role when not shouldering through the ice floes. The ship had secret listening equipment to monitor Japanese radio traffic when it was at the easternmost terminus of its long Arctic run.

Kranke gave the order to come 15 points to starboard. "We'll show them our bow," he explained. "That will keep them in a dark for a little while longer. Fire one warning shot this time. That is permitted under the rules of engagement."

He watched through his field glasses, seeing the dark uniformed crew scrambling to pull the tarps from their gun mounts and ready for action. As before, he waited until the Russians had sighted and aimed, a patient man as he sat in his armored conning tower.

* * *

Sasha's Captain, Anatoly Kacharava, was enjoying a small nip of Vodka as he pecked away at his typewriter in the ready room, writing the report he needed to submit when the ship made port. He had heard the signal sent by SKR-18 the previous day, and so he was taking no chances when the sighting was shouted out by senior signalman Alexeyev. He immediately ordered the radio room to send the contact information and stood his crew to battle stations. Then he told his radioman to request name and country of origin of the distant ship.

Captain Kacharava was in a real quandary. His ship was laden with supplies for the weather stations, including several hundred barrels of gasoline for the generators that powered their operations. With a top speed of only 13 knots, *Sasha* was a nice fat target, and very flammable. He had a crew of 104, including his 32 trained naval gunners. Fire crews had taken their stations, ready with hoses as they eyed the gasoline barrels on deck with some trepidation.

"They are ordering us to stop and be searched," said radioman Sharshavin, talking through the dark brown briar pipe that dangled from his mouth. The Captain wanted to see what he was up against here, and when he raised his field glasses to have a look his mood darkened considerably.

"A large capital ship," he said. "Send an emergency message to Port Dikson: large cruiser sighted... possibly a battleship from the size of those gun mounts. Country of origin unknown. Send it in the clear! And then request their name and origin again."

* * *

Far to the south the nervous radioman at Port Dikson heard what followed next. *"Ship closing range,"* he received. *"Shooting has begun... we will fight!"* Some minutes later. *"Siberiakov to any station.*

We are fighting!" Then again: "*German naval ensign spotted! We are damaged, on fire, still fighting…*"

Then he heard the powerful wash of a radio jammer clouding over the transmission. "My God," he said to his senior officer. Has the war started sir?"

"Something has started, Ludkov. Signal all ships in the Kara Sea to adopt radio silence. If the Germans have a warship up there they will be looking for targets. Then get a message off to Archangel and Murmansk—this time in proper code. Tell them there is Russian blood on the Kara Sea. Tell them *Sasha* is burning!"

Chapter 18

Yes, *Sasha* was burning, and Port Dikson was burning soon after. *Siberiakov* fired her two 76mm guns, but to no avail. Kranke was still well beyond range, and when he realized he would not make a harvest of any signals equipment here, he opened fire. Spouts of water were soon straddling the ship, and she was hit.

Captain Kacharava had attempted to lay a smoke screen, running for shore as fast as he could, but to no avail. Shell splinters sheared off the mast and radio antenna on the icebreaker, and cut down men on the decks. *Sasha's* chief stoker Vavilov was feeding coal to the boilers as fast as he could, and the sound of the ship's engines was deafening as they labored.

Admiral Scheer made short work of the icebreaker, and the gasoline on her decks went up like an inferno with Kranke's third salvo, which set off more explosions on the main deck as the splinters hit the gasoline barrels. Kacharava was struck in the arm, bleeding badly, and soon fell to the deck, lapsing into unconsciousness. Heavy black smoke mushroomed over the ship, and the next German salvo penetrated to the boiler room, stopping Sasha's fitful engines. Vavilov lay lifeless on the coal dark floor.

Yet topside, the brave Russian gunners continued to man a 76mm battery, firing impudently at the German ship. Krancke closed the range and his forward turret blasted again, finally silencing the enemy gun.

Chief Bochurko knew he must not allow the Germans to board the ship, and he worked his way past the licking flames to the radio room. There he found signalman Alexeyev, and radioman Sharshavin gathering up all the maps, weather data, ice floe reports and other code equipment. They threw everything into a rucksack and hauled it out onto the weather deck.

"No! Don't throw it into the sea," shouted Chief Bochurko. "Put it into the fire!" So they heaved the heavy bag down onto the lower deck and watched as it was consumed by the raging gasoline fire.

Then the Chief told the two men to get off the ship any way they could, and was last seen taking a ladder down into the dark recesses of the stricken icebreaker. The survivors believed he scuttled the ship, though no one ever really knew what happened to him.

At 15:00 *Sasha* gave up one last gasp with an explosion amidships, then rolled into the sea. The hiss of hot metal hitting the water was one of the last sounds the survivors could remember. Then they saw the Germans launching boats to rescue them, but stoker Matveyev would have none of it. He was shivering in one of the few lifeboats that made it away from the ship, but when the German boat came alongside, he threw an axe at the first man that tried to board.

There passed the first hand to hand combat of the war between Germany and Russia, with stoker Matveyev gunned down by a German officer wielding a luger, and the other crewmen fighting to resist capture. German Naval infantry leapt aboard the Russian boat, clubbing the sailors with the butts of their rifles. Three leapt overboard to avoid capture, braving the icy waters in the hopes of getting away. When it was over Kranke had fourteen prisoners, among them a man named Zolotov, who was being ferried to a distant weather station to deliver the new code books.

Kranke had his Kriegsmarine Funkaufklärung team interrogated the Russians, but learned nothing of value, so he determined to go after bigger fish, this time by making a raid on Port Dikson to the south. He loitered for a time, then satisfied that there was nothing else to be seen, he moved south, arriving off Port Dikson on July 8th. Little did he know that the course he set would soon bring him afoul of the Russian flotilla that had been hastily dispatched to the region.

"There will be better pickings ashore," said Kranke to his executive officer Heintz.

"Ashore?"

"Of course, Heintz. We get their maps, weather information, vital data on this northern convoy route, and possibly even their code machines this time. Just you wait!"

"But sir, we have already sunk two ships here! This will cause a major provocation."

"Yes," said Kranke coolly. "It will." He smiled, and Heintz immediately knew that there was more in the Kapitän's orders than he first revealed.

"That first ship fired on us," said Kranke. "We fired back. And you saw them train those deck guns on us just now. I took appropriate defensive action, and now we will punish the men ashore who gave the orders to attack the Kriegsmarine in these neutral waters."

"These are not neutral waters, sir. We are well within the territorial limit claimed by the Russians."

"That is not what the log books will read, Heintz. Get a head on your shoulders! It will be our story against theirs, but none of that matters. The important thing is that we have finally lit the match here, and now the fuse will be burning. Besides, we didn't start the shooting. The trouble started with U-46 and Oberleutnant Grau."

"Yes sir," said Heintz, feeling just a bit unsettled. "Grau started it, but one day it must have an end somewhere—in either Moscow or Berlin."

Kranke raised an eyebrow at that, but said nothing more.

* * *

The cruiser *Kalinin* was supposed to have had a sad and lonesome war. In Fedorov's old history it was built in Siberia, the steel, guns, and all other equipment shipped east on the trans-Siberian rail. Inactive during the war, the ship would later become a floating barracks until it was sold for scrap in 1963. But that history had changed in this new world. Instead the ship's parts were moved north to Murmansk, and the cruiser was commissioned into the fleet just weeks ago, on the 8th of May, 1940. Designated the flagship of the fledgling Red Banner Northern Fleet, *Kalinin's* history would be much more colorful.

At a whisker over 10,000 tons full load, *Kalinin* had a respectable battery of nine 180mm guns, a little over 7 inches and somewhat smaller than the typical 8-inch guns on a British heavy cruiser. There were also eight 85mm guns, twenty-two anti-aircraft guns, a pair of triple 21-inch torpedo mounts, fifty depth charges and over 100 mines aboard the ship.

Captain Koinev commanded the new ship, and he also had a pair of sleek hounds at his side that day, the destroyers *Kalima* and *Saku*. Originally meant for the Black Sea Fleet under the Project 20, class, these new designs weighed in at 3200 tons with a main armament of six 130mm guns and nine big torpedoes. They also carried eighty mines, and were perhaps the fastest ships in the world when commissioned into the Northern Fleet on direct orders from Sergie Kirov. The destroyers easily could run at 40 knots, and at trials the *Kalima* even recorded a 43 knot sprint. They were ships that had never been completed in the world Fedorov knew.

Now Koinev was pacing on the bridge, impatient in spite of the speed he was making. He was leading the cream of the Northern Fleet out to see about the numerous reports of ships and shore installations coming under fire from what was finally identified as a German raider. The war would not begin on the Polish frontier, he thought. No, it begins here, in the cold north, and this incident will soon be forgotten when the fighting starts on the ground. He knew the situation was very dangerous now, but he was determined to defend the motherland with all the skill he could muster.

The radio intercepts painted a grim picture by the time he reached the channel near the Port of Amderma after a 600 kilometer run east from Murmansk. The two destroyers had come up from Archangel to join him along the way, and by the time they reached Amderma the news of the loss of *Siberiakov*, old *Sasha*, had angered the crew when they heard it. The German raider had slipped away and had not been sighted since, but soon word came in from Port Dikson that a large warship had been sighted rounding Cape Anvil and heading into the port.

"We are under attack!" came the urgent warning, and the old port had little more to fight back with than three antiquated 152mm siege guns positioned by the quay at the edge of the harbor. There were no reinforced gun emplacements for them, and little ammunition, but the gunners rushed to man them and fired bravely in the hopes of warding the Germans off.

"Two ships sighted... boats in the water... they are coming!"

Admiral Scheer was at work again, her 11-inch guns pounding the harbor and providing ample cover while a detachment of 180 well armed naval Marines went ashore.

"Damn!" Koinev swore. "We are not ready!"

"There's a good local militia there," said Rykov, his gunnery officer. "Perhaps they can hold out until we get there."

"Yet what are we up against, Rykov? Reports are very scattered. They say the Germans have U-boats and fast cruisers running wild in the Kara Sea, yet not a single ship has been properly identified."

"We don't need to know a ship's name to put it at the bottom of the sea, sir. Just give me a target, and I'll drive them off. And let them try to run from *Kalima* and *Saku!*"

Koinev nodded, his confidence returning, but he was still pacing, restless on the bridge when another message came in: *Kuibyshev engaged and sinking! S.O.S!*

They had run through the pale Arctic night, still lit by the sun, and cut through the narrow Malygina Strait, heading due east for Port Dikson, but he was too late to stop the Germans. Word came that they had overwhelmed the militia, captured the port command buildings, and looted the place. Then they quickly withdrew, setting buildings afire and blowing up the piers as they went. *Kuibyshev* was sunk on the way out.

The watch soon spotted the mast and smoke of a ship, and the alarms sent all the crew to action stations. The Germans were trying to move west into the Kara Sea again, and a race ensued as Koinev turned up his speed and released the two hounds that were leading his flotilla. *Kalinin* quickly worked up to battle speed at 36 knots, but the new destroyers easily pulled ahead, both at just over 40 knots as they raced to run down the German raider.

But there were two ships now… The second sighting was called out almost immediately, and Koinev knew he now had a battle on his hands. Ready or not, he whispered to himself, here it starts, and here we come.

* * *

Kranke had a long look at the ships approaching off his port quarter. The Germans had pounded Port Dikson, stormed ashore and made off with a rich haul of intelligence, leaving the Northwest Naval Command headquarters there in a shambles. Now he was in the Kara Sea on a northeasterly course that would take him up above the great barrier island of Novaya Zemlya. He could see what looked like a pair of fast destroyers and one larger ship behind them, coming up off his aft port quarter.

"Those ships are fast," he said. "We are running at 28 knots and it looks like they will catch us in half an hour."

"We could turn northeast, sir," Heintz suggested. "It would be an hour before they could get close enough to engage."

"Too much ice there. We do not run, Heintz. Don't forget that. We will have them in range soon, but let's see what we have here before I show them my guns."

"It was only a matter of time before they came out to challenge us," said Heintz. "Soon we will see how the Russian Navy fights."

"Come 15 points to starboard. Let's make them work."

The two destroyers were closing on a converging course, exceeding *Admiral Scheer's* speed by over ten knots. They were outpacing the bigger ship behind them to the west, obviously with orders to run the German quarry down.

Kranke signaled *Nürnberg* to follow him. The light cruiser could run at 32 knots if it had to, but it was clear to Kranke that there was going to be a fight here. The Russian ships seemed much faster, and so he wanted to keep his ships together. The Kapitän slowly pulled on his leather gloves, his jaw set, a determined look on his face.

"They are requesting name and country of origin."

"Tell them to come and find out for themselves." Kranke was in no mood for the niceties of international protocol. *Admiral Scheer* remained silent after his curt reply. The next message would be sent with their 11-inch guns. At 11:00 he fired a single warning shot, and then sent a message for his log books: *Your intent appears hostile. Break off or be fired upon. This is your final warning.* The Russian destroyers replied with their forward deck guns, though the rounds fell well short.

"Well gentlemen, let us begin." Kranke nodded to his gunnery officer and *Scheer's* turrets rotated into position, their triple barrels training on the target. "Fire!"

The roar of the guns shook the ship, and even as the rounds began to fall the barrels were elevating to fire again. Kranke saw his spotting salvo was close enough, and now the targets turned slightly and looked to be positioning themselves for a torpedo run. The guns fired again, and this time he saw the tall splashes dollop the waters just ahead of the lead destroyer. The enemy would prove to be a fast and elusive target, zigzagging its way forward, and yet maintaining a speed of 40 knots the whole run in.

"Such speed!" Kranke exclaimed. "Those ships are faster than anything we have in the fleet. Engage with secondary batteries."

The smaller 15cm guns would fire faster and train better at a high speed target, and the Germans were going to need all the gunnery skill this ship and crew would become famous for if it survived this battle. A hit was finally registered on the lead ship, with smoke on the bow marking a small fire.

"They are firing torpedoes sir!" Heintz was calling from the weather bridge where he had been closely observing the fight. The Russian destroyers were equipped with a 21-inch torpedo, a design started in 1936 after the failure of an earlier model. This version was based on the Italian 533mm torpedo, bought from Fiume in 1932, and it became one of the main Russian torpedoes of World War II. It could range between 4000 meters at 44 knots out to 10,000 meters at 30 knots, but this first salvo had been fired with the jitters of a new ship in combat for the first time, and it was soon clear that the entire spread was going to be in *Nürnberg's* wake and miss both German ships badly.

The destroyers were turning to adjust their course and get a better firing angle when *Admiral Scheer's* 11-inch guns found *Kalima*. Two of the three rounds from Anton turret struck home, one forward where it smashed the second 130mm gun turret, and the second well aft where it exploded right between two torpedo mounts, destroying the torpedo firing director there and sending hot splinters and shrapnel in every direction. The aft mount had just been loaded and one of the torpedoes was struck right on the nose, causing the weapon to detonate, which set off the entire rack. The resulting explosion was catastrophic on the small ship. *Kalima* was finished.

Kranke looked at his Executive Officer, smiling. "Now they know who they are dealing with. We are not just another heavy cruiser! Look at that ship burn, Heintz!"

Kranke gave orders to shift main guns to the Russian cruiser farther west and leave the remaining destroyer to his secondary battery. Seeing the demise of their comrades, *Kalinin* was now opening fire with all nine 7.1-inch guns, and a running gun battle ensued, with both sides on a rough parallel course.

Destroyer *Saku* danced forward, making smoke to foil the gunners and put five torpedoes in the water. All but one would miss badly, and Kranke had to maneuver sharply to avoid the last, which was just astern, thrashing through his broiling wake. But it was *Admiral Scheer's* bigger guns that would make the difference. The German gunnery crews were seasoned and their optical sighting second to none. They found the range, put a good hit on *Kalinin* amidships that blew away her seaplane mount, and another just off the bow that sent the cruiser rocking wildly through the sea spray and dented the hull. *Kalinin* failed to score a hit, and now *Nürnberg* began to find the range, scoring twice with smaller 15cm guns.

When the Russian cruiser was straddled yet again by another salvo from *Admiral Scheer*, it appeared their Captain had had enough. Kranke saw the Russian destroyer swerve west, dancing through geysers of 15cm rounds with expert skill, but it was running. Moments later the cruiser turned as well, breaking off the fight. The first engagement of the war at sea for Soviet Russia had ended in defeat.

Heintz came in, congratulating the Kapitän, though he had a strange look in his eye. The shooting war had started and he seemed to have a sense of foreboding about it.

"Well," he said, "the madness has begun. What were those destroyers thinking? Any closer and we could have put rounds right through them."

Kranke laughed. "We are all mad men here, Heintz. No sane man would have come to this forsaken place just to kill or be killed here. I'm mad, you're mad, and the Russians are certainly mad as well. We call it war, but for now our purpose has been accomplished. Now we go home, thumbing our nose at them the whole long way."

Part VII

The Hunter

"If there is a sacred moment in the ethical pursuit of game, it is the moment you release the arrow or touch off the fatal shot."

— Jim Posewitz

Chapter 19

July 10, 1940

They saw it at a little after 19:00, high in the sky, gleaming with the light of the sun. At first the watchman thought it was a plane, but radar returns showed it to be moving far too slow for that. Kranke had a good laugh with Heintz and his senior gunnery officer, Helmut Schörner.

"Can you believe it?" he said as he took another sip of Merlot. "They have nothing that can bother us on the sea, so now they send that useless zeppelin!"

"Perhaps they have nothing else that can fly, Herr Kapitän," said Schörner. He was a short man, very proper, meticulous in his work and a stickler for cleanliness. Even as the Kapitän spoke he was slowly cleaning his butter knife with the linen napkin at the officer's dinner table.

Tonight they were celebrating the successful conclusion of Operation Wunderland. The Kapitän had ordered a nice roast beef with potatoes, peas and carrots. The Merlot was particularly good, vintage 1932, a bottle he had kept in his sea chest for some years waiting for a good night to celebrate.

Now his strange grey eyes were alight with jubilation, as if he were contemplating the medals he would win for this operation. "I told Hoffmann this was a good ship," said Kranke. "I told him we would have nothing to worry about. All this nonsense about a rocket cruiser has him whining like a schoolboy. Well, there is nothing of the sort here."

Kranke was a well respected officer in the Kriegsmarine, one who had fought with Admiral Hipper's Battlecruiser Squadron in the epic battle of Jutland. A torpedo man at heart, he cut his teeth in the navy in the torpedo boat flotilla, then served as an instructor in the Torpedo School.

The meal concluded, it was time now for drinks and smoke, and the mention of Hoffmann reminded the Kapitän that he had three fine cigars in his pocket. He produced them at once, handing one to each of the other men with a smile.

"Hoffmann gave these to me when I went over to see him on *Scharnhorst*. He said I was to smoke one for finding his ghost ship, the second for getting a good photograph, and the third for getting safely home. Well, I think we have more than enough reason to smoke them now, so light up gentlemen. Enjoy yourselves."

"Danke, Herr Kapitän," said Schörner, eager for a good smoke.

"Did you see how badly aimed those torpedoes were?" Kranke had another good laugh. "Ten fish in the water between the two destroyers and only one got close enough to ask us for a dance. It is clear the Russians have a lot to learn about warfare at sea. We will likely have free reign in these waters if this is all they have in the cupboard."

"Those looked like fine new destroyers," said Heintz. "Amazing speed!"

"But good for nothing unless you know how to properly fight the ship. They should have sprinted well ahead with their speed advantage and then fired right down our line of advance in a wide spread. But my god, Schörner, that was a tremendous hit you put on that lead destroyer."

"The guns are extremely accurate, sir. I believe I could have hit a fly on their mainmast if given just a little more time."

"Well," said Kranke. "Now that we have Norway, the Russians come next. They've were nipping at Finland's heels last winter, but the Führer will be sending troops there soon enough. In time we'll take these northern ports and then they'll be completely isolated, no navy to speak of and nothing but a few old zeppelins to bother us with."

Kranke had worked as Chief of Staff for North Sea Security in 1939 before taking his post on *Admiral Scheer*. When the pocket battleship went into the docks for a haircut and refit to officially become a heavy cruiser, Kranke was put to good use as Navy Representative on Special Staff *"Weserübung"* to help plan the naval portion of the invasion of Denmark and Norway. A man of 47 years, he was a tireless worker, always on the bridge, and taking little time for rest or leisure—except on a night like this.

"Suppose we send up our seaplane to harass that zeppelin, Kapitän?" Heintz had a derisive smile on his face.

"Good idea, Heintz," said Kranke. "That's a nice little slap in the face as we leave. They'll be remembering us for some time up here. Raeder was set to double down on this bet with Operation Doppelschlag, but I hardly think it will be necessary. Admiral Carls flew in from Wilhelmshaven with Vice Admiral Schmundt to plan the whole thing. Wait until they get my report! Yes, we were worried that the Russians had a few new ships up here, but it seems they haven't the faintest idea what to do with them."

Now he raised his glass in a toast. "Good shooting, Schörner. Congratulations! Now gentlemen, let us enjoy these fine cigars. Then we can go home and tell Herr Hoffmann that his rocket cruiser is nowhere to be found, and that from the looks of things, Murmansk will be even easier pickings than Norway!"

* * *

Even as Kranke raised his glass, a dark car rolled to a stop on a muddy road north of Murmansk. The front doors opened and the driver and a guard stepped out, the latter opening the rear door for the passenger, Vice Admiral Arseniy Golovko, his face grim and serious. The Admiral tramped across the road, folding his arms as he looked at the ship riding at anchor out in the bay.

Massive, he thought. Look at all those antennae! But where are the guns? I was told this ship would be very powerful, and it certainly looks threatening, but with just those three twin turrets? I have destroyers that are better armed.

He shrugged, sighing heavily. "That is the ship?"

"Yes sir. It has been here for several days, and the commanding officer is waiting to receive you ashore."

"We have nothing else that looks anything like this ship. Where did it come from? I know nothing of a special project to build of ship of this size."

"It's a bit of a mystery, sir," said the adjutant.

"Is it finished? They might have put some guns on the damn thing before they sent it to us." Golovko shook his head, discouraged and somewhat disappointed. The ship was beautiful, awesome in many ways. He found his eye sweeping over its trim lines as a man might regard the lean shape of a woman's leg. But nothing up front, he thought, noting the flat empty foredeck.

"Very well. Let us visit this new Admiral again. Kirov seemed fairly well taken with the man. And I see they have named this ship after him. Let's hope it has better luck for us than *Kalinin* had yesterday. That was a *Kirov* class cruiser too." He lowered his head, watching the mud under his boots as he walked.

They were in the small but rapidly growing settlement of Severomorsk. By order of the General Secretary a big buildup was now underway here. Trucks had been arriving day and night from the rail yard at Murmansk after a big shipment came all the way up from Leningrad. They were to construct new command centers, docks, berthing areas, a supply depot and barracks. Another base, thought Golovko, but nothing to anchor in it.

"Well, beggars can't be choosers. I come here with an empty teacup looking for help. Let us hope this ship will be of some use."

They made their way through the sodden ground to a newly built cabin, where the Admiral saw a detachment of security personnel waiting to receive him. He was ushered in to find Admiral Volsky and Fedorov waiting quietly in a simple room, with a table and chairs that doubled as a dining hall for staff officers.

"Forgive the accommodations, Admiral," said Volsky as he extended his hand. "We are just getting established here ashore, and the crews are busy with repairs on the ship."

"Quite a vessel," said Golovko. "I am told it was a secret project?"

"That is correct."

"Well I won't bother you with questions about it. I'm afraid I have come with some grave news. We received emergency alarms from our base at Port Dikson on the Kara Sea. The Germans have sortied with a squadron of warships. We got wind of it through naval intelligence last week—an operation Wunderland, as they call it. There has been fighting."

"Fighting? Then they have violated your neutrality?"

"If you want to call the sinking of three ships a violation, then you have it exactly." Admiral Golovko related the news, and Volsky could perceive his frustration at the end when he told the story of how his own warships had fared in their first encounter with the Germans.

"A destroyer sunk?"

"*Kalima.* One of our newest ships."

"And the ice breaker?"

"*Siberiakov.* We called her old *Sasha*, as that ship has made that high Arctic run east for years, but no longer. They tell me the Germans have taken prisoners, and one man in particular that raises some alarm. His name was Zolotov, and he was carrying the new code books for the weather outposts along that route. Now we will have to change the code yet again!"

At the mention of that name Volsky seemed very surprised.

"Zolotov… Georgie Zolotov?"

"Yes, that is the man. You know him?"

"I have heard of the man, though we have never met." Volsky seemed very upset now. "*Sasha*… yes, I have heard his name before. This is a very serious matter, Golovko. What do you propose to do about it?"

"That is the dilemma, Admiral Volsky. I have already sent the best ships at my disposal to find this German flotilla. *Kalinin* took three hits, *Kalima* was sunk and only *Saku* survived unscathed. We sent out the *Narva* to see if we could find and shadow the Germans, and this she has done."

"Another cruiser? I have not heard of this ship."

"It is an airship, Admiral. C-10, commissioned in 1938. We still have a few in the fleet, but it won't do us any good. There is nothing *Narva* can do to stop those German ships. Oh, it can catch them, but if it tries to fire on them they will blow it out of the sky with their secondary batteries. So here I sit, commander of the Red Banner Northern Fleet, and I have six older destroyers and another rusting cruiser moored at Murmansk. *Kalinin* will be in the repair dock for at least two weeks, not that it matters. I have nothing to throw at them but seaplanes and blimps!"

Volsky nodded, remembering his own frustration as he contemplated sending out his Pacific fleet against the powerful American Navy. His eyes narrowed, and he gave Fedorov a glance before he spoke.

"Perhaps I can be of assistance," he said. "My ship can finish up repairs and be ready to leave within the hour."

Golovko raised his eyebrows, for this is what he had come to ask, and it had been offered. Yet his own misgivings about the lack of firepower on the ship he had seen still nagged at him.

"I would hate to ask this of you, and put your ship and crew at risk. After all, *Kalinin* was a very capable ship—nine 180mm guns, good speed, torpedoes. I am told that your ship is very powerful, and forgive me now Admiral, but you do not seem very well equipped. Those guns you have cannot be more than 152mm."

Volsky smiled. "The British thought the same," he said quietly. "But I assure you, Golovko, they were quite happy when we helped prevent three or four German battleships from breaking out into the Atlantic. We are more than capable, and yes, we will help you restore the honor of the Red Banner Fleet. Wait and see."

Volsky stood up, decisively. "Mister Fedorov, have the men prepare my launch. We are returning to *Kirov* at once and the ship will sortie in sixty minutes."

"Aye sir." Fedorov said nothing more and went to see to those orders.

Admiral Golovko gave Volsky a smile and a handshake in thanks. "Go with God," he said, wishing the Admiral well.

"I'm afraid God will have nothing to do with it," said Volsky. "It appears the war has started. Yes? If so, then this is work for the devil."

An hour later, *Kirov* hoisted anchor and slowly slipped out of the long inlet, heading for the Barents Sea. Admiral Golovko watched it turn, again feeling something was very strange about this ship, ominous and threatening.

Other eyes were watching the ship as well, from a small trawler that was moored to the quay, an inconspicuous commercial fishing boat. There, a man sat quietly in the darkened cabin, the barest light of an oil lamp illuminating his work as he tapped slowly on a telegraph key. It was a coded message that would be heard by a relay station well ashore in an old hunting lodge in the hills. There another man would tap his wireless telegraph key, and hand off the signal to another relay station. The message would hop east, over the White Sea and into the wilderness until it reached another logging cabin on the foothills of the Urals. There it would be handed off to the Airship *Sarkand*, hovering over the icy peaks of the mountains on a standing patrol for just this reason. Soon it would come to the attention of Ivan Volkov himself. The ship—Karpov's ship—had finally been found!

Yet Admiral Golovko knew nothing of this as he turned and got back into his waiting car, wondering how long it would be before he received news that yet another Russian ship had been sunk.

Kirov must learn not to put his name on these ships until they can fight, he thought. But he did not know just how very wrong he was.

Chapter 20

On the bridge of his fighting ship, Admiral Volsky explained his urgency to Fedorov when they were underway. "Golovko says he will radio the position of the German flotilla," he said.

"We will most likely have them on long range radar as soon as we leave the Kola Bay," said Fedorov. "What is your intention, sir?"

Volsky gave him a long look. "Someone has just broken into our neighbor's house, Fedorov. No. That was our brother's house. It will not go unpunished. Beyond that, I was alarmed to hear the name of that man taken as prisoner—Zolotov."

"Who is he, Admiral?"

"You saw my surprise, yes? Well my father knew the man. Yes. Old *Sasha*. He told me stories of that ship when I was a boy. I used to imagine it pushing its way through the ice on the cold sea voyage east, a real pioneer ship. I often imagined I was there on the bridge, watching the ice crack under the ship's bow. Zolotov was a friend of my father, and so you see, it cuts a bit close to the bone to hear what happened to him. I can still remember the look in my father's eyes when he told me the Germans got him."

"They captured him?"

"You can probably look it up in your old history books, Fedorov."

"I did check on this operation, sir. It wasn't supposed to happen until August of 1942! It is very odd that it should occur so soon in this new time line, or even reoccur at all."

"Tell me about it. What ships were involved?"

"Just one, sir. The heavy cruiser *Admiral Scheer*. It did everything Admiral Golovko described—even the sinking of that icebreaker you mentioned. It's very strange how the history seems to echo the events of the world we came from, yet things have shifted, slipped. This time there is a second German ship, and that is a new variation."

"Just a piece of your cracked mirror that has moved out of place, Fedorov. Well, you will forgive me for what I am now going to do, and it may seem petty, but suddenly this little war has become personal for me. I will not allow this insult to stand. Do you understand?"

"Well sir," Fedorov thought for a moment. "If the Germans think they can come to our home waters and attack Russian ships with impunity, they will likely come to believe that they can easily close these ports and isolate Soviet Russia from any outside assistance. This may have been a reason for this operation, to test Russian resolve and measure our capabilities."

"They are going to need a very long measuring tape," said Volsky grimly.

Sometime later Rodenko reported to the Admiral where he sat in his ready room off the main bridge. They had just cleared the bay and were now entering the Barents Sea.

"Nikolin has received word on the German location, sir. They were hovering up near Franz-Joseph and Alexandria Islands. Now they are headed west towards Spitzbergen."

"That will put them some 400 kilometers northeast of us," said Fedorov. "If we steer due north we should be on a good intercept course."

"Make it so, Mister Fedorov. When do you anticipate contact?"

"We can be well within missile range in ten hours at 24 knots. Increase that a bit and I can put you on their horizon in that same timeframe."

"Do so, and inform me when we get within fifty kilometers. I think we will have a little chat with the German Captain and ask him to apologize for what he has done. Of course he will laugh that off. Then we will show him the error of his ways."

"It looks like they want to pass well north of Bear Island."

"Cold desolate waters there," said Volsky. "But it is July, and so there should still be plenty of sea room."

It was a time when much of the sea ice was broken into drifts, with occasional larger ice bergs leaving trails of open water behind them as they forged a path through the smaller floes, like ghostly frozen ships.

The senior officers rested, but were back on the bridge for planned operations at 18:00 on the 11th of July. By that time *Kirov* was well north, and had now turned west on an intercept course as the German flotilla approached Spitzbergen. Fedorov had increased speed to 30 knots to begin closing the range, and *Kirov* ran easily, the time at Severomorsk being well spent by Chief Byko to get much needed repairs completed on the ship's bow. Admiral Volsky was informed that the contact was being tracked on their Fregat radar, and he returned to the bridge, his manner serious.

"Very well," he said gruffly. "Mister Nikolin, you will begin hailing the Germans on an open channel. Tell them that they have violated Soviet territorial waters and neutrality, and that they are now holding our nationals as prisoners. They must stop. These men must be returned, or they will suffer the consequences."

"Do I send this in Russian, sir?"

"Yes. Fedorov tells me there is a good chance they have a team aboard that will understand you. Continue your hail and report any response."

* * *

When the message was heard on the *Admiral Scheer* it caused a moment of levity on the bridge. Kranke looked at the signalman with incredulity, then broke into a broad smile.

"Who is sending the message, that zeppelin shadowing us?"

"No sir, it is coming from a ship. They have identified themselves as the battlecruiser *Kirov*."

"The battlecruiser *Kirov*? My, my, the General Secretary of the Soviet Union is naming ships after himself. Well then, this must be the pride of the fleet, yes Heintz?"

Heintz stepped over, curious about the message. "What is it, Kapitän?"

"The Russians are not happy with our little foray into the Kara Sea. They want their prisoners back, or so they say." The Kapitän turned to the signalman now. "Tell them these men are now in the custody of the Kriegsmarine and will be interrogated at our leisure. If they want to do anything about it they are invited to try." He laughed, shaking his head. "The nerve of these Russians, eh Heintz? Perhaps they did not receive enough of a beating and we will have to take them to the woodshed yet again."

Time passed and the message returned. *"Stop and surrender all Soviet nationals or you will be engaged as a hostile ship."*

Kranke dismissed it as nonsense, thinking the transmission had to be coming from the Russian zeppelin that was still shadowing them, high above and just out of range of their guns. But the incident, a laughing matter to him now, was soon going to be more than he expected, and one that he would never forget.

At 21:20 hours the Germans spotted a contact off their port bow, and they knew that the Russians had indeed sortied another warship to challenge them. Kranke had a long look through the telescope on the weather bridge, returning somewhat bemused.

"One ship," he said quietly. "And it looks to be something more than a cruiser."

"The Russians *have* nothing more than a heavy cruiser, sir," said Heintz. "It must be the light and shadow at this distance. Shall we steer on an intercept course and have a closer look?"

"No, I think we will just continue on this heading. Let them come to us if they can."

"Battle speed, sir?"

"No need to rush, Heintz. Steady on at 24 knots."

"But they will catch us if this is a Russian cruiser."

"Then Schörner will deal with them."

Messages continued to stream in with the same demand: *Stop and surrender Russian nationals or be engaged.* Kranke ignored them, a wry grin on his face, though Heintz could see that the Kapitän seemed just a little more serious now, with an air of concern shadowing his bravado.

Then it began, they heard a distant thump, and then some time later the telltale approach of a naval shell that landed smartly in the water about a hundred meters in front of the light cruiser *Nürnberg* where it was steaming in the van.

"They say that was our final warning," said the signalman.

"Do they?" said Kranke. "What was that Schörner?"

"5.7-inch round by my estimation, sir, and very strange that they could get it anywhere near us at this range. We are over 26,000 meters away!"

Kranke began to slowly pull on his gloves. "The ship will come to battle stations. Hoist battle ensign and colors." His voice was flat, all business, with just a bit of annoyance in it now.

"The impudence," he muttered.

The sound of the alarm and the shouting and footfalls of the crew dominated the next few moments as Kranke stood calmly on the bridge, watching and listening. He saw the forward triple gun turret turn smartly and train on the Russian ship, the long barrels gleaming in the ruddy light. Soon the sounds diminished, and a hush seemed to fall over the *Admiral Scheer*, like the taking in of breath before some great exertion. The ship was ready, Kranke knew, and he turned to his gunnery officer.

"Schörner, announce us, if you please."

"The range is too far to hit anything, sir. All we will do is bother the sea."

"Give them one round in answer to their warning shot. I will not have it read that I did not follow protocols. They fired first, and we will answer."

"Very good sir."

The middle gun on the turret elevated in an obscene gesture, and fired. Kranke did not fail to appreciate the moment, smiling. "There, he said. "We have given them our middle finger and told them to fuck off. Now let's see if they want to do anything about it. Signal *Nürnberg* to come left fifteen, and we will follow."

* * *

The warning shot fell 3000 meters short, though it was well aligned. Volsky watched the round splash into the sea, tit for tat.

"They are turning on an intercept course," said Fedorov noting his new predictive plot for the German contact on the Plexiglas screen.

"Steer to maintain range," said Volsky.

"Aye sir. Helm, come left fifteen and ahead thirty." He re-established a parallel course, holding the range as the Admiral wanted.

"Mister Samsonov, how good is your eye these days?"

"Laser sharp, Admiral."

"Can you put one round on the lead ship in that formation?"

"Of course, sir. Do you want it forward, aft, or amidships?"

"That good, are you? Very well kick the lead ship on the ass. Put it well aft."

Fedorov had been studying the silhouettes of the German ships and now he spoke up. "Admiral, I believe that lead ship is a *Leipzig* class cruiser. The ship following is the *Admiral Scheer*, and that will be the flagship."

"I will knock on their door soon, Mister Fedorov. First let's see if Mister Samsonov can put on a little show. Their commander will have a very good view from his present location. You may open fire. One salvo please."

Samsonov keyed his target, integrating radar lock and his laser range finder into one position fix. The computers arrived at a decision in milliseconds, and the forward deck gun swiveled, trained on the target, the twin barrels elevating high before they cracked to life. Two shell casings clattered onto the deck and they waited. It seemed a long time, some 40 seconds before they saw the bright flash aft on the lead ship. Samsonov had scored a direct hit.

"A hole in one, sir!" he said, smiling.

"Your eye is good, Samsonov. Mister Nikolin, kindly ask the Germans if they would like us to continue."

Half way through Nikolin's hail they saw the second ship light up, both fore and aft. The rounds came in short again, but the sight of the six geysers in the sea prompted Fedorov to caution the Admiral.

"If I may, sir. Those are 11-inch guns, very accurate, and the same weapon that the battlecruiser *Scharnhorst* hit the British carrier with at 26,465 yards. We are just a few thousand meters outside that range."

"Which is exactly where we will stay, Mister Fedorov. Any answer, Nikolin?"

"No sir. No return on my hail."

"Mister Samsonov, again please. This time hit the bow of ship number two if you can."

"No problem, sir. Integrating data streams... Ready... Firing now." The crack of the deck gun sounded again, another long arcing fall of the shells, which resulted in a straddle this time, showering the bow of *Admiral Scheer* with seawater.

The game continued, with the German ships turning in an attempt to close the range, and Fedorov using radar to precisely determine their movement and dance away, always holding the range just outside 26,000 meters. Samsonov was ordered to fire three salvos at the lead ship, and three more at *Admiral Scheer,* and they soon watched as small fires broke out on each ship, the thin smoke trailing like blood. It was as if Volsky was hunting a whale, putting small harpoons into it, dancing away, then pricking it again and again. In all there were three more hits registered on *Nürnberg,* and two more on *Admiral Scheer.*

All the while the German guns barked furiously in return, but the range was just beyond their means. An hour passed, with Volsky scoring hits on the enemy ships every fifteen minutes, like clockwork.

Then he had Nikolin send another message. *I have hit you every quarter hour, and you bleed. Surrender our nationals, or I will now sink you.* In response the Germans launched a seaplane from *Scheer* and it slowly gained elevation and began to approach.

"They want to use the plane to try and improve their spotting, sir," said Fedorov.

"Do they? Mister Samsonov. Use the Klinok system and shoot that plane down. It's time we give them something more to think about."

The missile soon hissed into the sky, tracked relentlessly, and bored in on the seaplane. Fedorov looked at Volsky, surprised to see him make a small sign of the cross quietly on his chest as he sat watching in the Captain's chair. It was going to be a very unlucky day for the pilot.

Chapter 21

July 11, 1940 ~ 01:00 Hrs

Kranke was furious. The rounds had come like the chiming of a clock. Two hits at the top of the hour, another at quarter past, a fourth at half past the hour, and on it went.

"This is ridiculous, Schörner! How can they hit us like this at such range?"

"Amazing gunnery, Kapitän. I have never heard of a small caliber weapon firing with such accuracy. They must have superb opticals."

"What about *our* guns. Surely we can get them at this range. Elevate higher!"

"Sir, I am reading the target at 27,600 meters. If we hit them it will be one for the record books, and we do not seem to have the speed to close."

"Damn it, Schörner! They are hitting us! Signal *Nürnberg* to go to their top speed and close. They are four knots faster than we are. Get a seaplane up if you have to correct your sighting. I want hits!"

Nürnberg turned, but thirty seconds later the distant shadow on the sea turned as well, and Kranke could barely see it now on the horizon. The seaplane fluttered up, launching from the catapult amidships and slowly gaining altitude. It banked and began to head for the Russian ship, and then he saw it... Something erupted from the shadow, a white streak in the sky, a fiery light and then the explosion. The seaplane was gone!

Kranke slowly lowered his field glasses, a look of shock on his face. He kept staring at the sky, watching the fading contrail that connected the enemy ship to the place in the sky his seaplane had been flying. Heintz was quickly at his side.

"A rocket!" He pointed at the smoke in the sky, then lowered his arm and looked at Kranke. "Herr Kapitän," he said slowly. "I believe we smoked those cigars too soon."

* * *

"**That** light cruiser is turning on an intercept course," said Rodenko. The two ships are breaking formation."

"Yes, said Fedorov. If we maneuver to maintain our range then *Admiral Scheer* will slip over the horizon."

"I believe it is time for us to strengthen the brew," said Volsky. "How many of those P-900s from *Kazan* remain?"

"Six missiles, sir."

"Let us use one here on that light cruiser. That will get their attention, and I think we can use it in mode one with this ship, correct Fedorov?"

"Mode one?" Fedorov passed a moment of embarrassment, not knowing what the Admiral was referring to. He had never been a combat officer, and still felt more comfortable at the navigation station, in spite of his position as the ship's Captain now."

"On mode one this is a standard sea skimmer" said the Admiral. "It will not execute a last minute popup maneuver. Would you recommend this approach?" Volsky could see he had caught his young Captain at a disadvantage and he was wise enough to bolster him a bit by making it seem as though he was seeking his advice.

"There were only two ships in this class, and I believe this one is the *Nürnberg*, sir. If that is so it received the newly developed *Wotan Hart* steel instead of standard cemented armor. That said, the ship has only 50mm side armor. The P-900 should easily penetrate that and do considerable damage."

"Then we will fire one P-900 on mode one, Mister Samsonov, You may target and proceed."

"Aye sir. Setting mode command. Missile reports ready. Firing now."

The warning claxon sounded and the missile was up and on its way with a loud roar, climbing and then immediately dipping towards the sea to cross the short distance right over the wave tops.

Seconds later it struck *Nürnberg* amidships, just above the water line on her side armor, and Fedorov's assessment was on the mark as well.

The 200kg warhead easily penetrated the 2-inch armor there. *Wotan Hart* steel was much harder than cemented armor, but the ship would have needed at least six inches to have any chance of stopping the missile. The hull was badly breached, the explosive force ripping a hole from the weather deck to well below the water line. Fire broiled in the blackened gash, and heavy smoke engulfed the ship. *Nürnberg* rolled heavily as the sea rushed in, a benefit as well as a curse. The water helped to douse the terrible fire from all the excess missile fuel, but it was also dragging the ship into a bad list.

The ship would not recover, but counter-flooding would buy enough time to get most of the crew off safely. Volsky watched on the Tin Man display, his face serious, eyes troubled. The lessons of war were hard, whether you were the teacher or the student, he thought. Let us hope the Captain on this other ship does not need further prodding.

"That will be enough for the moment," he said to Samsonov. "Let's see if Mister Nikolin can get a response now."

* * *

Aboard *Admiral Scheer* Kranke was aghast. He had clearly seen the missile fire from the thick of the shadow that had been taunting him with small caliber fire, infuriated to think that this new Russian weapon could outrange his 11-inch guns. The rocket that took down his seaplane was shocking enough. He knew the old British battlecruisers once mounted a rocket system, but it was designed to deploy a small parachute and trail long cables at the bottom to act as an obstacle against planes. This was something else entirely, a lightning fast javelin that skewered his *Arado* and dropped it into the sea in seconds. Then came the rocket that struck *Nürnberg*, and he soon surmised that they were going to lose that ship. The Russians had evened the score.

So *this* was the ship Hoffmann warned me about, he thought darkly. Smoke one cigar if you find it, one if you can get close enough for a photograph, the third if you return alive. Now he knew just what Hoffmann meant, and it was a most uncomfortable feeling. One moment he was a jaunty, ebullient officer, fresh from victory, a good meal and a long sleep. Now he looked harried and anxious, struggling first to comprehend what he was seeing, weighing the implications of these new weapons. With each passing minute he realized the inadequacy of his ship now when pitted against this unknown foe.

"The battlecruiser *Kirov*," he said to Heintz. "Well now I can see why it gets the name. This ship is a little something more than we expected. They have saved the best for last."

"Schörner can't hit the damn thing unless we can close the range, sir, and it is obvious that they are faster than we are. There are probably 500 men going into the sea out there now, and if we continue this engagement we could lose most of them."

"Kapitän," the signalman called. "They say that if we do not cease firing and comply with the return of their nationals they will sink us too!"

"Calm down!" Kranke said sharply, hands clasped behind his back. "Alright then… first get a coded message off to Group North. Notify Hoffmann that we have found this ship. Call it *Fafnir*, he will know what I mean." He was referring to the legendary dragon in Norse Mythology.

"This one certainly breathes fire," said Heintz.

"That it does. Signalman… Tell the Russians they can have their damn prisoners. We have over 500 men on *Nürnberg* out there that will need our help. Ask them to cease fire." He shrugged, pulling his gloves off slowly, a defeated look on his face. Then the light of an idea kindled in his eyes.

"Let them come in to retrieve their comrades," he said to Heintz in a low whisper. "Then when they are nice and close, Schörner can blow them to hell."

Kranke would not be able to order his planned deception. The Russians were simply too cautious. The Germans were running past the long finger of Hopen Island off Svalbard, or Spitzbergen as it was then called. A signal came ordering them to set all the Soviet prisoners ashore there, saying their names and identities were known and stressing that they had best be unharmed and well treated. The Kapitän complied, then went about his rescue operation under the watchful eye of the Russian ship, always lurking on the horizon, a distant, threatening shadow.

Three hours later the Germans had recovered the great bulk of the crew of *Nürnberg*, and set off scuttling charges to make certain the Russians would not get the ship. Then, his decks crowded with cold, bedraggled men, Kranke turn and sailed on, a chastened man.

Fafnir, he thought. Yes, and now where is Sigurd? It will take something better than this old pocket battleship to get after that monster. Hoffmann fared no better, and he had both *Scharnhorst* and *Gneisenau* with him. And Lindemann had *Bismarck* and *Tirpitz* and he still broke off his engagement as well.

"I'm afraid they have evened the score," Heintz said dejectedly. "I wonder why they did not turn those rocket weapons on us? We've been in range for some hours, and they have every reason to avenge what we have done."

"This Russian Captain is a cagey and cautious man," said Kranke. "Yes, he's trumped us with these new weapons they've developed—for the moment. Lindemann turned for home on Raeder's orders, but I heard the damage to *Bismarck* was not significant. Against a lightly armored cruiser like *Nürnberg* those rockets were very effective. I doubt if *Bismarck* would be bothered by them, and that ship has 15-inch guns."

"I hope you are correct, sir."

Kranke gave him a long look. "Yes, I hope I am correct as well. Otherwise we may have awakened a sleeping bear here, and I was the man who gave the orders." He turned, walking slowly off the bridge, his gait slow and deliberate, shoulders slumped.

* * *

"Well," said Volsky. "I have accomplished my purpose here, and that was more than the recovery of Zolotov and the others."

Volsky waited until the Germans had completed their rescue operation and sailed off. They followed slowly, shadowing the Germans for some time, and then turned towards Hopen Island to pick up the Russians that had been taken from *Siberiakov* and Port Dickson.

"I know it appeared to you that all we did here is break another ship and crew," said Volsky. "But we have built something here as well."

"What is that, Admiral?"

"A reputation, Fedorov. It will precede us wherever we go now, like a long shadow. The next time a German Captain sees my ship on his horizon, they will remember us. Let us hope they respect the way this was handled."

"I would think they realized they were overmatched, sir," said Fedorov.

"Good. Fear is a useful weapon. Now when they see any Russian ship at sea they may not be so eager to engage. Perhaps they will think that all our ships might have the weapons we used. It could save some lives."

"Let us hope as much, Admiral, but in time they will see that is not the case. We will soon be deemed the exception, and not the rule, and that will deepen the mystery for them somewhat as well."

"They still have a lot to learn." Volsky nodded.

"Will we be returning to Severomorsk now?"

"No, I think we have other business at the moment, Mister Fedorov. "The ship has been well repaired, and we have replenished our stocks of food and fresh water. I know the men were eager for home, but in many ways, seeing it that way, barren, everything we knew gone... Well it may have done more harm than help."

"I understand, sir. Then what course should I set now?"

"I think we will continue west into the Norwegian Sea again. I told Golovko I would handle this matter and then scout the German buildup near the North Cape area. The KA-40 should be useful in that regard. After that we have business further south. I had a private talk with Sergie Kirov before he left. He has authorized me to make formal offers of Alliance with Great Britain, and to reinforce the diplomatic talks now underway in back channels with an official visit."

"I see," said Fedorov, very impressed by this, and heartened by the news. "Then we are going to rendezvous with the British? Where sir? Scapa Flow?"

"We can arrange that soon enough," said Volsky. "Plot a course for the Faeroe Island Group. I think that would make a convenient place to have another chat. I think you might also see what you learn with signals intercepts and use that gizmo you have."

"Gizmo, sir?"

"That application that deciphers the German Enigma Naval code. I think Admiral Tovey might be pleased to learn that we have broken that code."

'That would be a major development, sir. It was instrumental to the British war effort."

"Yes, well that will be a nice little cherry we can put on the ice cream, yes?" Volsky sighed. "It was my intention to find friends here, Fedorov. That we have done, but I'm afraid that every choice has its implications, and we have made enemies here as well."

"The Germans may have been surprised and intimidated here, sir," said Fedorov. "But they will not give up easily. They've lost a destroyer and a light cruiser, but all their other capital ships will return to service. I think things should quiet down here for a while. They will want to make those repairs and the winter ice will be setting in sooner than we realize."

"Where is the hot table in the casino now, Fedorov?"

"Sir? If you mean the history, the British are worried about Operation Seelöwe now, and the French Navy."

"I will tell Admiral Tovey that they need have no worry over the prospect of a German invasion. That I could easily prevent. As for the Battle of Britain, I'm afraid we don't have enough SAMs to stop the Luftwaffe just now."

"Agreed, sir. Unless you are willing to reconsider another shift attempt, I think we must be very conservative in the application of our remaining missile inventory. We have 23 SSMs remaining."

"You say the British are worried about the French?"

"Yes sir. The center of gravity now shifts to the Mediterranean for the balance of this year. France has just capitulated, and the French have some very powerful and useful ships. The British may have settled the matter. The attack on the French fleet at Mers-el-Kebir took place on July 3rd in our history, but this recent German operation may have changed that. I doubt if it occurred. Most of the ships that were to be assigned to Admiral Somerville to create Force H at Gibraltar were up here for this operation, including HMS *Hood* and the two carriers that were supporting Tovey's operation against the Germans. But all things considered, the British will now be looking south. They could be planning an operation against the French fleet even as we speak."

"Let us hope they sort it out. You have the bridge, Mister Fedorov. I'm going below to see Zolotov and the other Russians we took aboard. They may be with us for some time, and that may require a little management."

"I understand, sir."

Fedorov saluted as the Admiral left, thinking. It appears that everyone has finally chosen sides. Soon the real fighting will begin.

Part VIII

Vulture's Feast

"Here is a list of fearful things:
The jaws of sharks, a vulture's wings,
The rabid bite of the dog's of war,
The voice of one who went before.
But most of all the mirror's gaze,
which counts us out our numbered days."

— Clive Barker

Chapter 22

July 15, 1940

Admiral Tovey sat at his desk, a dejected look on his face. Britain was also in a quandary over what to do about the powerful French fleet. While the French Army had been shattered by the German blitzkrieg, the Navy survived largely intact, with strong capital ships scattered throughout ports from Alexandria to Dakar. Soon the Italians and Germans will realize what is there, he thought. Then they'll descend on those ports like vultures.

Even as he thought that, he realized what lay ahead, and what they would have to do about it. Sadly, we'll have to be the vulture too, and get whatever we can off the carcass. We've already grabbed the few ships that were in English ports, and at Alexandria we were lucky to get our hands on the old battleship *Lorraine*, and three heavy cruisers. But that is only the first bite. There are ships at Toulon, four heavy cruisers, fifteen destroyers. There are submarines in Beirut, Bizerte, Casablanca, Oran and Dakar, but the real prizes of war here are the newer battleships. If we cannot secure them, then no one must.

The older French battleships, *Lorraine, Provence, Bretagne, Paris* and *Courbet*, were of little concern. The last two were old enough to be called "Dreadnaughts" and all the others were laid down before the outbreak of WWI. They might be useful as floating batteries when permanently moored in a friendly port but, as for naval operations, their sluggish speed and the necessity of keeping them supplied outweighed their usefulness.

But France had also participated in the big pre-war naval buildup, experimenting with several new designs to meet the 35,000 ton treaty limitations, until Admiral Darlan got word that the German Z-Plan ships were now openly being built in violation of all agreements. France had built some fast and capable ships, designed to hunt down and kill Germany's early pocket battleships like the *Graf*

Spee. These were fast battlecruisers, yet with very good armor and eight 13-inch guns, *Strausbourg* and *Dunkerque.*

Two knots faster than the German raiders, and much better armed and protected, they were also capable of standing with *Scharnhorst* class ships, and with a good chance of coming out the victor. Only the German *Bismarck* class bettered them, and both these new French ships now sat in Oran. They were accompanied there by two of the older battleships, *Provence* and *Bretagne*, along with four light cruisers, sixteen destroyers and a handful of submarines and other minor ships.

Two other newer battleships had been completed just before the war, well ahead of schedule in the history Fedorov knew. They had been built in answer to the Italian naval buildup more than anything the Germans were doing, up-gunned to eight 15-inch guns in two quadruple turrets mounted forward, and state-of-the-art armor protection that still allowed them to work up to 32 knots. *Richelieu* fled to Dakar, and *Jean Bart* was at Casablanca with a light cruiser, seven destroyers and eighteen submarines.

There were also a few hidden gems in the French Navy, ships that had been planned and built in answer to the German Z Plan naval buildup. One was now at Casablanca, moved there hastily in the twilight of the war from her moorings at Saint Nazaire, where the ship was being provisioned after fitting out. The shipyard crews sailed with her, still feverishly working on equipment installation. Yet ready or not, she was the grand duke of the fleet, built under the codename "Project C" with the early name *Alsace* that had since been changed to *Normandie.*

The ship was bigger and heavier than anything else in the fleet, a truly formidable design on the scale of Britain's own HMS *Invincible.* The same quadruple 380mm gun turrets used for *Richelieu* and *Jean Bart* were used, but instead of only two forward, a third turret was also added aft, up-gunning the design to twelve 15-inch guns, 33% more raw big gun firepower than on the German *Bismarck* class battleships. Only one ship in this project was ever laid down, and was still somewhat raw and incomplete when France lost her war in 1940. Sadly her maiden voyage would see the *Normandie* flee the shores of her homeland, never to return. The ship was a prize that Germany, Italy, and Britain would have dearly liked to take if they could, and one that Fedorov was delighted to read about as he poured over the altered history of this world as written and known in the books the Russians had given him as a parting gift.

Yet perhaps even more enticing to the naval high commands of all the nations that now looked hungrily upon the French fleet, were the two incomplete designs that still sat in the shipyards in various stages of completion. One was the fast anti-aircraft cruiser *De Grasse*, a sleek design capable of over 33 knots and bristling with eight twin 127mm AA guns and another ten twin 57mm Bofors.

The other was the real jewel, the large fleet aircraft carrier *Joffre* that was presently in the yards at Staint Nazaire-Penhoët, about 80% complete. Also designed to achieve 33 knots, the 20,000 ton full load carrier could carry 40 aircraft and run with the fastest battle fleets any nation might assemble. Adding such a ship to the fleet suddenly became a top priority after the proven utility of carriers, and Admiral Raeder was pleased to know that it was already within his grasp. It was this plum that he pulled out of his hat in the meeting with Hitler, and it lightened the Fuhrer's mood even as it darkened that of Admiral Tovey where he sat at his desk back at Scapa Flow, meeting with his Chief of Staff, Daddy Brind.

"My God, Brind. We were very narrowly handed our hat in the Denmark Strait. Were it not for that Russian cruiser I wonder how much of the Home Fleet we would still have out there."

Brind nodded, grey haired, dour faced, and fully aware of the gravity of the situation they were now facing. "The Russians certainly lent a hand when we needed one," he said. "Yet I find it nigh on to impossible that we didn't even know this ship existed."

"Yes, and the First Sea Lord is quite beside himself. Churchill with him. One look at *Hood* was enough when it pulled in to Rosyth. Admiral Pound went out to see for himself, Whitworth too."

"That was his old ship, sir."

"Right, and I can only imagine what they're saying about me now. *Hood* beaten, *Birmingham* sunk, sorry for that one, Brind. I know that was your last command."

"I'm sure she went down fighting, sir."

"She did, and *Renown* and *Repulse* both fought their way into the shipyards too. They simply haven't the armor to stand with these new German ships. HMS *Invincible* lived up to her name—at least I've got that much to crow about, but very little else."

"We hurt them as well, sir."

"Did we? The Russians hurt them, Brind. There wasn't a Royal Navy ship that had anything at all to do with the sinking of any ship they lost in that engagement. This Russian Admiral said there was more to his ship than meets the eye, and now there will be no one inclined to pass that off as mere braggery, least of all Admiral Holland."

"How is the Admiral?"

"Recovering well. We've that to be thankful for. He'll mend quicker than we can patch up *Hood*. If not for these two new battleships coming off trials the cupboard would be all but empty here."

"We've still got *Nelson* and *Rodney*, sir."

"They did us very little good. I can use them to close the leeward passage, between the Shetlands and Faeroes, but get them out on the open sea and they are just too damn slow. I'd happily trade them both for another ship in the G3 series. We need speed, Brind. These new Germans ships can outrun most anything we have. *Invincible* is the only ship in the fleet on active duty now that could catch a ship in the *Bismarck* or *Scharnhorst* class. The rest of the Battlecruiser Squadron is on crutches for the next weeks and months, and now we have the French to worry about."

"That would seem to be the primary concern of the Admiralty at the moment, sir. They have grudgingly come round to the notion that you fought to a bloody draw in that engagement. I'm not quite sure they know just how much a part was played by this Russian battlecruiser. I'm told Churchill was simply happy that *Bismarck* and *Tirpitz* were sent packing."

"For the moment, Brind. We'll have to face them again one day. This issue is far from decided. Beyond that the Germans have a couple of real cherries in the shipyards at Lorient and Saint Nazaire."

"Those ships aren't seaworthy yet, Admiral."

"That could be a different story come next year. As soon as we get Goering off our backs here we'll have to get Bomber Command busy with that."

"Yes sir, and we must also consider what to do about all the rest. The French have ships scattered from Dakar to Alexandria. Most of the ships we were planning on sending to Gibraltar for Admiral Somerville's Force H got caught up in the maelstrom here. How did *Illustrious* fare?"

"Well enough. Those Messerschmitts from *Graf Zeppelin* mostly fell on the boys off *Ark Royal*. If nothing else, they have convinced me that we need a new carrier based fighter, and quickly. These new Fulmars might not even be able to stand with the Messerschmitts. Thank god that when *Illustrious* put in her attack most of the German planes were already heading home. Good for us, because we put a torpedo into *Tirpitz*, and that may have persuaded Lindemann to turn. It was Lindemann, yes?"

"Correct, sir. Intelligence says he was on *Bismarck*."

"Strange that they gave the operation to a Captain. Not an Admiral in sight."

"Lütjens is thought to be on the *Hindenburg*. There's another nightmare waiting in the wings."

"Yes, a real phantom in the opera, Daddy. Let's hope that damn ship stays put in the Baltic for a good while longer."

"I doubt if they will attempt another major operation this year, sir. Which may give us just a little time to get up off the canvass and catch our breath."

"What can we send south to Somerville?"

"Well, sir. May I suggest *Rodney* and *Nelson*. As you say, they're not much good up here. The Germans would never attempt to force the inside passage. Every breakout attempt they have made has run out west to the Denmark Strait."

"Agreed, Brind. *Nelson* and *Rodney* will be a good fit for the Med. We'll send them, and we shall have to come up with another aircraft carrier as well."

"Both *Ark Royal* and *Illustrious* were nominated, sir."

"Yet I can't really spare them yet," said Tovey. "I need fast carriers here as well. What about *Glorious?*"

"She's patched up and ready now. The last three weeks have done her a world of good, and the shipyard gave her top priority."

"Good then. HMS *Glorious* goes to Somerville."

"And who do we give her to, Admiral? There's been no appointment for her next Captain."

"I have a man in mind for the job, Mister Brind. Yes… I have just the man in mind, the very same man that delivered her safely home."

"Wells? He's a Lieutenant Commander. No experience at all."

"You forget that he was a serving officer on *Glorious*."

"No, I haven't forgotten that, sir, but is he ready for such an assignment?"

"Was I ready when they gave me Home Fleet? Not by a long shot. Were you ready when they gave you your first ship, Brind?"

"HMS *Orion?* Well I can't say that I was, sir."

"No man ever is. Yet we all start somewhere. I had this young man at my arm as Flag Lieutenant's assistant on *Invincible*. He has a good head on his shoulders, a bit excitable at times, but he knows the ship and her crew, and he's got one battle star on his chest with *Glorious* as it stands. Make the recommendation to the Admiralty."

"Very good, sir."

"Right… Then we hand off the torch to Somerville for the moment. Let's send him a pair of nice fat battleships and another carrier and see what he can do about the French. As for my watch, I plan on taking our newest ships out for a stroll to shake off the goblins. We've received a request to meet with this Russian Admiral Volsky on the Faeroes. I shall take the opportunity to thank him personally, and perhaps this time we may add a few other ships to our side of the ledger—the Russians!"

"They do have a few ships worth the name," said Brind.

"Particularly the ship we encountered—that rocket cruiser. Have you ever heard of anything like it?"

"Not on my watch, sir."

"Well call me an old fool, but I have the strangest feeling that I have seen this ship before. When we invited the Admiral over for lunch I simply could not take my eyes off that ship. I could swear I'd run across it once, in the far east when I was a young Lieutenant. But that is clearly impossible."

"It's also quite a black eye for Bletchley Park," Brind put in. "They should have had eyes on that ship, and long ago."

"Quite so. It's all very bothersome, Daddy. All I can say about it is that I'm glad that ship is on our side." He was going to add 'this time around,' almost reflexively, but stopped himself. He could simply not place his finger on any firm recollection concerning this ship, yet it continued to nag him. In a fitful dream the previous night he saw the ship looming on the horizon of his mind, saw those fiery rockets, felt the jarring sound and concussion of an explosion. It was so compelling that he sat up in a cold sweat, breathing hard with his nightmare. Yes, this strange ship was giving him bad dreams, though now he hoped he could forget them.

"The Russian Admiral seems quite accommodating," he said.

"Whitehall has also received high level official contacts regarding this meeting," said Brind.

"So I've been told. That incident involving the *Admiral Scheer* and *Nürnberg* is a hot potato now. It's come to blows up north, and this could be something to move the Russians our way. I have every hope that it is."

"Agreed," said Brind. "It could also give the Germans just the excuse they need to attack Soviet Russia."

"Well that will happen one day, Brind, you can bet on it. If not this autumn, then next year."

"It really comes down to what the Germans plan for us, sir. We've got most of our cruisers tied up in home waters on invasion watch now."

"And that will have to continue."

"Do you think they'll have a go at us?"

Tovey thought, then shook his head. "I doubt it, Brind. Try that and we blast them in the Channel, and they damn well know it. Bletchley Park believes the Germans are focusing their effort on trying to break the R.A.F. at the moment. I think they'll see if they can pound us into submission with the Luftwaffe. They know they can't cross the channel unless they do that first, and then they'll still have the Royal Navy to deal with. Frankly, I don't believe the Germans will attempt an invasion here. It's the Mediterranean we have to worry about for the foreseeable future. But we must remain vigilant in any case. That's why I'll want *King George V* and *Prince of Wales* working out with me as soon as possible. In the meantime, I have other beasts to slay."

"Sir?"

"They want me in the lion's den with a full report. I've been summoned to Whitehall, Daddy. And in case I don't come back in one piece it has been a brief but pleasant duty here."

"Chin up, sir," said Brind. "But bring your whip and chair."

Chapter 23

July 18, 1940

Raeder and Doenitz sat at the conference table, waiting nervously for the meeting they had both come to dread. The Führer himself was coming to assess the plans now being laid for the continuation of the war, and determine the role the Kriegsmarine would take as they developed. Abwehr Intelligence Chief Canaris sat in his dignified silence, an aristocrat, ever scheming, and holding far too many reins of power as far as Raeder was concerned. Lastly, Luftwaffe Air Chief Hermann Goering was also present, sitting like a sullen bullfrog at the other end of the table, his arm resting on a fat binder that Raeder eyed suspiciously from time to time.

No doubt I will first receive a scolding over what has just happened in the Denmark Strait, thought Raeder. Canaris is here to sort out the intelligence. Well, I have read Lindemann's report ten times, and still cannot believe what he asserts. Hoffmann said the same, and the damage to *Gneisenau* was plain to see. Then comes Kranke's ignominious performance in Operation Wunderland and the loss of the *Nürnberg*. He was sent there with explicit orders to scout out the state of Soviet naval development in the far north, and to find this ship Hoffmann and Lindemann have been bawling about—not to start a war!

Raeder had spent a full hour scouring Kranke after ordering him to take the first plane from Narvik and return to Wilhelmshaven to account for himself.

"A 5.7 inch gun that could hit you at over 26,000 meters? I find that difficult to believe Kranke."

"Then come and look at my ship! We took seven hits at that range. Seven!"

"All from secondary batteries?"

"Thank God, yes. They would engage us and then slip away, every quarter a hour. It was as if they were simply playing with us.

But they had something more at the end. I detached *Nürnberg* to get after that damned marauder… and then the missile came."

"And why were they shooting at you, Kapitän? Enlighten me on that, for I gave you specific orders to scout the area, and *not* to engage." It was only then that Raeder learned of Kranke's hidden agenda, and one given to him by highly placed officers in OKW.

"Was Jodl privy to this? Keitel? Yes, they were. Am I correct? They put you up to this, did they not? They would like nothing more than to start things boiling along the Polish and Russian frontier. They don't believe we can get their troops across the Channel, and so they look East, to Soviet Russia. But I tell you now, Kranke. A two front war is the last thing we need. I have argued it endlessly. Why should we repeat the same mistakes that were made in the first war? Surely Hitler must see this, and if he has been poisoned by the likes of Jodl and Keitel, I must do everything in my power to get him to see reason. Then you go off taking pot shots at Russian ice breakers! Are you insane? Those were not your orders!"

On and on it went, until Raeder determined that those *were*, indeed, Kranke's orders, even though they had not come from him. He had half a mind to tender his resignation then and there, and to tell Hitler that if it were not his to command the navy then he should find another. Now he looked suspiciously at Canaris.

That man knows entirely too much, he thought. And one thing he knows is that I am determined to force the issue of the war into the Mediterranean. Could the Abwehr Chief have been behind Kranke's insubordination? Perhaps, he thought. Canaris is a navy man. He knew Kranke, and if anyone could get to that man it would be Canaris.

The more he thought about this, the more he began to see a devious plot here. Why would Kranke listen to Jodl or anyone else at OKW? But Canaris is another kettle of fish. Yes, he could have been the one that put Kranke up to this deliberate provocation. Canaris has been busy in Spain since the Spanish civil war. He speaks the language fluently, is very cozy with Franco, and I have heard that he has been quietly working to maintain Spanish neutrality.

Yes… Canaris. This was the man behind everything, the man with a hand in everyone's pocket. If Spain remains neutral, then my plans for an attack on Gibraltar will be compromised. We need access to Spanish territory to do that. So what does Canaris do? He arranges this little dance with Kranke when he gets wind of my Operation Wunderland. He knows the kindling is piled high along the Russian border, and now he lights the match. Look at him, sitting there as if this were an afternoon tea. I must be very careful here. I am already on thin ice now after Lindemann's failure and the loss of *Nürnberg* and *Sigfrid*, not to mention the *Altmark*. I have much to account for, and Canaris is going to enjoy watching me squirm. The question is how to prevent this incident from becoming a pretext for war against Russia? How to prevent it from destroying my plans in the Mediterranean?

The sound of heavy footfalls echoed in the hall and seconds later the door burst open. The SS guards surveyed the room darkly and announced the arrival of the Führer of the German Reich, Adolf Hitler. He stepped into the room, giving the three men there a narrow eyed look as they all stood to attention.

"Very well," Hitler looked immediately to Raeder, as if the other men were not even present, and spoke the words the Admiral knew he would hear this day. "Explain yourself, Raeder. Tell me… why do all the new ships you've been building have holes in them? Tell me why there has not been a single British transport ship sunk during your operation. Tell me what this nonsense is about a British ship firing rockets, and driving off the finest battleships in the world! And when you are done with that, tell me why, after six years of steel and sweat in the shipyards, all these ships seem good for little more than running home for repairs?" The Führer folded his arms, his eyes smoldering, standing like a carved statue, implacable.

"My Führer," Raeder began, not knowing where in the list he should start. Begin with any success you have, he realized, and hope you can somehow get this man to learn the lessons you yourself have taken here with this hard medicine.

"The operation was not without its successes. It was never designed to seek an all-out engagement with the Royal Navy, but merely to test the mettle of their strengths, and stand as a trial for our own ships, some fresh from the shipyards and entering battle for the first time. The experience we have gained was invaluable, particularly regarding the use of aircraft carriers in operation with the fleet."

"Oh? What about *Gneisenau*? Where is the *Nürnberg*? Where's that nice shiny new destroyer you built for me? Thank god only two of these ships were sunk!"

"That was regrettable, my Führer, but combat at sea always entails the risks that ships engaged may be damaged or sunk. This is why I gave specific orders to Lindemann not to seek a major engagement that would place our capital ships at risk of sustaining severe damage."

"But they *were* damaged, Raeder. *Bismarck, Tirpitz,* and *Gneisenau* are now in the repair yards."

"Yet none hurt seriously enough to impede their operations in the near future, my Führer. *Tirpitz* sustained a minor torpedo hit, but one that proved again the necessity of protecting the fleet with additional air power." Raeder glanced at Goering as he spoke. "In like manner, the damage to *Bismarck* simply involved the loss of a single secondary battery which can be replaced in a few weeks time. As for *Gneisenau*, the hit that ship sustained was more significant, and will take several months work to repair, but otherwise the ship is sound and seaworthy. Yet in taking this blow, we have discovered that our enemies may now have achieved a level of technical proficiency in another area that can pose a grave threat." He looked at Canaris now.

"You are speaking of these rockets?" said Hitler.

"What else, my Führer? Yes, the rockets! We are working on them ourselves, so do not be surprised that our enemies have done the same. Only they appear to have achieved something here that is well beyond our capabilities at this moment. These were shipborne missiles, and they proved to be decisive in each and every engagement, as much for the initial shock value as anything else."

"What about this, Canaris?" Hitler looked to his Abwehr Chief now. "Why is it we have heard nothing of this?"

"Because there has been nothing, sir. My agents have found no evidence that the British have an advanced rocket project ready for deployment."

"Then who was firing at my ships? The Americans?"

Canaris shifted, poised, a half smile on his face. "My Führer, we have no information that would in any way confirm that."

"Raeder? Tell me more about these rocket weapons. Clearly my intelligence Chief can tell me nothing!" Hitler's displeasure was obvious, but Canaris sat unmoved.

"I have interviewed all the senior officers involved in the operation," said Raeder, chastened but yet determined. "They described these weapons as fast, accurate, and having great range—a range exceeding that of our most powerful naval guns. They were undoubtedly a secret project. These missiles move like lightning. They strike with pinpoint accuracy, and the one that nearly hit the *Graf Zeppelin* was fired from well over 100 kilometers away." He left the full weight of that statement out there, watching the reactions of the other men.

"From a ship?" Now it was Goering who spoke, a look of astonishment and disbelief on his face, cheeks red, and the light of enjoyment in his eyes flickering behind it all. "You expect me to believe that the British have a missile that can fire at such range and still hit anything? This is ridiculous! If they could fire such a missile from a ship, then they could line them up all along the English Channel and rain them down upon our troops in France, yet we have seen nothing."

"The survivors from the destroyer *Sigfrid* will beg to differ with you, Aviation Minister Goering. They clearly saw something. That was the reason *Sigfrid* was sunk. It was cruising right alongside the *Graf Zeppelin* and took the blow that was intended to strike the carrier. Yet there was no enemy ship within 100 kilometers at the time. Böhmer's planes searched for an hour, and yet saw nothing. It has been suggested that the ship was sunk by a submarine, yet reports from over 100 eyewitnesses all clearly state that the weapon was airborne, a rocket. Admiral Doenitz has assured me that no submarine in the world today could have carried or launched a weapon with sufficient fuel to achieve that range, and a warhead heavy enough to do what we saw happen to *Sigfrid.*"

"The British have these weapons on all their ships?" Hitler tapped the table impatiently, looking from Raeder to Canaris.

"We were not certain," said Raeder. "At first we believed at least one ship was equipped with them, perhaps one of their battleships being held in reserve, or even one of their carriers. This is what we thought—until the loss of *Nürnberg.*" There is no way around the ice pond now, thought Raeder. I will just have to skate across.

"Sunk by a British ship?" Hitler waited.

"Not the British, my Führer," Canaris said quietly. "We believe this ship was Russian."

"Russian? You are telling me that Russians have these weapons? They cannot build anything that would remotely challenge our battleships. How could they do this?"

"The question of how is no longer relevant, my Führer. It is becoming more and more apparent that they were, indeed, behind these missile attacks which so confounded Admiral Raeder's plans here. And they were clearly responsible for the *Nürnberg* incident. Air Minister Goering may shed some light on this."

Goering nodded. "We had planes out from Narvik and Tromso, covering the withdrawal of Raeder's ships after his failed operation." Goering twisted the barb a bit, his eyes alight. "A ship continued north, shadowing our own units and eventually moving around the North Cape to Murmansk, and was photographed during that transit on two occasions. The naval ensign of Soviet Russia was clearly evident. I have the photographs with me if you would care to see them. More photos were obtained during Operation Wunderland, which was undertaken, in part, to obtain more information on this ship and the new weapons it employed. Am I not correct, Raeder?" Goering tossed the hot potato back, smiling.

"Of course we were suspicious. We knew there was a ship, but it was not clear as to the nationality. So yes, I told Kranke to see what he could find out with Operation Wunderland."

"And we paid a very high price for that information," Hitler was not happy. "The loss of *Nürnberg* was shameful—an embarrassment! Now to hear this may have been a Russian ship makes the sting and the insult even worse. This is clearly an act of war! Are you telling me the Russians have now openly sided with the Royal Navy in combat against our ships?"

"That appears to be the case, my Führer," said Raeder. "Yet the incident can also be interpreted as a simple act of self-defense. Kranke was given no order to engage Russian shipping in the far north—at least not by me. In fact, I ordered him to avoid engagement. If he was given those orders by someone else then let that man account for the loss of *Nürnberg*." He glanced at Canaris now, his suspicion obvious. "If Kranke had followed my instructions we would not even be discussing this."

"Oh, but we *would* be discussing it, Raeder," said Hitler. "The damage to all those other ships was more than enough reason. If it was caused by a Russian ship, then I will have the head of Sergei Kirov on a platter!"

Hitler seemed to simmer with that, his eyes shifting from Goering, to Canaris, to the map on the table in front of them. He knew that Raeder had long opposed open hostilities with the Soviet Union. The Admiral much preferred a strategy that would see the navy lead the fight against England. He had been given Operation Seelöwe to chew on, but nothing was discussed concerning Barbarossa, and Hitler did not want to open that can of worms now.

"Are you certain this was a Soviet ship?" asked Hitler, folding his arms again.

"Admiral Doenitz concurs with the assessment of our analysts in section I-M," said Canaris, referring to the naval intelligence arm. "The ship is not of British design. It is something entirely new, completely unexpected. We can only conclude that it was a highly secret project, perhaps being tested on a maiden voyage even as we thought to blood our ships with this operation."

"Not quite," said Hitler. "We thought to blood the *enemy's* ships."

"And this we did," said Raeder quickly. "One of their fast battlecruisers, HMS *Hood*, was battered to a near hulk in the engagement with *Bismarck* and *Tirpitz*. It was also struck by our *Stuka* dive bombers! Another, HMS *Renown* was sent to the shipyards in a successful air strike by the brave pilots and air crews of *Graf Zeppelin*. Hoffmann had good hunting with *Scharnhorst* and *Gneisenau* as well. His detachment sank *Birmingham* and heavily damaged the *Manchester*, a pair of cruisers to put on the scales for *Nürnberg*. *Dorsetshire* and *Sussex* were driven off as well, and with damage. The battle would have been a complete victory, were it not for the sudden appearance of this mysterious ship—this Russian ship, as we now have come to believe."

"Then why was it not sunk?" Hitler was struggling to contain his anger, but it was apparent.

"These weapons it deployed, missiles with such accuracy and power, were not something to be trifled with. Until we could learn more about them I wisely chose to cancel the planned breakout into the North Atlantic and return our fleet to friendly ports. I stand by that decision, because this development concerning the rocket weapons deserves our most serious consideration. If the Russians have such weapons we must learn everything possible about them, particularly if war may come of this incident. But I must advise extreme caution here, gentlemen. Until we know what we are up against, no open declaration of war should be made against Soviet Russia. Remember also that Britain is isolated. If the war moves East,

Soviet Russia will surely choose to ally with the British…" The implications were obvious and did not need to be spoken.

There, thought Raeder, a little butter on the bread at last. For that is the point of all this. Someone got to Kranke to stir things up, but now I have said it, as plainly as I could. This war must not move East.

Chapter 24

"This was not a defeat," Raeder continued. "Quite the contrary. It was a strategic decision to preserve the fleet until such time as we can determine the nature and scope of this new threat. I would have been foolish to proceed in any other manner, just as it would also be foolish to consider war with Russia now when we have the British on their knees waiting for the death blow."

"What do you think, Doenitz?" Hitler looked to the head of his U-Boat fleet now, sitting quietly, saying nothing.

"I must agree with Admiral Raeder, my Führer. When facing an unknown threat such as this, caution and discretion are well in order. Now we have some idea what we're up against. We know these weapons are sufficiently powerful to damage and sink a destroyer, and with the loss of *Nürnberg* even a light cruiser."

"But not the battleships," Raeder put in quickly. "Yes, there was damage, but it was not significant. This is a tribute to your own vision, my Führer. The armor protection we have built into the ships has proved invaluable."

"Only if they choose to stand and fight, Raeder," Hitler admonished.

"And I might add," said Doenitz, "that none of these rockets would have been able to put a scratch on one of my U-boats, would they?"

"A point well made, Doenitz." Hitler nodded in agreement. "I have read your latest budget request and in light of what has happened here I'm inclined to approve it. As it stands, I do not think we can complete many more battleships in the short run."

"*Hindenburg* will be ready in a matter of months," said Raeder, "and *Oldenburg* soon after."

"Yes, yes, *Hindenburg* and *Oldenburg*. Will they run from the rockets as well, Raeder? Would they be chased from one end of Norway to the other by a Russian cruiser?"

"Of course not, my Führer. I will make it a top priority to find and sink this Russian ship, and we will show Sergei Kirov who he is dealing with, if you so order it."

"See that you do!" Hitler rapped the table top with the palm of his hand to emphasize his order. "Yes, I want that ship found, and I want it sunk."

"We can certainly do so, yet in light of the political situation…"

"Leave the politics to me, Admiral. They sink one of our ships, so we will sink one of theirs."

"Might we attempt to capture it, my Führer?" Doenitz proposed the obvious alternative. "That way we could have a look at these weapons and that could be very useful."

"Of course," said Hitler. "But if it cannot be taken, then it must be sunk. That will settle the matter."

"I give you my pledge on that," said Raeder, "but there is something that cannot be overlooked in all these events, and that was the outstanding performance of the *Graf Zeppelin*—two attacks, two British capital ships hit and seriously damaged." He wisely decided to say nothing of the abortive third attack. "We must not overlook the lesson here with all this furor over rocket weapons. Admiral Canaris is correct, it does not matter who or how the enemy got these weapons—they clearly have them, and they are not shy about using them. We will get them soon enough," Raeder shook his finger confidently.

"I will see that the research into this area is tripled," said Hitler. "Yes, we will get them ourselves, Raeder. I like your spirit!"

Raeder nodded his appreciation, seeing an opening here. "Yet in the meantime, we already have a weapon that can find and hit an enemy ship over 200 kilometers away, twice the range of these rockets—the *Graf Zeppelin!* Seeing what it was able to do in this engagement has convinced me that we may have relied too heavily on our battleship program. A few more aircraft carriers to match the British may be the key factor now. We have the battleships. Yes, we already know we can match them ship for ship, rockets or no rockets. Now we must look to the development of more aircraft carriers."

To Raeder's great relief, Hitler did not disagree. "This is what I had hoped to have in place before the war," he said. "Yet events and resources did not permit that. The Japanese have six fleet aircraft carriers, do they not? The British have many such ships, as do the Americans. For a navy to sail where it wishes, we must have them as well. Yes, Admiral, *Graf Zeppelin* has showed us that much, if nothing else. How soon will we have another of these ships ready?"

"*Peter Strasser* is nearing completion. I believe it may launch with the *Hindenburg*. But there is nothing else in the shipyards."

"Nothing else?" Hitler frowned.

"Allow me to correct myself, my Führer. There is nothing else in *our* shipyards. Nothing more was ever authorized from our Z-Plan. There was simply no time. The Flugdeckkreuzers were not approved. That said, we have other ships that might easily be converted to the role of a carrier. I will submit a full report on this with detailed plans in just few days. In the meantime, there are ships already afloat that could prove decisive in this area."

Raeder's eyes gleamed now. First the butter, now the jam. Now was the time to steer the conversation south, away from the icy north and talk of war with Russia and back to the nice warm and inviting waters of the Mediterranean.

"The French," he said calmly, his voice steady with newfound resolve. "Yes, the French fleet. There are all the battleships, cruisers and destroyers we might never be able to build in time, and they are just sitting there in the Mediterranean waiting for anyone to come and take them. And one, my Führer, is a nice new fleet aircraft carrier, the *Joffre*."

Hitler dimly recalled that the French had been working on carriers as well, though he could not remember the details. He had his mind set on the battleships for so long that he could see nothing else when it came to operations at sea. In fact, while he agreed that Germany needed more aircraft carriers, that was only to provide the necessary protection and support for the battleships in his thinking, only because his enemies were doing the very same thing, and Germany could not be left behind.

The Third Reich had achieved a remarkable and swift victory in Europe. The lightning war had toppled a mortal enemy in a matter of months. Now it was only England standing defiantly in the West, and Soviet Russia in the East. He was close now, so very close to a position of such dominance that no enemy could ever challenge him—except for the Royal Navy. This is why, as much as he wished his troops could simply wade across the English Channel, he knew the Kriegsmarine was an essential element of his power, and would be in the years ahead. Yet how best to use it?

"If this is true," he said slowly, "then I must assume you have plans to secure this French aircraft carrier before the British. Yes?"

"No, my Führer. I have no such plans." Raeder was ready to for his final act.

"What? No plans?" Anger flashed in the Führer's eyes.

"They will not be necessary," said Raeder quickly, holding up a hand. "We already *have* the French aircraft carrier. It is sitting in the shipyards at Saint Nazaire, surrounded by elements of our Panzer Army. Yes! We already have a ship it might take us another four years to build ourselves, and that is only the beginning. Now we must set our minds on how to get our hands on the rest. Clearly there is nothing to be gained by contemplating war with Soviet Russia now. But look south and we find enormous military resources just sitting there for the taking. Add key units of the French fleet to those we already have, then throw in the Italian Navy and we will be invincible, my Führer. We can roll the British, and the Royal Navy, right out of the Mediterranean and establish good bases all along the North African coast. We can take Alexandria, Cairo, the Suez canal, and cut the British Empire in two! Then it is merely a matter of shaking hands with Ivan Volkov in the Orenburg Federation, and all the resources we need will come flowing through the Bosporus and into good ports in southern France. This will smash Great Britain once and for all, and we do not even have to consider an invasion of England to do so!"

There, he had said it all, laid out his vision for how Germany could now proceed to win the war. "Do this, my Führer, and the Third Reich *will* last a thousand years." He looked at Canaris, who now sat in sullen silence. You wanted to push my nose into a bowl of cold milk, thought Raeder as he saw Canaris slowly reach into his pocket for a cigarette. Eat that!

The question now was: what to do about the French fleet? Raeder had led with his ace, revealing Germany's de facto control over two fine new French ships, cruiser *De Grasse* and the carrier *Joffre*. But Hitler raised a delicate political point.

"You propose we simply seize those ships? It was you who argued the French fleet could be left on its own and that it would behave itself, Raeder. Our armistice states we would not attempt to seize control of Darlan's Navy."

"I understand, my Führer, but the situation has changed. Certainly we cannot consider the seizure of the entire French fleet. It would take years just to train men to crew those ships. But the ships I just mentioned are presently in the occupied zone, not the Vichy sector. In effect, they are not under Admiral Darlan's control. The ships are incomplete. They will need work, and there is no risk that they might flee. Taking them as a prize of war may be controversial, but necessary—particularly the aircraft carrier."

There came a knock on the door, and Hitler looked over his shoulder. The SS guard entered, saluting crisply. "Forgive the intrusion, but I was told this was a matter of some urgency. Message for Admiral Canaris." He handed off a folded paper and made a quick withdrawal."

"Dinner invitation, Canaris?" Hitler smiled for the first time in the meeting, and Goering laughed appropriately. Canaris, however, seemed to know what he had been handed, and he sighed heavily as he read the note.

"I hardly think we will want a seat at this dinner table," he said with an edge of warning in his voice. "This is a message from my network in Spain. As you know, we keep a good eye on ship movements at Gibraltar. It appears that a big British buildup is underway. Two more battleships and another aircraft carrier have arrived."

Raeder nodded his head, raising a finger as he spoke. "I am not surprised to hear this. Was your man good enough to determine what ships these were?"

"Battleships *Nelson* and *Rodney*, along with the carrier *Glorious*."

Hitler listened closely, his dark eyes moving from one man to another. "Gibraltar," he said gruffly. "Ever a British thorn in the underbelly of Europe. If I could convince Franco to acquiesce, I would take the place and be done with it."

Raeder's ears perked up at this, his eyes alight. "These ships can be assembling for only one reason, my Führer—the French fleet. Now the British have the firepower necessary to force the issue. There were already three battleships in Gibraltar, now they have five."

Hitler shook his head, a frustrated look on his face. "All our ships laid up after this disastrous operation, and yet the British have sufficient resources to send five battleships to Gibraltar! That is more than we have in the entire Kriegsmarine, correct?"

"Do not concern yourself with numbers," said Raeder. "Most of those ships were built during the first war, and these latecomers soon after, in the 1920s. They are old and slow, nothing like our new ships. Yet it is not any threat to our operations they now pose. No. The British mean to bring the French fleet under their guns, and if they cannot capture them or force them to demilitarize, they will destroy them." He folded his arms with an air of finality. "And here we sit worrying about a clause in the armistice!"

Hitler looked at him, his eyes fierce now. "At last you are completely correct, Raeder. The British have no qualms. They do what is in their own interest, and the niceties of politics be damned. So we will do the same. Take those ships in occupied ports. I order it this very minute! Then put any resources you have available and get them ready for operations as soon as possible."

"As you wish, my Führer, and this is a wise decision in light of these developments. I will admit my caution earlier regarding the French fleet, but events have proven me wrong."

"Then what about the remainder of their ships? What can we do about this, Raeder?"

"Frankly, there are only a few we might wish to get our hands on—the fast new battleships, perhaps a few cruisers and destroyers."

"Certainly any submarines we can secure," said Doenitz.

"What are we now, a pack of scavengers? Saying is one thing," said Canaris, "doing quite another. How do you propose to get these ships? Yes, the carcass is there for the pickings, but soon the British will be circling like vultures. Toulon is Vichy controlled. The rest of the French ships are in African ports. I'm sure you don't plan on sailing *Bismarck* and *Tirpitz* down there after you patch them up."

There was just a bit of a smirk in that, and Raeder bristled, but calmed himself. Canaris won't give up easily, thought Raeder. I must be very careful in the way I handle him.

"No Admiral, we'll concern ourselves with operations in the north for the moment. As for Toulon, I'm afraid I have no solution for you. Might something be done politically? After all, we remain in a position to exert considerable influence on the Vichy French. They exist only by our leave, do they not?"

"Correct again, Raeder," Hitler's eyes were that dark well again, vast, deep, endless darkness there. "The bar fight is well under way, and now Franco and Pétain want to sit quietly and watch. These little men should be of no concern to us, nor will they impede me in any way that matters. If they will not join us they will be dealt with. We could demand the surrender of all French ships at Toulon, or threaten to rescind the occupation and our agreement not to divide France permanently."

"But my Führer," Canaris began.

"Not now, Canaris. I know you are quite comfortable with your arrangements in Spain, and nice and cozy with Franco. Set your mind to discovering his intentions! Will he join the Axis, or not? Find out, because once I am through speaking with the French, he will be next. Then this fellow in Russia. First things first. The British are the real problem now. But let us see how things look if we can get these ships you speak of, Raeder. Yes, and things will be quite different once our ships are anchored in Gibraltar instead of the Royal Navy."

The Führer smiled, a cold, evil smile that made every man there uncomfortable. This was the twilight of the British Empire. It was fading and failing, descending into the dark night that would be ruled by the iron hand of the Third Reich. Gibraltar, Malta, Alexandria, Suez…. It would be just like shooting birds on a wire, thought Hitler. But first things first, the French fleet.

Part IX

Doppelganger

"In a world where the dead have returned to life,
the word 'trouble' loses much of its meaning."

— Dennis Hopper

Chapter 25

July 24, 1940

They spent some days in the harbor at Severomorsk, and Fedorov was making good use of every minute of free time he had. He was in the officer's mess hall, the table covered with the cache of books he had been given by the Russians, and was happily perusing one after another.

Much had changed, but he was still amazed to find that other parts of the history remained remarkably consistent with events he already knew so well. The history of his own homeland was badly fractured. Stalin's death was a backwater footnote now, the assassination of a minor figure on the fringes of the incipient revolution, well before it had taken real form in 1917. Stalin had been relatively obscure in the early years, gaining prominence in revolutionary circles only after Lenin's return to Petrograd in April of 1917. In his place it was Sergei Kirov who shined by the borrowed light of Lenin.

The twin defeats at the hands of the Japanese in 1905, and again in 1908, had humiliated Russia. Karpov's great dream of Russian Pacific power had completely backfired. The Japanese Empire was catalyzed by the events in 1908, and incursions into mainland Asia, on both Chinese and Russian territory, soon followed.

This crisis did much to cause many defections in the military, eroding the power base of the Tsar, but the nation was still swept into the gathering maelstrom of the First World War, and continued to bleed. The revolution happened right on schedule, between February and October of 1917. A few faces were different, but it all played out much the same.

The civil war that followed, however, was suddenly overshadowed by the rising figure of Volkov in the White movement. After an abortive bid for power in Moscow, Volkov withdrew through the Ukraine and into the Caucasus and border states that now made up his Orenburg Federation. There were periods of tentative peace as Red and White struggled to find balance, but the fighting invariably re-ignited, spurred on by much foreign interference.

By 1924 the borders had cemented again. There were seven years of truce, seven more of war until 1938, when the Siberian Free State began to organize into a third major entity. Remnants of Kolchak's White movement there were joined by Kozolnikov, yet information on what was happening in the far east was very sketchy. None of the books had covered any recent events there. Siberia had been a wild frontier, a loose confederation of warlord states with a few centers of Kolchak's White movement in the major cities. No one seemed to want the place, not even the Japanese who exerted nominal control all along the frontier of the Amur River, but with little real strength.

Fedorov spent some time reading on Volkov, watching his slow rise to power, first as a master of intelligence under Denikin, then slowly co-opting that man's authority. The Bolshevik Red Army had gained the Ukraine, but could not seem to make inroads into Kazakhstan, the Caucasus, and the Caspian region. Instead of trying to defeat one another, both sides entrenched and consolidated their power, and the long civil war dragged on and on, a simmering conflict that spilled across one border or another, then cooled until the next incident stoked the fires.

Volkov eventually secured power and established his seat of government in the growing city of Orenburg. He then changed the White movement to the Grey Legion, breaking ties with remnants of Denikin's supporters. There had been fighting back and forth along the Volga with Kirov's Soviet State ever since.

Fedorov was finishing up his research, thinking of the implications on the war that was now unfolding. Surely Volkov knew this history as well, or at least knew the general outcomes of the 'Great Patriotic War.' Even against a united Russia ruled by one strong hand, Germany devoured half the nation. Was he doing this to finally destroy the Bolsheviks under Kirov? Did he think he would somehow find a way to manipulate Adolf Hitler in the end? These questions and so many others percolated in his mind, but weariness overcame him, and the tea he was drinking was not helping. He was just about to finish up and get some sleep when Orlov happened along.

"What are you doing, Fedorov? Nose in the books again? You should have been promoted to the ship's librarian." Orlov said that with a grin, realizing, after all, that he was speaking to the ship's Captain now, and remembering the humiliating lesson Troyak had taught him about showing due respect when he had been busted to the Marine detachment. He had come to the officer's dining hall for a cup of coffee before going on duty, and found Fedorov sitting at a table reading.

"The world has changed, Orlov," said Fedorov. "I did not realize just how much has gone awry."

"I know you are wanting to blame me for that, yes?"

"What? No Chief. I think I got to you in time, or at least those British commandos did. Besides, most anything you may have changed would have had to occur after 1942. The altered state of affairs I am reading about now all happened well before that. I think it was Karpov who had a great deal to do with some of the changes, and I must also confess that I am equally to blame."

"You, Fedorov? What did you do?"

Fedorov confessed his crime, that errant whisper, and he told Orlov that it ended up resulting in the death of Joseph Stalin himself.

"My god!" Orlov exclaimed. "Here I was worried a bit about choking Commissar Molla, and you took a contract out on Stalin!" As always, Orlov interpreted the events in light of his own life experience, running with the Russian mob for so many years before he had joined the navy had left him very jaded.

"So you see, Orlov, you can sleep easy now. I'm the real culprit."

"And that bastard Karpov. He sleeps easy too—with the fishes!" Orlov grinned again.

"Yes, I suppose so. In fact, as to that Commissar you speak of, remember, in this world now it is only 1940, so he may still be alive out there somewhere, though if he is he will be working for Volkov, and not the Bolsheviks."

At that Orlov's face and mood darkened. "Still alive? But I killed him."

"In 1942, but that world, those events that saw you make your way to the Caucasus… well, they might never occur. This is a new world, Chief. Another life altogether, for you, and I suppose for Commissar Molla as well."

"Sookin syn!" Orlov swore, clearly unhappy with what he was learning now. "I wondered about that. Was another Orlov going to appear and do everything we just lived through?"

"We've all wondered about it."

"It is not possible, right Fedorov?"

"Director Kamenski does not think so. He believes we are in a completely altered world now, separate from the one we left. So come July 28, 1941 when we first appeared here, nothing will happen. In his mind we have trumped all our previous exploits."

"You mean none of it counts? Molla is alive, none of those ships we hurt are sunk?"

"That could be so, Chief. Our appearance in 1908, and now here in 1940 predates all that experience. Perhaps it counted in the world we left, but not this one. It hasn't even happened yet, at least according to Kamenski."

"Is that what you think?"

"It does sound reasonable. Otherwise we will have a real paradox on our hands in another year."

"Yes," said Orlov with a smile. "One ugly mug like this one is enough for the world." He tapped his own cheek. "So that means we are living in a world where Karpov doesn't exist any longer. There is one good thing about our fate, eh?"

"I see you still have hard feelings about him."

"I hold a grudge, Fedorov. That's why I killed Molla. Frankly, to learn he is still alive makes me want to go and kill him again! But don't worry. I'll stay put this time."

"Please do, Chief. We need you here."

"Now that you mention it, I have duty on the bridge in ten minutes. Keep reading, Captain!" Orlov clapped Fedorov on the back and went on his way, shaking his head and muttering under his breath.

Fedorov smiled, putting the book he had been perusing aside, entitled *Rise of the Orenburg Federation.* The photographs there had convinced him that the leader of that state was indeed the same man they knew and met on the ship with Inspector General Kapustin.

He went down those stairs, he thought. So it wasn't just what Karpov did, or even what I did. It was Volkov too. Yet it all comes back to me again. If I hadn't insisted on retrieving Orlov, leaving as I did with Troyak and Zykov, then Volkov would have never tried to find me along that route, and never had a chance to take that trip down those stairs. Then again, Orlov's recent visit put him in the spotlight again. If Orlov did not go missing... No, I was Captain, he thought. I was the one who gave that order to fire on the KA-226, so it all comes back to me again.

He passed a moment wondering what might have happened if he had not fired. If there had been a fire on the helicopter as Orlov claimed, they might have made an emergency landing. They could have even parachuted to safety, and we could have rescued them by zeroing in on their service jacket transponders in both cases. It was only because we thought those missiles made an end of both the helicopter and Orlov that we failed to mount a search—that and the urgency of the hour with that race to Gibraltar underway.

I was sloppy, he berated himself. I was too inexperienced to take on the role of ship's Captain at that time. I wasn't thinking clearly as to proper procedure. All I could do was think about avoiding any contamination to the history, but there we were, ready to slug it out with the *Nelson* and *Rodney*. How foolish I was! That duel seems to have caused very little change, but the little things—my failure to search for Orlov then and there—that's what really put a missile into it all, and ripped the history open from bow to stern.

Orlov slipped away, I hatched my plan to go after him, and then that stairway at Ilanskiy changed everything. There was the death of Stalin in one errant whisper. There was the rise of Volkov and the deadlock in the civil war that shattered my homeland. Now that will have a dramatic impact on the outcome of this war. How can Britain survive without a united Russia fighting against Germany on the Eastern Front? We have chosen to place *Kirov* on the scales of Time to try and help, but we are just one ship. How can we possibly counterbalance the grievous harm I have done?

Feeling very dejected, and harried by a nagging sense of guilt, he reached for another book, a study of the French naval buildup between the wars. Then his eye fell on a plain manila envelope, and he opened it to see what the Russians had tucked inside. It was marked, "Free Siberian State," and Fedorov found that it contained a few folded newspapers, some very recent by the dates. He found himself drawn to the headlines and photos, turning the page on one issue and then nearly choking on a sip of tea as he did so.

Another man would have cursed, or invoked the deity, but this time Fedorov just stared in shocked silence, slowly lowering his teacup, his hand noticeably shaky as he did so. A sense of rising apprehension gathered like a sickness in his belly and rose like bitter bile in his throat. His impulse was to sound battle stations, raise the alarm! There, standing on an airfield tarmac beneath a massive tethered zeppelin, was a man in a uniform that Fedorov clearly recognized, right down to the pips on his collar.

Fedorov leaned forward, his pulse racing, a rising sense of distress in him now that bordered on panic. He squinted at the photograph, the man's face, his stance, the cut of his shoulders. His eyes scanned and rescanned the photo caption, as if he was simply unwilling to believe or admit what he was reading there. "Air

Commandant Karpov inspects the fleet flagship *Irkutsk* as operations begin on the Samara Front."

Air Commandant Karpov... It *was* him!

Fedorov stood up, stiff and alert, looking about him as if to seek help. He stared at the newspaper again, noting the date as April 10, 1940. How? How? *How* could this be? Were his eyes deceiving him? Was he seeing something here born of his own fear and recrimination? Could this be nothing more than a coincidence, another man, a mistaken appearance?

He sat down again, his hands shaking as he fished out all the other newspapers in the large envelope. Then he began to go through them, page by page, his eyes dark with misgiving. He soon found that he was not imagining anything at all. There were three other articles referencing the man, and one giving his full name: Admiral Vladimir Karpov, First Air Commandant of the Siberian Aero Corps.

Vladimir Karpov...

He was up, quickly gathering and folding all the newspapers again, and tucking them under his arm. His footfalls were quick and heavy on the deck, his breath fast as he went. Where was the Admiral? He found himself almost running now, racing to the officer's deck and down the long hallway to the Admiral's cabin. Resisting the urge to simply barge in with the urgency of his news, he stopped, took a deep breath, and then knocked on the door.

There was movement from within, then the door slowly opened and he saw a red-eyed Volsky peering at him, a look of surprise on his face.

"Excuse me, Admiral," Fedorov gasped, still breathless. "Something very important has come up."

"Another contact? Is the ship in danger?"

Is the ship in danger, thought Fedorov wildly? My god, the whole damn world was in danger now! "No sir, but I have found something in the research that you must see at once."

Volsky looked a bit disheveled and weary, but he opened the door, beckoning for Fedorov to enter. The young Captain could not help but notice the small glass of Vodka on the Admiral's desk near the photo of his wife, the letters there.

The Admiral gestured to the other chair by the wall, and shuffled to his desk, reaching to put away the letters. "You will forgive an old man a moment of sentiment, Fedorov," he said quietly. "I was just reading the last letter I had received from my wife before things started going crazy at Vladivostok. And I suppose I was drowning my sorrows in a glass of good Vodka. Don't worry, I am not one to overindulge, but we all have places to hide and heal, do we not?"

"Of course, sir. Please forgive me for barging in like this. I can come another time—"

"No, no, please be seated. I can see by the redness in your cheeks that you have run all the way here, and you can barely catch your breath. Very well. Let me hear what you have found. Sit please. Take a moment if you must." The Admiral eyed the newspapers under Fedorov's arm, a squall of trepidation on his face now, yet curious.

Fedorov composed himself, looking at the photo of Karpov beneath the looming hulk of the airship, seeming a doppelganger, a dark shadow of the man he was, something born again of trouble and the whirlwind of chaos.

"Sir," he began haltingly. "Have a look at this!"

He handed the Admiral the paper.

Chapter 26

Doctor Zolkin was surprised to see them when Volsky and Fedorov arrived at the sick bay hatch. Shocked by what they had discovered, the two men immediately sought out Director Kamenski, learning that he was in for a medical check.

"More headaches?" said Zolkin as they entered. But Zolkin new the Admiral well enough to know that something was very wrong. He had been listening to Kamenski's heart, satisfied with what he was hearing. Now he set his stethoscope aside and folded his arms, waiting.

"Misery loves company," said Kamenski. "Did you have a restless sleep as well, Admiral?"

"I hope nothing is wrong, Director." Volsky glanced from Kamenski to Zolkin as he spoke, civility trumping the news they carried in that bundle of newspapers under Fedorov's arm. Here they were, huddling in the sick bay again with Zolkin, the place they had discussed the business of the ship so many times, and Karpov more than once.

"He's fit and likely to live another hundred years," said Zolkin with a smile. "Nothing to worry about beyond a bit of indigestion."

"Glad to hear some good news for a change," said Volsky, looking sheepishly at Fedorov. The two men sat down near Zolkin's desk, and then Volsky simply looked at Fedorov.

"Out with it, Fedorov. Tell them."

Fedorov cleared his throat, looking from one man to the next. Just say it, he thought, and then he spoke, certain of what he was now about to assert.

"I believe Captain Karpov is alive."

"What is that? Alive?" Zolkin's hand strayed unconsciously to his arm where he had only recently recovered from the gunshot wound during that wild moment on the bridge.

Fedorov just handed him the newspaper, and gave another to Kamenski, watching them take in the information with growing surprise.

"Excuse me, gentlemen," said Zolkin, "but now you have gone and made the Doctor ill. If Kamenski thought he had trouble with his dinner, my indigestion will be worse. How could this be?"

"Your guess is as good as mine, Doctor."

"We think Karpov must have been thrown clear of the weather bridge. Perhaps he even jumped," said Volsky, putting forward the only logical explanation he and Fedorov could come up with.

"Jumped?"

"Yes," said Fedorov. "If he fell into the sea just as we shifted, he would probably have been pulled forward in time with us as well, just as we pulled that trawler forward with us when the *Anatoly Alexandrov* shifted back from the Caspian. That was how we eventually reeled in Orlov."

"But look at the date on this article, Mister Fedorov," Kamenski pointed with his finger as he spoke. "It reads May of 1940."

"This one reads April of that same year," said Zolkin, trading newspapers with the Director.

"Yes, well that is before we appeared, correct?" Kamenski pointed out the obvious key fact. "It was June of 1940 according to our calculations."

"Correct, sir," said Fedorov, a question in his eyes as if he were hoping the Director would solve the puzzle for him.

Kamenski gave him a wan smile. "Big fish, little fish," he said calmly. "The ship moved, and it obviously pulled this man along in its wake. But the little fish get thrown away, yes? We made it all the way to 1940. He was thrown out earlier. For him to be standing in these photos—in Siberia—and in the spring of 1940... Well that means he would have had to appear some time before that. It would take time for him to get there, yes?"

"That is what I thought," said Fedorov. "From what I can make out in those photos, he does not seem to have aged much. I was also thinking he may have fallen out of the shift we made from 1908 and arrived some time before us. Who knows why? He might have arrived years before. That would account for his present position as these articles indicate."

"My, my," said Zolkin. "So he's given himself a promotion now. Admiral Karpov, is it? First Commandant of the Siberian Aero Corps?"

The men just looked at each other, each one hoping the other would know what to do next. Then Volsky raised the obvious question. "Gentlemen," he began. "Those articles make it obvious that Karpov has survived, and he has deviously been able to get himself mixed up with Kolchak in the Free Siberian State."

"They consolidated power in the far east," said Fedorov.

"Kolchak?" said Zolkin. "But he should have died in the 1920s?"

"A lot of things should have happened that did not happen," said Volsky. "Now I fear that the presence of this man in a position of power there is going to change quite a bit more."

"Indeed," said Kamenski. "It is clear that events we are witnessing now clearly derive from the death of Stalin, and from the foolish prank I thought to play on Volkov. I wanted to get him out of our hair, so I sent him east to look for you, Mister Fedorov."

"That was all my fault," said Fedorov, looking at the floor as he spoke. "I caused all of this."

"Now, now," Volsky tried to console him.

"No sir. It was all my doing." Fedorov unburdened his guilt, confessing all that had so bedeviled him of late, but Kamenski gave him a forgiving smile.

"Listen now, Mister Fedorov. You want to count the dominoes and you just pick out the ones that *you* have tipped over. What you must realize is that the row goes on and on. You think your insistence on finding Orlov caused the fall, but this man used his parachute to jump to safety, did he not? He had a service jacket on just like the one this Karpov is wearing in that photograph. Why did he not call for help?"

"He thought we were trying to kill him," said Fedorov, still sullen. "A logical assumption after we fired five missiles."

"Perhaps he did, but he still had the choice as to what he should do—to call and clear the matter up, or to slip away. Something tells me your Mister Orlov didn't really want us to find him, and it was not because he thought we were trying to kill him. Something tells me he wanted to get away on his own. So you see, there are just too many variables at play here. Remember, it was Orlov who wrote that journal note that you discovered. Without that you would have never launched your mission to rescue him."

"I suppose Orlov would have had good reason to jump ship," said Volsky.

"He might have," said Kamenski. "But not unless this Karpov here had hatched his little plot to take the ship. So you see, Fedorov, you want all the blame to begin with you, but nothing you did would have ever occurred if not for Karpov's little rebellion, or Orlov's strange letter. He is more than a little fish, I think. Karpov is a free radical, a wildcard, an unaccountable force in all of this history we've been writing and re-writing. Everything that has happened, except perhaps that first explosion on the *Orel*, can be laid at Karpov's feet, so do not be greedy in taking all this on yourself, Fedorov. You were just reacting to events he had already set in motion."

"But if I had not spoken to Mironov—to Sergie Kirov—then Stalin might have lived and the nation would not be fragmented."

"Don't think you killed Joseph Stalin now, Fedorov," Kamenski chided. "Sergie Kirov has already confessed to that crime, or so I was told. Correct Admiral?"

"That is what he told us."

"So you see, Fedorov, Kirov is not a puppet. Your whisper in his ear decided nothing. He used his own free will to do what he did. He made choices too, another free radical in the stew."

"But if I had not warned him as I did, he might have died as in our history."

"If, maybe, perhaps." Kamenski held up his hands. "Nothing is certain, Fedorov. Things happen, and all this history we now find ourselves reading about in those books and newspapers is the result of millions of tiny choices and actions taken by people all over the world. Yes, we single out a few and claim they are the ones that matter, but I have not found that to be the case. We want certainty. We make big plans and hope things will all turn out well, but life seldom cooperates. Just when you think you have it all tied off and ready to slip into a drawer, the story continues. It resists resolution. It evolves to something new."

"But I must be responsible for the things I caused," said Fedorov.

"Did you cause them? I wonder. This is where you make your mistake in thinking about all of this. The dots *seem* to be connected. You want to move from point A to point B and feel that one thing caused another, but it does not work like that. It's human nature, I suppose. We want everything tidy, with a nice beginning, middle and end. Believe me, I was in the same distress you were in when I first found my history books were telling me lies. Things change, Mister Fedorov. Things begin from unseen causes. They spin off in unexpected directions. They end up places no one ever thinks they could go. Look at this ship and crew for the truth of that. You see, there are no happy endings in stories like this. Things just continue. They go on and on, just like this little adventure you have all found yourselves in these many months. This isn't just *your* story, Mister Fedorov. It's everyone's story, yours, mine, the whole world's. Yes, you have your part to play, but there are other actors on the stage, and they speak for themselves."

He folded his arms, satisfied that he had done what he could to relieve the other man's burden, but knowing that it was entirely up to Fedorov as to whether he would continue carrying it.

"Now," said Kamenski. "This Karpov is back again. It appears his part in the story is not yet finished. In fact it seems he never left the story at all! The only question we have before us is what do we do about it?"

Volsky nodded. "What *can* we do about it? I do not believe I can simply send a radio message and tell Karpov to return to the ship!"

"No, it is clear that he has made good use of his time since he arrived, whenever that was. This is a man who aspires to reach the top. He will always be uncomfortable standing in any other man's shadow, so trying to bring him back into our family here may be useless."

"Karpov is Karpov," said Zolkin with finality. "We were foolish to ever think he would really change. The man is a megalomaniac!"

"A very dangerous one," said Fedorov. "What you say is true, Director. He is a bit of a wild card in the deck now, as is the Free Siberian State. I've been reading those books we got from the Russians at Murmansk. Last winter Volkov's regime made a major incursion east and took the city of Omsk. It has been a point of contention between the Siberians and Orenburg ever since, but now Nikolin tells me he has received news feeds indicating that the Grey Legion is withdrawing from the city."

"The Grey Legion?" Zolkin had not heard any of this.

"That is what the troops under Volkov's regime call themselves. Yet, from what I can see, Volkov could have held on to Omsk easily enough. The fact that he is pulling out could hint at an accommodation with the Free Siberian State."

"You believe they may have negotiated a settlement?" said Volsky, knowing where this might be leading them.

"It is very possible, sir. Volkov is already at war with Kirov's Soviet Russia. The last thing anyone wants is enemies on two fronts. He may have chosen to end his operation at Omsk to appease Kolchak and the Siberians. Kolchak had a residence in that city for many years, and I do not think the Siberians would have given it up easily."

"My God," said Volsky. "Do you think the two of them might ever get together?"

"Karpov and Volkov?" Zolkin smiled. "They would mix like gin and vermouth, eh? What a nice little martini they would make together."

"Yes," said Fedorov, "and the olive would be the outcome of this war. If those two states ally, then Soviet Russia is isolated. They are already at war with Volkov on one front. If he is reinforced by the Siberians that will be a major strain on Soviet resources and manpower. Add to that the fact that Germany could invade Russia at any time, and I do not think Kirov's Red state can survive."

The implications of what Fedorov was saying were now evident to them all. "And there is one other thing," he said, his face betraying real fear now. "Karpov knows about us—the ship. He knows we are adrift in time, and a possible player in all these events. I have little doubt that he has wondered often what happened to us. If he suspects that Rod-25 was used as we planned it, then he also knows that control rod has a habit of stopping off in the 1940s on the way to 2021."

"Yes, I have worried about this," said Volsky.

"Well sir," Fedorov continued. "He may be watching for us... waiting, and looking out for any sign of our appearance."

"But would he not assume we were still in the Pacific?"

"Perhaps, but this ship can move. He obviously made his way to Siberia somehow, so he learned that his plans all backfired and that the Japanese Empire controls Vladivostok and the far east now. He would realize we would have discovered that as well. Then where would we go?"

"I see your point," said Zolkin.

"He may not know we are here yet," said Fedorov. "We have only been here a few weeks, and I do not think much news has leaked out on us yet, but it will. The British intelligence has good photos of this ship already, and so do the Soviets. In time our presence here will be known, and don't forget that Volkov was a Russian Naval Intelligence officer too."

"The bear is out of his cave," said Kamenski. "Yes, they will soon learn we are out on the tundra looking for fish and berries."

"But that is not all I'm worried about," said Fedorov. "There is something else we have to consider now. What if they discover that stairway at Ilanskiy?"

"Ilanskiy?" Volsky spoke up. "But Karpov knows nothing about that. He was out to sea with the Pacific Fleet when you launched the operation to rescue Orlov."

"What about Volkov?" said Fedorov. "He went down those stairs too. Might he not wonder about that place?"

They were all silent, thinking it through. Then Kamenski spoke.

"Gentlemen, the young Captain here makes a very telling point. That stairway at Ilanskiy may still exist in this world. If it does, it might even still connect the year 1908 to this time, and even extend to the year 2021. It did that in the world we came from, and it may do so here. Think about this for a moment. If we could go back up those stairs, to our time…" The implications were blooming in all their minds like black roses in the Devil's Garden.

"What would a man like Karpov, or Volkov do with the power that stairway represents?" Kamenski was thinking out loud now. "Would they go forward to escape this mad world? Yet what if they had grown all too comfortable running things here, then what? Would they go up those stairs and bring things back… Weapons? Technology? Or perhaps they might simply have a look at how things might turn out?"

"Or worse," said Fedorov. "What if someone goes *down* those stairs, returning to 1908 to start this all over again? That stairway represents a very grave risk. It must not be discovered or ever used again by either of these men."

"What do you suggest?" asked Volsky.

"We must destroy it," said Fedorov. "Destroy it and forever close the breach in time there, if we can. Or God help us if we cannot, because that will either become the stairway to heaven, or the stairway to hell."

Chapter 27

The airship emerged from thick overhead clouds, a monstrous thing in the sky, big as an ocean liner, brooding over the sallow landscape as it slowly descended. *Abakan* glided gently down, following the steel railway line as it wound its way through stands of pine. Behind it came a second zeppelin, lighter in color than the dull slate grey of *Abakan*, the *Angara*. It followed in the air wake of the command ship, a pair of bulbous behemoths gliding through the lowering sky.

Negotiations at the Omsk meeting had dragged on for days on the lower levels as arrangements were made for the withdrawal of Volkov's forces, and re-occupation of the city by Siberian troops. Karpov supervised everything, tirelessly seeing to the smallest detail to assure that there were no hidden cadres left behind in the city, and that adequate security was in place. Then, satisfied that all was in order, he boarded *Abakan* and turned east for Novosibirsk.

There Karpov disembarked to rejoin his commiserate headquarters. After working late, filing his report and communicating with Kolchak in Irkutsk via telephone, he took a fitful sleep, rising early to make ready for a another secret foray into the skies, his curiosity driving him east with the wind.

The sun rose at a little after 5:00 in the morning of July 27th to begin its long journey, climbing up through the low clouds and arcing high overhead. It would not set that day until two hours before midnight, and the weather and winds out of the west seemed favorable for a speedy journey. *Talmenka*, the third zeppelin in Karpov's flotilla, remained at Novosibirsk. The other two airships replenished and carefully checked for any maintenance needs before their next flight. They continued east, following a course that would take them over Kamenka and Krasnoyarsk to Kansk, some 800 kilometers distant.

The airships slipped their mooring cables, rose into the sky and were on their way an hour after dawn, rising up to pierce the cloud deck like whales breaching the surface of the ocean. The upper level winds were very steady, allowing Air Commandant Bogrov to make a hundred KPH and cut their flight time to just eight hours. Karpov had spent most of that time in his air cabin, thinking, planning, wondering.

So now Volkov and I are two peas in a pod, he thought. Be careful. That man is not to be trusted. That theater at the end of our discussion was good warning. Pull a revolver on me, will he? No doubt he was infuriated by the fact that his security men had failed to find my own weapon. But he would not have killed me, any more than I would have killed him. It would have upset everything he was planning. Yes, I think he took Omsk last winter simply to give it back this summer and buy himself a tentative peace.

Yet we are stronger together than either state could be alone. Siberia has just dragged itself up off its knees, and we still see the shadow of the Japanese Empire darkening our borders. Volkov knows that is our primary concern for the moment. That *vranyo* I gave him about putting half a million Tartar cavalry in the field was enough to give him pause. He really may not know how strong we are just now. One day he will find that out.

Yet how shocking it was to learn who this man really is! Ivan Volkov, Kapustin's lapdog. It seems the dog has become a wolf here, even as I have become a bit of a Siberian Tiger in these two short years. Volkov's presence here was shocking, completely unexpected. Once I had time to think about it, I knew what my next move was at once. Here… this place.

He had come onto the gondola bridge after taking a light breakfast. "Where will we tether, Air Commandant Bogrov?"

"Sir? We could use the tower at Kansk by the river. I have radioed ahead to arrange for a car. It is just a twenty kilometer drive east from that point."

"Good enough. I will want a full rifle squad in escort, as always. And scout the road ahead with the motorcycle platoon."

Twenty minutes later the *Abakan* was tethered to the tall steel tower near the river at Kansk, while *Angara* continued on. It would arrive at their planned destination first, hovering on overwatch, the eyes of its watchmen scanning the surrounding countryside, gunners at the ready. One never knew when a roving band of raiders might emerge from the thick woodlands.

Karpov made the long walk along the keelway of the ship to the nose. Being a minor air receiving station, this was a small tower, with no elevator, so he had to make the climb down some 200 feet using the interior metal ladder. His security detachment went before him, and he was pleased to see that Bogrov had doubled the guard by having men from the Kansk militia at the ready as well. There were two trucks and a motor car waiting. His Siberian Rifles took the lead truck, his car following with his personal guard of two men, the militia following behind.

A small motorcycle detachment had been lowered by winch and cables and was already well ahead, scouring the road east by the time Karpov settled into his motorcar. It was a short, bumpy ride over a plain dirt road, but it had not rained in recent days and so the mud was not a problem.

They pulled into the small hamlet of Ilanskiy half an hour later, the security men leaping from the lead truck and fanning out, eyes dark and threatening as they began to search the warehouses by the rail yard. This was the very same place Fedorov had come to with Troyak and Zykov, the place where he had faced down Lieutenant Surinov and tried to secure just a little fair treatment and comfort for the prisoners moving east on the railway cars. This time there were no NKVD men, and no prison camps, and not even a train car to be found in the desolate little town. Stalin's gulags were not blighting the land as they did in Fedorov's journey. Stalin was dead.

Karpov stepped out of the car, squinting at the dilapidated buildings. With so few trains making the run east to Irkutsk these days, places like this were like withered, leafless branches on a barren tree. There were few travelers in these dangerous lands, and therefore little business for the inn at Ilanskiy.

"Where is it?" Karpov said to Tyrenkov, his lead security man.

"Right this way, sir. That building there." The man pointed to a squat two story inn, looking much like most other buildings clustered about the rail yard. In better times it would be a rail holiday house for the train workers, but these were not better times.

Karpov tramped up to the front entry with three men, seeing it was boarded up. The building appeared to be completely abandoned.

"Open it," he said curtly to his men, and they set to work batting aside a few obstructing two-by-fours with their rifle butts. The way cleared, Tyrenkov tried the handle, then simply kicked the door open when he found it locked. He was through the entry and into what was once the front lobby of the inn.

Karpov waited, while his men made certain no one was lurking inside, then stepped through the entry, noting the thick layer of dust on the floor, disturbed only by the footfalls of his men. No one had been there for some time. Pale light filtered from an overhead skylight. He walked up to the front counter, noting the date on the calendar there. 8 DEC 28. Apparently the inn had been abandoned for the last twelve years.

He looked around, seeing nothing of interest here. What was so special about this place? Volkov said it had happened here—the madness, as he called it. It was here that he claimed he suddenly found himself lost in another time. He did not say the year and day. The story was fantastic, but Karpov knew better. Yes, he knew how easily a man could find himself in another world—just like this one.

"There is no one here, Commandant," said Tyrenkov, returning. "My men took the main stair way up. There are eight rooms, all empty, just like everything else."

Karpov said nothing, giving the receiving desk a frown and striding slowly into the next room, a dining hall where several bare wood tables sat without chairs. An empty stone hearth yawned in stony silence at the far end of the room.

"What is there?" Karpov pointed to an alcove to the right of the hearth, sending Tyrenkov striding across the room towards the location. He found another locked door, but it soon gave way with a hard kick of his heavy booted foot. Karpov saw him peer inside, emerging with a scowl, brushing a cobweb from his face.

"It is just an old back stairway, he said gruffly."

"Up or down?" Karpov was at his side now.

"Up, Commandant. The men found an upper landing on the second floor. This is probably the servants stairwell."

"Very well," said Karpov, reaching into his pocket and drawing out a cigarette. It was a habit he had cultivated upon his return here, and he found it calming when he wanted to think quietly for a time. "Cigarette?" Karpov offered, but Tyrenkov saw it was the last one in the Commandant's pack, and politely declined.

"Find out if there is anyone else in this hovel of a town. Have the guards wait at the car. I'll be along shortly."

"Sir!" Tyrenkov saluted, off to round up his detachment, still searching buildings near the rail yard.

Nothing here, thought Karpov. What did I expect? The place is just an old run down inn, and hardly worth the time and fuel I wasted coming here. What could have possibly happened to Volkov to send him back in time? That was 2021 when he arrived here. There was a war brewing. Who knows, perhaps it started. In that year there are several targets near this place that might have interested an American warhead. The 10th Naval Arsenal was just outside Kansk where *Abakan* was tethered. The 23rd Guards had bases here, and there were also mobile ICBM sites scattered around the area, the trucks waiting in underground bunkers… Eighty years from now.

He passed a moment thinking about that, taking a long drag on his cigarette. Then he heard what sounded like a dull rumble. At first he thought it was coming from outside, but when he took a step or two away, he could immediately tell that the sound was echoing from the stairwell! Surprised and curious, he stepped closer to the broken door, leaning into the darkened stairwell. Yes… there was a distinct rumbling sound, a distant growl as from a broiling explosion. He thought the stairway might be focusing sound from above, and without thinking, he started edging up the stairs following the sound and noting that it grew more distinct, louder with every step he took.

Seventeen steps...

It was very dark, and he could feel the discomfiting, trailing caress of old cobwebs as he went. When he reached the top there was another door, split right down the middle, one half askew and broken as if it had sustained some powerful shock.

The sound was very loud now, and he saw an eerie red-yellow glow. He slipped through the broken door, squinting in the light, and was completely astounded by what he saw.

The entire upper floor had been mostly blown away. He found himself on a tenuous perch, a part of the upper floor that still remained standing. There were loose shards of shattered glass under his feet, dust everywhere, blown by a foul wind that seemed to chill his soul with its heartless sound. What had happened?

There! He saw the source of the angry light as the dust cleared, shielding his eyes. There! It rose up in a seething dark column of destruction, unmistakable in its shape and form, a broiling mushroom cloud with a livid white top, lit by an evil glow. He knew what it was at once, for he had set loose that same hammer hand of doom on the world many times himself. Yet this was impossible! How could this be happening, here in 1940? Nuclear weapons would not be developed for years and he knew there were no such projects underway in the wild lands of Siberia.

Then it struck him—jarred loose by the sight of that terrible mushroom cloud. He had come here looking for the reason Volkov might have shifted in time, and he had found it! Yes, that could not be happening in 1940, which meant...

With a sense of rising panic Karpov looked over his shoulder, staring back at the broken door, aghast. He took one last look at the roiling detonation, knowing it would have been right over the Naval Arsenal near Kansk. Then, like a man who had stumbled upon the entry way to hell itself, he took one backward step, edging slowly away, back to the broken door, back to the darkened stairs.

Shaking with fear and shock, he turned and hurtled down the steps, shouting for Tyrenkov. Half way down the awful rumble of the explosion diminished, becoming a muffled background sound, and then fading away altogether when he reached the bottom landing.

He stood there, shivering, his eyes still wide with fear. The sound of a barking dog came from far off, and he took two steps, out from the shadowy alcove on unsteady legs. Then he started, reflexively jerking his hand to see that he still had hold of his cigarette, and the ash had burned down to singe his fingers. The sound of men shouting...

He stepped into the dining room, making his way slowly toward the front desk of the inn, and seeing there the same calendar, the same date: 8 DEC 28. As he stepped outside he saw one of his guards, who turned, face alight when he saw Karpov.

"Commandant!" The man looked over his shoulder, waving at someone. "Lieutenant! I have found the Commandant!"

Karpov heard men running, fast booted footfalls on the ruddy ground. Then up came Lieutenant Tyrenkov, his dour face registering surprise and relief.

"There you are, sir. We thought something had happened to you. I've had men searching for you the last hour." Now he looked at Karpov, somewhat shocked. The Commandant's uniform was soiled, a sheen of chalky dust on his shoulders. Karpov just stared at him, his mind finally starting to function and think again. The sound... that distant rumble, the stairway.

"Tyrenkov," he said, his voice hoarse. Karpov looked over his shoulder, to the northwest, the place where he had seen the terrible mushroom cloud just minutes ago. There was nothing there, only the pallid sky and the distant shape of *Abakan* gleaming from the tether at Kansk, the sunlight finally breaking through and reflecting off the airship's smooth surface.

"You say you have been searching an hour?"

"Yes, sir. I came to give you my report. The town is abandoned, but you were not where I left you at the inn." He noted the diminishing ash on the Commandant's cigarette, a strange look on his face now.

"Sir, what happened to your uniform?"

Karpov now took notice of the dust that lay on him, his shoulders and cap all covered with a sheen of chalky white. He removed his cap, slapping it on his pants leg to clear the soot, and brushing off his shoulders.

"Filthy place," he said. "That damn back stairwell. Cobwebs everywhere!"

Tyrenkov surmised that the Commandant must have gone up those stairs, but where he had been the last hour still befuddled him. He had a man up there, searching every room, and he had shouted into that stairwell calling for the Commandant himself. Why did he not answer? Perhaps he was simply enjoying his smoke and did not wish to be disturbed, he thought. The sight of the cigarette still burning in Karpov's hand drew his gaze again, and he remembered that it had been the last one in the pack when Karpov offered it to him an hour ago. He dismissed the thought, realizing the Commandant must have had another pack in his coat pocket.

Karpov could feel his weight on his feet again. His breath calmed, eyes narrowed. That damn stairway, he thought. One minute I am here, and the next I am somewhere else! This is the madness that Volkov described. What did he say? He struggled to remember the man's exact words.

"The little railway inn just east of Kansk near the old naval munitions center. That's when the madness started. I was searching the premises with my guards, and thought I discovered a hidden stairway at the back of that inn. I found someone was hiding there, and herded the rascal down to the dining hall. The next thing I know I encountered men who seemed completely out of place ..."

Tyrenkov saw Karpov reach into his jacket, fishing out the cigarette pack. He found it empty and threw it away, then turned and walked slowly to the waiting car.

Karpov looked at his Lieutenant. "Bar the entry to this inn—every door and every window. Leave two men here and no one is to enter—absolutely no one. And get me some cigarettes. Understood?"

Part X

Vengeance

"To choose one's victims, to prepare one's plan minutely, to slake an implacable vengeance, and then to go to bed ... there is nothing sweeter in the world."

—Josef Stalin

Chapter 28

July 28, 1940

In spite of the grave danger the stairway at Ilanskiy represented, Admiral Volsky could think of no way they could do anything about it. He paced for days, postponing his movement south into the Norwegian Sea as he considered the situation, realizing the danger and the need to act soon. Fedorov was patient, but he could see his young Captain was still concerned. Finally he raised the matter yet again, and Volsky had come to a decision.

"Let us now consider an operation, Fedorov. How far is it to Ilanskiy?" He soon got the answer he already knew intuitively.

"Just over 3000 kilometers, Admiral. But if we sailed to the deep inlet south of Port Dikson, we could trim a thousand kilometers off that range."

"That still leaves 2000 kilometers. And what is the maximum range of our KA-40? That is the only way we could get men there any time soon, yes?"

Another quick check with the helo bay brought no discouraging news. Even with external reserve fuel tanks mounted, the KA-40 could range no more than 1200 kilometers.

"So if we were to attempt a mission with the helicopter, we would also have to abandon it at the 1200 kilometer mark. Where would that leave the men, Fedorov? In the middle of the Siberian wilderness, with an 800 kilometer hike in front of them. A man might be lucky to get twenty kilometers a day in such terrain, particularly now, in July. The place is a morass of bog and marshland, with no roads and little to eat. They might make good sport for the wolves, but it would probably take them months to reach Kansk. Then what? They could blow that railway inn to pieces, but there they would be."

Fedorov frowned. It seemed hopeless, until he suddenly remembered what Admiral Golovko had told him. "Just a moment, sir." The light of a plan was in his eyes again, and Volsky recognized it at once.

"Admiral Golovko said that they were able to find and shadow the German ships with a zeppelin—the *Narva*. The later German models had tremendous range, over 16,000 kilometers. If *Narva* could do the same it could easily get an assault team to Ilanskiy."

Volsky folded his arms, looking at his ex-navigator, slowly nodding his head. Then he smiled. "Mister Fedorov... Another of your missions to the heartland of Russia, is it?"

"It sounds like a job for Sergeant Troyak, sir. I'm sure he could do it. Then we would at least know that the history we are dealing with here will stay put for a while. As it stands, if the nature of that stairway were to be discovered, and a man knew what he was about, why he could go down those steps, appear in 1908 and change everything."

Volsky's eyes narrowed. "Yes... he could. He could find the man you met there, for example, Mironov, the young Sergei Kirov, and he could kill him. What would happened then?"

"Sir? Kill Kirov? Then we get Josef Stalin back."

"Yes, we do. Does that mean we also see him unite Russia under his iron fist—that these altered states will no longer exist? Have you considered that, Fedorov?"

"Frankly I haven't considered it, Admiral. It never occurred to me. But killing Sergei Kirov? Somehow after meeting the man he became, I think that would be very hard to do, sir."

"Yes, I agree. Who in their right mind would want to replace him with Stalin? We might re-unite our homeland. I don't think this Volkov character could even stand against him, but we get all the rest with him—the detention camps, the purges, the millions dead in the Gulags. Which world would you prefer to live in, Fedorov?"

"I see your point, sir. Yet every coin has two sides. Suppose a man were to go down those steps and find Ivan Volkov instead? That is how he moved in time, sir. We are certain of it now. Volkov went down those steps, and if another man followed him down, perhaps this Orenburg Federation would never arise? Perhaps Kirov could then unite the country under his banner."

"An interesting proposition." Volsky shook his head. "Here we stand, two fools, one old and weary, one young and eager. Here we stand considering how we might change all modern history in a single stroke. At the moment we have placed this ship and crew on the scales, but I wonder if we are heavy enough to shift the balance, Fedorov. We have only so many missiles, and while we can decide the fate of naval engagements, that does little to determine the outcome of the land war. Yes, we still have our special warheads, but that is a fairly radical lever on events that I would hope I never have to use. Yet here we calmly discuss how we might do more than every missile in our dwindling magazines with just a single bullet from Sergeant Troyak's rifle. It's maddening. Kill this man and one thing happens. Kill another man and the world spins off its rocker. How can we make such decisions?"

"Sir… We would not have to kill anybody," said Fedorov. "Apprehending Volkov in 1908 would do the job well enough, would it not?"

"Capturing him?"

"Yes, sir. We just bring him back—a rescue mission. In fact, I can imagine he was quite disoriented after he went down those steps. He might welcome anything that anchors him to the reality he knew. The sight of Russian Naval Marines sent to rescue him would be a great relief."

"One might think so…" Volsky was considering this deeply now. So if we remove Volkov, can we be sure this Orenburg Federation never arises? What if another man takes Volkov's place?"

"This we cannot know, Admiral."

"Yes, it's like reaching into a dark cupboard for a cookie, and finding a rat. More meddling. The world is shattered as it stands. Who knows what might result if we do this?"

"We do not have to decide that now, sir. We could assemble the mission team and then see if we can get *Narva*, or some other zeppelin. Admiral Golovko owes us a favor, does he not?"

"He does. How surprising that these old airships could be the key to everything now."

"Actually, I'm not surprised they are still in use here, sir. Even in our time they were setting up the Krylo Airship project at Omsk. Zeppelins are the perfect transportation solution for the Siberian heartland. They can go where no road or rail can, and with good speed. Our modern designs will make 280kph."

Volsky considered. "I have arranged a meeting with the British at the Faeroes. We must get ready to depart in a few days, but I would like to linger here if we attempt this operation. I don't know what good it would do, but I would feel better seeing to this before I meet with the British again."

"I understand, sir."

"And what about Karpov?"

Fedorov stumbled in his thinking a bit. Karpov… Another rogue was at large in the history as well. It wasn't just Volkov they had to worry about.

"I see that gives you pause," said Volsky, "Yes, what about Karpov? *Admiral* Karpov, if your intelligence is now correct. He has zeppelins too. I think we need to know more about the dangers such a mission might face. That said, I think we must also give it every consideration. Select the mission team, and have Mister Nikolin see if he can reach Admiral Golovko. I will also have to request a brief delay with the British. In the meantime, we have a great deal to discuss."

* * *

The old "B-Series" zeppelins built by the Russians were long gone. They had all crashed into mountains, failed in storms, or simply run afoul of power lines to catch fire. One had its ballast tanks sheared off an ascended so rapidly that it's inflation bags exploded. Another fell prey to simple incompetence when its service crew forgot to remove the caps from the exhaust valves, which resulted in a rupture of the hull.

In their place, however, the much more successful "C-Series" had corrected many of the problems pioneered in earlier decades. They successfully converted to helium lifting gas, incorporated the new Duralumin frames and Vulcan self-sealing gas bags, and proved remarkably durable. But there were only five ships left in Soviet Russia. Three were serving on the Black Sea Flotilla, *Odessa*, *Sevastopol* and *Rostov*. Only two remained in service in the north, *Narva*, and *Riga*, and the latter was far to the south in the Baltic Military District.

"*Narva* will have to do, Mister Fedorov. Admiral Golovko says it is a solid ship, and one of the biggest in the fleet. It is as big as the old German *Hindenburg* class zeppelins, 200,000 cubic meter gas capacity and a useful lift of over 232,000 kilograms." He was reading from notes he had taken. "Half of that capacity is in the guns they have mounted on the damn thing—recoilless rifles! Golovko says each one has 200 rounds. Those guns and other equipment leave you about 120,000 kilograms for your mission lift."

"That will be sufficient, sir." Fedorov was excited at the prospect of another mission, though he had more than a few worries about it.

"Yes, these airships were designed as cargo lifters and troop transports, among other duties. You can carry a full battalion."

"I think a few platoons is all we have in the Marine contingent, though Karpov was running basic crewmen through combat training and trying to make naval infantry of them."

"I think our Marines will have to do. I assume Troyak will lead the mission?"

"Both Troyak and Zykov have been to the location, sir. That was in 1942, but it should be much the same in this year. In fact, its basic structure was the same from 1908 to modern times, hiding that fissure in time for decades."

"I wonder if the innkeeper knew about it?" Volsky was curious.

"I met his daughter when I was there, sir. She said there were stories about that stairwell, and that they were never allowed to play there. It was often sealed off and shunned, and for good reason. I can imagine that inn might have lost more than one visitor on that back stairway."

"Amazing to think of such a thing." The Admiral shook his head.

"One other thing, sir. It's about Orlov."

"Orlov? What's the problem?"

"He heard about the mission from one of the Marines and he has asked if he can join the team."

"What do you think, Fedorov? Is this risky? After all, we never quite got to the bottom of his disappearance from the ship."

"I know that, sir. It's just that he's been going from one duty to the next, and his mood has been souring. I think he still feels diminished and discarded in many ways. After all, he was Chief of Operations."

"He still is. You restored his rank and position and I let that stand."

"I know, sir. But his heart is no longer in it, if that makes any sense, and he's been drinking again. He knows he doesn't really have any part in the real decisions these days. His morale has obviously suffered."

Well... I suppose Troyak can keep him in line if we do approve this request. I will leave this decision to you, Fedorov. You are ship's Captain now." The Admiral suddenly had a question.

"Fedorov, I hope you are not thinking of joining this mission."

"I considered it, sir, but as you say, I am the Captain of this ship, and proud of it. My duty is here."

"Agreed," said Volsky. "Troyak is the sort we need for this mission, and in many ways Orlov too. Have you set the objectives?

"Get to the site, secure the inn, and report back. At that time, if the situation is favorable, we can give the order for the descent."

"The descent—oh yes, you mean that trip down those stairs. This is very risky, Fedorov."

"I know, sir. Many things could make that mission impossible.

Troyak—and he's the only man I would trust with this—well he could arrive before Volkov, or well after. It could take time to find him, and we don't know how much time will transpire here while that is going on."

"What do you mean?"

"Time seems to pass differently at both ends of that stairway. When I went down those stairs I was only there a few minutes, but Troyak said I was gone for over an hour from their perspective. Suppose it takes Troyak days to locate Volkov. That could mean the team we leave at the top would have to hold that location secure for weeks."

"That could be a problem."

"Yes sir. That zeppelin is not very inconspicuous. The mission is likely to be discovered soon after the team arrives on site."

"And what will you find there, Fedorov?"

"That remains to be seen. It is likely that station will be little used. From what I have been able to determine the Trans-Siberian rail is not well served these days."

"It seems this mission is best suited for a quick in and out."

"I know, sir. That may end up being our only option. What we could do is see if Troyak can do a reconnaissance down those stairs, and then report back on the general situation he finds there. We know he is likely to arrive sometime after 7:14 in the morning on the 30th of June, 1908."

"How can you know this?"

"That is the time of the Tunguska impact, Admiral, and I believe that is what caused this fissure in time. I discussed this with Director Kamenski and he agrees. Whatever caused that detonation, it had some exotic material in it that breaches time, particularly in a nuclear environment."

"So you think Troyak can go there, have a quick look around and then scoot back up? What if he finds himself having breakfast with Mironov again? Something tells me finding Volkov will not be so easy as we might hope. My inclination is to simply destroy the inn and be done with it."

"Then we lose any option of reversing what Volkov did."

"True, but sometimes you must close a door in life, Fedorov. Close the breach and end the matter. Then we play with the hand we have been dealt, and no one goes back to 1908 again. That seems to be a very critical juncture in the history. Karpov sinks a few of Admiral Togo's old ships, and we lose Vladivostok and all the eastern provinces. You are there for just a few minutes and look what has happened! Then Volkov... No. That stairway is dangerous, and I think it must be destroyed, just as you first said."

"We can do that, but we may not be able to close the time breach, sir. All we will be doing is destroying access to it. That stairway just happens to be precisely positioned along the line of the breach, right down to the number of steps and the exact angle of ascent or descent. It was just happenstance, but there it is. Kamenski says this is not the only instance. There are others, but that was all I could get out of him. We may be able to close the easy access to this one, unless someone can rebuild that inn exactly as it was, in exactly the same place. This is why I'm sending along a good demolition squad. I think we'll have to blow that inn to a million pieces. That way, putting the puzzle back together again may be next to impossible."

"Fedorov... I know you would dearly love to see Troyak get hold of Volkov by the ear and drag him here, but it may not be possible. I will keep the option open pending the mission team's initial report. Then we will decide. For now, however, this mission is a search and destroy."

"I understand, sir." Fedorov had a grave expression on his face, fully appreciating the danger ahead.

Chapter 29

August 1, 1940

Fedorov was standing on the weather bridge, and he could not resist the urge to wave the mission on, raising his arm to the massive hulk of the zeppelin overhead as it slowly ascended, pumping his fist. They were on their way.

The ship had returned at high speed to Severomorsk, and the *Narva* was waiting there for them, hovering over the scene and tethered to a large mooring tower. It was every bit as big as the ship, nearly as long and much wider abeam, its shadow darkening the harbor as it waited. Admiral Golovko had been elated by the news that *Kirov* had done the job and forced the Germans to pay for their incursion.

"I do not know how you managed it," he said gratefully, "but we are in your debt. *Narva* is yours, and any other resource we can provide."

Sergeant Troyak had selected the men and established three teams. He would lead the first assault team, and for this he chose his toughest and most experienced Marines. Zykov would lead the support and holding team, reinforcing the position after Troyak gained entry. The third team would remain as a reserve aboard the *Narva*, the extraction and support group, and it would be led by Operations Chief Orlov. There were seven men in each group from the Marine detachment, including Orlov.

"How do you feel about the mission," Fedorov had asked.

"Back to Siberia, sir. It will feel like home." Kandemir Troyak, was a Siberian Eskimo from the Chukchi Peninsula in the far east. He was a short, broad shouldered man, very stocky, yet all muscle and all business, particularly with an assault rifle in his hands. Fedorov recalled how easily Troyak had lifted that oil barrel for the train when it was needed at the coaling car, and how he had backed down the NKVD Lieutenant and his squad with the sheer force of his intimidating presence. His organization and conduct of the rescue mission to the Caspian had been exemplary. Troyak led the assault that held off a full regiment of a German Panzer division while they desperately searched for Orlov, and that was no small accomplishment. He had every faith in the rock-like Sergeant, and knew he could count on him.

"There is one thing I need you to know, Troyak. We have made no general announcement to the men, but as mission leader I must tell you that we now know Captain Karpov has survived. He must have been thrown clear of the ship and shifted forward to 1940 in our wake. The strange thing is this—we think he fell out of the shift before we appeared here, and so he arrived earlier in time. We aren't sure exactly when, but his name first appears in 1938."

Troyak listened, his eyes registering surprise, but saying nothing.

"The thing is this, Sergeant. Karpov has wormed his way into a position of authority in the Siberian Free State. He is now commander of the Siberian Aero Corps, and we have learned they have at least eight zeppelins."

He explained the flight plan was to cross the White Sea and stop briefly at Port Dikson on the Kara Sea to drop off mail, supplies, and take on fresh water and diesel fuel. Then they would vanish into the sprawling wilderness of Siberia, planning to approach Ilanskiy from the north. He wanted them to take the stealthiest approach possible, and also loaded portable jamming equipment just in case any of the Siberian zeppelins had mounted radar.

Chief Byko also suggested they use an Oko Panel radar set connected to a portable receiver. They could mount it easily on the bottom of the main gondola, and it could detect any hostile aircraft long before they would become a potential threat. Byko also nudged Fedorov with a wink and told him he could sharpen the *Narva's* teeth a bit if necessary. The Marines ended up taking some reserve hand held 9K338 *Igla* missiles. The name meant "needle" in Russian, and NATO called the infrared seeking missile the SA-24 *Grinch*, but by any name it was a very capable infantry operated SAM system.

These advantages, and the normal thick cloud cover over Siberia, gave them every hope that they could reach the objective site undetected. They also hoped that they would learn the outcome of the mission before they met with the British.

"And what if we encounter Karpov in one of his zeppelins?" Troyak asked the obvious question.

"You will have to use your best judgment, Troyak. The Admiral hopes to avoid engagement. We do not want to let Karpov know we are here just yet. Admiral Volsky is considering the matter. But you must protect the airship, and your men. This mission is very important. Coordinate with Captain Selikov. He knows how to fight the airship. You handle ground operations with your Marines. For the moment it is Volkov that we are worried about. If the situation allows you to reconnoiter down those steps and find him, report and Admiral Volsky will give the final order. And Sergeant, no one needs to know about Karpov for the moment, particularly Orlov."

"I understand, sir."

"One other thing…" Fedorov did not quite know how to say this, but struggled on. "If you should go down those steps, and for any reason cannot return, then realize that you are at a very decisive point in history. We know what Volkov does, and what we are trying to prevent here. How you accomplish that is up to you, Sergeant. But I realize we are asking a great deal of you. The fate of the world, of all our lives, and the life of our homeland, will be on those broad shoulders of yours."

Troyak took that in for a moment. "I will do everything in my power to complete my mission, sir. You can rely on me."

"But… we may not ever see you again, Troyak."

The burly sergeant smiled, shouldering his automatic weapon. "Don't worry about me, Captain." He saluted, and for the first time Fedorov knew what that salute was all about as he returned it.

"God be with you."

Now they were committed, up in the long steel gondola beneath the *Narva*, the tether released and the airship slowly ascending into the grey skies. Fedorov waved, pumped his arm, and saw a man return the gesture from above, a distant salute. They were on their way.

And we will be on our way as well, thought Fedorov. *Kirov* was already turned around, the ship's nose pointed north again in the Kola inlet, and starting to work up speed. They would be 36 hours at full speed before they reached the meeting place with the British, sailing up around the north cape of Norway, then down through the Norwegian Sea to the Faeroes. *Narva* had a longer journey, some 3600 kilometers, but they expected to average at least 100kph and should make it to Ilanskiy within that same 36 hour period.

"Will we get this man Volkov?" The Admiral had asked him. "What do you really think our chances are if I give the order?"

"I don't know, sir. In fact, I don't know what we can possibly expect here if Troyak succeeds. Suppose the Orenburg Federation never arises. Would we suddenly forget about it? Would all the references and history I've been reading in those books we were given suddenly change? What about all the Soviet troops along the Volga facing down the Grey Legion? I just don't understand how any of that could be affected. Are they all just going to appear somewhere else as we sit down to tea with Admiral Tovey? Will we be able to remember we even launched the mission? Why would we? There would be no reason to go after a man who was never there—do you see what I mean, Admiral?"

"Madness, Fedorov. I don't understand any of it. Every time I lay my head down to try and sleep I keep thinking that I will awaken to the old world, before we left Severomorsk the first time."

"There is one anchor I have tried to use for my thinking on this. The work of that American physicist—Paul Dorland. He was talking about something called a Heisenberg Wave."

"What in God's name is that?

"Werner Heisenberg, sir. He was a German theoretical physicist and one of the creators of the theory of quantum mechanics. Now that I think of him, he must be alive even now, working in what was called the German Uranium Club. They were trying to develop nuclear fission and an atomic weapon. In fact, Heisenberg came to believe that the war would eventually be decided by the bomb."

"Yes, they are all working to lay their eggs," Volsky shook his head. "And here we sit with three already in the nest. But how does this relate to this wave business?"

"The Heisenberg wave was not his idea. It was just a name given to a theory proposed by the American physicist, Paul Dorland. Heisenberg once proposed what he called the Uncertainty Principle. In effect, he claimed that events in the subatomic world, the world of quantum mechanics, were not certain. The movement and orbits of particles were not there unless and until they were observed. It is like these possible changes we've been discussing. Perhaps they only take real form the instant we observe them. Once a change has been made in the past, then its consequences sweep forward in time, like ripples from a stone thrown in a pool of still water. This is the Heisenberg Wave. Dorland theorized that it literally re-arranged every quantum particle it encountered as it migrated out, though its range was unknown. He carried this idea further by saying that only the knowing observer would realize the change had taken place, and in order to be able to make such an observation, he would have to be in a safe place, one that would keep them from becoming swept up in the wave of change itself. He called this a Nexus Point."

"You and Kamenski should have a long talk, Fedorov. He tried to explain this to me once, but I have no mind for it. We seem to remember things that others forget, or have never even known. We knew about the Japanese attack on Pearl Harbor, and how that war ended, but if I asked anyone at the naval headquarters at Fokino, they all talked about the bombing of Vladivostok. Now here we are again in a world where that has never happened. Are we in one of these Nexus Points?"

"I don't know, but this time I have my doubts. We have always been the ones making the changes in the past. We were the stone thrown into the water, and the Heisenberg Wave swept away from us, leaving us unaffected. Yet this time, if Troyak goes back and changes something, then we could very well be at risk."

"It is too much for me to keep track of all these things. I have enough trouble trying to keep the ship and crew on a steady course. Yet what you say here gives me much to think about."

"I understand, sir." Fedorov recalled how Kamenski had described it before they set out on *Kazan* to try and stop Karpov in 1908... *Time is not the nice straight line from point A to point B that you think it is. It is all twisted and folded about itself and, in fact, any two points on that squiggly line could meet and be joined. This is why I say we are all together now, in one place, a nexus point where the lines of fate meet and run through one another like a Gordian knot, and we sit here trying to figure out how to untangle it....*

"Perhaps we will know if anything happens," he said at last. "Perhaps we just need to have faith, and do right as we see it, moment to moment. Then let God, Fate, and Time sort everything out. We'll just have to do our best and see what happens, sir."

* * *

Even as the *Narva* lifted off the mooring tower and climbed into the sky, Vladimir Karpov was musing in the gondola bridge of airship *Akaban*. So I have finally seen the end of all my mischief, he thought with some foreboding. The war in 2021 reaches its awful conclusion. What else could that have been? I was watching a nice fat nuclear warhead going off, right over the 10th Naval arsenal on the other side of the river.

He could see the place where it would be built, just a thicket of pine and taiga now, where the rail line curved towards Kansk. He was suddenly beset with the feeling that nothing mattered any longer. No matter what I do here, he thought, I cannot save the world. Or is it the things I do here that bring that awful vision to life in the future? Which is it?

Face it, Karpov, he chided himself. You are not busy here trying to save the world. You are only interested in saving your own skin, and the world be damned, eh? Another voice argued in his mind. No, it said, that wasn't true. I have been fighting for Russia all along. I fought the British, Germans, Japanese and the Americans—all our enemies, all with a mind to exploit us and take from us. Now I fight for Russia, and not simply my own ambition. If no one here has the mind or will to pull this country together again, then I must do it.

Yes, he thought, give yourself a noble purpose, but look how it ends? What are you doing, you fool! You were once Captain of the most powerful ship on earth. The possibilities were limitless. You could have done anything. Now here you are flitting about in these antiquated old blimps, a self appointed Admiral of a phantom fleet of airships. What in God's name do you think you are doing?

I'm doing *this*, the other voice answered. There's more in my grasp now than the reins of this old airship, or even the entire fleet. No. I have more at my command than the hordes of Tartar Cavalry I threatened Volkov with. I've got that damn stairway under my thumb! Volkov doesn't know what really happened to him. He never made the connection between this place and his movement in time, a connection that was almost immediately apparent to me. What a fool I was—I very nearly spilled the beans when I suggested that to him in our meeting. I can only hope he doesn't put two and two together like I did and get curious. Otherwise he would likely move his entire air fleet to secure this place.

That is why I must secure it first! I'm here, now, and I have two airships and a full battalion of the 18th Siberian Rifles with me. That will be enough for the moment. I'll offload that entire force here, and lock that railway inn down tight as a drum. I can make this a new regional headquarters and bring in more troops in the weeks ahead. This place is perhaps the most strategic soil in all of Russia, and it's mine! Let Volkov and Kirov squabble over the rest.

He remembered how he had figured out what must have happened to Volkov. The man started at the top of that stairway and he claimed he was interrogated by NKVD at the bottom. That had to be in the 1940s. There were no NKVD operating back in 1908. The

Tsar was still in power then. So how did Volkov end up in 1908? He must have gone down the stairs a second time! You go up those stairs and you move forward in time. You go down those stairs…

Now the full implications of what he had just worked out in his mind struck him. My god, he thought, I have even more power here than I realized! I could go back there right now, with Tyrenkov and some of his very best men. We'll go up the main stairway and then the whole lot could follow me down that service stairway to the dining room—but to where? Would it work? Would we end up in 1908, or some other year?

If it did work… If I could go farther back… Why then Volkov was small potatoes, wasn't he? Kirov would be no problem either. I could go back and get rid of them—pull the weeds before they ever get a chance to spoil my garden.

He smiled, thinking how easy it would be to do away with his enemies. Then I'll handle the matter, won't I? I'll be the one who gets rid of Stalin, Volkov, Kirov and anyone else who gets in my way. Then I could just come back here and see what has developed. I'll be the most powerful man in the whole world!

He passed a moment imagining it all. I was thrown off the back of *Kirov* for a reason, he now believed. That old Japanese fisherman did not know what he was doing when he pulled me out of the water, that he had fate himself in his fishing net! Look how they brought me home. Those few rubles the pilot of that steamer handed me will end up buying much more than he could imagine. Now I can be the one who takes control, not just here in Siberia. From 1908 I can manage everything. I'll even be able to take an occasional walk up those stairs to see how the cake is baking, eh?

It was a heady toxin, and he seemed to delight in the thought of quietly eliminating his enemies. Yet now he was strangely drained by what he had experienced. So he decided to savor the moment, let it simmer in his thoughts for a time, and then go to bed.

There would be time enough tomorrow to reshape the world.

Chapter 30

More than one man was thinking that night. Ivan Volkov was also awake, turning fitfully in his sleep as he thought about the presence of Karpov here. The news he had received about the location of that ship—*Kirov*—had shaken him further.

So Kirov has hold of the ship they gave his name. Or does he? What was that ship doing at Murmansk? Clearly whoever is now commanding it must have had a mind to go home. Yet how did it get there? Karpov left to fight his battle in the Pacific. He claimed he was blown into the past, but still in the Pacific. My intelligence network is very good. I built it, and it has served me well. There was a squabble between the German navy and Russian ships in the Kara Sea some days ago. Now I learn that the Germans ran into trouble and got a nice kick in the pants as they tried to slink away. What Soviet ship could have backed the Germans off? Was it this ship?

Who would be in command there? Not fat old Volsky. He was stuck at Naval Headquarters at Fokino. So it must be one of the other officers, the *Starpom*—the ex-navigator. Yes, he was the one who was promoted so oddly, skipping three full ranks. I knew something was amiss with that. Is he working for Sergie Kirov now? Are they in league? That would certainly be a problem. That ex-navigator, Volsky's resident historian... Yes, it all makes sense now.

My god... that seems so long ago. Yet I can remember it. Yes, it is as clear to me as if it were just yesterday, and when I saw Karpov's face it all came flooding back. I wonder what really happened to Karpov. Was he lying? Did he really find himself in 1938 as he told it? Was he sent there to perform a mission of some kind? But he seemed genuinely surprised to learn I was still alive—that I was the Volkov at the heart of this Federation. Was that all an act?

Yes, Karpov seemed quite astonished to see me here and learn who I really was. He could simply not understand how I came to be here. That is no surprise to me. I still don't know what really happened. What was it Karpov suggested? He asked me if I had ever considered that my strange movement in time had something to do with the place where it happened, that old railway inn.

The news he had received earlier that night pricked at him now. It was most unsettling. His intelligence network said that Karpov had taken his airships back to Novosibirsk, but two set out almost immediately and headed northeast. His operatives had spotted them overflying Krasnoyarsk, still heading northeast. Why?

He sat up in bed and reached for the lamp switch, squinting at the harsh light in the darkened room. Immediately he heard movement at the door, and a quiet knock. "Is anything wrong, sir?" came a muffled voice from the guard outside.

"No, nothing." He said, shuffling to his writing desk across the room and turning on another light. He looked at the clock there, seeing it was five in the morning.

"Coffee," he said at the door. "Hot coffee." He had always had a taste for the bean, eschewing tea and needing something stronger to stimulate his thinking.

"I'll send for it at once, sir."

Back at his desk Volkov opened a drawer and took out a map and ruler. He laid one end on Novosibirsk, and then lined the ruler up on Krasnoyarsk, following it on to see what lay beyond on that heading. There it was! Of course! Kansk, the river, and then just a little ways beyond—there was the tiny hamlet of Ilanskiy! His operatives had been very specific. Two zeppelins continued northeast. They did not turn southeast for Irkutsk, so Karpov wasn't running home to Old Man Kolchak to get another medal pinned on his chest.

No, he was up to something else, and his course points right to Ilanskiy. There's nothing else beyond that town of any import for hundreds of kilometers. *Sookin Syn!* He's curious. That son-of-a-bitch has gone to stick his nose in things and see what he can find. But what *would* he find there?

There was a quiet knock on the door, and a servant came in with a tray and two coffee cups. He poured coffee into both, drank one, and left the second filled on the table. Volkov looked at the guard and gave him a terse order.

"Send for Kymchek. Tell him to bring anything he has on what those zeppelins are doing, the ones Karpov brought with him. I want to know where they are and what they are up to—understand?"

Even as he said that a cold thought occurred to him. What would I be up to, he said to himself? Karpov and I are two fish from the same pond. If I were him I would be trying to figure out how I got here… Ilanskiy. Yes, he's trying to see if there's any connection with that place and my strange appearance here. I'm almost certain of it. Kymchek will come in and tell me exactly what I already know.

He walked over to the coffee tray and poured a fresh cup, using the mug the servant had drunk from. There could have been poison at the bottom of that other cup. One could never be too careful, could he? Karpov would certainly like to serve me a spiked coffee if he could, wouldn't he? The grand admiral of the Siberian Aero Corps is probably already planning my undoing. I could crush him like a bug. My fleet is three times the size of his little airship navy.

Now Volkov remembered a lesson he had learned and put to good use many times over the decades in his rise to power here. First, know what the other man wants to know—and get it before he does. Information was power. Second, kill your enemies before they are powerful enough to kill you. Sergei Kirov had plucked Stalin out of the stream when he was just a tadpole.

This Karpov has made remarkable strides if he only showed up here in 1938. The man's ambition is impressive. So now is the time to get the bastard—now while he thinks we're all nice and friendly, now while he can crow that he liberated Omsk with a simple threat. Did he really think I bought that *lozh* about half a million Tartar Cavalry?

Volkov smiled. Planning the demise of one's enemies was such a satisfying endeavor. So what should he do now? Find out what Karpov knows, and why he's squatting on that railway inn if that is where he went. I'll know soon enough. If he finds nothing he will simply leave and stick his nose somewhere else. But if he sees an egg or two in that nest, then he'll sit on them. Yes, he'll sit there, and I should begin to see a buildup in that sector soon.

He did not have long to wait. Kymchek was very efficient, at any hour. The telephone rang and the voice of his Intelligence Chief gave him a satisfied smile.

"The zeppelins you have inquired about are at a small hamlet east of Kansk."

"Ilanskiy?"

"Yes, Governor-General, that is the place."

"What are they doing there?"

"We do not yet know. But Karpov is there with Abakan and Andarva, and he is disembarking the entire battalion he had with him during the negotiations. There is a good deal of activity around the rail yard. They could be setting up a new military depot or command center."

"At Kansk? That makes no sense. It is too far behind the front to perform either role effectively. Why set up facilities there when he has them in abundance further west at Krasnoyarsk?"

"We are looking into the matter, sir."

"Please do. Now tell me what airships we have available to operate east of the border."

"Sir? We have Pavlodar, Astana, Oskemen and the Alexandra still in the Eastern District."

"Anything north of Omsk?"

"Alexandra is presently at Tyumen, en-route to Perm. Oskemen is at Petropavlovsk. A little south of the city, but close enough."

"Who commands?"

"Symenko is senior officer aboard Alexandra. A bit surly these days. He wasn't happy about having to rename the ship."

Volkov laughed. "He'll get over it. Form a long range reconnaissance group of those two ships. I'll send the flight plan and orders through normal channels. I'll want a full battalion with each. Understood?"

"Very well sir."

"And put all the other airships in the Northern Division on

standby alert, including the *Orenburg*."

"*The fleet flagship, sir?*"

"Are you going deaf, Kymchek?"

"*I will see the orders go out immediately, sir. Anything more?*"

"That will be all."

Even as he hung up the telephone something told Volkov that it would not be all, that there was much more that would come of this. What he contemplated now was very risky, and as he looked at the map lit by the wan light of his desk lamp he began to consider how best to make this approach.

I cannot send them due east. The *Alexandra* is already well north, so I will send *Oskemen* to rendezvous here, at Tobolsk, but it must not overfly Omsk along the way. These are good, fast airships, and well gunned. Will two battalions be sufficient? Anything more might cause a major incident, particularly if Karpov stays at Ilanskiy for any length of time. So I will send these two ships northeast across the Ob River all the way to the Yenisey River. They can follow that south and then skirt over to Ilanskiy from the north. The area is a complete wilderness. If they stay above the cloud deck there is every chance for them to arrive undetected.

Yet this is risky. It could upset everything I have just negotiated with Karpov. It will definitely upset Karpov himself. He smiled. Too bad in that case. Perhaps I should have killed him the minute I realized who he really was. Curiosity stayed my hand. I need to know more about why he is here, and about that damn ship he was on. There are just too many unanswered questions. He was wearing a service jacket. Why did he not use it to contact his ship? There is more to this story than I know now, and if Kymchek cannot find out what is happening at Ilanskiy, I want a detachment ready to see firsthand.

This must be done carefully. I must plan it well.

* * *

Orlov was standing on the Gondola bridge of the *Narva*, watching the long ragged coastline off the starboard side viewports, amazed by the vastness of his homeland. He had never seen it quite like this, drifting a few thousand feet up, slipping through the mist and clouds and then breaking into the clear to see the sunlight dappling the Barents Sea. He had always enjoyed flying, his face at the window seat of any flight he ever booked. The vastness of the sky and the landscape below him were an altogether different experience from that aboard the ship. He felt airy light, like the zeppelin that bore him, with a sense of freedom that he had not felt since he took that fateful jump from the KA-226 helicopter in the Mediterranean, so long ago as it seemed now.

He had been very excited to learn his request to accompany the mission had been approved by Admiral Volsky. Duties on the ship had fallen into that old tedious routine for him again, checking ship's rotations, assigning crews to maintenance details, knocking a few heads together when the work was slack. He missed the freedom he felt when he was at large in the world, this time, the 1940s, and with his head full of information that he knew he could use to become as rich and powerful as any man alive.

He remembered how he felt, almost invulnerable, a kind of demigod among these unknowing men. He never worried for one minute, not when the British found him, then when the NKVD had him, or even after those commandos pinched him. Persistent little rats, weren't they? Why was everyone so interested in him, he wondered? But he really didn't care. He had his own mission at the time, and he never doubted for one minute that he would do what he set out to accomplish—find Commissar Molla and choke the life out of the man before he could harm anyone else like he hurt his grandmother. Yet that conversation with Fedorov had left him feeling strangely perturbed. Molla was still alive! *Sookin Syn!* The son-of-a-bitch was out there somewhere—or was he?

Commissar Molla was one of Beria's men, working in the Caucasus regional commiserate. From what Fedorov had told him he had learned that whole area was now controlled by someone else, a man named Volkov. Would Molla still be up to no good there? Stalin was gone, killed long ago, so was Beria working for this Volkov figure now? He didn't learn much about him, but it was clear that Fedorov was very upset about that man. He could see it in the young officer's eyes, hear it in his voice.

If Molla was still alive, would things happen as his grandfather had told him? Would he still find his grandmother and do what he did before? If that is so, he thought grimly, then I am going to have to enjoy choking him again. He smiled at that, still seeing the Commissar's red face turn slowly purple, his eyes bugging out and his smart ass mouth shut once and for all. He finished what he came to do, then walked calmly out of that prison to freedom—until the Russian Marines found him.

Damn Fedorov had the balls to come all the way across the continent just to bring me home. He scouted on ahead for 2000 miles to sniff out my trail and then brought in the Marines! And all of that coming from the year 2021, or so he knew now. Pretty damn ballsy, eh? Fedorov was a hard-nosed boss when he had to be. He got things done too.

Orlov shook his head, but he could not help but admire Fedorov. The man had trail blazed a path all through his own damn history books to find me, and then to get after Karpov when he learned he had the ship way back in 1908. The men had told him all about it.

"Hey Orlov," they said, "you missed all the fun. Karpov was kicking every ass we ran into, throwing missiles everywhere—nukes too! But this damn ship just wouldn't stay put. We kept slipping farther and farther back. Can you believe it? 1908?"

No, he still couldn't believe it. The whole thing was too confounding and mind boggling to contemplate. Orlov believed in very few things to a certainty—a good steak, vodka, a nice piece of ass when he could find one, and a hard fist when he was real pissed off. Those were the bounds of his reality. All this business about traveling through time was more than he could think about or comprehend.

He never understood why all this happened, but he had come to accept it, because there was still vodka in this world, good food, and there were still women there too worth the trouble. 1940 wasn't so bad. He would get on quite well here, but look at me now, he thought. Here I am floating over the Barents sea in a blimp! What are we really after this time? Why is Troyak here with all his men?

He had been in on the main briefing, but Fedorov seemed deliberately vague about what they were doing this time. They were to go east to Port Dikson, a place Orlov had visited only once in his day, then from there they would turn south and vanish into the endless taiga wilderness of Siberia. What was the name of the place? Ilanskiy. Orlov had never heard of that town, just another desolate hamlet on the edge of nowhere, like so many lost and forgotten settlements in Siberian Russia.

We go there, Troyak and Zykov go in to scout the place out and take down the objective. They brought enough explosives with them to leave a crater ten feet deep! I asked why they were doing this, but Fedorov just said it was classified. What the hell was that? Well I'll classify this whole situation in two seconds. It's got something to do with this time travel crap. Fedorov wouldn't say anything else, but that's what I think. What could it be?

In once sense it did not matter. Orlov knew he was just along for the ride. He was given command of the reserve squad, and it was to stay aboard the zeppelin unless Troyak and Zykov got into trouble down there.

Trouble... Yes, that was going to be his only ticket off this blimp this time. Trouble. Well, if there was one thing Orlov was good at, that was high on the list. I'll find some way off this ship, he thought, just like I found a way off *Kirov*. I jumped ship before and I can do the same now if I want to. And this time I'll be a little more careful and no one will ever find me.

Russia is a very big place

Part XI

Hammer & Anvil

"Life's a forge. Yes, and hammer and anvil, too.
You'll be roasted, smelted, and pounded, and
you'll scarce know what's happening to you.
But stand proudly to it. Metal is
worthless till it is shaped and tempered.
More labor than luck.
Face the pounding, don't fear the proving;
and you'll stand well against any
hammer and anvil."

—Lloyd Alexander

Chapter 31

When Lieutenant Commander Wells got the news he had been nominated for a promotion and appointment to his first ship he was elated. Then he learned he was to be reassigned to HMS *Glorious* and his mood dampened. He had his hopes set on a fast cruiser, and might even have been more pleased to Captain a destroyer. He knew they would never give him anything bigger, and was very surprised when he learned he would now be commanding his old carrier.

At least Woody will be there, he thought. Old Woodfield. What will he say now that I'm sitting in Captain D'Oyly Hughes chair? Well I can start changing things right off, the minute I set foot on the ship. I'll coordinate well with the Air Wing Commander. I hear Heath was exonerated and returned to the ship after Lieutenant Commander Stevens went down in that brave attack against the Twins. My Executive Officer is a good man, Alfred Lovell, and then there is Mister Barker to be relied upon, as good a Lieutenant Commander as they come.

So he thanked Admiral Tovey for the internship aboard HMS *Invincible*, and even more for his faith in him at the helm of *Glorious*.

"You'll have a tough job ahead down there, Wells," said Tovey. "Somerville is a no nonsense admiral, professional through and through, but with a good heart and outstanding character. I'm sure you will learn much more from him than I could ever teach you here."

"Yet one day I might be glad to be back aboard a battlecruiser, sir," Wells smiled, shook the Admiral's hand and he was on his way.

Once he found himself in the Captain's chair he became a no nonsense Captain as well. They had sailed south with two venerable old battleships, *Rodney* and *Nelson*, and a pack of destroyers. Wells made sure he had planes up in every direction, mostly on U-boat watch for he knew the German capital ships were all up north at the time. Yet he would certainly not ever allow himself to be caught flat footed, and always had a good watch posted on the mainmast and a second squadron spotted on deck at all times.

It wasn't the Germans he had to worry about for the moment, he thought. Strange to think it was the French now! That navy has some fine ships in it. What if they fight? Will it come to that? One look at those two fat battleships out there told him all he needed to know about what might happen. So now he set his mind on planning what his role would be in these operations.

Soon they reached Gibraltar, the men glad to feel the warm July breeze of the Mediterranean as the ship pulled into the harbor. It was not long before he was summoned to present himself to Admiral Somerville, who now set his flag on HMS *Nelson*.

* * *

"**Mers**-el-Kebir, gentlemen," said Somerville. "That is the primary French base in French Algeria, Oran, and I am now in receipt of a message from the Admiralty directing me to take immediate and drastic action against French ships remaining in Oran. "

The Flag Officers and senior Captains were all meeting on HMS Nelson for the final briefing prior to the launch of what was now being called "Operation Catapult." Somerville opened with a brief rundown of what Force H might encounter.

"A pair of older battleships are presently there, *Provence* and *Bretagne*, but also the two new battlecruisers, *Strausbourg* and *Dunkerque*. They are accompanied by four light cruisers, sixteen destroyers and a fist full of submarines. The rest is riff raff. Now while I should be delighted if Admiral Gensoul decides to join with us, we must be firm in insisting his ships are demilitarized, and that failing, scuttled in place should he decline other options. Any questions?"

Wells immediately raised his hand. "Have we communicated with Admiral Gensoul on this matter, sir?"

"Not yet," said Somerville, tall, trim, his uniform immaculate and every bit the English gentleman that he was. A navy cadet at the age of just fifteen, he made Lieutenant in only five years, a specialist in radio signals and communications. He won the DSO at the Dardanelles campaign in the first war, then commanded a destroyer squadron during the Spanish Civil War before coming home to study radar applications. In 1940 he had served in the evacuation at Dunkirk before being sent to the warm Med again to organize Force H at Gibraltar. Churchill had now handed him the first real heavy lifting for the new battlegroup, a showdown with the powerful French Navy. He had requested *Hood* and *Ark Royal,* but they sent him *Nelson, Rodney,* and *Glorious* instead. That was good enough.

"No," he continued. "We want to maintain the element of surprise. Once we appear off shore at Oran, then we have a good man slated to go in on a destroyer and may the initial contact. We will give the French a list of reasonable alternatives, but must be prepared to act decisively, and in a timely manner, if they are not accepted… as distasteful as this prospect seems. I must also tell you that Admiral Cunningham at Alexandria has expressed strong opposition to the proposal that we resort to force, and while I am inclined to agree with him. We could make a defeated ally into an active enemy if this operation spins out of control. I have expressed these views to the Admiralty and I have been informed that the civilian leadership, remains adamant on the matter."

Everyone there knew that the civilian leadership meant Churchill, and the word adamant was well applied

"Then we are to attack the French by surprise, sir?"

"We intend to arrive by surprise, Mister Wells, and then give fair warning. I must place Force H in a position to have every option available, and therefore this movement will benefit from the element of stealth. We will leave at dusk, steam throughout the night rigged for black, and expect to reach our destination at dawn."

"Sir, should our proposals be rejected, am I to expect orders to coordinate a torpedo attack?" Wells wanted to know just what he was in for, as distasteful as it seemed to be planning the betrayal and demise of a former friend and ally. All the other senior officers were equally bothered by the prospect, yet ready to do their duty if so ordered.

"You opinion on that, Captain?" Somerville handed the question back to him.

"Without some supporting fire to silence enemy flak guns protecting the harbor, sir, it would be very risky, and could be a costly option."

"Admiralty was of the same opinion," said Somerville. "The presence of netting at the harbor entrance also precludes the use of destroyers to make such an attack. You should, however, be prepared to execute mining operations so as to prevent any French ships from leaving port. Yet do not be too eager, Mister Wells, even this option will likely be an order of the last minute. To do so too soon could be perceived as a hostile act at a most delicate moment, and prevent the French from accepting our proposals."

"I understand, sir. May I suggest that our first operation be limited to reconnaissance? This would allow us to determine if any of the French ships are making steam or hoisting boats to indicate signs of imminent departure."

"A good point, Mister Wells, and so ordered. It would also be wise to keep a close eye on the submarines present. Should any be seen to slip their births, 8th destroyer flotilla will be prepared to handle the matter. Your aircraft should be prepared to support this action. Now then, I think it best I read to you the ultimatum I have drafted, if you will all bear with me. I think it's fair, and I hope it will be well received."

Somerville took up a typewritten page and began:

"It is impossible for us, your comrades up to now, to allow your fine ships to fall into the power of the German enemy. We are determined to fight on until the end, and if we win, as we think we shall, we shall never forget that France was our Ally, that our interests are the same as hers, and that our common enemy is Germany. Should we conquer, we solemnly declare that we shall restore the greatness and territory of France. For this purpose we must make sure that the best ships of the French Navy are not used against us by the common foe. In these circumstances, His Majesty's Government have instructed me to demand that the French fleet now at Mers el Kebir and Oran shall act in accordance with one of the following alternatives:

(a) Sail with us and continue the fight until victory against the Germans.

(b) Sail with reduced crews under our control to a British port. The reduced crews would be repatriated at the earliest moment.

If either of these courses is adopted by you we will restore your ships to France at the conclusion of the war or pay full compensation if they are damaged meanwhile.

(c) Alternatively if you feel bound to stipulate that your ships should not be used against the Germans unless they break the Armistice, then sail them with us with reduced crews to some French port in the West Indies—Martinique for instance—where they can be demilitarized to our satisfaction, or perhaps be entrusted to the United States and remain safe until the end of the war, the crews being repatriated.

If you refuse these fair offers, I must with profound regret, require you to sink your ships within 6 hours.

Finally, failing the above, I have the orders from His Majesty's Government to use whatever force may be necessary to prevent your ships from falling into German hands."

Somerville put the paper aside. "That was the easy part," he said. "The real work is in your hands, gentlemen. Should all else fail the code word signaling opening of hostilities is Anvil, and the guns of the battleship squadron shall be the hammer. We sail for Oran in three hours. That will be all."

Those three hours never went by so quickly. The destroyers were out first, eleven in all. Then came the light cruisers, *Arethusa* and *Enterprise*. Behind them the big battleships moved in a stately procession, *Resolution, Valiant, Nelson* and *Rodney*. Wells was to bring up *Glorious* in the rear, with a flotilla of destroyers waiting in escort when the ship cleared the harbor. It would be a journey of 420 kilometers to Oran, which was over twelve hours sailing time east into the Alboran Sea and the Mediterranean.

As the ships steamed out of the harbor, a man was watching from the Spanish coast sitting lazily on the beach at the little coastal town of Concepcion, north of the isthmus of Gibraltar. He raised a brown hand, squinting, then stood up slowly, brushing off his white trousers and slipping his sandals back on. It was a beautiful hot late July day, and he wished he could stay longer, but now he had business to attend to.

Juan Enrique Calderon had sat on that beach every day that month. The show he was watching now was supposed to have been staged much earlier, on July 3rd in the history Fedorov knew. Instead the action in the Denmark Strait had delayed these events, and shuffled the cast a bit, but the script of the play would remain the same, right down to each letter and period in Admiral Somerville's note of ultimatum.

Now Juan had his little part to play, just a note scribbled on the margins of these great events, but one that would have a most dramatic effect. He walked into the little hotel there on Paseo Martimo, and slipped into the telephone booth, his brown finger dialing quickly.

The voice on the other end of the line answered with the familiar greeting, and Juan Enrique spoke his quiet message. "Just calling to confirm that I will definitely attend the event tomorrow morning. Please tell my friend that it is a beautiful day here. The birds are lovely off the coast, I saw four white doves and a nice fat goose! I wish he could see it."

That was all.

Yet it was enough to change all the history that would be recorded on the following morning, for Señor Calderon was working for a deeply nested intelligence section keeping a close eye on British ship movements at Gibraltar, and the four white doves were the four battleships out there on the horizon now, with one fat goose behind—HMS *Glorious*.

* * *

When Admiral Marcel-Bruno Gensoul received the news that a large British task force was now heading east from Gibraltar, he was understandably tense and upset. What would a British force of that size, four battleships and a carrier, be doing? He knew before he had even finished asking himself. The question now was what would he do? He looked out on the fleet where it lay at anchor and realized his predicament. The guns of his most modern ships were pointing landward. *Strausbourg* and *Dunkerque* had two quadruple turrets both forward of the conning tower. If caught in their present position they would have no chance if hostilities were to break out.

A disciplined and efficient man, Gensoul was under no illusions about his situation now. Unless he took his fleet to sea, and quickly, it would not survive. He immediately sought instructions from the French Admiralty, pacing as the sun hung lower in the sky, knowing that the British had departed from Gibraltar at 15:00. At 17:00 he was informed by cable that Darlan could not be located, and that the French Chief of Staff, Vice-Admiral Le Luc at French Naval headquarters at Nerac, was now issuing an order for all French naval forces to prepare for imminent hostilities.

Admiral Gensoul was in a quandary. He knew what the British really desired, not conflict but alliance. They hoped his fleet would be sailed to English ports, but this would clearly be impossible. To do so would immediately violate the terms of the armistice signed with Germany and could lead to the complete occupation of all free French territory by the German army. Yet to turn his guns on the British was also an agony. It would create a situation where Vichy France became a de facto ally of Germany, in full cooperation with the Nazi regime, which was a proposition he knew Darlan was strongly considering.

His third alternative would be to try and sail to a neutral port, perhaps Martinique in the Caribbean, where the Old French carrier *Béarn* had sailed after secretly hauling a load of gold bullion from the Bank of France to safety in the United States. In return *Béarn* was receiving a new air wing from the Americans consisting of 27 Curtiss H-75s, 44 SBC Helldivers, 25 Stinson 105s, and also six Brewster Buffaloes. The planes were to be loaded and delivered as part of the Belgian Air Contingent, but that was over now. There was no free government in Belgium any longer. He could not sail west in any regard. Not without the likelihood of encountering the Royal Navy and a battle at sea.

That left the sour alternative of scuttling his ships in place, and he knew that this is what the British would demand in time. Refuse that and their guns would fire soon after. He had little doubt of the outcome should he leave his ships where they were.

Vice-Admiral Le Luc sent a further message at 17:20 indicating he was planning to send the French squadrons at Toulon and Algiers to Oran as an immediate reinforcement, but Gensoul knew this would also be a mistake. Mers-el-Kebir could not accommodate these additional ships, and this move would only lead to another battle at sea. The only alternative he could think of was to reverse that order, and take his ships to Toulon. Yet he knew if he sat there, sending messages to Nerac, waiting for Le Luc to respond, arguing the matter should his suggestion be rebuffed, the British would draw nearer with each passing minute. He knew what he had to do—order the fleet to action at once! He must present Le Luc with a de facto situation that he knew would be the only solution now.

And this is exactly what he did.

Chapter 32

Newly promoted Captain Wells received the message from the W/T room with some surprise. *'MOST IMMEDIATE – Admiralty informs the French fleet at Mers-el-Kebir has worked up steam and is now moving out to sea. Course and destination unknown. Imperative you ascertain location and intentions of the French Oran Squadron.'*

Wells looked at the chronometer, 21:10, and the sun was just on the horizon behind them, setting in minutes. He would have twilight conditions for the next hour, but if he wanted to have any chance of spotting the French fleet he had to get his planes up immediately. The moon would not rise until quarter after one, a half moon that would provide some light. Should he launch now, or just before moonrise?

"Mister Lovell," he said quickly. "Send down to Air Commander Heath and get that flight of *Swordfish* up for extended search to the east at once. The French have put to sea." He had two *Skua* fighters on the forward catapults ready for immediate launch, and a squadron of four *Swordfish* aft on ready alert.

A signalman ran in with a further message, breathless from his trip up the ladder, and Wells took it quickly, raising an eyebrow at what he saw. *'Considering gravity of present situation, HMS Glorious is herewith detached with DD Flotilla 8 and will make best practical speed ahead in effort to effect contact with French fleet. Main battle squadron will follow at best speed.'*

Flotilla 8 consisted of six destroyers, *Faulknor, Foxhound, Fearless, Forrester, Foresight,* and *Escort.* They had been steaming off both sides of the carrier in two lines of three, providing a very effective ASW screen for the valuable ship. The remaining five destroyers of Flotilla 13 were attending to the four battleships.

Wells felt the rising adrenaline as he realized what was now happening. *Glorious* was the fastest ship in Somerville's squadron, ten knots faster than any of the battleships. The situation had obviously changed. Somehow the French must have gotten wind of our operation, he thought quickly. We've lost the element of surprise, and they are slipping away. But where are they sailing? Suppose they are coming west in an attempt to reach Casablanca or Dakar? In that event I'll have *Glorious* out in front and run into the entire French battle squadron! Would they sail west? The more he considered it the more he thought that unlikely. No, they will go home to a French port now, or further east to Algiers. Nothing else made any sense.

Yet he knew what that might mean, and the urgency that was now in the order for *Glorious* to move on ahead. They will order me to strike, he thought. It's all on me now, the whole bloody mess.

"Mister Lovell, the ship will come ten points to starboard and increase to 30 knots."

Lovell hesitated, ever so slightly, then the reflex kicked in and he quickly repeated the order. "Aye sir, starboard ten and ahead full."

"Lampsmen, signal destroyers on our starboard side and order them to make way."

Wells walked quickly to the chart room, remembering how he had assisted Admiral Tovey in the fleet flagship aboard *Invincible*. He had to now make some very quick calculations, and an equally quick decision. They were still west of Melilla, and 124 miles from Oran. His fairy *Swordfish* had a range of about 475 miles out and back, which might be extended to 525 with additional fuel, and no torpedo. This was a good deal more than the two Blackburn *Skuas* he had on the catapults, so he would go with his *Swordfish*.

If he launched now he could have his planes move ahead at their best speed and in an hour they could be just north of Oran with a little light before complete darkness set in. The *Swordfish* might then have another hour loiter time to shadow the French before they had to turn for home. It would be enough to at least find and mark the position and heading of the French fleet, which is what he had been ordered to do. So he would let his order stand. The planes would launch immediately.

The *Swordfish* were already sputtering to life, and he quickly had Lovell send down instructions as to his intentions for their course and mission. Come first light, he thought, the decks would likely be crowded with the whole of 823 Squadron, armed and ready. I have better inform Mister Heath, he thought.

"Mister Lovell, please ask Mister Heath to come to the bridge at his first opportunity."

* * *

The calculations Wells had made were spot on. His *Swordfish* thrummed away east, vanishing into the twilight and labored off at their best speed. It was no more than an hour later before they reported back. '*Spotted large flotilla, four capital ships, heading 030 degrees NW. Speed 20. EST - My position follows.*'

"See that is forwarded to Admiral Somerville at once."

"Aye sir."

The French were just north of Oran, and if there were four battleships then they had emptied out the harbor. He had little doubt now. They were most likely running for Toulon. He passed a moment of relief, glad to know he might not blunder right into them as Glorious sped east at 30 knots. In the plot room off the bridge he was working out the situation on the chart, marking off the range with a compass. It was immediately obvious to him that Admiral Somerville's battleships were not going to catch up.

His good friend Lieutenant Robert Woodfield had come onto the bridge as senior officer of the watch, relieving Lovell, and he waved him over.

"Have a look here, Woody. The French are slipping away like a proverbial thief in the night. Our search detail is already turning for home, but if they stay on their present heading I've worked it out that Somerville hasn't a chance to ever catch up."

"Not a very satisfactory turn of events," said Woodfield.

"You know what this means," said Wells. "If the Admiralty remains determined to get at these ships, we'll be the ones they tap on the shoulder."

"Does Heath know?"

"Yes. I spoke with him half an hour ago and he's down there arming 823 Squadron with torpedoes even as we speak. I have little doubt I'll have a launch order well before dawn."

"Right," said Woodfield. "Well we'll just have to make the best of it, hard as it may be."

"Sun will be up at 07:20, but I'll have everything ready to go in another hour. We'll recover our search detail a half past midnight. I've plotted their farthest on circle here," he pointed to the chart. "So if we steer this course and swing up near Cartagena, we could be about 90 miles west of them if they have turned north towards Mallorca."

"And if they turned east for Algiers?"

"Then I'll have to steer 040, right down the middle. In that instance I think we can get even closer. We're closing the range on them at ten knots per hour."

"My guess is that they will run parallel to the coast to a point north of Algiers before they head north, if Toulon is where they are really headed."

"I thought the same. So I'm steady on for the moment unless I hear anything to compel me to move north."

"Right you are, Welly... You don't mind my calling you that, Captain?"

"Perhaps not best in front of them men," said Wells, "but between the two of us I'll miss it if you don't."

The signal Wells had been waiting for, and mostly dreading, came shortly after midnight, just as the *Swordfish* were beginning their approach for a night recovery. *'Considering present situation, and decisions taken by the Admiralty, Case Anvil is hereby ordered for 04:00 hours. Imperative you give main battle squadron every chance to catch up.'*

Woodfield was still at his elbow when he received the message, and he handed it off to his friend, saying nothing.

"You know what this means," said Woodfield quietly. "Have we even given them our ultimatum?"

"I can't see how." Wells had a look of anguish on his face.

"Some Anvil," said Woodfield. "That squadron out of Oran may be joining up with ships from Algiers."

"And we're the hammer now, Woody. 823 and 825 squadrons against the whole French fleet!"

* * *

July 28, 1940 was a hard day. The leading *Swordfish* of 823 and 825 squadron had assembled on deck, two groups of eight spotted for takeoff, two more groups waiting on the hanger deck below. *Glorious* had closed to a range of just 60 miles, and so eight *Skua* would also be added to the strike, for a total of 40 planes. Their engines were spinning up and sputtering to life at 05:00 And the whole formation was aloft and assembled over the next twenty minutes.

Wells had been informed that the demands to be made of Admiral Gensoul had been directly transmitted to the French Admiralty, now modified to require the French ships immediately proceed to either Alexandria to come under British control or to Algiers where they were to be scuttled within six hours. An affront to French honor, and in accordance with Admiral Darlan's orders that the French fleet would not comply with orders from any foreign Admiralty, the offer was rejected. Now well out to sea and still over 150 miles ahead of Somerville's battleship squadron, the French did not believe that the British could back up their threats any longer.

At 05:40 that morning, the pre-dawn quiet was broken by the low, distant drone of the *Swordfish*, coming in over the wave tops after finally locating the French fleet again. Gensoul knew he had been spotted, but was so confident that the British no longer posed any real threat that he remained on his heading, taking no further evasive action.

Following orders, Wells transmitted the follow up sighting report, indicating his planes now had Gensoul's squadron in sight. Five minutes later the signalman handed him a one word message:

Anvil, which was in turn immediately transmitted to Commander Heath. The Old Stringbags were going in.

823 Squadron broke formation, approaching from the left, with 825 Squadron on the right. The heart of the formation was a line of four large capital ships, the primary targets. Ahead of them was a second formation of six light cruisers, three from Oran and three more from Algiers. Eight to ten destroyers were steaming on the fringes of this grand formation. As they approached, the *Swordfish* pilots claimed they could hear the sound of alarms and sirens blaring on the bigger ships ahead, and soon cold fingers of white light probed the darkened skies as the ships began to switch on searchlights.

Guns began to fire, almost randomly at first, puffing up the sky with white explosions. Three ships launched flare rockets, which whistled up and descended on slow parachutes, illuminating the targets more than affording any aid to the gunners. By the time the planes were actually seen, and not simply heard, the *Swordfish* were already well lined up on the end of the formation, closing on the lumbering battleships *Bretagne* and *Provence* like a pack of hyenas stalking water buffalo on the African savannah.

The pilots took aim at the leading battlecruisers, but their torpedoes would not find them that dark morning. *Strausbourg* in the van of the battle squadron immediately accelerated to its top speed of 32 knots, *Dunkerque* following in her frothing wake. A gap appeared between those sleek new ships and the old WWI era battleships behind them, already struggling along at only just 20 knots.

The first eight planes on either side had little luck. One torpedo struck a fitful destroyer running alongside *Bretagne*. Another hit the battleship full amidships. The second wave got in much closer, braving the thickening AA fire as the French finally focused their defense. Two planes were hit and felled, the remaining fourteen all getting torpedoes in the water. Of these eight would find their targets, four plowing into *Provence* at the rear of the formation and four more striking *Bretagne*.

The explosions rocked the big ships from side to side, and it was soon apparent that they had both taken severe damage. *Bretagne*, hit five times now, was quickly listing to her starboard side. *Provence* had taken one hit that disabled her port side engines. She wallowed in the sea, down at the stern and the last ignominious attack was put in by the escorting *Skuas*, which swooped down from above to deliver bombs. Three more hits were obtained and it soon became obvious that neither one of the battleships would survive the attack.

Like bees that had delivered their only sting, the *Swordfish* could do little more. They fluttered about, some making a vain attempt to get after the faster French ships with bombs, but to no avail. When all was said and done, the sun rose over the scene to reveal that the British attack had claimed the two old battleships, the destroyer *Mogador*, and the lives of over 1300 French sailors.

By 08:00 the planes were being recovered and Wells messaged Admiral Somerville with results, asking if another strike should be mounted. The British had learned that the incident had stirred up the Italians on Sardinia, and that planes were up from Cagliari, the humpback three engine bombers out to see what they could find. The French had another 380 sea miles to go before they were safely home, but now, with Italian bases active at Cagliari, Sassari and Ajaccio it was deemed imprudent to allow the sole carrier to linger. Somerville signaled that the ship should turn and rejoin his battle squadron, which proceeded to Oran, finding no more than a few submarines, minelayers and Colonial Sloops remaining there. Algiers was also abandoned.

In the end the British were left with a result that was 90% of what they had accomplished in the history Fedorov knew, and with the same consequences. The attack was reviled in France, lining up all the remaining French naval units in sworn opposition to the Royal Navy from that day forward. It also dealt a hard blow to General Charles De Gaulle's efforts in organizing his Free French resistance, but Operation Catapult did accomplish one thing politically by proving the resolve of Great Britain to fight on without scruples, which immediately stiffened the flagging morale at home and did much to bolster Churchill's position.

Yet the real prizes within the French fleet still remained at large. The fast battlecruisers *Strausbourg* and *Dunkerque*, and all the light cruisers and remaining destroyers made it safely to Toulon where they would continue to pose a dangerous threat. More than this, the operation had not challenged the three modern French battleships, *Richelieu* at Casablanca, and *Jean Bart* and the late arrived *Normandie* at Dakar. These five ships would loom ever larger over the scene in the months ahead, though Britain had achieved at least one thing by preventing the concentration of all these powerful ships in one location. Three of the five were east of Gibraltar at Casablanca and Dakar, potential prizes for the British if they could be obtained, certain enemies otherwise. The last two were At Toulon, potential prizes for the Germans and Italians that would cause much strife in the days ahead as Britain considered how it could maintain the long supply line through the Med to Cunningham in Alexandria.

As a adjunct to Operation Catapult, a small British detachment under HMS *Hermes* had mounted an air raid on the *Richelieu* in conjunction with a mining operation by frogmen, but failed to inflict any serious damage. This served only to telegraph future British intentions to Rear Admiral Plancon, Flag Officer, French Navy West Africa. He called an emergency meeting with Admiral Laborde on the *Normandie*, and Captains Barthes and Marzin on the other two battleships in French West Africa. The universal consensus was that Vichy France should extend their armistice with Germany to the status of alliance, and forsake Britain and the West altogether.

Admiral Darlan had been leaning this way for some time, believing England's days were numbered and wanting to place the last of his dwindling chips on a winning number. He met with Marshall Petain, and a delegation was sent to Berlin. Three days later the news shocked the world and rattled the grey heads in Whitehall. France had not only fallen as an ally, it had now become a foe.

Chapter 33

"What have we done, Woody?" said Wells when it was all over. "We sink a pair of old hulking dreadnoughts that would probably have spent the entire war rusting in port, but the fast battlecruisers got clean away!"

"We did what we had to," said Woodfield. "You weren't flying the planes, Wells. All you could do was get the ship in close and carry out your orders, and that you did well enough."

"Yet we were supposed to try and stop them, weren't we?"

"You got hold of their leg and took a good bite, Captain. Then you were out there, well in front of the rest of Force H with Italian bombers inbound and only 8 fighters for air cover. What more could you do? Somerville was simply too far behind to finish the job."

"Yes we did, but it's my name written in the history books this time, isn't it. I'll go down as the man who ordered the dastardly deed. I got hold of Admiral Gensoul's leg alright, then stabbed our former friend and ally in the back. Now look what has happened. The Vichy government is in cahoots with Hitler, and it's all my fault." He felt that, of all days, this surely must be England's darkest hour.

"Don't get a big head on your shoulders, Welly." Woodfield jabbed his friend in the shoulder. "That order came from well above your pay grade."

"I suppose you're right," said Wells, but the thought of all those French sailors that went down with those ships would haunt him for the rest of his days, and he was ever bothered to think that his actions had tipped the delicate political balance that was teetering in the operation, and made a new enemy out of England's old friend.

Germany expressed immediate interest in the overtures put forward by Petain and Darlan. They had already seized control of the fast cruiser *De Grasse* and the nearly completed carrier *Joffre*. Now a pair of fast battlecruisers and a gaggle of other ships were nesting at Toulon, within easy reach of either Germany or Italy. The Vichy French knew they had a strong bargaining chip in the navy, and in the considerable holdings they now still controlled in North Africa. In exchange for full wartime cooperation with Germany, they would ask for governing authority over all of France.

Hitler equivocated, then decided that as long as the Germans would be permitted free and unfettered access to all French Territory, with a German minister placed as a kind of *chargé d'affaires* overseeing policy decisions and representing German interests, the arrangement was entirely to his benefit.

As for the French Navy, the ships would remain in French hands, except the two vessels taken at Saint Nazaire. German naval "advisors" would be placed at the Flag Officer level at Toulon, Casablanca and Dakar, and all French controlled ports would be open to the Kriegsmarine and accept a German contingent in garrison. It was a hard blow to the British hopes for holding on to Egypt in the long run. It was, indeed, their darkest hour, with no other friend in the world, standing alone against an array of foes that now seemed unconquerable. Now, more than ever before, they set their minds on the destruction of the entire French fleet.

* * *

Admiral Somerville was initially pleased with the results of Operation Catapult, in spite of the fact that his own squadron had been prevented from engagement due to untimely withdrawal by the French. The political consequences had been catastrophic, and his greatest fears about the operation had been realized. That, however, was beyond his control, though he knew the job of cleaning up the mess they had made of affairs would also fall to him soon enough.

First things first. He had summoned the young Captain of HMS *Glorious*, receiving news that Wells was brooding over what had happened. Now he looked up at Wells, who had just submitted his report to the fleet offices at Force H headquarters, Gibraltar.

"All things considered, Mister Wells, I find your actions and deployment entirely consistent with the guidelines for fighting instructions involving fleet action with a retiring enemy."

"I wish we could have done more, sir," said Wells, still beset with mixed feelings over the engagement.

"We all do, and I regret that I was unable to lend a much needed hand. The task assigned you was arduous, not only from a tactical standpoint but also considering the fact that you were asked to raise your hand in anger against a former friend and ally. We all felt the same way, Mister Wells. Most every senior command level officer in the Med expressed strong reservations over what we were ordered to do. I can imagine your stomach was in your throat when you received code 'Anvil.' To ask you to break formation, move out ahead of the battlefleet, and find and strike the enemy was a hard task, and it was one you performed admirably."

"Thank you, Admiral, but I must point out that the bulk of the French fleet was able to reach Toulon safely in spite of our actions. Now look what has happened."

"That may be so, but your tactical approach was correct. You followed section E guidelines regarding air striking force operations, to the letter I might add, by correctly attacking the rear enemy capital ships with the objective of reducing their speed. In this case your attack produced stronger results in the sinking of two battleships which would otherwise now be at large."

"Yet the consequences, sir…"

"The consequences are not your consideration, Mister Wells. They were not my consideration either after Whitehall and the Admiralty had set these orders in stone. Had I come up on the French, my intention and effort would have been to do exactly what you accomplished. The French rejected all our fair terms. It was therefore our objective to sink those ships."

"I understand, sir."

Somerville gave Wells a long look, a sympathetic light in his eyes. He knew exactly what the younger man must be feeling now, that it was all on his shoulders, the burden of all the consequences that might result from this operation, the alienation of Vichy France and the deep feelings of resentment and ill will that this engagement would foster between former allies.

"I know you put men in the water yesterday, Wells, and a good many lost their lives. Take my advice and try not to think you put your hand on each one's head and held the man under. This is war. It's cruel, mindless violence at root, ever so carefully planned but yet wholly unreasonable. I will tell you that the Germans gave no quarter during the recent evacuation forced upon us. We lost a good many men, civilians too. I would be foolish to say we could put those French sailors on the scales to try and balance that. They were simply doing their duty, as you were. We did not want to make an enemy of them, but this war has done as much, and I'm afraid this is only just beginning. You will find yourself in similar circumstances again, Captain, perhaps even more trying. I know this is the second hard blow you've been dealt."

"Sir?"

"I am aware that the ship you now Captain is only on the fleet active duty roster because of your actions in getting her to safe waters under equally trying circumstances. That was the hot fire of war, and you weathered it when you were on the anvil. This time you were the hammer. So you've seen both ends of it now, and that is what really shapes the metal of a man's character. Stand proud, Mister Wells. That will be all."

"Sir!" Wells saluted, feeling just a little better about what had happened, yet not knowing which was worse—to be on that anvil, or to be the hammer.

Life is a forge, he thought, and he put the matter out of his mind.

* * *

Alan Turing was having a very bad day. Thankfully his hay fever had abated somewhat, and he could at least breathe again. And he had managed to keep his coffee mug chained up until he wanted it. But the pressure was now mounting, as one intercept after another began to pile up on his desk, in a well named German naval code that was proving to be a real enigma.

Admiral Tovey had been on the hot seat at Whitehall over losses and damage to the Home Fleet in the recent duel with the Germans in the Denmark Strait. Questions had been asked about the W/T intercepts of German command level signals, and why they were not deciphered, but more so about the strange decision to parlay with the Admiral of a Russian cruiser—the very same ship that Peter Twinn had dropped in his lap with that handful of photographs. Now they wanted to know more, and Turing was back in the storeroom rummaging through boxes of old photo reconnaissance material. And that was when his day went completely bonkers.

How could we have missed the construction and commissioning of such a ship, he thought? They were saying that it must have been a secret project, possibly built in Odessa or the shipyards at Nikolayev South, also known as Soviet Shipyard No. 444. It was certainly not laid down in any of the Baltic shipyards, and we have no evidence to suggest that the Soviets could build a ship of that size at any of their northern ports. If it was laid down at Shipyard 444 then they damn well must have had a magician's cloak over it the whole time.

I was never on ship watch. I'm here to sort through the signals intelligence and decipher the damn things. And that is all I'll be doing for months now—going over anything they pile up from three and four years back to ferret out the trail on this ship. Surely there were orders, message traffic, commercial contracts, personnel assignments, materials acquisitions. It would simply be impossible to hide all that for very long. We should know about this ship, chapter and verse. But yet I find nothing; nothing at all in the archives here.

He stood up, frustrated, and ready to call it a long afternoon and go unchain his coffee mug. Then he saw it, the box tucked discretely away behind the last indexed photo box on the reconnaissance shelf. Someone got hasty, or very sloppy, he said to himself. Here they've gone and mislabeled a photo box. He stooped down, leaning in and wishing there was better light in the musty old storage room of the archive. Well, what is it then? He pulled the box out, sliding it in to an open space on the hard tiled floor, right beneath the bare light bulb hanging from a cord above.

We simply must find a better way to keep track of things. Now where does this belong? The box was very odd, and it left him feeling strangely unnerved. No label at all… Just stuck in here in a nook against the wall behind that entire indexed series of photo boxes, and taped up rather well.

Curiosity got the better of him now. If had always been one of his salient personality traits, or flaws—that persistent curiosity that so often accessorized the mind and character of a scientist and intellectual. Wondering about things was always the first step down the garden path to the roses of understanding. Now he wondered what he had dragged away from the old daddy long-legged spiders, layered in dust and looking like it wanted nothing more than to be left alone—for another century or two.

But to Alan Turning a closed box wanted opening, just as any puzzle or chess problem needed solving. He reached for the tape and had it off in a minute, slowly opening the lid to the box and setting it aside. A last bit of masking tape clung plaintively to one end of the lid as he did so, but Turing had his way.

Now what have we here, he said to himself, his curiosity redoubled? There was a nice fat row of well stuffed manila envelopes, typical of the sort they all used here to store files and reports and photos pertaining to one thing or another. This one did have a label, which he read, though it rang no bell in his mind as he did so. Must have been before my time here, he thought, though the writing did not look all that weathered. Strangely, each and every envelope bore the same label.

There was no good trying to get into all that in the middle of the storeroom floor, so he took a single envelope, the first in the series, and retreated down the long aisle toward the light of the open door. It would make for a brief diversion while he took a brief time out for some much needed coffee.

He set the file down on his desk, fished about in his pocket for his padlock key, and then slowly unchained his coffee mug, heading for the pot brewed fresh at four in the afternoon, along with plain hot water for tea. Back at his desk he settled in, enjoying those lingering first sips and the aroma of good hot coffee as he picked up the manila envelope.

He was not surprised to see what looked like typical aerial reconnaissance photos, and as was his habit, he turned the first over without really looking at it to note the location, source and time stamp.

No wonder, he thought, as it was clear that someone botched the time stamp, fat fingered the numbers and stamped the wrong year. A quick look at the back of all the other photos in that envelope reinforced that, all misdated. Someone was getting sloppy, he thought. They botched the labels on all these photos and probably had to re-do them all again. But we never throw much of anything away here, do we? So they bloody well threw them into an envelope and thought to hide it all away in the back. He smiled, like a school master who had just caught one of the students cheating on an exam, and turned the photo over to have a look.

And his heart nearly stopped dead.

There was a ship… a ship at sea, making a wide turn, its wake curved out behind it. It was obviously photographed by an aircraft, probably a seaplane out on a scouting and recon mission. But that ship… He leaned in closer, squinting, reaching for his magnifying glass, his pulse racing though he could not think why. Yet it wasn't a matter of thinking at that moment. It was all something in the pit of his stomach, a feeling, a dark intuition, laden with misgiving and an edge of fear.

A ship… the ship… the ship that Peter Twinn had clued him in on! It was unmistakable, the silhouette, high swept bow, long foreword deck that was strangely empty, the strange domes and antennae mounted all about the dark superstructure, and more, that feeling of dangerous menacing power, yet he could not see why— there were hardly any guns worth the name to be seen.

What is this, he thought? Has Peter been holding out on me? I told him to let me know the moment we had anything more on that ship, and here's an nice fat envelope... in a *box* full of nice fat envelopes, all taped off in the storeroom. Perhaps they did get wind of this ship years ago, and this was the mother lode of information he had been looking for!

He looked at the photos, each with a date in August of 1941, a full year off due to that dodgy rubber stamp. Let's have a look at the others, he thought, his curiosity rising again.

And it was a very long and harrowing afternoon from that moment on, ending with Turing sitting alone, a look of perplexed astonishment on his face that soon gave way to white faced fear. It was completely unreasonable, this feeling that had come over him, a feeling that he had seen these photos before, though he knew he had no recollection of ever doing so... Until he saw the unmistakable scrawl of his own handwriting on the back of photo five next to a string of numbers he had written there: *Length, 820ft; beam, 90ft; displacement, Estimate 30,000 +,* and there were his initials, claiming the note and hand dating it himself, in August of 1941!

He looked over his shoulder at the open door to the storeroom, his eyes dark with apprehension. Then he reached for the telephone on his desk, thinking he had done exactly that once before... exactly that...

"Turing here. Hut Four. Secure line to Whitehall please. Admiralty office of the Home Fleet Commander."

As he waited on the line he turned the manila envelope over again, noting the single word on the typewritten label there, all capitals.

It read, GERONIMO.

Part XII

Anomalies

"Through every rift of discovery, some seeming anomaly drops out of the darkness, and falls, as a golden link into the great chain of order."

—Edwin Hubbel Chapin

Chapter 34

Siberia was the greatest wilderness on earth, vast, desolate, a seemingly unending stretch of pine and birch forests that stretched from the Ural Mountains to the Pacific. The land was dotted with a hundred thousand marshy bogs, traversable only when frozen over in winter, and broken by steep ridges and deep valleys cut by the aimless wandering rivers that had remained largely unexplored, even to modern times. In all that space, over five million square miles, there were just a scattering of tiny hamlets, and no more than a few thousand people.

Only along the Trans-Siberian rail line were their towns and cities worth the name, but north of that thin steel corridor the wilds of Siberia were largely uninhabited. A few that did live there had passed decades in complete isolation. One family of six, the famous Lykovs, would live more than 40 years without seeing another human being, completely oblivious to the course of modern events, the war and all that followed it, until they were eventually discovered by chance in a remote river gorge by geologists.

So the Siberian wilderness could swallow whole armies if it wished, and they could vanish never to be seen again. The stolid stands of larch, spruce, pine and birch sat in their unknowing silence, and the centuries passed, largely without witness by human eyes. To this day it is said that the wilderness hides undiscovered mysteries, and few have received more speculation than the strange event on the morning of June 30, 1908.

On that day something came from the deeps of outer space, streaking across the Siberian sky, and blasting into the valley of the Stony Tunguska River. One of the few humans that saw it descend described it very strangely: "a flying oblong body that narrowed towards one end, and light as bright as the sun." Some said it left a trail of smoke and dust behind it, and appeared in the shape of a pipe or fiery pillar. Another described it as a tube, and one claimed it actually changed course as it approached!

Whatever fell there was preceded by a strange magnetic storm that was detected on instruments in European universities for several days before the event. The impact explosion, thought to approach 20 megatons, was seen 1500 kilometers away, and the eerie light in the sky that lingered for days was noticed as far away as London. It devastated the 2150 square kilometers of the taiga forest in every direction, blowing them flat and burning them. It sent seismic waves trembling through the earth and atmosphere that were felt half way around the world, and the sound of thunderous explosions continued for fifteen minutes and were heard 1200 kilometers away.

The magnetic storm persisted another four hours after the impact. Optical anomalies were seen in the night sky all over Europe, along with strange Noctilucent clouds. Radiation was found at the site of the impact, and other anomalies in genetic mutations of the local Tungus people were reported over time. Yet trees that survived the impact went into a sudden, unexplained period of accelerated growth.

The site lay undiscovered for years, but an enterprising Russian scientist named Leonid Kulik had mounted four expeditions, the first in 1927, and the last in August of 1939—at least in the world Fedorov had been born to. He had found an old Siberian newspaper dating from 1908 that made a very unusual claim: "*...a huge meteorite is said to have fallen ... beyond the railway line near Filimonovo junction and less than 11 versts (12 kilometers) from Kansk. Its fall was accompanied by a frightful roar and a deafening crash, which was heard more than 40 versts away. The passengers of a train approaching the junction at the time were struck by the unusual noise. The driver stopped the train and the passengers poured out to examine the fallen object, but they were unable to study the meteorite closely because it was red hot...*"

If the report was true, the object or meteorite, perhaps a fragment of the larger Tunguska object, would have fallen very near the place where the Airship *Abakan* was now tethered to the tall mooring tower at Kansk, perhaps 25 kilometers from the small hamlet and rail station called Ilanskiy.

* * *

What was out there, thought Orlov as he gazed out the main gondola windows. What was causing the strange anomaly in the compass room? The Airship *Narva* had left Port Dikson, heading south to follow the broad gleaming course of the Yenisei River south. Many other rivers would feed the mighty Yenisei as it wandered north to the cold Kara Sea. They had passed these tributaries as they cruised south, using dead reckoning and compass navigation, and the visible track of the river itself to guide them. On the fifth tributary, the Angara River, they would branch away to follow that east briefly, and then look for the twin tributaries of the Burisa and Cuna rivers that would lead them southwest to a point just above Ilanskiy.

But something had gone wrong.

A day out of Port Dixon they had covered some 1600 kilometers when the skies began to thicken with rafts of dark, threatening clouds. Orlov saw streaks of white lightning rippling on the flanks of the storm, and the ship's Air Master, Captain Selikov, seemed worried.

"That's the problem out here," he said to Orlov. "No good weather maps, so we have to take things as they come. Now we shall have to climb," he said to his Elevatorman where he stood at the broad metal wheel. "Ten degree up bubble. I want to get above that storm front."

Narva had become much lighter by burning fuel over the last 1600 kilometers, and there was a fuel weight panel that calculated this, and allowed a man to select just the exact amount of water ballast to be dropped, lightning her further. The airship slowly nosed up into the grey sky, but the storm clouds towered up and up, rising in huge angry anvils hammered by some unseen god that sent thunder and lightning crackling through the sky. For a time they seemed to be navigating a great canyon of angry clouds. They had to get higher, and Selikov nervously watched the altitude increase.

Theoretically, an airship could climb to any height as long at the pressure between its helium gas and the reserve air sacks could be carefully balanced. Helium expanded as the atmospheric pressure weakened with altitude, which is why the helium gas sat inside a larger air filled bag where the air could be pumped out to a reserve air sack at the tail to allow the helium sack to expand. When the ship descended the process was reversed.

Even though it was late July, it was very cold as they gained elevation. The crew of the airship tramped about in their heavy woolen coats, hands tucked into mittens and thick gloves, heads lost in dark fleece hats. Orlov was no stranger to these conditions, having stood many a watch on the cold Arctic Seas, and he was wearing his thick leather service jacket and Naval Ushanka. As they climbed, he watched the ribbon of the river below them grow smaller, then cloud over, until they were lost in the thickening sky.

The Rudderman was standing with a firm grip on the wheel, feeling the winds beginning to buffet the airship's tail. The wheel itself vibrated in his grip from the pressure exerted on the rudder, over 600 feet behind them. The Elevatorman, a *mishman* named Yeseni, was exerting himself, spinning the wheel to maintain the inclination and trim of the ship.

The winds became more intense, and Orlov could feel the Duralumin frame of the airship shuddering and creaking as its great mass was moved by the storm. The Captain's eye strayed to the gas board, where the pressure in each of the big gas bags could be constantly monitored and vented if necessary, though with the rarity of helium that was seldom done, except in emergencies.

They were skirting the north edge of the storm, an old trick the airship captains had used known as 'pressure pattern navigation.' Winds in the northern hemisphere circulated around a low pressure center in a counter-clockwise rotation, so by skirting north they would move in the same direction of the winds around the storm.

"Rudderman, ten points to port," said Selikov. "We're drifting." The Carl Zeiss Drift indicator would normally scan the movement of terrain beneath the ship through a downward facing telescope, and the blur of the passing terrain would appear as a streak between two lines on the readout, which were rotated to match the desired course. As long as the streaks were within those lines, the course was true, and a nearby compass allowed the Captain to adjust his course magnetically as well.

With thick clouds and altitude there was little or no terrain to be seen, so the drift indicator became less useful. Selikov kept his eyes fixed on the compass instead, until it began to shudder and quiver oddly within its casing. He looked up, thinking it was only a temporary vibration caused by the buffeting winds, and when he looked at the compass again the needle was spinning wildly.

"What's this?" He tapped the compass, thinking to stabilize the vibration, but to no avail. Then he walked to the voice pipe and shouted down to the navigation room.

"Navigator, what is your main compass reading?"

There was a long pause before he got the answer he feared. *"Captain... I can't read anything. The compass needle is all over the dial!"*

Selikov frowned.

"What is wrong?" Orlov asked.

"This storm has the ship's compass all fouled up. We can't read our heading accurately. I will have to attempt radio direction finding if this keeps up. That might help, assuming we can pick up any stations in this region."

This was tried, but the same odd magnetic interference that had the compasses in a dizzy spin was also clouding over all the radio equipment. Then Troyak came up from the auxiliary crews cabin where his Marines were quartered, and huddled with Orlov over the situation.

"We cannot navigate," Orlov explained what had been happening. "What about your equipment, Troyak? Our transmitters are quite powerful."

"All of my equipment is fouled up too. We lost contact with *Kirov* half an hour ago, and now I can't raise them on any bandwidth."

"We must get clear of this damn storm," said Selikov. "Our only option now will be to descend to lower altitudes and see if we can spot the river again. Otherwise we are just flying blind here, and we could end up anywhere—miles from the river until we find another tributary to follow."

Selikov was able to steer wide of the storm cells, but new formations seemed to loom up, forcing him to some very tense moments in the navigation of the ship. It took some physical exertion to turn the rudder or elevator wheels, and the men there were soon drenched with sweat, in spite of the cold. The storm was much bigger than they had first believed, and it was long hours of harrowing flight before they could break into clear air again.

Captain Selikov was frustrated and ill at ease. "Well," he said finally. "We've got clear air for a descent. The only problem now is that I haven't the slightest idea where we are. Our heading has been unreadable since the compass failed, and it is still spinning like a top! We could be anywhere inside that circle, by my calculations." He pointed to a 'farthest on' circle he had drawn around their last known position on the chart, with a double line on one side indicating the probable direction.

"To make it simple, gentlemen," until I get down and find a recognizable river, we're lost. At the moment we can descend, but we're losing light fast and the moon will also set with the sun, so it's going to be a very dark night for the next six hours, and navigation will be almost impossible, even if we do find the river. Without that compass, we'll simply have to hover until daylight."

Orlov folded his arms, frowning.

"Welcome to Siberia," Troyak said gruffly.

It was only necessary to become ever so slightly lighter than air to climb, and heavier than air to descend, but the process often took time. It would take three hours of careful maneuvering and ballast recovery via the air condenser equipment and rain collectors, but they eventually secured enough new ballast to begin a steady descent.

At about 6000 feet the landforms were clearly visible again, and they maneuvered towards the gleaming course of a distant river, thinking they could now get back on track. Though the storm had abated, the magnetic disturbance was still giving their compass equipment fits, but the river would take them where they needed to go—or so they believed.

The light faded with the setting sun at 21:30, and it would not rise again until almost five AM. With shadows lengthening on the landforms below, Selikov drifted lower, safely above the forest but at an altitude where he could try and keep the river beneath them. Speed was reduced to the bare minimum as darkness folded over them like a heavy quilt.

It was a very long wait for the sun, even if the night was fleeting by normal standards. They drifted over the endless dark wilderness, hovering with the passing clouds, lost in the realm of osprey and eagle. The crew slept fitfully that night, with Orlov huddled in his cabin trying to keep warm with a good wool blanket.

Hours later a weary Selikov was back on the bridge with Orlov and Troyak, shaking his head as he studied his charts, then scanned the surrounding terrain beneath them. They had found the river, but Captain Selikov remained troubled, shouting back and forth with the navigation room, and finally going there himself for a lengthy conference. When he returned he had a crestfallen expression on his face.

"Good news, and bad news," he said to Orlov and Troyak. The good news is that we have finally determined where we are. That fork in the river two hours back at sunrise was the village of Bajhit. I hoped it might be Motiygino on the Angara, which is why I steered to follow the course of the lower tributary. That was supposed to take us very near the objective."

"And the bad news?" Orlov wanted to know the score.

"We have drifted off course during the storm. That river we were following was not the Angara and we are well to the northwest of where we wanted to go."

"Can't we follow this river south?"

"No, I'm afraid we would not wish to follow this river, Mister Orlov. It has haunted the nightmares of children in Siberia for generations now. Perhaps you know it, Sergeant Troyak? This is the Stony Tunguska."

"Tunguska?" Orlov had heard the name. "Isn't that the place where the asteroid fell? Scientists have been trying to figure out what it was for years."

"Yes, something happened there, but I am not a scientist," said Selikov. "Science has always been too strong a drink for me. There was a German physicist who put it very well. I think his name was Heisenberg. He said: 'The first gulp from the glass of natural sciences will turn you into an atheist, but at the bottom of the glass God is waiting for you."

"Or the devil," said Orlov.

Selikov smiled, rolling up his navigation chart. "Well, gentlemen, I prefer to find God in a cathedral. And I think we should get as far from this place as we possibly can, and that soon."

Chapter 35

Admiral Tovey was not at his office when the call came in, but the secretary took down the note and placed it in a pile of ten others just like it on his note needle. Tovey came in and sat down that evening, frustrated and bothered by the grilling he had been through in the Admiralty offices. The First Sea Lord, Admiral Dudley Pound, had been particularly trying with his questions and innuendo, intimating that the entire operation had been blighted with incompetence, that the fleet flagship had gone running about like a chicken with its head cut off—those were the man's exact words—a chicken with its head cut off!

Whitworth had been somewhat more lenient, sizing up the situation in light of the odds we were facing and putting a better hat on it. "Damn lucky we made port with anything at all," he said. Four German battleships, with two heavy cruisers, three new destroyers and an aircraft carrier—all coordinating in one sweep south—it was something the Germans had never attempted, and a harbinger of hard time ahead for the Royal Navy if they ever tried it again.

"To think that we turned that German fleet for home is certainly the best we could have hoped for," said Whitworth, god bless the man. But Pound was steaming over a thick report from Rosyth on the damage sustained by *Hood*, materials needed for repair, time to be laid up. He was so single minded about it that they never did get round to the matter of the aerial rocketry they had observed, and the role it may have played in the outcome of the battle. That was another battle he would likely fight with Pound at tomorrow's meeting. It was all very, very frustrating.

Tovey looked at the stack of messages, reaching for them out of habit, or a pathetic attempt to chase his discomfiture over the meeting by seeing what else was on his plate, unattended while they had him on the chair. He would normally start from the bottom of the pile, the oldest messages that might need his attention first, but instead he just took up the first one there and saw a name he was not familiar with, yet it was noting a call from a place that immediately got his attention.

The note read simply: *Turing, Alan. Regarding Kirov incident.*

That had to refer to the Russian cruiser, and it was coming from Hut Four, Bletchley Park. Why did he feel this odd sense of familiarity in that brief message. Was it the name? Alan Turing... Yes, he had heard of the man, one of the boys at BP sorting out the German Naval code.

Tovey raised an eyebrow, curious. He should have put the matter aside and called for a cup of Earl Grey to settle himself, but there was something about that name, about that note, that made him very curious. There was no other way to describe the feeling, a kind of breathless anticipation, a feeling of stony presentiment settling over him. So he reached for the telephone and had them ring this man back on a secure line. The voice at the other end sounded thin and high, and beset with a nervous edge. He introduced himself politely enough, saying he had been asked to help sort out the matter of the Russian ship that had been encountered just before the recent engagement.

"This may be an odd question, Admiral," said Turing on the line, his voice sounding distended, as though stretched by time and distance, a crackle of frosty interference clouding the end. *"May I ask if the word Geronimo means anything to you in regards to this ship?"*

The word... The word Geronimo... *Geronimo!* Tovey put his hand on his forehead, and he almost dropped the receiver. What was it? Yes, he had heard that word. It struck a deep nerve, jarring him, yet where? What was it? He immediately arranged to go and find out.

That afternoon a car pulled up beneath the stately green bell dome and high arched entry to the estate of Bletchley Park. Tovey had wriggled out of his meeting with Admiral Pound, informing him that BP had special intelligence regarding the subject of that day's discussion. He requested a 24 hour delay, and went straight to the horse's mouth.

Tovey entered the simple office, noting the plain map on the wall behind Turing's desk, the standard black telephone, the odd goggles resting on a pile of papers in his inbox tray—and Turing. He was hunched over a photograph, making a close inspection with a magnifying glass and completely oblivious to the Admiral's presence.

"Mister Turing?"

The man looked up, surprised. "Oh… Excuse me Admiral." He stood up immediately. "I was so focused on my work that I did not even hear you come in. People shuffle in and out of here all day and I hardly give them any notice. Please be seated."

Turing extended a handshake and Tovey sat down, feeling like he had sat there many times before, still strangely familiar with this man in spite of the fact that he knew this was their first meeting.

"I assume those are the photographs we sent over from our encounter with this Russian cruiser?"

"Some of them…" Turing gave Tovey a look that seemed to harbor a warning. "I turned up the others in an old box that was stashed below the bottom shelf in our photo archives." The man seemed to hesitate, as if he were uncertain of himself, like a man edging out onto frozen ice and hoping it would not give way beneath his feet and send him plummeting into frigid water.

"Then you've turned up good information on this ship? That's precisely what I am here to see. Admiral Pound is already beside himself over recent events, this business with the French now becoming a major blow up as it has."

"That was most regrettable," said Turing.

"What was this reference to Geronimo about, Turing? When you mentioned it on the telly I thought I had it right at the edge of my mind, on the tip of my tongue, as it were, but then it completely eluded me."

"Strange you should say that, Admiral. I felt the same way. It's just that this box I pulled out was given that label, and taped up as if it were not to be opened again anytime soon."

"I see. And the contents?"

Turing gave Tovey a lingering look, then averted his eyes, deciding something. He simply handed the Admiral the photograph he had been scrutinizing, and let it speak for itself.

Tovey raised an eyebrow. A ship, making a wide turn, and it was clearly the battlecruiser that had come abeam of HMS *Invincible* for that unusual meeting at sea with the Russian Admiral.

"Where did this come from? Was it one of the air reconnaissance photos taken by the boys off *Ark Royal?* I haven't seen it before." Yet even as he said that he knew he had seen it. Yes, he *had* seen it, though he could not remember when. The feeling was very frustrating.

"No, Admiral. That photograph was taken by an American PBY, if you'd care to have a look at the label on the back."

"American?" Tovey flipped the photo over, quite surprised to read the notation. "It's misdated," he said flatly. "August 4, 1941? They've got today's date correct, but a full year on."

"That is what I first thought," said Turing, still somewhat hesitant. "But do note the other information provided. You'll see the notation PBY-6B, Squadron 74, Vosseler. That's the plane and pilot."

"Out of Reykjavik?"

"That is what the photo label indicates, sir."

"I wasn't aware there were any American planes operating out of Iceland. We've barely got our own trousers on there. I requested Fleet Air Arm units, but they've only just arrived at Reykjavik."

"Indeed, sir." Turing said nothing, simply handing Tovey yet another photo.

This time the image was a typical gun camera still. "My God," he said. "When did this happen, during the recent engagement in the Denmark Strait?"

"Not according to the photo label, sir."

Tovey flipped the image over again, his eyes darkening as he read the information: *Bristol Beaufighter VI-C – 248 Squadron, Takali, Malta. Melville-Jackson - August 11, 1942 – Tyrrhenian Sea."*

"Misdated by two years this time... And what's this rubbish about the Tyrrhenian Sea?"

"I have five more photos with identical labels."

"248 Squadron?"

"I went to the trouble of looking them up," said Turing. "They were operating with Fighter Command as of 22 April, 1940, flying fighter patrols over the North Sea from R.A.F. Dyce, Aberdeen, and R.A.F. Montrose. They have since been returned to Coastal Command control as of 20 June. Latest information has the squadron at R.A.F. Sumburgh in the Shetland Islands as of 31 July 1940, flying reconnaissance and anti-shipping missions off the coast of Norway." Turing let the facts speak for themselves.

"I don't understand. Then why would this photo be labeled this way and show this unit at Takali airfield on Malta?"

"My question precisely, sir."

Tovey gave him a frustrated look. "See here, Mister Turing, we generally come to you people for answers, not more questions. This is obviously nonsense."

"Quite so, sir. The entire box." He now pointed to the box beside his desk where Tovey could see many more fat plain manila envelopes in a row."

"The entire box? What are you saying?"

"I wish I knew, sir. What I have found here makes no sense. It's either complete rubbish and nonsense, as you have put it, or perhaps someone's idea of a very bad joke. Yet I have opened several of these envelopes and all I have found within was a mystery so profound that I find myself completely shaken. It was then that I made my call to you, sir."

"A mystery? Explain yourself."

"I have studied photo after photo from that box, sir. They are all arranged, nice and neat, very proper, and following all established protocols for labeling and attachments."

"Except for the rubbish."

"Exactly, sir. Yet the photographs... A picture is worth a thousand words, is it not? A foolhardy man might label those photos any way he pleases, but the photographs themselves do not lie. That gun camera shot for example, the one purportedly taken by this Melville-Jackson, well it would be very difficult to fake such an image. I'd say impossible."

"Are you saying someone deliberately mislabeled the photographs? I'll have the man's head!"

"Unfortunately that will be somewhat inconvenient for me, sir, as I found several photographs where I, myself, appear to have completed the labels."

"You?"

"Yes sir. This one here, for example. See the notations? It looks like someone was using a shadow cast on the forward deck of the ship in that image to work out its dimensions—nearly 900 feet long, a hundred feet abeam—big as *Hood*, sir, or even HMS *Invincible*. That someone was me. Those are my initials there at the bottom."

Tovey steamed. "Have you summoned me all the way from Admiralty headquarters to make a confession, Mister Turing? Are you telling me you botched the labeling on these photographs, or worse, that you did this for sport?"

"Quite the contrary, sir. I must tell you now that I have never set eyes on any of the material in that box—yet the evidence of my own eyes now tells quite another story. A man knows his own initials when he sees them. Those are mine, but I swear to you, sir, that I cannot recall ever seeing that photo, or making those notations."

Tovey listened, shrugging, and clearly unhappy. "I was told you were somewhat absent minded at times," he began. "A bit of an eccentric, or so the rumors go. You've heard them."

"Of course, Admiral. But I can now hand you five or ten other photographs labeled by Peter Twinn, also initialed. He's an associate here. There are numerous others, all processed and labeled by trusted men here, and a few by people I have never heard of."

"This is a group effort at mayhem with the files? Outrageous!"

"It would be if the men in question were foolish minded individuals, sir. But I am not a fool, and contrary to anything you may have heard, the only games we play here are a good spot of chess from time to time. Otherwise, I assure you we take to our work with the utmost seriousness. Yet I do not have to defend myself here, or anyone else. That box contains photographs that will astound you, sir. Quite shocking, really. How many *King George V* class ships do we now have in the fleet?"

"What? Just the two newly commissioned ships. Three more in the shipyards."

"Well have a look at this, sir." Turing handed over another photo, and Tovey spent a very long time with it, holding it up, his eyes reflecting a gamut of emotion from surprise to recognition to fear.

"God in his heaven…"

"And all's well with the world," Turing finished. "Well not quite. As you can see there are four *King George V* class ships in that image, all at sea, and the label will indicate that photograph was taken in the Western approaches to the Straits of Gibraltar… in 1942."

"That simply cannot be. It must be a double exposure." But even as he said that Tovey knew that *King George V* and *Prince of Wales* were only now scheduled for a good active duty shakedown cruise. When might that photo have been taken to find them at sea like that? The photos next in that series were equally astounding. There was the ship, the Russian battlecruiser, clearly photographed as it emerged from the Straits of Gibraltar. He could make out the distinctive landform of Isla de las Palomas on the far left, and something about that island stirred a deep memory, more a feeling than anything he could really recall.

"There's more, sir," Turing said quietly. "The entire box—gun camera footage, film reels, and voluminous reports and other attachments." Now he handed Tovey a sheaf of plain typewritten papers, and if Tovey thought he was flummoxed before, this was the final straw.

Chapter 36

He looked at them, unbelieving, yet utterly convinced on another level as to what he was seeing. To the Admiral's profound amazement he was soon reading what appeared to be his own reports, dated from August of 1941 through August of 1942, regarding a coded series of incidents under the broad designation *Geronimo*. Where Turing had gaped at his own initials on the back of reconnaissance photos, Tovey now stood dumbfounded to see his full signature, unmistakably affixed to the reports Turing had handed him. If this was an elaborate ruse, a forgery, it was expertly done. Tovey recognized his own unique style in the way he would format his briefings and reports, and his 'voice' in the text itself.

He sat, stupefied, bewildered and badly bothered, speechless for some time. "This is absolutely impossible," he said at last. "Impossible… Yet here it is. This is my signature, yet it is quite obvious that I could not have written any such report. Royal Navy ships dueling with this Russian battlecruiser?"

"It was more than a duel, sir," Turing ventured. "I've been reading all morning, and this documents involvement by the American Navy, the use of some rather amazing weaponry, action against the Italians, a full out running gun battle with our own *Nelson* and *Rodney*, and more. Apparently that little war was ended by truce in a meeting between you and the commander of this mystery ship designated *Geronimo*, and it was at that meeting that the ship was finally determined to be of Russian origins—a ship firing advanced rocketry that was effective against both aircraft and surface ships."

"Someone has a rather bold imagination," said Tovey at last. "This sounds to me like a rank and file effort at drafting up an alternate history, a work of pure fiction, yet so chillingly real. I could swear that report you just handed me was written by my own hand, and the signature certainly was. What could this possibly be about? Are the two of us completely daft?"

"This evidence is simply too authentic in format and detail, sir. No one outside Bletchley Park could have done this, and I can assure you that no one inside it has the slightest bit to do with it. We would have neither the time nor the inclination to produce such a complex fabrication. And yet, my initials are there as plain as your own signature. This may also seem odd, but I have the distinct impression that you and I have discussed all this, in great detail, at some time in the past."

"Mister Turing, correct me if I may have forgotten a prior encounter, but is this the first time we have ever met in person?"

"It is, sir, and I thank you for coming, and putting up with what must certainly seem a complete crock of mad hatter stew. I am as perplexed about all this as you are, yet the details presented in these documents are chillingly accurate—units, designations, officers involved. Whoever wrote these documents would have had to be privy to information that no one head might hold. That aside, the photographs, sir. These images simply cannot be fabricated."

"I should think not."

"If you think you are confounded now, I dare you to venture further into the contents of that box. Things begin rooted to the here and now, familiar names and such. There is, indeed, a Melville-Jackson, for example. I looked up his service record. The man is presently posted to No. 236 Squadron R.A.F., flying Bristol Blenheims on convoy patrols and escort sorties over the Channel and Western Approaches. Then there are references to Royal Navy Fleet operations that are either top secret, in the works, or completely fabricated. One was called 'Jubilee,' another 'Pedestal.' There are documents referring to a FRUMEL unit in Australia, an acronym for Fleet Radio Unit, Melbourne, yet no such unit exists. I looked into that."

"Australia? What would the Aussies have to do with any of this?"

"This ship apparently went round the Cape of Good Hope to the Pacific and tangled with the Japanese navy as well."

"The Japanese?"

"It's right in the box, sir. Envelope number seven. You will find photographs taken by coast watchers near Darwin—of the same ship. The really alarming thing is that the reports reference action by the Japanese against Darwin, and against the American Navy in the Solomons. Yet we both know there is no naval war underway in the Pacific, at least not yet."

Tovey reached up, took off his hat, and set it quietly in his lap. He knew all of this, on some deep unfathomable level of his being. It was all true, yet impossible. It could simply not be possible in any wise. It was madness, sheer lunacy, an anomaly so impenetrable that it numbed the mind. It was *Geronimo.*

"Alright," he said, his mind settling on the only thing left that might explain the situation, like a man scuppered into the sea grasping at any floating spar he could reach. "Suppose all this is some complex deception plan, aimed at throwing off the Germans. Suppose these reports were prepared by some secret arm of the government, and there are many, Mister Turing."

"How would you explain the uncanny resemblance to reports you might draft yourself, Admiral?"

"It would be challenging, but it might be mimicked. And the signature could have been forged."

"The photographs?"

Tovey stumbled at that. The photographs were the bulk of the information. There were images of the ship in many different settings. Was it possible that some photo alchemist in a hidden special section was turning them out, superimposing negatives, conjuring this all up in a darkroom witches brew of deception?

"The photographic evidence is daunting, but I must admit the possibility of tampering and tomfoolery before I can go down the lane to the next house, Turing. For to knock on that door admits to sheer bedlam. You and I both know that these cannot be images and reports from 1941 or 1942! That is madness. So it must be something else, correct?"

"Yes, it must be, but I cannot shake the awful feeling I have about it all, Admiral. It's as if we have had this discussion before, and bent our minds around it at the edge of that insane conclusion that we cannot admit to here and now. I can say nothing more than that, but I have the most nagging feeling that something is terribly amiss here. Have a look at some of that gun camera footage and you will be utterly amazed, as I was. The question now is what do we do with all this?"

"Assuming the only logical explanation that I have put forward, that this is material prepared as a deception, then we should keep it safe and very secure. Say nothing about it to your colleagues, Turing. The fewer cooks around this kettle, the better. However, I should like it if you would select four or five photographs for me. Choose images you think are particularly compelling. In a few days time I have scheduled a meeting with the commander of that ship—*Kirov*. Yes, it is a Russian ship after all, in truth as well as in that fiction we've uncovered from your storeroom."

"One remark, if I may sir. This ship first appeared just a few weeks ago, right in the middle of your recent operation against the Germans. Before that time nobody heard of this ship. Are we to assume that all this material was doctored up in the last week or two, then tucked away in this box and hidden in the archive? I must tell you that when I first dragged it from its shadowed resting place, it was covered in dust as if it had been sitting there for years, completely undisturbed."

Tovey did not quite know what to say to that. Turing made a telling point. How could all these reports and photographs have been assembled, all about this ship, and in so little time. There were only a very few men that even knew about the meeting he had with the Russian Admiral, though many had seen the ship when it came alongside *Invincible*.

"Half my squadron had a good long look at this ship, Turing. Word gets out. In any case, I will be meeting this Russian Admiral again in a few days time, that is unless I find myself beheaded by Admiral Pound, or locked away in the Tower of London."

He stood up, putting his cap back on and straightening his jacket, as if to set all right again, smoothing out the impossible wrinkle this box had introduced. He pointed to the box.

"Let's keep that material safe, shall we, and just between the two of us for the time being."

"Of course, Admiral. I'll see to it. Shall I select a few photographs for you now?"

"Take your time, but send them to my Admiralty office by special courier. Mark it eyes only, and to my attention."

"Of course, sir."

Tovey nodded and began to leave, but Turing cleared his throat, needing to say one last thing. "Something else, Mister Turing?"

"Well sir, in considering your assumption, that all these documents and photos were prepared as part of a deception plan, how could anyone predict these events? These photos and reports are all detailing things that have clearly not happened, but in a manner that suggests they *did* happen, that all the material in that box is history. Why would anyone create material about an engagement in the Pacific that they could never know about in any wise? It would all be a wild guess and a terrible waste of time."

Tovey looked at him, thinking. "Interesting point," he said quietly. "Yes, I suppose it would be a waste of time, and I can't see why anyone would do such a thing."

"Oh, that question is answered in envelope nine, sir."

Tovey raised an eyebrow. "Envelope nine?"

"Yes sir. There is one final document there that may be of interest to you. It indicates that the events documented in these files are to be classified top secret, so secret that only a handful of people would ever know about any of it. That code word I telephoned you about—*Geronimo*—well it was supposedly known to no more than ten men, a group known as 'the Watch,' and you may be surprised to learn that the First Sea Lord, most everyone else of note in the Admiralty, and the Prime Minister are not on the list."

"The Watch?"

"Yes sir, and as to the mystery of who might have wasted their time with all of this, the rascals are clearly identified."

"Out with it, Turing. Who's behind all this?"

Turing smiled. *"We* are sir… You and I—at least according to the report, and the two signatures affixed to it, in envelope nine."

"You mean to say that someone is trying to use our names and reputations in an attempt to lend credulity to this box of fairy tales?"

That wasn't exactly what Turing meant to say, but he decided to be very discrete here, and simply smiled. "Apparently so, sir."

Tovey shook his head, clearly bothered by all of this. As he reached the door he stopped, not knowing why, a rhyme in his head that he could not account for, like something that had just welled up from some deep, unconscious pool in his mind. He looked over his shoulder at Turing, a strange light in his eye.

"Byron," he said quietly. "Do you read poetry, Mister Turing?"

"Sir? Well, now that you mention it, I do. Yes, I am particularly fond of Lord Byron's muse."

Tovey smiled.

"I thought as much," he said with the nod of his head. "Good day to you."

Turing watched him go, feeling himself to be the biggest fool in the world. Here was the Admiral of the Home Fleet, and what did I summon him here to see? That box full of parlor tricks and deceit— fairy tales as he called it. Of course his explanation is the only possible answer to all this. It may even be that there is some secret operation on and I've gone and stuck my thumb in the pie. There is simply no other way to think about this.

He looked at the box, frowning, feeling the red heat of embarrassment rise on his neck. The Admiral must have thought he was a complete idiot. Yet on another level he could sense something more had transpired here. Tovey was genuinely shocked by the evidence contained in that box. The word *Geronimo* seemed to jolt him with an almost electric current. Those photographs deeply disturbed him.

What was that bit at the end about Byron's poetry? Ah, the photos. Well I'll fish about a bit more and find the best of the lot. As he did so, his hand fell on something cold and hard at the bottom of the box. When he pulled it out he was struck yet again with that same feeling of profound anomaly. It was a watch, and not just any watch. It was his own Gallet Multichron Astronomic! He had been missing it for a month! What in the world was it doing here in this old box?

Then he noted the date and time the watch had stopped. The calendar window read September… In the year 1942. What in God's name was going on here? Was he being framed? He knew there were men spreading rumors, talking about his strange ways and habits. He knew there were other men keeping a close eye on him—on all of us here at Bletchley Park.

He sighed. Looking again at some notes he had scribbled on the back of a photo. Yes, he clearly recognized his handwriting there. How could anyone mimic it with such uncanny accuracy? Why they would have to fish about in my waste basket and find all my doodles and notes, wouldn't they? Just like this bit here on this photo.

He read the note: *Dilly's 'L' Crib!* What was that about? The words meant something to him. Dilly Knox was one of the team members working on Enigma. 'Cribs' were little lapses and errors of judgment that the Enigma machine operators might use in the formatting of their messages. They might always start a message with the same word, for example, or make careless and repetitive keystrokes that could become clues as to how the code could be interpreted. But he could not think what Dilly's L Crib might be. Knox had been active as a cryptologist since 1914 when he worked in the Royal Navy's cryptological effort in Room 40 of the Old Admiralty Building. He was apparently on to something again.

That was another thing that bothered Turing. If this was some elaborate hoax, a planned deception, the perpetrators had seen to the smallest of details, like that errant scribble of a note that was all too typical of his own habits. They might have fished it out of the waste bin, he thought again. It might have been something I wrote days or weeks ago. I can hardly remember half the mumbo jumbo that I run through my own head on any given day.

He finished up, selecting his photos and pocketing his Gallet watch, glad to have it back again, but very suspicious as to how it went missing now, and how it found itself in that hidden box under a patina of dust that looked to have accumulated over long years. It was more than strange. There was an eerie quality to his feeling about all this now, and one that got his hackles up, chilling him with implications he did not wish to even consider.

He sent off his envelope to the Admiralty as Tovey asked, put the box right back where he found it, and went about his business again, a good deal more edgy and ill at ease for all his trouble.

The next time he saw the tall bespectacled Dilly Knox, he remembered the note. In a very casual manner he asked his colleague a brief question. "How goes it, Dilly? Any Cribs this week?"

"What's that, Turing? Oh yes! It seems we picked up a test message from a German operator who must have been all thumbs. I was just looking over the message when it occurred to me that there wasn't a single instance of the letter L in the whole damn message!"

Turing knew immediately what that meant! Any time an Enigma machine key was depressed, it would return any letter of the alphabet except the one letter labeled on the key being used. If there were no instances of the letter L in the message, then it was a clear tip that the key labeled L had indeed been used, and most likely multiple times.

"On a hunch I assumed this operator had gotten very lazy and just kept using that single key. Well we broke that whole message, and sure enough, I was correct. It just read LLLLL." Dilly smiled. "I'm calling it my L crib, Alan. Make a note of it. It will likely go down in history!" Knox laughed and was on his way.

Turing did not laugh.

Apparently I *did* make a note of it, he thought darkly. Right on the back of that bloody photo. And yet I've heard this from Knox for the very first time, and just this minute.

Just this minute…

His hand fell on the watch in his pocket now.

Yes! It was all about time!

The Saga Continues…

Altered States: Volume III ~ Hinge of Fate

As Turing and Tovey pursue the mystery of the strange mother lode of information on the Russian ship, Admiral Volsky sails to meet with the British on the Faeroes, bearing an offer of formal alliance between Soviet Russia and Great Britain. Meanwhile, the Germans plan a fateful meeting of their own, at the small village of Hendaye on the border near Spain. There Hitler hopes to secure another vital ally so that he can breathe life into Admiral Raeder's long advocated plan for a Mediterranean strategy. It will begin with 'Operation Felix' the assault on Gibraltar, and only one man stands in the way, el Caudillo himself, Francisco Franco.

As Britain steels itself for possible invasion, Tovey must now rally his battered fleet to the defense of Gibraltar, England's Rock in the Mediterranean and the hinge of fate that could turn the entire course of the war should it fall. Opposing him are the powerful new French battleships at Casablanca and Dakar, and a resurgent Kriegsmarine led by a fearsome new gladiator, the *Hindenburg*.

Meanwhile, The airship *Narva* faces danger and mystery on the Stony Tunguska, even while elements of two other airship fleets converge on another hinge of fate, the inn at Ilanskiy. Action, mystery and intrigue pulse through this compelling continuation of the amazing *Kirov Saga!*

THE KIROV SERIES ~ BY JOHN SCHETTLER

Kirov

The battlecruiser *Kirov* is the most power surface combatant that ever put to sea. Built from the bones of all four prior *Kirov* Class battlecruisers, she is updated with Russia's most lethal weapons, given back her old name, and commissioned in the year 2020. A year later, with tensions rising to the breaking point between Russia and the West, *Kirov* is completing her final missile trials in the Arctic Sea when a strange accident transports her to another time. With power no ship in the world can match, much less comprehend, she must decide the fate of nations in the most titanic conflict the world has ever seen—WWII.

Kirov II – *Cauldron of Fire*

Kirov crosses the Atlantic to the Mediterranean Sea when she suddenly slips in time again and re-appears a year later, in August of 1942. Beset with enemies on every side and embroiled in one of the largest sea battles of the war, the ship races for Gibraltar and the relatively safe waters of the Atlantic. Meanwhile, the brilliant Alan Turing has begun to unravel the mystery of what this ship could be, but can he convince the Admiralty? Naval action abounds in this fast paced second volume of the *Kirov* series trilogy.

Kirov III - *Pacific Storm*

Admiral Tovey's visit to Bletchley Park soon reaches an astounding conclusion when the battlecruiser *Kirov* vanishes once again to a desolate future. Reaching the Pacific the ship's officers and crew soon learn that *Kirov* has once again moved in time. Now First Officer Anton Fedorov is shocked to learn the true source of the great variation in time that has led to the devastated future they have come from and the demise of civilization itself. They are soon discovered by a Japanese fleet and the ship now faces its most dangerous and determined challenge ever when they are stalked by the Japanese 5th

Carrier Division and eventually confronted by a powerful enemy task force led by the battleship Yamato, and an admiral determined to sink this phantom ship, or die trying. In this amazing continuation to the popular *Kirov* series, the most powerful ships ever conceived by two different eras clash in a titanic final battle that could decide the fate of nations and the world itself.

Kirov Saga: *Men Of War ~ Book IV*

Kirov returns home to a changed world in the year 2021, and as the Russian Naval Inspectorate probes the mystery of the ship's disappearance, Anton Fedorov begins to unravel yet another dilemma—the secret of Rod 25. The world is again steering a dangerous course toward the great war that blackened the shores of a distant future glimpsed by the officers and crew. Fedorov has come to believe that time is waiting on the resolution of one crucial unresolved element from their journey to the past—the fate of Gennadi Orlov.

Join Admiral Leonid Volsky, Captain Vladimir Karpov, and Anton Fedorov as they sleuth the mystery of Orlov's fate and launch a mission to the past to find him before the world explodes in the terror and fury of a great air and naval conflict in the Pacific. It is a war that will span the globe from the Gulf of Mexico to the Middle East and through the oil rich heart of Central Asia to the wide Pacific, but somehow one man's life holds the key to its prevention. Yet other men are aware of Orlov's identity as a crewman from the dread raider they came to call *Geronimo*, and they too set their minds on finding him first...in 1942! Men of war from the future and past now join in the hunt while the military forces of Russia, China, and the West maneuver to the great chessboard of impending conflict.

Kirov Saga: *Nine Days Falling, Book V*

As Fedorov launches his daring mission to the past to rescue Orlov, Volsky does not know where or how to find the team, or even if they have safely made the dangerous transition to the 1940s....But other men know, from the dark corners of Whitehall to the KGB. And other men also continue to stalk Orlov in that distant era, led by Captain John Haselden and the men of 30 Commando. The long journey west is fraught with danger for Fedorov's team when they encounter something bewildering and truly astounding, an incident that leads them deeper into the mystery of Rod-25.

Meanwhile, *Kirov* has put to sea and now forms the heart of a powerful battlegroup commanded by Captain Vladimir Karpov. He is soon confronted by the swift deployment of the American Carrier Strike Group Five out of Yokosuka Japan in a tense standoff at sea that threatens to explode into violence at any moment. The fuse of conflict is lit across the globe, for the dread war has finally begun when the Chinese make good on their threat to secure their long wayward son—Taiwan. From the pulsing bitstream of the Internet, the deep void of outer space, the oil soaked waters of the Persian Gulf and Black Sea, to the riveting naval combat in the Pacific, the world descends in nine grueling days, swept up in the maelstrom and chaos of war.

This is the story of that deadly war to end all wars, and the desperate missions from the future and past to find the one man who can prevent it from ever happening, Gennadi Orlov. Can the mystery of Rod-25 and Orlov be solved before the ICBMs are finally launched?

Kirov Saga: *Fallen Angels ~ Book VI*

The war continues on both land and sea as China invades Taiwan and North Korea joins to launch a devastating attack. Yet *Kirov* and the heart of the Red Banner Pacific Fleet has vanished, blown into the past by the massive wrath of the Demon Volcano. There Captain Karpov finds himself at the dying edge of the last great war, yet his own inner demons now wage war with his conscience as he contemplates another decisive intervention.

After secretly assisting the Soviet invasion of the Kuriles and engaging a small US scouting force in the region, Karpov has drawn the attention of Admiral Halsey's powerful 3rd Fleet. Now Halsey sends one of the toughest fighting Admirals of the war north to investigate, the hero of the Battle off Samar, Ziggy Sprague, and fast and furious sea battles are the order of the day.

Meanwhile tensions rise in the Black Sea as the Russian mission to rescue Fedorov and Orlov has now been expanded to include a way to try and deliver new control rods to *Kirov* from the same batch and lot as the mysterious Rod-25. Will they work? Yet Admiral Volsky learns that the Russian Black Sea Fleet has engaged well escorted units of a British oil conveyor, Fairchild Inc., and the fires of war soon endanger his mission.

All efforts are now focused on a narrow stretch of coastline on the Caspian Sea, where men of war from the future and past are locked in a desperate struggle to decide the outcome of history itself. Naval combat, both future and past, combine with action and intrigue as Volsky's mission is launched and the mystery of Rod-25 and Fedorov's strange experience on the Trans-Siberian Rail is finally revealed. Can they stop the nuclear holocaust of the Third World War in 2021 or will it begin off the coast of Japan in 1945?

Kirov Saga: *Devil's Garden ~ Book VII*

The stunning continuation to the *Kirov* saga extends the action, both past and present, as the prelude to the Great War moves into its final days. The last remnant of the Red Banner Pacific Fleet has fought its duel with Halsey in the Pacific, resorting to nuclear weapons in the last extreme—but what has happened to *Kirov* and *Orlan*?

Now the many story threads involving Fairchild Inc. and the desperate missions to find Orlov launched by both Haselden and Fedorov all converge in the vortex of time and fate on the shores of the Caspian Sea. Fedorov and Troyak lead an amphibious assault at Makhachkala, right into the teeth of the German advance. Meanwhile, Admiral Volsky and Kamenski read the chronology of events to peek at the outcome and discover the verdict of history. Can it still be changed?

Turn the page with Admiral Volsky and learn the fate of Orlov, Fedorov, Karpov and the world itself. Follow the strange and enigmatic figure of Sir Roger Ames, Duke of Elvington as he reveals a plot, and a plan, older than history itself on the windswept shores of Lindisfarne Castle.

Kirov Saga: Armageddon ~ Book VIII

The lines of fate have brought the most powerful ship in the world to a decisive place in history. Driven by his own inner demons, Captain Karpov now believes that with *Kirov* in 1908 he is truly invincible, and his aim is to impose his will on that unsuspecting world and reverse the cold fate of Russian history from 1908 to the 21st century. But it is not just the fate of a single nation at stake now, but that of all the world.

Shocked by Karpov's betrayal, Anton Fedorov plans a mission to stop the Captain before he can do irreversible damage to the cracked mirror of time. Now Admiral Volsky must do everything possible to launch this final mission aboard the nuclear attack submarine *Kazan*. The journey to the Sea of Japan becomes a perilous one when the Americans and Japanese begin to hunt *Kazan* in the dangerous waters of 2021.

Join Anton Fedorov, Admiral Volsky, Chief Dobrynin, and Gennadi Orlov aboard *Kazan* as they launch this last desperate mission to confront the man, and the ship, that now threatens to change all history and unravel the fabric of fate and time itself.

Kirov Saga: Altered States

Kirov and *Kazan* move forward yet find themselves stuck in the midst of WWII once again, only the world is not the same! The consequences of all their interventions in history have now calcified to a new reality. The political borders of nations have been re-drawn, Colonial powers vie for control of the undeveloped world, and Russia itself is a divided nation. Discovering they still possess a decisive edge in weapons technology they must now decide which side to take to end a long and terrible war that threatens millions more lives.

Altered States ~ *Volume II: Darkest Hour*

The first rounds have fallen, heavy shells smashing against the armored conning tower of HMS *Hood*, stunning the ship and its stolid Admiral Holland. Yet *Hood* fights on, her guns raging in reprisal as the pride of two navies meet in the largest naval engagement since Jutland. Even as Admiral Tovey reaches the action, the shadow of Hoffmann's battlegroup looms over his shoulder and the odds stack ever higher against the embattled ships of Home Fleet. Off to the north the *Stukas* rush to re-arm aboard carrier *Graf Zeppelin*, while far to the south another ship hastens north to the scene, from a time and place incomprehensible to the men now locked in a desperate struggle raging on a blood red sea that may decide the fate of England in 1940. Can they engage without shattering the fragile mirror of history yet again?

Learn the outcome and follow *Kirov* north as it heads to home waters, determined to meet the man that may have changed the course of all history, Sergei Kirov. Meanwhile the action moves to the Med where the young Christopher Wells is dispatched to Force H. The British must first prevent the powerful French fleet from falling into enemy hands. The fighting has only just begun as *Altered States* continues the retelling of the naval war in an exciting second volume.

The *Altered States* segment of the *Kirov Series* continues in the book you now hold: *Darkest Hour,* to be followed by Volume III: *Hinge of Fate.* Further titles are planned as the days slowly tick off toward "Paradox Day" the fateful day and hour when *Kirov* was to have first arrived in the Norwegian Sea on July 28, 1941.

Like Alternate History / Time Travel by John Schettler?
Don't miss his five volume *Meridian Series!*

The Meridian Series (Time Travel / Alternate History)

Book I: *Meridian – A Novel In Time*
ForeWord Magazine's "Book of the Year"
2002 Silver Medal Winner for Science Fiction
The adventure begins on the eve of the greatest experiment ever attempted—time travel. As the project team meets for their final mission briefing, the last member, arriving late, brings startling news. Catastrophe threatens and the fate of the Western World hangs in the balance. But a visitor from another time arrives bearing clues that will carry the hope of countless generations yet to be born, and a desperate plea for help. The team is led to the Jordanian desert during WWI and the exploits of the fabled Lawrence of Arabia. There they struggle to find the needle in the haystack of causality that can prevent the disaster from ever happening.

Book II: *Nexus Point*
The project team members slowly come to the realization that a "Time War" is being waged by unseen adversaries in the future. The quest for an ancient fossil leads to an amazing discovery hidden in the Jordanian desert. A mysterious group of assassins plot to decide the future course of history, just one battle in a devious campaign that will span the Meridians of time, both future and past. Exciting Time travel adventure in the realm of the Crusades!

Book III: *Touchstone*
When Nordhausen follows a hunch and launches a secret time jump mission on his own, he uncovers an operation being run by unknown adversaries from the future. The incident has dramatic repercussions for Kelly Ramer, his place in the time line again threatened by paradox. Kelly's fate is somehow linked to an ancient Egyptian artifact, once famous the world over, and now a forgotten slab of stone. The result is a harrowing mission to Egypt during the time frame of Napoleon's 1799 invasion.

Book IV: *Anvil of Fate*

The cryptic ending of Touchstone dovetails perfectly into this next volume as Paul insists that Kelly has survived, and is determined to bring him safely home. Only now is the true meaning of the stela unearthed at Rosetta made apparent—a grand scheme to work a catastrophic transformation of the Meridians, so dramatic and profound in its effect that the disaster at Palma was only a precursor. The history leads them to the famous Battle of Tours where Charles Martel strove to stem the tide of the Moorish invaders and save the west from annihilation. Yet more was at stake on the Anvil of Fate than the project team first realized, and they now pursue the mystery of two strange murders that will decide the fate of Western Civilization itself!

Book V: *Golem 7*

Nordhausen is back with new research and his hand on the neck of the new terrorist behind the much feared "Palma Event." Now the project team struggles to discover how and where the Assassins have intervened to restore the chaos of Palma, and their search leads them on one of the greatest naval sagas of modern history—the hunt for the battleship *Bismarck*. For some unaccountable reason the fearsome German battleship was not sunk on its maiden voyage, and now the project team struggles to put the ship back in its watery grave. Meet Admiral John Tovey and Chief of Staff "Daddy" Brind as the Royal Navy begins to receive mysterious intelligence from an agent known only as "Lonesome Dove." Exciting naval action and top notch research characterize this fast paced alternate history of the sinking of the *Bismarck*.

Golem 7 Introduces Admiral John Tovey as a primary historical character, and he figures prominently in the long Kirov Saga novels that followed this book.

Historical Fiction

Taklamakan ~ *The Land Of No Return*

It was one of those moments on the cusp of time, when Tando Ghazi Khan, a simple trader of tea and spice, leads a caravan to the edge of the great desert, and becomes embroiled in the struggle that will decide the fate of an empire and shake all under heaven and earth. A novel of the Silk Road, the empire of Tibet clashes with T'ang China on the desolate roads that fringe the Taklamakan desert, and one man holds the key to victory in a curious map that guards an ancient secret hidden for centuries.

Khan Tengri ~ *Volume II of Taklamakan*

Learn the fate of Tando, Drekk, and the others in this revised and extended version of Part II of Taklamakan, with a 30,000 word, 7 chapter addition. Tando and his able scouts lead the Tibetan army west to Khotan, but they are soon confronted by a powerful T'ang army, and threatened by treachery and dissention within their own ranks. Their paths join at a mysterious shrine hidden in the heart of the most formidable desert on earth where each one finds more than they imagined, an event that changes their lives forever.

The Dharman Series: Science Fiction

Wild Zone ~ Classic Science Fiction – Volume I

A shadow has fallen over earth's latest and most promising colony prospect in the Dharma system. When a convulsive solar flux event disables communications with the Safe Zone, special agent Timothy Scott Ryan is rushed to the system on a navy frigate to investigate. He soon becomes embroiled in a mystery that threatens the course of evolution itself as a virulent new organism has targeted mankind as a new host. Aided by three robotic aids left in the colony facilities, Ryan struggles to solve the mystery of Dharma VI, and the source of the strange mutation in the life forms of the planet. Book I in a trilogy of riveting classic sci-fi novels.

Mother Heart ~ Sequel to Wild Zone – Volume II

Ensign Lydia Gates is the most important human being alive, for her blood holds the key to synthesizing a vaccine against the awful mutations spawned by the Colony Virus. Ryan and Caruso return to the Wild Zone to find her, discovering more than they bargained for when microbiologist Dr. Elena Chandros is found alive, revealing a mystery deeper than time itself at the heart of the planet, an ancient entity she has come to call "Mother Heart."

Dream Reaper ~ A Mythic Mystery/Horror Novel

There was something under the ice at Steamboat Slough, something lost, buried in the frozen wreckage where the children feared to play. For Daniel Byrne, returning to the old mission site near the Yukon where he taught school a decade past, the wreck of an old steamboat becomes more than a tale told by the village elders. In a mystery weaving the shifting imagery of a dream with modern psychology and ancient myth, Daniel struggles to solve the riddle of the old wreck and free himself from the haunting embrace of a nightmare older than history itself. It has been reported through every culture, in every era of human history, a malevolent entity that comes in the night…and now it has come for him!

For more information on these and other books please visit:
http://www.writingshop.ws or http://www.dharma6.com

DEAR READERS:

"All good books are alike in that they are truer than if they had really happened, and after you are finished reading one you will feel that all that happened to you and afterwards it all belongs to you: the good and the bad, the ecstasy, the remorse and sorrow, the people and the places and how the weather was. If you can get so that you can give that to people, then you are a writer."

— Ernest Hemingway

Thank you for reading! I hope I have given you something here that rings true as I continue that never ending journey, and hope one day to call myself a writer.

JS